KISS HARD

A HARD PLAY NOVEL

NALINI SINGH

OTHER BOOKS BY NALINI SINGH

Play of Passion

Kiss of Snow

Tangle of Need

Heart of Obsidian

Shield of Winter

Shards of Hope

Allegiance of Honor

The Psy/Changeling Trinity series

Silver Silence

Ocean Light

Wolf Rain

Alpha Night

Last Guard

The Guild Hunter series

Angels' Blood

Archangel's Kiss

Archangel's Consort

Archangel's Blade

Archangel's Storm

Archangel's Legion

Archangel's Shadows

Archangel's Enigma

Archangel's Heart

Archangel's Viper

Archangel's Prophecy

Archangel's War

Archangel's Sun

Archangel's Light

Thrillers

A Madness of Sunshine

Quiet in Her Bones

For detailed descriptions of these books, as well as additional titles, visit Nalini's website: www.nalinisingh.com.

PROLOGUE

TEN YEARS AGO...

Catie stared out the rain-washed window.

The deluge was so heavy that it blurred the outside world, turned it into a scene from a Renaissance painting she'd seen in a textbook, all soft and out of focus, but one thing was clear: it was bad out. The increasingly violent winds had half bent the trees in the yard and water was starting to collect on the lower part of the driveway.

Her heart thudded, her muscles all tight. "Dad's fine," she muttered, reminding herself that the last time she'd freaked out about her father, Clive, he'd been having a great time gambling it up at a casino in Sydney, Australia. It just hadn't occurred to him to tell his teenage daughter that he was leaving the country. He'd been too excited to "meet up with an old buddy and hit the blackjack table while his luck was running hot."

Still, her hand clenched on the phone.

The weather was worse than awful—complete with a dangerous gale-force-wind warning from the national meteorological agency—and Clive had left for his trip yesterday morning. It was now past four in the afternoon, the storm turning the world dark at the edges.

Dad, she messaged, *can you message back so I know you're okay?*

No response. Not then, and not for the two hours that followed. Not even to her multiple calls. She knew he wouldn't mind. Her father never minded anything— mostly because he just ignored stuff he didn't want to handle.

"Catie, dear." Martha poked her head into Catie's room. "Come on, it's time for dinner." Her face was warm with love, her brown skin aglow and her black hair in loose curls that held the shine of her favored leave-in conditioner. "I made spaghetti with meatballs."

One of Catie's favorites. Poor Martha. Having to pick up the pieces once again—and stuck with a silent Catie. She flushed, immediately ashamed of her stressed preoccupation. "I'm sorry, Martha. I should've helped."

The near-to-fifty-year-old woman deserved all of Catie's respect. Not only because Martha had been Catie's caregiver since the day Catie was finally discharged from the rehabilitation center two years ago, but also because she was kind and had done everything in her power to help Catie on her path to independence.

At fourteen, Catie no longer needed Martha as she had back then, but since neither Catie's big sister nor her mother were about to chance Catie ending up alone when Clive pulled a disappearing act, Martha stayed.

Truth was, Catie would miss her so much if she left.

"You can do the dishes." Martha walked over to ruffle Catie's messy hair, her dark eyes heavy with worry she tried to keep from her voice. "Trust me, you'll definitely earn your dinner scrubbing the pot."

Catie laughed, more to ease Martha's mind than because she felt anything beyond the knot in her gut. And though she could barely taste the dish Martha had prepared with love in her heart, she cleaned her plate.

Her phone stayed silent throughout, and the knot... it grew and grew until she had no room in her stomach for anything but fear. Clive had taken off plenty of times, but he usually messaged her back within a few hours. She'd been very clear with him after the Sydney thing.

"I'm your kid," she'd pointed out in a calm tone she'd practiced in her room—because Clive blanked if anyone got too emotional. "I need to know my dad is safe."

Catie didn't expect Clive to be like her friend Laveni's dad—a jovial and warm presence who came to school meetings and drove her places and scowled at boys who wanted to hang out with her. Catie had Issie for that; her sister was the best and even more protective than Veni's papa. But Catie did expect Clive not to scare her.

That was normal, wasn't it? She loved Martha but knew that Martha had her own daughter and a grand-child on whom she doted; Catie tried not to ask for anything from her beyond what was in her duties. When it came to family, Catie only had Clive and Issie. Okay, she had the Dragon, aka Jacqueline, too, but her mother —who'd married and then divorced Clive within a few short years—didn't really like to spend time with her children.

Ísa was the one to whom Catie went with her problems and questions. Ísa's husband was pretty neat, and he treated Catie like family too. So yeah, she had him as well. That was four people. Plenty enough. But only one was her *dad,* and she didn't know what she'd do if anything happened to him.

The knot was a rock by now, her throat all choked up.

Bedtime came without any reply from Clive, though Veni messaged her a pic of a cute boy she liked from school—he wore glasses, played chess rather than sports, and was almost as smart as Veni.

Catie answered her friend with a heart eyes emoji, then took a deep breath and began calling hospitals to check if Clive had been in an accident. She still had a kid's voice, so the busy people who answered the phones were nice to her where they might not have been as welcoming to an adult.

"Oh, honey," one nurse said. "Is there no trusted adult who can do this for you?"

Yes, she thought. Issie would help her in a heartbeat. So would Martha. But Martha should've been off-shift *before* dinner today. Catie had apologized for that and said it was okay if she wanted to clock out. At fourteen, it was no longer illegal for Catie to be left alone at home.

Scowling at the very idea, Martha had kissed her on the cheek and said, "Not on my watch, hon. You're a child, not an adult. And Jacqueline pays me triple when I work overtime, so I'm doing just fine."

Catie hadn't argued, though she knew full well that Martha had been planning to have dinner with her daughter's family. As for Catie's big sister... Catie didn't want Ísa to know how bad Clive had begun to act. She was scared her sister would try for custody out of worry for Catie. But though Catie *loved* Issie more than anyone else in the whole world, she couldn't leave her dad.

Clive would be devastated by her defection. He wouldn't eat properly, wouldn't sleep, wouldn't make any good choices at all. Because though he was a bad father, he loved Catie in his own mixed-up way.

"No," she said to the nurse who'd asked if anyone could help her. "My dad's usually the one who'd handle things." That was a full-on lie. Clive was the least responsible person she knew; the only reason their bills got paid was that Issie had set them up as direct automatic payments—it hadn't always been that way, but then Clive had taken off with the bill money one time and the electricity company had almost cut them off. The money came from the dividend account Jacqueline had established for her children—an account Clive could never access.

Their mother was rich, but even rich women wouldn't want to support their ex-husband. "I'm not supporting him," the Dragon had said coolly the one time Catie brought up the topic. "I'm supporting my daughter. Leaving him penniless would affect you, and for all his faults, he's a loving father."

Loving but unreliable. Yet Jacqueline had given him custody of Catie. Which made Catie think that a big part of the reason Jacqueline didn't mind footing the bills was because she saw it as a fair trade for not having to raise a child.

Tonight the nice nurse confirmed that Clive hadn't been brought into the hospital, and after thanking her, Catie continued to ring around. She'd called all the hospitals she could find in the phone book by the time she hung up.

Tomorrow she'd ring the police and ask if he'd been

arrested.

The stone in her gut got even heavier. Because maybe the police would tell her they'd found his vehicle down a ravine or in a gorge. Just because he wasn't in the hospital didn't mean he wasn't hurt. It could be that he just hadn't been spotted. The weather would turn his black car all but invisible if he'd gone off the road along the way.

Eyes gritty and bile in the back of her throat, she was staring at the ceiling when her phone beeped at four in the morning. Snatching it off the bed stand, she sobbed out a breath when she saw the message was from her dad.

It read: *Sorry, baby girl. Got busy with my mates. All good here. Back when I'm back. Love ya.*

Cheeks hot, her eyes afire, she dropped her phone onto the designer white-on-white duvet he'd bought her with his last gambling winnings. On the ceiling, shadows prowled in the light thrown by her phone screen before it went black. As it did so, something inside her snapped in two.

"No more," she whispered. *"No more."*

From now on, she wouldn't worry over her father. She'd be zen. She'd go running. She'd learn a new language. She'd call Veni or Ísa to chat. Hell, she'd even call the Dragon and pretend she wanted to pick Jacqueline's brain about an economics project for school.

No matter what it took, she'd create new habits to deal with her anxiety when her father vanished on her— until she had no anxiety at all.

"I. Am. Done."

Tonight was the last time she would lie awake worrying over Clive.

1

KNIGHT IN GLITTER EYE SHADOW AND SHINING TITANIUM

Catie narrowed her eyes when she saw Danny stumble against the bar inside the thumping Dunedin club. If there was one thing she knew about her number one nemesis, it was that he was about as clean-cut as they came—especially when he was representing his team.

Oh, he knew how to party, but he kept it strictly to the off-season—and even then indulged only rarely. Danny was too committed to his sporting career to risk damaging either his body or his reputation. He certainly wasn't one to get stumbling drunk in public. Which was why, though she and Danny had an avoid-ignore-or-irritate relationship most of the time, she got up off her chair and headed toward him.

She heard her friends calling after her, turned to say, "I'm checking something out."

"Some*one* more like it!" Alina giggled, raising her glass.

The others—including Catie's best friend, Veni—cheered Catie on.

Most of the girls were a touch tipsy, but Veni would make sure they didn't overdo it, not with the lot of them booked to take a charter flight home in a couple of hours. Veni didn't drink and never had—she hated the taste of alcohol—but she was a demon on the dance floor and was only seated now because she abhorred this particular track.

Catie herself had only had a single fruity cocktail for the same reason that Danny controlled his intake: sports and alcohol didn't mix long-term. Her reflexes were as quick as usual, but the place was packed, making it impossible to avoid all contact.

She didn't often do the club scene because of exactly this—she hated being jostled by people. While she was a pro on her prostheses by now and most people couldn't even tell she had two artificial legs if she wanted to play it that way, it was difficult in places like this. The last thing she wanted was for some drunk groper to shove her off-balance.

Speaking of which...

Instead of telling Mr. Gary Groper to get his hand off her, she just twisted his thumb until he went to his knees, whimpering like a baby. Leaving him there for his laughing buddies to collect, she finally reached Danny.

"Hey, hotshot!" she yelled over the beat of the music. "You need to cut off the alcohol! You know the media's camped outside!"

Danny had, last week, signed a massive sponsorship deal with an international corporation. That particular corporation expected its brand ambassadors to be the perfect athletic role models, including when it came to alcohol and drugs.

It was open knowledge in sporting circles that the "moral turpitude" clause was in their actual contract—and that they weren't shy about enforcing it.

Danny put one big hand on her hip, a bit too close to her butt.

Catie's concern spiked. Danny did not hit on her. Ever.

Instead of pushing him off, she slid her arm around his back, over the top of his short-sleeved black shirt with stud detailing, and really looked at him for the first time.

Panic. A lost kind of panic.

That was what she saw in Danny's brown eyes. His hand fisted on the back of her sparkly, strappy top even as she came to the realization that something was seriously wrong. He was almost twice her size, as sleekly muscled as a hunting cat, and he was clinging to her.

"Catie, I don't..." His words faded off into confusion, but she'd caught a whiff of his breath when he'd come close to her face and there hadn't been even a hint of alcohol in it. He smelled only of plain soap and that fresh aftershave he preferred, his hair still damp from the shower he must've taken after the game tonight.

Rage boiled through her. "Danny, did someone roofie you?"

The panic in his eyes was increasing by the second, but it would be invisible to anyone who didn't know him. Though he was somehow managing to keep it together, she could tell he was losing physical coordination from the way he was leaning more heavily on her.

She could also tell that he was fighting it—Danny

knew she couldn't deal with his weight, that it'd take her to the floor. However much they annoyed each other, she'd never worried for her physical safety around him.

He was in serious trouble.

She had to get him out of here, and in a way that didn't set the media on him. If she didn't, they'd plaster his face all over the papers and magazines, make him the next "bad boy of sport." It'd savage his aspirations. More, it'd hurt his family—and Danny loved his aiga. So did Catie.

But she wasn't going to be able to pull this off on her own.

"Hold on," she said against his ear, then looked around.

If only Jake had come out with them, but Danny's brother had flown home straight after tonight's midweek charity match, and Veni was out of sight beyond the dance floor. That was when she saw Viliame "Vili" Serevi.

While Vili now played for the Harriers' archrival, the Southern Blizzard, he, Jake, and Danny remained tight— she knew it was at Danny's place that Vili had crashed when he flew up to Auckland for a wedding. And, regional rivalries aside, all three played together on the national team. The Fijian-Kiwi winger also hated the gossip media and would never betray one of his friends to them.

Catching his eye, she jerked her head.

He wandered over, a big smile on his handsome face and his usual quietness diffused by the fact they'd met multiple times over the years. "Hey, Catie. You and Danny finally hooking up?"

"He's been slipped drugs I think," she said to him

under the cover of music. They both knew Danny would never do drugs on his own. "Can you help me get him out the back somehow?"

Expression changing so quickly that it was obvious he was sober, he nodded. "Let me go check out the exit there."

She found herself stroking Danny's back in the interim, his muscles flexing under the contact. "Hold on, hotshot. I've got you."

Catie could murder the asswipe who'd dared do this to him. She and Danny might be frenemies at the best of times, but even she'd admit he was one of the genuine good guys. Smart, loyal, trustworthy—and irritating as all fuck. But when the shit hit the fan, Danny Esera would be the man you'd want beside you.

Danny mumbled a response, but she couldn't make sense of it. What she didn't miss was the fact that—even drugged and out of control—he was trying to brace himself on the bar so he wouldn't push her off-balance.

"It's all good," she said against his ear—which she could reach because he was kind of bent over the bar. "I've got excellent upper-body strength."

He didn't scowl at her subtle reference to the time she'd beaten him not once but twice at arm wrestling. They'd been in their teens at the time, and he'd muscled up considerably since then, but she liked to mess with him by pulling out that factoid, did so now in the hope it would spark emotion, clear out a little of the fog. But his eyes stayed dazed as his hand clenched desperately on her top.

Catie stroked his back again on a roaring wave of protectiveness.

No one was allowed to do this to her people. And nemesis or not, Danny was one of Catie's people. "Where the hell is Vili?"

The other man appeared out of the mass of people at that moment and gave a short nod before putting one thickly muscled arm around Danny's waist and pulling Danny's arm around his shoulders. Though Vili was as tall and well-built as Danny, Danny was having so much trouble holding himself up that Catie stayed at his other side, her arm around his waist and his other arm around her shoulders.

To outside eyes, it'd look like the three of them had had a few too many drinks—enough to get a little loose with their bodies but not enough to get Danny any bad press.

"You're heavy, hotshot," Catie muttered in an effort to keep Danny awake.

He was fighting the drugs, but it was obvious they were starting to win. And even Viliame couldn't get Danny out if he became dead weight. Danny might be one of the fastest people on the team, his ability to side-step opposing players legendary, but he was still a rugby player. The man was muscle on muscle in a way that was quite different from Catie's runner's physique.

"Come on," she said as they weaved through the crowd; the happy partiers provided excellent cover for their stumbling progress. "You can do this, Danny."

Her use of his actual name seemed to get through, and he managed to help them the last few feet off the dance floor. Probably because she mostly called him anything but his name. Hotshot, GQ, Skinny, and her favorite, Cutie. That last one always made him growl because he knew she was poking him just to get a reaction—and still he'd react.

Never would Catie tell him, but that growl thing *was* actually cute.

Once out in the dimly lit back corridor, she and Viliame only had to go a short way to get Danny to the back door. When Vili pulled it open, she saw why he'd been gone so long—a rugged dark green Land Cruiser sat by the back door. Right, of course. Vili was based in the region, must've driven tonight.

"No Ferrari?" she huffed out, aware of his love for that sleek bullet of a car.

"This rig is Romeo's," he said, naming another teammate. "I'm the designated driver for a bunch of us—but don't worry, boys'll be in the club for hours yet."

The two of them managed to get Danny into the back seat. "I'll get in with him," Catie said, suiting action to words. "Just in case he throws up or has another reaction."

"Hospital?" Vili glanced in the rearview mirror. "I don't like how he's looking."

"Yes, head for the emergency department." Catie had managed to belt Danny in, and he was now lying with his head on her shoulder. "I wish we could protect him from the media, but his health comes first." For whatever reason—whether his rugby royalty family, his natural charm, or his gorgeous face and body—the entertainment media had decided that Danny Esera was their current "It" boy.

When she'd needled him about it, he'd given her a wry half-smile. "You know they build people up to tear them down, right? They'll be on me like a pack of hyenas if I so much as stumble."

That was the thing with Danny; he could be weirdly wise.

"Yeah," Viliame murmured as he pulled out. "I mean, the doctors take oaths to keep things confidential, but there's going to be a bunch of the public in ED." Pulling to a stop at a red light, he added, "His team doctor is still in the city and is a good man, but I don't know if he'd feel obligated to report this to the higher-ups. Especially with Danny having been selected for the national squad."

Catie's mind flashed. "Wait," she said, digging out her phone from the small purse of glittery gold that she wore slung across her body. "I know a doctor here. Maybe she can help. Hopefully she hasn't put her phone on silent and gone to bed."

Dr. Priya Chauhal was thirty years Catie's senior and a woman Catie had first met during her major surgeries as a child. They'd stayed in touch through the years, even after the doctor moved cities, and tonight she answered the call at once.

The noise in the background told Catie that Dr. Chauhal was on shift at the hospital. When Catie explained the situation, the doctor told her to bring Danny around to a back entrance of the hospital.

"I'll get him into a private area for the assessment and make sure it's a very small team that interacts with him. All of them far too old and dedicated to their careers to get starstruck and make a stupid decision."

"Thanks, Dr. Priya." It was what Catie had called Dr. Chauhal back when Catie had been a shocked and scared child; that it came out tonight was no surprise.

While Viliame got instructions from the doctor on how to find the correct entrance, Catie brushed back Danny's thick hair with its slight hint of curl. Girls loved that midnight-black hair and so did all his sponsors.

No reaction from Danny. He was unconscious. And his skin didn't feel right.

Face tight, Catie looked up after Viliame hung up the call with Dr. Chauhal. "Is it far?"

"No, we're almost there."

When they pulled up in front of the right entrance, it was to find Dr. Chauhal waiting for them with a stretcher and a couple of nurses. One of them was as big a man as Viliame, and together, they were able to get Danny onto the stretcher.

Catie stuck to Danny's side while Vili went to park the Land Cruiser. Goose bumps broke out over her skin as they navigated the hospital corridors. She'd forgotten her jacket back at the table she'd been sharing with her friends, and her pretty, sparkly top, devoid of a back and sleeves, was meant for the heat of a club.

It was no match for this institutional building.

But they were in a warmer patient room soon enough —a room far from the hustle and bustle of the ED. Minutes later, Dr. Chauhal led another woman into the room. Tall, her golden hair threaded with the odd strand of silver that caught the light, she had the kind of elegant bone structure that made it impossible to pinpoint her age. Her expertise, however, was clear the instant she began to examine Danny.

"Drug reactions of this kind aren't in my bailiwick," Dr. Chauhal told Catie as they stood back and let the other doctor work. "Dr. Smitherson is one of the best in that area."

"Thanks for doing this." She was very conscious it wasn't procedure. "I hope it doesn't get you or Dr. Smitherson into trouble."

Hands tucked in the pockets of her lab coat, Dr. Chauhal shook her head. "Perk of being extremely senior and actually willing to take night rounds. No one's going to piss us off over something so small."

Dr. Smitherson cracked a smile but kept her attention on Danny.

"And," Dr. Chauhal added, "the only favor he's received is a private way in. We'd give the same care to anyone who came in exhibiting the effects of a drug of this kind."

"Is it very busy out there?"

Dr. Smitherson was the one who answered. "Not quite yet. We'll start getting the weekend rush come eleven p.m. If this had happened then, I couldn't have come up and Mr. Esera would've had to take his chances entering the public way."

She rose from her examination of Danny. "His heart rate is a little concerning but nothing dangerous. I don't like the fact he's lost consciousness, however—I'm going to have the lab run his blood as a priority. He stays here with full monitoring in the meantime."

Catie settled into the chair beside Danny's bed after the medical staff vacated the room; prior to leaving, they'd drawn his blood, then hooked him up to various monitors. She was just pulling out her phone when Viliame walked in.

"I found Danny's jacket in the car," he said, holding it

out. "I gave him a ride in tonight. Anyway, figured you might need it."

"Thank you—you're a lifesaver." Shrugging into the fleece-lined corduroy jacket that Danny somehow pulled off, she was immediately overwhelmed by the warm, masculine scent of Daniel Esera. It was... comforting. Scowling at her own thoughts, she said, "I can hold the fort here. You okay to head back to the club, run interference so no one starts to wonder where Danny disappeared to?"

Lines forming above the dark brown of his eyes, Viliame folded his arms across his chest. "I don't want you here alone."

"I'm surrounded by doctors and nurses," she reminded him. "And you know people will've noticed us cutting out. Better to head off the gossip or they'll have us in a threesome and the Vilimaidens will murder me with a hatchet." To say Viliame's fan club was devoted was a *vast* understatement; his future girlfriend or wife would be in for a hard time.

"Seriously, Vili," she added. "You know there are people out there just waiting for Danny to slip up, make an ass of himself." Those hyenas, waiting for him to fall. "It doesn't need to be true to stick—the worst would be if the person who dosed him takes advantage of his sudden exit to start a rumor about him doing drugs. Making him seem drugged out might've been the whole point of this."

Catie's anger was a hot blade, her need for revenge a cold determination. The latter had to be a genetic trait she'd inherited from Jacqueline; her mother was definitely one for revenge being a dish best served cold.

Viliame shoved a hand over his tight black curls.

"Shit. Yeah, I see where you're going." Lips pursed and eyes narrowed, he said, "I have an idea that'll blow all other rumors out of the water—I could make it sound like we were going to hit another club but then you two ditched me and went off together."

The usually reserved player waggled his eyebrows.

2

VILIAME THE GOSSIP COLUMNIST

Catie rolled her eyes. "Like anyone is going to believe that." The fact that she and Danny were *not* friends was well known. Possibly because they kept snarking on each other's social media posts.

Take Danny's last comment: *Oh, going for the princess look today, I see. In my considered opinion, you need more gold eye shadow, and wow, go you for not hesitating to glue spider legs to your eyelids. That's true commitment to fashion.*

Danny thought he was a genius.

Not that she was any better.

Bit light on the weights today, Daniel. Tut-tut. Got a little lazy on holiday, huh? It's all right. That's why I got you the flamingo-pink kiddie weights for Christmas. Always thinking of what's best for you. xoxo

It was a good thing Danny's mum, Alison, wasn't on the social media platform the two of them preferred for their mutual mockery. She'd twist both their ears for behaving like children rather than the full-grown adults they were supposed to be. As it was, Danny's brothers found it hilarious and Catie's sister just shook her head at each new dig they made.

"Um." Viliame unfolded his arms and winced. "I mean, everyone thinks you two are flirting with the insults, so yeah, it'll fly."

Catie shuddered even as she pulled Danny's jacket closed around her upper body. "I will never flirt with Daniel Tana Esera." The idea was so ridiculous that she couldn't even be insulted. "But go for it. Whatever works. Tomorrow I'll post that he made a move, I kicked his ass, and we'll be back to all systems normal."

"I will never understand you and Dan," Viliame muttered, then held out a fisted hand. "Look after my brother from another mother?"

She bumped her fist with his. "He's annoying, but I love his family."

Viliame just shook his head, then said, "Talk to you soon, brother" to Danny before leaving.

Only then did Catie give in to her worry and stroke Danny's hair back once again. "Hey, hotshot. Sorry to break it to you, but the nurses didn't swoon over you." Her stomach was all twisted up. She hated seeing him this way, so still and pale. Danny was energy and life. He was the guy who'd hauled her onto his back during the beach races at last year's family camping trip and run so fast that they'd smoked the other teams.

As the others were coupled up, the two of them usually ended up paired together unless her brother Harlow could make it or they had another friend join them. And because she and Danny were as competitive as all hell, they won more times than not.

Danny was also one of the few people whose back she

had no problem jumping onto and riding. Growing up, she'd gone out with a few boys who'd thought it the height of romance to sweep her off her feet and carry her around, forget about the fact that (one): Catie hated being startled and off-balance, and (two): she'd spent literal *years* learning to walk on her own two prosthetic feet.

With Danny, it was different. He'd seemed to understand from the first that her prostheses were an indelible and treasured part of her, not attachments to be ignored or seen as lesser. When they raced, *she* was the one who usually suggested she take them off so she'd be lighter and he could run faster.

"Still a cheater," he'd said with a grin last summer, hailing back to the very first time she'd joined the family camping trip—after Ísa met and fell for Sailor, one of Danny's two older brothers.

Danny had been bare chested that summer's day, all gilded brown skin and sleek muscle as he grinned down at her. Bare feet, board shorts, saltwater-tangled hair, and sand stuck to his calves, he'd struck her as beautiful.

Quickly shaking off that random thought, she'd pointed at him. "You want to win or not?"

"I always want to win, princess." He'd watched her remove her legs. "That foot's new, right?"

"Yep. The lab's testing a new everyday foot and asked if I wanted to be a guinea pig." Thanks to her mother's insane wealth, Catie had never had to fight to pay for a prosthesis, a privilege she never forgot and that she did everything in her power to pay forward—including by funding continuing research on low-cost prostheses that could be built from scratch by those on the ground in the developing world.

That day Danny had picked up the foot, examined it. "Has a futuristic look to it. Robotic stuff in there?"

"Microprocessors." She'd grabbed back her foot. "You can ogle to your tech-geek heart's content later. It's race time."

He'd gone down on one knee, she'd hauled herself onto the smooth warmth of his back, and they'd run to the starting line. Sea winds riffling his hair, he'd been all fluid muscle and strength against her—and when he'd laughed at a comment from his brother Jake, she'd felt the vibration in her bones.

Danny was meant for sunlit beaches and rugby fields, not a stark hospital bed.

After shifting her hand to wrap it around his, she made a call she didn't want to make—but his family wouldn't thank her for keeping them in the dark.

Her sister picked up the phone, sounding breathless. "Catiebug!" Love, so much love in that single word. "How's it going down there? I hear the temperature's dived. Oh, did you run into Danny?"

Wrapped up in the warmth of Ísa's affection, Catie told her what had happened. "Doctors are running the tests now, and from what I can see on the monitors, his vitals are steady." Catie had spent enough time in hospitals to have picked up the basics of reading the onscreen output.

"Oh, sweetheart." Ísa's shaken response. "Let me get Sailor." Half a minute later, she said, "I've put you on speaker. Sailor's here."

"Catie, darling." Sailor's deep voice. "I'm searching for tickets for the next flight down. Mum and Dad are going to want to be there for Dan."

Catie's heart squeezed. Sailor was surely her first real crush—but not in a weird way. She loved how he loved her sister, loved how he was with their children, Emmaline and Connor. Sailor Bishop had spoiled Catie for dickheads and losers. She wanted a man who loved her the way Sailor loved Ísa.

No holds barred. Now and forever.

Sailor was part of why she'd been able to kick Ward to the curb without regrets. He'd somehow slunk in past her dickhead radar, but she'd seen him for who he was in the end and she'd known she deserved better.

"Danny's going to be mad at the fuss," she said.

"Yeah, Mum is *real* scared of his wrath."

Laughing softly at Sailor's deadpan tone, Catie squeezed Danny's hand. "I'll keep you updated on his condition."

"Looks like there are no flights till morning," Sailor said. "You'll probably get a call from our parents soon. He look okay?"

"Yes." Not like himself, but his color seemed better.

"How are you doing, Catie?" Ísa, the mama bear. "Do you have support? Laveni's there, isn't she?"

"I haven't had a chance to tell her what's going on, but Viliame's been amazing. He's currently out spreading the rumor that Danny and I vanished together because we're hooking up." She made gagging sounds.

A male snort came down the line. "Danny must be looking okay if you're being your usual self with him. Make sure you take care of yourself too while you're looking out for him."

"Yes, boss."

She didn't have to wait long for the call from Alison

and Joseph. It always made her heart ache, seeing how they were with their boys. Warm and loving while raising them to be tough, independent men. You'd never know that Joseph was Gabriel and Sailor's stepfather—he treated all four boys as his own, and the brothers never used the word "half" for each other. They were brothers. End of story.

When it came to the parent thing, Jacqueline had gotten better over the years, but she'd never had and never would have this kind of love for her children. Not her fault. It was the way she was built: for creating empires and being CEO.

The problem was that instead of falling in love with men who loved children and would do the heavy lifting in the parenting department, she'd picked Stefán, followed by Clive. Her current husband, Oliver, a man Jacqueline had married after her daughters were too old for it to matter, was actually a gentler, kinder sort of man, but Ísa's dad was also an empire-builder while Catie's was... less than reliable.

Leaving no safety net for Jacqueline's daughters.

Back after that truck ran onto the curb and crushed Catie's legs, her mother had turned up at the hospital. Of course she had. Jacqueline wasn't a monster. But she'd disappeared the minute the doctors pronounced that Catie was out of the woods.

Jacqueline wasn't a keeping-vigil-by-a-hospital-bed-type person.

It was Clive who'd taken that role. Her flake of a father hadn't let her down at that critical time in her life, when she'd been so afraid and hurt, her dreams of a running career in apparent tatters at the ends of where her legs should've been.

That was why she could still love him even though he'd broken her heart so many times. Because she remembered waking up from sedation after yet another surgery to find always-spick-and-span Clive passed out in the hospital chair, unshaven and wearing dirty clothes.

He hadn't missed a single hospital day, had spent hours keeping her entertained and laughing. But it was Īsa who'd been there for the months and years of rehabilitation that followed, Īsa who'd come to all the appointments with the prosthetic specialists, Īsa who'd made sure Catie didn't derail her progress by attempting to skip stages.

Jacqueline, in contrast, had paid to have Clive's entire home reconfigured so Catie could navigate it. She'd also set in motion the beginnings of a company to build cutting-edge prostheses. Looking after Catie in her own way—just not the way so desperately needed by the wounded child Catie had been.

Her mother was a complicated woman.

"We'll be on the first flight out," Joseph said toward the end of their call. "Make sure you get some hot drink and food into you since you're staying up with Danny, or you'll be answering to me."

Catie's eyes burned. "Yes, sir."

Slipping the phone back into her pocket, she swallowed hard. "I hope you know how lucky you are, hotshot." All those people, ready to drop their lives to come to him. The surreal thing was that they'd do it for her too.

She'd spent so much time with the Esera clan after

Ísa hooked up with Sailor that Veni had once said, "With you and Danny so close in age, you must feel like brother and sister."

After gagging, Catie had—very firmly—said, "No. Daniel Esera is not my brother. I'm not sure he's even human."

Veni had burst out laughing, her giggle an infectious thing, but truth was truth. As for Sailor and Gabriel, they did treat her like a kid sister, but she didn't mind—they were older, had been adults when she first met them. Jake, closer to her and Danny in age, was a friend.

It was only her and Danny who'd rubbed each other wrong from their first meeting. "And I'd still stab the loser who did this to you," Catie muttered, her hand yet locked with his. "Don't let it go to your head. I'd do the same for anyone who had drugs slipped into their drinks."

Then she squeezed his hand and watched his chest rise and fall.

3

(STRICTLY) TEMPORARY CEASE-FIRE

Danny woke up feeling like shit.

His head was all fuzzy, his mouth tasted like he'd snacked on a furred animal of indeterminate origin, and his body felt like it had taken tackle after tackle in a bruising battle of a game. The only point of warmth, of softness, was in his right hand.

Looking down, he saw a tumble of hair made up of so many shades of red and brown that to call it auburn felt like an insult. That hair was captured sunsets and autumn fire; he loved watching it blaze in the sunshine.

"Catie?" His voice came out low, gravel-rough.

It didn't wake her where she lay sleeping with her head against the side of his bed, her hand curled into his. No, not curled into his. Gripping his tight.

Why was Catie in his room?

That was when he noticed the curtain around the bed. Another breath and the scent of antiseptics and who knew what else flooded his system. Hospital. This was a hospital. No mistaking that smell or the medical items nearby—including what looked to be an empty nurse's cart. And yeah, this skinny thing with a metal frame definitely wasn't his bed.

He went to look at Catie again, was distracted by the bright white light coming through the window behind her. So bright it hurt his eyes.

Frowning, he went to lean forward.

Catie jolted up. "What? I wasn't asleep!"

All huge brown eyes and golden skin creased with sleep wrinkles, she glared at him before breaking out into a sudden, dazzling smile that threatened to steal his breath. "Hotshot." She used the knuckles of her free hand to knock gently against the side of his head. "You have all your marbles?"

He scowled. "Why the hell am I in the hospital? Did you run me over?"

"Ha ha. *I'm* not the one with three speeding tickets." Reaching over, she pressed something beside the bed. "Got told to buzz if you woke up." Then she squeezed the hand she held. "Some asshole slipped a drug into your drink last night. You were out of it."

Danny's blood ran cold. Jerking up into a straight-backed sitting position, he tried to think back to the night, hit a blank wall. His heart thudded, his mouth dry. "I can't remember anything after the game." He'd been buoyant, delighted at their win against the Southern Blizzard.

"I looked it up on the web when I couldn't sleep," Catie said. "Being roofied can result in retrograde amnesia."

"Roofied?" Mind spinning, he tried to make sense of what she was saying. "Why—?"

The curtain rustled to reveal a small-boned woman in scrubs. "Good, you're awake," she said. "And perfect timing. Dr. Smitherson is doing her final rounds before heading out."

He didn't have to wait long for the doctor.

After checking Danny over—including testing his cognition and motor skills, she slipped her hands into the pockets of her lab coat. "Your friends were right—and wrong," the doctor told him.

"You were slipped a drug, but it wasn't what's colloquially called a roofie. Rather, it was a downer cut with another drug." She rattled off the technical names. "Tests show you were dosed with a relatively small amount comparative to your physical size."

Danny tried to think. "Why would anyone do this?"

"Given the circumstances—that you were surrounded by friends who would and did notice that something was off with you—it might've been for no reason but that certain individuals get a kick out of it." Her face reflected her distaste. "Last month we had five people come in sick and vomiting after a supposed friend spiked their drinks with an illegal substance simply to see how they'd react."

"It could've also been an unscrupulous reporter," Catie put in. "Photos of Danny out of it would bring in serious bucks, and all they'd have had to do was bribe a member of the bar staff or a groupie who could get close to you."

"Shit." Danny shoved both hands through his hair, only then realizing he'd been holding on to Catie all this time. "This could get me thrown off the fucking team. Zero tolerance to drugs, that's the policy."

"It's all confidential," Dr. Smitherson told him. "It

won't leak from here. But if it does ever come up, I'm more than willing to testify that you didn't voluntarily take the drugs. I also suggest you file a police report."

Danny's mind was a huge roar of noise.

"Can he go home?" Catie asked, taking charge.

For once he didn't argue. Didn't have the capacity to argue.

"Yes, but I don't want him alone for the next forty-eight hours. The effects can linger."

"No problem. I'll stick with him until his parents arrive from Auckland."

"If they were planning to fly in, they're out of luck." The doctor nodded to the window behind Catie. "Big, once-in-a-century snowstorm swirling outside. All flights grounded. It's forecast to get worse before it passes. I'm discharging you now so you can get home before it gets too dangerous on the roads."

Dr. Smitherson was as good as her word, and Danny walked out of the ward only minutes later.

"I called one of those fancy executive cabs," Catie told him. "You know, the ones that advertise about being super confidential. If the driver blabs anyway, we'll pretend I fell and had to get my prostheses checked out and you came with me."

Danny was used to Catie's quick mind, but it was too quick for him today. "Catie, I can't think quite right."

She slipped her hand into his, slender and warm and with calluses from her weight work. "Lingering effects, remember? Doc also gave me a bit of advice about food and drink while you were in the bathroom, so we'll start that, try to get your body into the right state."

He looked down at their clasped hands. Funny, how

delicate she was, though he never thought of her that way —but while Catie was honed and sleek, a bullet on the race track, her hand was all slender bones, and it held his with fierce power. Telling him it was okay if he leaned on her; she could handle it.

Curling his bigger, browner, blunt-tipped fingers around hers, he said, "I'm incapacitated. This doesn't count."

No one else would've understood. Catie grinned. "Granted. This does not go on the scoreboard."

The taxi driver proved to be an older guy who was far more interested in Catie's prosthetic feet than anything to do with Danny. She'd worn skin-hugging black capris that exposed her high-tech ankle joints, her equally high-tech feet clad in gold-sequined sneakers.

Catie chatted away to the driver as the taxi crawled through the snowy streets, the silence beyond a soft hush. She'd told him once that she liked talking about her prostheses. "As long as people aren't rude and are just curious," she'd said. "I figure if I can help them see prosthetic limbs as nothing strange, just a normal aid, it might help another amputee who isn't as comfortable talking about this stuff. Plus, I mean, my hardware is wicked cool."

By the time the taxi came to a stop outside a building Danny didn't recognize, the driver had asked for a selfie with Catie and was planning to tell his grandchildren about the famous runner he'd met. He ignored Danny.

Thank God. Or thank Catie. Better not tell her that. She'd probably command him to refer to her as God from then on.

After paying—and after the selfie, for which Catie leaned forward into the gap between the two front seats—

they got out under the shelter of an awning. Danny automatically held out an arm in case Catie wanted to take it. She usually didn't, but she curled her fingers around his biceps today. It wasn't until they were inside the lobby that he realized she wasn't holding on to him. She was holding *him*.

His cheeks burned.

Aggravated at the continuing heaviness in his head, he said, "Where are we?"

"Jacqueline has an apartment in the city." She gave the crisply uniformed front desk concierge a cheery wave before heading to the elevator. "My girls and I were staying here."

He froze. "Your girls?"

A roll of the eyes, the glitter on her lids sparkling. "No need to hit the panic button. They flew out after the club last night—I was supposed to go with them, but I made an excuse." A disgusted face. "Do you know they actually believed Viliame's stupid rumor about the two of us hooking up?"

"Vili what?" Danny felt like his head was exploding.

"I'll catch you up upstairs."

Upstairs ended up being the penthouse. Of course it did. This was Jacqueline Rain's place after all. "It smells like women." He sniffed the air, his eyes narrowed. "All perfumy and soft." Then he turned to sniff at her. "Ugh, you smell like a woman too."

Catie snorted at him, laughter in her tone. "You want a shower? Viliame grabbed your stuff from the team hotel and dropped it off, and I asked the concierge to put it..."

Stopping, she went back out into the small entrance area... and returned with his bag. "Voilà!"

The shower did help, and he was feeling much better by the time he walked out, dressed in a clean pair of gray sweatpants and a white tee. Catie, her hair damp from her own shower, wore a velour sweat suit in eye-searing purple as she stood at the kitchen counter scrambling eggs.

The outfit, with its gold zips and epaulets on the shoulders, should've been a monstrosity, but she made it look kick-ass. But, of course, he could never allow her to know that.

Raising his hand to his face, he said, "My eyes, my eyes!"

"Shut up or no eggs for you." She pushed over her phone. "And call your parents. They just rang to say their flight was canceled. I told them you were fine, but they want to talk to their baby boy." She smirked. "Coochie coo."

"Bite me." But his lips twitched—he knew just how much she loved his folks; last month she'd taken them out for lunch for no reason but that she enjoyed their company.

Instead of taking her phone, he went back to the guest bedroom and dug into the pockets of his jeans. "I still have my wallet and phone," he called out, "so at least I didn't get robbed."

"I'd have loaned you some dollars," Catie said when he emerged from the room. "At a generous interest rate. Nothing over twenty-five percent."

"The Dragon would be proud." Walking over to the counter, he made the call as he began to pour himself an orange juice from the bottle Catie had put there.

33

His mother answered on the first ring. "Danny, sweetheart."

His mum and dad's concern wrapped him in a familiar warmth. He knew other guys his age might've been annoyed at their worry, but Danny made no bones about being close to his parents. Joseph and Alison Esera were his rocks, and they understood the line between caring and hovering. That was why they had four strong, independent sons who adored them.

After the two pronounced themselves satisfied that he was all right and that Catie was "looking after him"—he narrowed his eyes at that—they told him to call Gabriel.

Danny took their advice, and his big brother helped break it all down for him. File the police report, contact his sports agent so he could talk to team management on Danny's behalf, and touch base with the hospital to authorize the release of his medical report from tonight's incident to the team.

"That way no one can accuse you of drug taking," Gabriel said. "It ever comes up, it's all documented."

Being labeled a drug cheat could be the kiss of death for a sporting career, but Danny hesitated. "Gabe, no one knows. I just want to forget it." Forget being out of control when he'd spent a lifetime learning to be disciplined, to color within the lines.

"This is your call," his brother said. "But if you don't report it, it becomes a hidden thing you're going to worry might come back to bite you. Better to be up front as close to the incident as possible, when all the data is there to back you up—including a respected ED doctor and her colleagues. Also, you're going to go to therapy."

Danny's jaw dropped. Striding to the balcony doors,

he opened them and stepped out into the icy chill. "Hell I am!" He never yelled at his big brother—he had too much respect for Gabriel. But this was ridiculous. "It was one night and nothing bad happened!"

Gabriel let him go on for a bit before quietly saying, "You're angry, little bro. Listen to yourself. Sort it out by talking to a professional before the anger goes toxic inside you."

Chest heaving, Danny pressed his back against the outside wall. "Shit. I just— I was surrounded by friends, Gabe. The idea that one of them might've done it..." There was a strong likelihood that it had been a stranger, but still, the thought haunted him.

"That's exactly why I want you to talk to someone. Look, Mum shoved me into therapy after my injury. I whined like a baby, but it was the best thing she could've done for me. If you don't listen to anything else I say, listen to this."

"Yeah, okay, I'll think about it." After hanging up, he stared out at the snow for a while until Catie stuck her head outside.

"Hey, I didn't know you wanted prostheses too."

"What?"

"I mean, since you're trying your best to get frostbite and lose your feet."

"Funny." But realizing she was right about him freezing off his feet, he walked in and slid the door shut.

His stomach rumbled.

Catie didn't take the chance to razz him, and together, they dished out the eggs and bacon she'd made along with slices of what looked like fresh bread. When he held it up with a raised eyebrow, she said, "It's a premade kind that you keep frozen, and when you want a bit, you chuck it in the oven for fifteen minutes. Jacqueline's private chef stocks it."

Not for the first time, Danny wondered how Catie had turned out so normal after having Jacqueline Rain for a mother and a womanizing gambler for a father. "Eggs are good," he mumbled after shoving a huge portion into his starving mouth.

"I know." Catie took a sip of the coffee she'd refused to give him, citing doctor's orders. "What did Gabe say?"

He told her. No point keeping secrets from Catie when she was a vault where family was concerned. And to her, the Eseras were family—except for him. He was her chief nemesis and vice versa.

His friends got on his case all the time, asking if he had blue balls by now what with how long the two of them had been flirting. Idiots didn't get it. He and Catie didn't *flirt*. It didn't matter that she was hot—he had eyes in his head, could see why several of his single teammates tried to hit on her every chance they got.

Only to get shot down. Boom.

His enjoyment of their misfortune might have been assholish behavior if they didn't spend so much time ragging him on his "unrequited crush." Hah! The idea was ludicrous. Catie would fall down dead of laughter if she heard it.

He shoved more eggs into his mouth.

4

MR. SIZZLING BACHELOR OF THE
YEAR AND THE DRAGON'S DEN

"Gabe's right." No laughter in those brown eyes, nothing but the understanding of a fellow athlete. "Secrets just come back to bite you." She pointed her fork in his direction. "I say put it out there to nip off any rumors of a cover-up down the line. You know how things are—just takes a whisper to threaten to ruin a good career. Then there's your squeaky-clean sponsorship deal."

"Shit." He'd known his brother was right, had still hoped she'd disagree. "I guess I better get myself to the police station."

Catie glanced at the snow falling beyond the balcony doors, the world outside blurred white. "See if they'll log the complaint over the phone—they can't want people out in this weather. Especially when no one's used to snow in the city. It's usually limited to the higher elevations."

Antsy now that he'd made his decision, Danny picked up his phone.

"Wait. How's your head?" Catie tapped the side of her own temple. "All marbles retrieved?"

Scowling, he checked those marbles. "Heaviness is gone," he confirmed. "I'm fucking pissed off but not feeling dull and foggy."

He made the call and—once he got through to a detective in drug crimes—received an unexpected response: "We're still mobile. I'll come out to you to take the report."

Danny stared at his phone for a second before putting it back to his ear. "You sure? I know you have far more serious drug issues on your plate."

"I'm positive."

Not certain what to make of that, Danny next called his agent, Matthew. He and Jake had different agents—on their big brother's advice.

"Stop any conflicts of interests before they arise," Gabriel had said, the steel gray of his eyes holding the calm that came with years of experience. "Any decisions you two make over whether you both want to angle for an opportunity or not will be between brothers. You don't want to put that on an agent."

Today Matthew was in full agreement with Danny's decision to put it all on the record. Most players would've contacted their agent first, before they did anything else, but Matthew knew Danny—and he understood that on certain things, Danny would make his own call. That was why their relationship worked.

"It'll be fine," the agent added. "Similar thing happened to another player on an international tour a few years before your time, and it was classified as a medical incident. No one's going to be idiotic about it. I'll touch base with team management now."

Feeling better with all that done, Danny got stuck into his food. When he looked up to find all the scrambled eggs and bacon gone, he made a mournful face.

Catie laughed. "I'll make you more."

"No, I can do it." He'd been raised by parents who both pulled their weight, had seen the same thing in the marriages of his older brothers.

Not only that, after Danny was chosen for the national squad at a bare nineteen years of age, his father had taken him aside and given him a piece of advice that Danny had never forgotten. "This kind of fame and money so young," Joseph Esera had said in his quiet way, "it can change you. Especially when it comes to how you treat others."

He'd patted Danny on the shoulder, his stubble already more salt than pepper and his eyes warm with pride. "I can't see you ever going that way, son. You have your mother's heart. But I wouldn't be a good father if I didn't warn you of the dangers—I've seen too many young players fall victim to it, end up surrounded by people who only wear the mask of friendship. In the end, it's a hollow life."

But Catie waved him down today. "Special dispensation on medical grounds. One time only." A glare. "If you ever tell anyone I was nice to you, I'll kick you where it hurts—with my pointiest prosthetic foot."

He winced. "You're mean in the morning. But I like your eggs."

"Humph."

Watching her in motion was a pleasure he didn't deny

himself. She moved like a dancer, no trace remaining of the awkward teen who'd transitioned from prosthetic limb to prosthetic limb through her erratic growth spurts. At least she'd had an excuse for her awkwardness; he'd just been all skinny arms and legs and a total lack of coordination.

"You feeling okay after having your legs on all night?" He knew she was a full-time user of prostheses, but that didn't mean twenty-four hours a day.

"I'm fine, but I'll probably take a little time-out after breakfast." As she sprinkled herbs into the eggs, she said, "I forgot how much you can eat. Are you still on like six meals a day?"

"Yup. Where do you think this big, beautiful body comes from?" Leaning back in the chair, he spread his arms wide.

A jaundiced look up and down. "Seen better."

"Oh, ouch." Grinning, he rubbed a hand over his abdomen. "You have a gym in this building?"

"Building?" A snort. "Have you met my mother?" She pointed to the corridor that led in the other direction from the kitchen area. "The Dragon never does anything by halves. Her private gym's thataway."

When Danny rose and wandered off to check out the exercise area, Catie let him go without comment. He was wound up, stressed, needed the familiar. And for an athlete, a gym was familiar territory.

She heard his admiring whistle from the kitchen.

"Damn, princess," he said when he walked back

down the corridor. "You've got over a hundred grand worth of equipment in there."

"Probably closer to a quarter mil," she said. "I told Jacqueline I didn't need all that, but you know how she is." She shrugged, well used to her mother's way of throwing money at her children in lieu of affection.

In fairness, she *was* better these days, and a good grandmother to Ísa and Sailor's two demons—said demons having learned all their tricks from Catie—but Catie couldn't simply forget her own childhood.

Danny grimaced. "Money talks and emotion is for sissies, right?"

Oh yeah, Danny knew Jacqueline.

"Don't get me wrong." Catie put a little bit too much power into mixing up the eggs. "I'm grateful for her money and all it's meant for me." It had given her a quality of life she'd never otherwise have had, especially after the accident.

That was indisputable fact.

"But I still resent how it's always been her first priority." She threw the egg mixture into the pan, began to move it around using the cooking spatula. "Then I hate myself for being an unappreciative brat." It messed her up at times, that confusion inside her. "I know exactly how much others in my position would give for that kind of financial support."

Walking around the counter, Danny leaned against it with his back, his hands braced behind him. "I dunno," he said. "I think you can be mad. I mean, your mum already had two gazillion dollars by the time you were born. Even if she had to duck out on Ísa to build her empire, she didn't need to do the same with you."

Catie made a face and waved the spatula at him. "See, that's when I hit the wall. Because why *should* it have been on her to raise me and do all the kid-friendly stuff? I have a father who had plenty of time on his hands."

Danny, who'd been a part of her life for so long that he was like furniture—annoying, irritating furniture with sharp edges that snagged her favorite sweaters—made a face back at her. "Yeah, but you didn't choose Clive. She did. And she knew who he was—er—how honest can I be without you throwing my eggs in the garbage disposal?"

"It's fine. I know who my dad is." A good-looking gambler and cheerful companion allergic to responsibility. "He hit me up for money yesterday."

Danny straightened, his expression tight. "Jesus, Catie. That is not on. The man needs a swift kick in the ass."

Catie dumped Danny's eggs onto a plate. "Shut up. Only I get to dis my dad."

Not calling her out on her sudden about-face, Danny took the plate and went back to the table. Though he ate in silence, she could all but hear the gears turning in his brain, could predict what he was thinking. Because Danny had grown up in a wholly different kind of family. Far more traditional than her own if you wanted to put labels on it.

Catie had picked up enough bits and pieces over the years to know that, prior to marrying Joseph, Alison had worked her fingers to the bone to support herself and her two boys by her first husband.

Danny, however, had been born into a family where the father was the breadwinner while the mother took charge of the household and the children. More, he'd been raised by a man who believed the care of his family was his responsibility, making sure they were provided for an integral aspect of his masculinity.

It was as old-fashioned as anything... but it was nice too. Catie could still remember how she'd almost cried the first time Joseph Esera had hugged her, then given her five dollars to go buy herself an ice cream from the ice cream van that had stopped by their beachside campsite.

She hadn't needed the money. It hadn't been about that. It had been about seeing how a dad could be— giving, responsible, *stable*.

"Enough about my hang-ups," she said as she stacked the dishwasher while Danny finished up his food. "How's your mum doing in her studies?" Alison had gone back to university the previous year, was in the midst of a history degree.

"Loving it." Danny's scowl melted away. "I always knew she was into ancient cultures, but man, she glows when she talks about that stuff. She's started writing a historical novel—fiction based on actual history with a bit of a romantic thread in it."

"What? I didn't know that!" Having finished with the dishes and wiped down the counter, Catie grabbed a seat at the table. "Tell me everything!"

"I don't know any specifics yet. I think she's a bit shy about it."

"What's your dad think of her being so busy?" After all, Joseph was used to a stay-at-home wife.

"He bought her a brand-new laptop for her birthday, loaded with special writing software he asked Ísa about." Danny's grin was wild with affection. "My dad's not a reader, but he's been asking to read her draft chapters as she finishes them—only Mum says he's a terrible critic because he tells her he loves every word."

Again, Catie felt that heart squeeze. "Jeez, you realize your parents are disgustingly adorable?"

"Nah, they're real," he said with the easy comfort of a man who'd grown up surrounded by an enduring love. "They have their arguments—last time I was home, Dad was in the doghouse because he forgot to line the bin with a bin liner and Mum dumped a bunch of gross trash in it before she realized and it got all filthy."

"World War III right there, hotshot." She'd been a toddler of three when her parents divorced, and while Clive was too charmingly slippery a character to get into fights, she'd seen the look on Jacqueline's face when Clive dropped Catie off for visitation with her mother: a kind of pained disappointment that went to the core.

At some point in her teens, Catie had put a label on that look—it had been of a woman who knew she couldn't rely on this man. What kind of mother, Catie sometimes wondered, would Jacqueline have been if she'd had a true partner for a husband—someone who not only pulled his weight but who called her to account when necessary? Instead, it was Ísa who'd been thrust into the role of ensuring Jacqueline didn't totally abdicate her responsibilities as a parent.

Danny had parted his lips to reply when the intercom buzzed, and suddenly there was no more smiling. Rising, he went to answer and let the detective up. She cleared the table in the interim, not wanting this stranger to see any hint of vulnerability. Danny was feeling exposed enough.

It turned out Detective Green had brought his partner along with him.

Catie figured the heavy presence had to be because of Danny's status as a well-known athlete, but after the two had taken their statements and gotten Viliame's details so they could interview him as well, the younger of the pair —Detective Shan—put away her notebook and said, "I don't know if this'll make you feel better, but you're not the first person this has happened to in the past month."

Danny's face was granite. "I figured it happens."

"No, this specific drug combination at this specific bar," she clarified. "All males with no associated assault or theft. One target was out alone and collapsed in the street; a few inches to the right and he'd have hit the curb, almost certainly suffered a severe head injury. Then there's the problem of dosage—the individual doing this is getting reckless, might accidentally give someone too much."

Seated right beside Danny, their bodies touching, Catie fisted her hands on her thighs. "You mean some sicko is doing this for the hell of it?" Exactly as Dr. Smitherson had theorized.

"That's what it looks like," Shan confirmed. "The good news is that there are a lot of photographs of you at the bar." A nod at Danny, her hair a shining black pulled back in a neat bun. "All over social media. We're trawling through them to see if we can pinpoint anyone also caught on camera at the previous scenes."

She'd felt Danny's body tense at the mention of social media, took the lead. "The photos—any of them—?"

Detective Green was already shaking his head, his scalp a freckled paleness where it showed through his

extreme buzz cut. "No compromising shots," he said, then
glanced from Catie to Danny and back, one eyebrow
slightly cocked. "Unless you're concerned about the
images of you two with your arms around each other.
Those are blowing up on every network that we
checked."

That was when Catie realized her phone was still on
silent; she'd forgotten to switch the sound back on after
leaving the hospital. Because no freaking way Veni
wouldn't have called her by now. Especially since the last
message Catie had sent her best friend had been to tell
her that she'd be missing their flight.

"We can handle that," she said, nudging Danny's
shoulder—or, more accurately, a lower part of his arm.
Seated, she was *still* shorter than him. "As if anyone
would believe I'd hook up with hotshot here."

Danny shot her a narrow-eyed look. "Did you or did
you not see that I am considered the Sizzling Bachelor of
the Year according to the biggest women's magazine in
the country?"

"The editors obviously need glasses."

Coughing into her hand in a failed effort to hide her
grin, Detective Shan rose to her feet. Beside her, Detective
Green was making no such effort, his grin creasing his
cheeks and bringing an unexpected twinkle to the hazel
of his eyes.

However, that amusement had faded by the time they
reached the door. "I'm sorry this happened to you," he
said to Danny. "But by reporting the incident, you've
helped us gather more evidence."

Shan nodded. "It might be exactly what we need to
stop anyone else being ambushed."

Catie saw a little of the tension go out of Danny's spine. Again, she thought of Joseph and how he'd raised his boys. As protectors. It would matter to Danny that his actions might help someone else escape the same sense of violation.

"That does help," he said to the detectives and held out his hand.

After everyone shook, the cops left. But Danny's work wasn't yet done. For one, he had to organize a copy of his medical report for both the cops and his agent.

While he disappeared into his bedroom to do that, Catie sat down on the living room sofa with her legs stretched out in front, the snow a steady fall beyond the balcony doors, pulled a cozy blanket over herself, and decided to see how bad it was on social media before she returned all her—*many*—missed calls and texts.

What she discovered almost set her phone on fire.

5

TINGLES, PRIMORDIAL TINGLES

"People are nuts," she muttered to herself as she scanned the explosion of heart emojis and smug "I told you so" comments alongside the gushing hope that their "new love" would last so the fans could enjoy the "wedding of the year."

All because someone had caught her looking up at Danny in concern while he leaned into her. Okay, she could see how her concern might be interpreted as intense interest in the gems of delight falling from his lips —while the way his body was positioned made it seem like he was being all protective.

Meanwhile, he'd been trying not to fall over, and she'd been stressed out over how long Viliame was taking to get back to them.

Rolling her eyes, she took a quick peek at her diary and saw that her memory was spot-on: Veni was doing a partial shift at the hospital today. Since she didn't carry her phone with her on the ward, Catie sent her a quick text saying she'd call once Veni was back home.

Then she got to returning work calls. Including one from her sports agent, Soraya, who immediately looped in Catie's publicist, Ani.

"This is uh-mazing, babes!" Ani gushed. "The coverage is fantastic and so positive!"

"We are not together," Catie muttered.

"Keep saying that." Soraya's far more pragmatic tone. "It'll just make everyone speculate. I've already had multiple companies get in touch about the possibility of dual marketing deals with you as a couple."

Given Jacqueline's wealth, Catie didn't need sponsorship. She accepted it because she wanted to support herself and because it allowed her to help fund smaller charities that Jacqueline had declared not worth the tax deduction. Also, her mother had a way of trading money for control, and while Catie gritted her teeth and bore it when it came to major charitable endeavors, she refused to permit it in her private life.

"Listen to me," she said, word by word, "we are not together. There will be no couple deals."

Ani paused in her ecstatic burbling. "Really? Babes, a one-night hookup between you two will be a *catastrophe*! People are *invested*. They need at least a short-term relationship." Her voice was suddenly two pitches higher. "I need a drink."

"Hey, it's not the fall of the Parthenon," Catie muttered. "It's just social media gossip."

Ani made a strangled sound. "Catie, darling, I love you. So let me make it clear—the public has Daniel Esera on a pedestal, so you'll take the fall."

"If Ani's right," Soraya said, "and I happen to agree

with her, the fallout could impact your other sponsorships."

"Bullshit. This isn't the 1800s."

"Kiddo, people suck," her agent drawled. "And the patriarchy is alive and well. You'll be the hoyden who broke his bright young heart. He'll get aw-baby sweetie, what did that meanie Catie do to you while you'll be cast as the villain. Think about it."

Catie was still fuming ten minutes after the call ended.

When Danny finally emerged from his bedroom after taking care of all the admin, she said, "According to social media, we're getting married any day now and our babies will be the cutest!" She said the last in her peppiest voice.

Mock horror on his face, he collapsed onto the other end of the sofa after patting the blanket to find out where her feet ended. "Matthew gave me the heads-up. Says he's had calls from every possible media outlet."

Catie scowled as a message popped up on her phone, sent through by a girlfriend. "Egad." She turned the screen so Danny could see it. "We are not famous enough for this." It was the online front page of one of the biggest tabloids in the world.

"Apparently, together, we are." He looked a bit ill before suddenly brightening. "Hey, we're snowed in. The assholes can't stalk us!"

Catie stared out at the snow falling beyond the balcony, felt her eyes go wide... and started to cackle. Danny joined in, and the next thing she knew, they were both laughing so hard that she made him look away from her so she could catch her breath.

Of course, that only lasted until he looked back. They set each other off again.

Exhausted afterward, her stomach muscles aching, she thought about what Ani and Soraya had said. She wasn't about to put that on Danny. Not when he was already dealing with shit. "Did you make a therapist appointment?"

"Do I have a mother named Alison Esera who will not stop calling me her baby boy?" Despite his grumpy words and the muscled arms folded across his equally muscled chest, there was love in every word. "I have a remote session this afternoon."

"Good. Better to get it all out there straight off the bat. Don't let it stew."

"You sound like you know what you're talking about."

Catie pointed in the direction of her legs. "Jacqueline has her flaws as a mother, but she made sure I had a therapist in the room the day after I woke up. Ísa had already interviewed the woman to make sure our personalities would mesh. Anyway, I got it all out there, about how scared I was, how I was terrified I'd never run again, and I did feel better."

Danny slumped down farther on the couch. "Shuddup. Your inspiring kid tale is making me feel like a big baby."

Laughing, she threw a cushion at his head. Most people got real quiet when she referred to her accident or its aftermath—or they began to call her brave, or they just didn't know where to look. If there was one thing about Danny that she didn't find nemesis-worthy, it was that he'd always seen *her*—the whole person—her legs or lack of them only one part of her.

The first time they'd met, as young teens, he'd been outraged because she'd dared wear makeup on a beach holiday. He'd spent the entire time fluttering his eyelashes and pretending to put on mascara or otherwise being an insufferable teenage boy. Never once had he treated her like glass, treated her as *other*. To him, she'd just been a teenage girl he wanted to annoy.

Catching the cushion with the same wild grace he showed on the field, he said, "I mean, I did a whole degree in sports psychology, and I've had psychobabble stuff for the team health checks, but this..." He thrust down the cushion and rose. "Can I dig around in your kitchen?"

"Sure." Curious about what he was planning to do, Catie got up and shifted to the other end of the couch so she could watch him while maintaining her laziness. "Chocolate raisin cookies?"

Once, long ago, Danny had thought cooking was for girls. That, however, had changed deliciously as he grew up.

"We'll see," said the grumpy rugby player in the kitchen as he opened the pantry to check out her supplies. "Jeez, princess. Who the fuck stocks this? Saffron strands? Fine dark cooking chocolate? Dried *truffles*? It must all go to waste half the time."

"Nah, housekeeping has instructions to go through the cupboards on a regular basis and donate things to the local food banks at least a month prior to expiry. Gives them a chance to get it out to people who need it. Then housekeeping restocks—except for fresh produce. They're on speed dial to provide that anytime it's required."

When Danny just stared at her, she shook her head. "I did try to convince my mother that it doesn't need to be fully stocked all the time, but she said, 'Caitlin, if I wish to fly to Dunedin on a moment's notice, I expect the pantry to be stocked for my chef.' So this is our compromise."

She held up a finger. "To be clear, I go out and get my own damn fresh stuff—there should be some stuff still in the fridge from the shop I did when I flew in. The supermarket's just down the road. If the snow lets up, we can walk there for anything else you need."

"Humph." With that, Danny began to pull out baking supplies.

"I wonder what would happen if I posted a shot of you baking?" she said, just to rile him up. "All grumpy and moody and with flour on your hands." His fans would combust.

"What would happen is that you'd never again get those chocolate raisin cookies."

"Good threat. I fold." He made *really* good chocolate raisin cookies. Better than any store-bought or bakery ones.

Another message pinged her phone, this one from Ísa. *Catiebug, have you seen the recent speculation? Gabriel's been in touch to say the media might try to get to the family.*

Yup, Catie answered, her heart a big ball of mush for her big sister. *Ani and Soraya and Danny's team are on top of it. They're fielding all inquiries.*

Okay, good. You just call us if you need any help. Love you.

Love you more. She added the heart emoji. *Hug my favorite demons for me.*

Ísa sent through an image of Emmaline and Connor

in response. Both in their pj's, they were tumbling around on the living room floor with their dad, clearly "wrestling," their arms and legs every which way while a grinning and outnumbered Sailor tried to keep them from doing bodily harm to themselves.

Never to each other, however, as nine-year-old Emmaline was fiercely protective of her toddler sibling, who, in turn, thought Emmaline hung the moon. Exactly as Catie had done with Ísa. Still did, to be honest.

Catie immediately saved the photo to her folder for the children of the family.

The mixer started up in the kitchen. Danny wore a look of intense concentration as he added whatever it was he was adding to the mixer—it was the same look he wore on the field at times, usually right before he slipped one of his teammates a pass that no one on the opposition had seen coming.

"Why do you never post online about your baking?" she said when the mixer stopped. His close friends knew about his hobby, but that was a small and tight circle.

A scowling glance before he returned to his wizardry. "It's an image thing, princess. Does your exhausting pixie-bunny of a publicist teach you nothing?"

Catie fought not to laugh at his all-too-accurate description of Ani. Tiny and determinedly cute in her aesthetic, Ani was a rottweiler as a publicist, absolutely brilliant at her job—but she also had no off switch. Her battery was at a hundred percent every minute of every day.

"Do you know about toxic masculinity?" she asked sweetly after she was no longer in danger of bursting into laughter.

"Yes, you tell me every chance you get."

"Guys who cook are hot." In evidence, she pulled up a familiar profile, then held up the phone so he could see. "See? Romanos Cavalier cooks and he's a total thirst trap."

"Are you calling me a thirst trap?" He shot her a grin over his shoulder.

"Not even if I was gasping for a drop of water in a godforsaken desert in the middle of nowhere, *Daniel*."

Laughing that big, warm laugh he'd inherited from his father, he began to chop up something on the board. "Okay, *Caitlin*."

She decided to ignore him in favor of reading a sponsorship contract she'd intended to get to today. But even as she did so, she found herself thinking about what Soraya and Ani had said. The money she might end up losing would mean a loss of independence, not just for her but for the other amputees she supported via her donations to various small organizations.

"What's going on?" Danny said after sliding a tray into the oven. "You look like you're sucking on lemons."

Catie thought about it, pride coming up against practicality and the need to protect Danny. Though... he did look much better, and this wasn't only about her. "According to Ani, I'll bear the brunt of the backlash if we try to walk back the relationship rumors—especially if the public gets the idea that we had a one-night hookup. Could affect my sponsorships."

Danny, who'd begun to whisk something, the veins on his forearms standing out against the brown of his skin, paused, looked over. "You serious?"

"You're the golden boy of Kiwi sport, hotshot, part of a

family that rose from humble roots to become rugby royalty. I'm the poor little rich girl." She shrugged. "I get a little leeway because of the whole not-having-legs thing, but put us side by side in a situation like this, and I'm the one who'll be cast as the bitch."

Hands braced on the counter, he stared at her with pure thunder on his face. It startled her. She'd seen Danny angry, but never at her. Not this way. Their anger toward each other had always been more on the aggravation end of the scale.

Then he said, "People are assholes if they think I've walked a harder road than you. My big brother is *the* fucking Bishop, a straight-up legend in the game. One of my other brothers is the vice-captain of the national squad—and a shoo-in for the captainship when our current captain retires. My father is a former regional player turned senior-level coach."

He barely paused for air before continuing. "Hell, Gabe is over ten years older than me. I was playing with a rising star when I was a skinny primary school kid— where the fuck do they think I learned my skills?"

Something inside Catie went sideways. Just a little bit. But enough to make her breath catch. "Sorry, Danny —to the fans, you're the battler from the streets who made good while I was born with a silver spoon in my mouth."

He narrowed his eyes. "Let me think about this." Then he went back to his whisking, all muscles and veins and concentration.

She took a sneaky pic. Not to put up anywhere. Just to keep for herself as a memory of this unexpected week- end. It had nothing to do with the fact he looked hotter than her favorite chef. Of course not. Danny was not hot. Not to her.

Frowning at herself but oddly relaxed after sharing the problem with him, she went to settle back down and read the contract but made the mistake of glancing at her social media first.

Danny looked up right then. "Are you trying to smite me with that glare?"

"One of your floozies just spammed my socials with a diatribe about how you're hers and I'm a homewrecker."

"She's lying. I'm not going out with anyone."

"I didn't say she was your girlfriend. Did you recently sleep with an eighties-style big-haired brunette with knockout boobs?" Catie took a closer look at the other woman's profile pic. "Ooh, she's gorgeous. Cuckoo bananas stalker given what she's written, but also gorgeous."

Danny looked like he wanted to brain her with the whisk in his hand. "I haven't slept with anyone in the past few months." Red heated his cheekbones. "Jeez, Catie, I can't believe you made me say that." A shake of his head. "There's a reason I avoid you. You make me crazy."

Catie smiled proudly. "Thank you."

Daniel Tana Esera, pinup boy for the masses, national sweetheart, and gifted rugby player, snarled. "No cookies for you."

"Hey!" Pointing her phone at him, she snapped a shot. "Gimme or I'll post this with a sappy heart emoji." No need to tell him he had a murderous glint to his eye that would shoot down any idea of romance.

Not the least worried, Danny checked what he'd put in the oven, then returned to his current work in progress, his biceps flexing as he began to whisk again. "Go away." A growl in his tone that threatened to cause a tingle inside her. "My genius needs space."

Catie wanted to get up and—

Eyes wide, she pulled back her thoughts with a painful screech.

Tingle? What the hell?

Her cheeks flushed. It was the whole cooking thing, she told herself as she picked up the contract again. It was stirring a primordial part of her nature. It had nothing to do with Danny.

Nothing at all.

6

WHEREUPON WE LEARN THAT DANNY IS A HIGH-MAINTENANCE CASANOVA

Delicious smells permeated the air by the time she finally finished reading the contract—she refused to think about why it had taken her so long to concentrate. Putting it aside, she typed up an email on her phone asking for clarification on a couple of clauses, pushed Send, then looked up.

To see Danny walking over with a plate of cookies.

"Eee!" Sitting up, she made gimme hands.

Lips curving, he put the plate on her lap, then placed a glass of milk on the coffee table next to her. "Don't inhale them! They're meant to be savored."

"Mmm-hmm," she said around a mouthful of warm cookie.

Shaking his head, he returned to get himself a glass of milk and his own plate of cookies. Because he knew Catie wouldn't share hers. Then he sat at the other end of the couch, and they ate cookies and drank milk like any other hot young twentysomethings who were having a flaming affair.

Despite Catie's speed eating, he was done before her.

She still thought it sucked how much he could put away and not gain a freaking ounce. That they were both athletes with intensive training schedules just made it worse.

After drinking his milk, he stretched an arm out along the back of the sofa and turned to her. "I've been thinking about what you said, about the whole public backlash."

"Uh-huh." In a sugar-chocolate-raisin haze, she licked her fingers.

Danny's eyes followed the movement before lines formed between his eyebrows and he flicked his attention back to her face. "I have a problem too—the fact I haven't been in a steady relationship is becoming a PR issue."

"You're a twenty-four-year-old star rugby player," Catie said dryly. "No one expects you to settle down."

"Twenty-five in just over a week," Danny pointed out.

"My argument stands. Lots of people our age are single." She pointed at herself as an example.

"That's what I said, but apparently I'm meant to have had a serious girlfriend at least." He shrugged. "I dunno who makes the rules. I mean, with my recent sponsorship deal and how conservative they are, I just laid off on hooking up with anyone. And I'm training right now. Focus is on that. Don't have the attention to spare for women."

"You sound like a grade-A arrogant ass."

"Hey, I can't help it if I'm irresistible." His grin was young and wicked. "I only accept invitations, princess. Can't help it if they keep on coming... and coming."

60

Catie pretended to throw up. "Stop, or I'll have to take off a leg and massacre you with it." The worst thing was that he was right; she'd seen how women drooled over him. "Why did you agree to that sponsorship deal anyway?" The company was well known for being sticklers when it came to the "morality" of their athletes. "Gabe advise you to do it?"

Smile fading, he shook his head. "No, he told me he didn't think it would be a good fit, but it's a shit ton of money." He blew out a breath. "Enough to give me a solid foundation if I suddenly have to stop playing. And all I have to do is walk the straight and narrow for a couple of years."

Catie didn't make a snarky remark, well aware that Danny had watched a career-ending injury fell the big brother he idolized. That he had family support didn't matter, not in this. It was a thing of pride, but not the bad kind. No, it was the kind that made for a good man—one who wanted to stand on his own feet.

"I get it," Catie said, thinking of her own fight for independence against Jacqueline.

Their eyes met, understanding passing between them.

Until she couldn't take the intensity of it, broke the contact. "You've still got the clean-cut image even if you haven't had a steady girlfriend. You must have good taste in hookups since no one has sold their story to the magazines."

"Hey, it's not like I'm—what's his name?—Casanova. I don't have time to be juggling women. I just have the odd night out like any normal guy my age." He pointed a finger. "And I'll have you know, the women I've been with don't want relationships either. I'm considered too high-maintenance."

Blinking, Catie tilted her head. "Say what?"

"The fame thing." He twisted his lips. "Lots of women don't want to have cameras shoved in their faces, lose their privacy. And the ones who *would* be okay with it... I dunno, I feel like they're after me for the fame, not for me."

Catie got it; she'd been chased by her share of fame hounds—in her case, it could get even grosser. Because too many times, said hounds were "willing" to date an amputee to get their shot at the spotlight. As if she wouldn't kick their loser asses out the door if they came anywhere near her.

"Still," she said, "your shtick is that you don't break women's hearts or roll out of clubs at three in the morning." No woman in Danny's orbit ever had anything bad to say about him.

"My shtick?" Chest rumbling, he grabbed her blanket-covered foot—but didn't pull or do anything else rough. "Do you just sit around thinking up ways to annoy me?"

"You're not that interesting, so don't flatter yourself." She held out the plate. "More cookies."

He glared at her but rose to refill her plate. The instant his back was turned, she took a long, shaky breath to calm herself down because the tingle had returned, and it was in her breasts now.

And she was *not* okay with it.

"I'm only giving you two," he said. "I don't want your nutritionist blaming me for your diet."

"What she doesn't know won't hurt her." Catie's heart

thumped as he walked toward her; she told herself it was just a thing of circumstance. After all, they were literally living a romance novel—snowed in, just the two of them, with him making delicious baked goods.

She'd have to be superhuman to resist.

The tingles would pass with the snowstorm. She just had to make sure not to do anything stupid in the interim —because wow, how horrific would it be to walk it back in the cold light of day? And to know she was just another notch on the bedpost?

A shudder rolled through her.

Yeeeaaaah. Nope, nope, nopety nope.

Taking a small bite of cookie to savor its chocolatey raisin deliciousness, she got back to those notches that had successfully killed the tingles dead. "Shtick or brand or whatever, yours doesn't involve a parade of bitter women. They should be happy about that. Why are you getting blowback?"

"You know I don't take dates to awards ceremonies or other formal events. I mean, I took Mum that one time, and that was cool, but apparently the fact I've never taken anyone else is starting to be noticed and maybe not in the best way. 'Commitment issues.'" He curved his fingers into air quotes.

"Why haven't you?" she asked. "Taken a date to a fancy shindig?"

"Because dates come with expectations." He grimaced. "Especially a date on a stage that big, and even more because I haven't done it before. It's a serious decla-ration—and I haven't been with anyone long enough to get anywhere *near* that point."

Catie nodded slowly. "I see the problem, hotshot. By

going solo most of the time, you've now set yourself up so you can't take anyone without it being a major deal."

"Exactly." He pointed at her. "Which leads me to the solution to our mutual problems."

"I'm listening."

"I promised Leon I'd show up to the premiere of his play. He's wrangled a theater outside the city for it." He paused, frowned. "You ever met him? He came to a couple of barbeques at Mum and Dad's, but I think it might've been while you were training out of the country."

Catie shook her head. "I definitely don't remember a friend of yours who's involved with plays. You said he booked the theater—do you mean he's actually putting on the play? Producing the whole thing?"

"Yeah, he's fucking talented. Wrote the script, too." Pure, generous warmth. "Anyway, his premiere deal's meant to be tomorrow—if it manages to go ahead." He nodded at the falling snow. "But if it does"—he lifted crossed fingers—"you could come with me to that. And later to a couple of other things, and I'll be your fake boyfriend for whatever length of time is enough to protect you from any backlash."

Catie chewed on that. "I have to pretend to adore you?" she asked dubiously.

Throwing back his head, Danny laughed so hard that she tried to kick him. "You're not that good an actress, princess," he said, catching her foot with a careful hand, his eyes dancing. "Just be your usual annoying self— according to everyone, that's a sign of twuuu wuuuv anyway."

Catie snorted out a laugh. "The fam won't go for it."

They knew the two of them too well. Even Jacqueline. "Veni either. She's already suspicious."

"We'll bring them in on the act. I do not want to try lying to my mother—or yours. And I have no problem with Veni knowing—when we were kids, I tried to bribe her with chocolate to play a prank on you. She dumped a glass of ice water on my head."

Catie felt zero surprise at the latter. As for their parents... Alison just *knew* when you were bullshitting. It was like a superpower. And Jacqueline was relentless. "They'll think it's weird."

"Nah. They've seen all the media crap with Gabe and Jake. They'll get it."

"Hmm." Catie considered his idea, thought of all the money she could make for the organizations that relied heavily on her support. "You up for doing a few couple-type sponsorships?"

"Yeah, if you want. You want to bulk up the funding to the camp?"

Catie nodded. "Partially. So many kids have told me they'd never have been brave enough to use prostheses without the camp." Jacqueline had sent Catie to a similar international children's camp when she first began to wear prosthetic legs, and though Catie had already been determined to use them full time, meeting older kids who were already living that life had helped her an incredible amount.

Especially after she was introduced to her mentor, Posey, who, at twenty-three, was already a champion skier.

Catie's future dreams had suddenly taken concrete form.

The New Zealand version of the camp, which ran for a full month over the summer holidays, was the first thing she'd set up on her own—from contacting the large international camp to get advice on how to start, to touching base with local amputee services to spread the word about the initiative.

Jacqueline had offered to fund it, but it meant so much to Catie to have built the entire operation from the ground up exactly as she envisioned, and she was determined to maintain its independence. She had, however, made it clear to her mother that she'd never forget the gift Jacqueline had given her by sending her to that international camp.

Her mother, tough as steel, had actually looked nonplussed when Catie hugged her in thanks... but then she'd hugged Catie back and said, "I'm glad I got it right that time," her voice quieter than Catie had ever before heard it.

That same voice had rung with open pride the last time she'd visited the camp. "Look at all this, and you'd never know you began as an eighteen-year-old with five kids in a day program."

The Dragon might like control, but she also appreciated the fact her children—stepson Harlow included—had spines.

"It's fucking amazing what you do." Danny's smile made his eyes light up, the reason he was the pinup of so many. When Danny Esera smiled with his whole heart, he was absolutely beautiful.

Not that Catie was affected.

At all.

"We need ground rules if we're going to do this," she

said and picked up her tablet and electronic pen off the coffee table. "First rule: no PDA."

"Vetoed." Danny slashed out a hand. "There has to be some PDA if we're going to sell it, but nothing like tongue kissing. That's a step into nightmare territory."

"I am never tongue kissing you, so don't worry about that." Skin unexpectedly hot, she considered his rejection of her suggested rule, decided he was right. "Minor PDA only. Hugs permitted. Arms around waists, that kind of thing. Kiss on the cheek is the closest you get to my mouth."

"Agreed. And same. These luscious lips are off-limits to you." Danny rubbed his bristled jaw. "Since we're both pretty private on our socials, too much PDA would look suspicious anyway."

"If we have to be in a place where we have to share a room to sell it, you get the couch."

"No way." Danny scowled. "We're sharing. We've done it before."

"That was outside, in sleeping bags on the beach."

"Same diff." He waggled his eyebrows. "Unless you think you won't be able to keep your hands off me."

"You wish."

"Most hotels have rooms with king beds," he pointed out. "They're huge. We'll build a pillow wall and that's it."

Catie paused. This wasn't about her snowbound-induced awareness of Danny. Fact was, she didn't like just anyone seeing her stumps. Not that she hid them—for one, she gave regular talks to children where she showed them how her prosthetic legs worked so they could be more comfortable with other children who had to wear artificial limbs.

And Danny had seen her without her prostheses plenty of times.

But being *in bed* without her prostheses... that wasn't the same as horseplay on the beach. It was a whole different level of vulnerability. Of intimacy. "No, Danny," she said, readying herself for an argument. "I need the bed."

7

HERE BE DRAGONS

Danny frowned, parted his lips, then looked into her eyes. "Okay, you get the bed." A gentleness to his tone that made her cheeks flush, but he carried on before she could get uncomfortable. "I'll see if I can find an air mattress small enough to smuggle in a suitcase. Most of the fancy hotel couches are insanely tiny."

Fighting off her hot cheeks and the urge to be annoyed with him for getting it—getting *her*, she said, "Or you can be a diva and ask for a custom 'rugby player suitable' couch."

"Will work on my soprano."

Heart dangerously softer toward her childhood nemesis—a nemesis she was starting to see had grown into the best of men—she looked at her list. "We have to have an end date." For both their sakes. "Six months?"

He shrugged. "Sounds okay. That's like a real relationship that just happened not to work out. And after, we can still do our usual social stuff so people don't think we're enemies."

"Except we are."

"Exactly."

Laughing, happy, content in this moment, she said, "What else?"

"You don't look at me with dagger eyes everywhere we go."

"No one will believe it."

"In fact, I want goo-goo love eyes."

Catie would've thrown a cushion at him, but she liked the one she was sitting against. "Shall we tell the family now, before we do anything else?"

"Yeah, might as well bite that bullet."

They decided to do it on a visual conference call, complete with the Dragon. Who said, "A wise business decision for both your brands."

Catie had never before seen her mother's business brain as an emotional asset.

The rest of the family laughed and took bets on how long Catie and Danny could keep it up.

The longest bet came from Charlotte, who said, "They'll go all the way." The hazel of her eyes sparkled behind the clear lenses of her spectacles.

Everyone else told Gabriel's gentle, strong wife that she was going to lose all her money.

"O ye of little faith," Danny said. "Catie and Charlie and I are going to take *all* your money. Put it on the line if you're so confident."

They all did except for Jacqueline, who just raised a single eyebrow. "Caitlin is my child. She will ensure Daniel follows through."

Ducking out of camera angle by pretending to reach for something, Danny mouthed a dragonish roar.

Catie gave him a smug smile.

Charlotte, meanwhile, was laughing, Gabriel's deep voice tangling with the sound as he tried—and failed—to convince her that she was throwing away her money. Charlie might be the quietest member of the extended family, but she knew how to hold her own—especially with her big, brash husband.

"So you'll all back the story in public?" Danny asked after returning into the shot.

"Of course" was the response from so many throats that Catie couldn't separate them out.

Not that the backup had ever been in question. The family might razz them in private, but in public they'd be an impenetrable wall. It was only after they'd hung up that Danny said, "You didn't add your dad to the call." His gaze was gentle.

Irritated, she shoved off the blanket and swung her legs to the floor. "Clive would sell the story to the highest bidder."

"Hey." Danny reached out to grip her arm, his hold warm and loose enough for her to break at will. "I wasn't poking at you. I thought I heard that, you know, he'd gotten a bit better. Not the money stuff obviously, but the rest."

Catie shrugged off his hand, but she couldn't keep up her anger. Because it wasn't about Danny. Dropping her head, she shoved her hands through her hair. "He's older, not wiser, Danny."

Catie would never trust Clive—and that hurt her heart. But she had enough of Jacqueline in her to understand that emotion couldn't reign supreme—not when it came to something this important. She'd always love her father, but trust was out of the question.

"The whole leopards don't change their spots thing?" she said, staring at the wall rather than at Danny. "That's Clive in a nutshell." She wished she was wrong, that her father was a better man, but she wasn't and he wasn't. "I stopped expecting more from him a long time ago."

She got up. "I need to move." And she didn't need to see compassion in Danny's eyes. He'd never get it, not when he'd been raised in the most stable family situation Catie had ever seen. His older brothers though, Gabriel and Sailor, they got it.

That wasn't just supposition. A year after Sailor married Ísa, he'd found Catie crying after Clive pulled some stunt Catie could no longer remember. Her brother-in-law had hugged her with those big strong arms, rocking her like she was a little girl; then he'd told her about the deadbeat who'd been his mother's first husband, a man who'd walked out on his family after cleaning out their accounts.

"He came back into our life toward the end of his," Sailor had told her. "Though I could allow that, allow compassion for a dying man, I couldn't forgive him for all that he'd done. Trust was never going to happen between us."

He'd squeezed her tight against the protective warmth of his chest. "I loved him as a kid, really loved him, even when he broke promises, even when he was never there when he said he would be.

"It's okay to love the screwed-up people in our lives, Catie. But you have to also understand that they are who they are and learn to stop expecting them to change—that's the only way you can survive without being hurt over and over again. You have to learn to create a distance between their actions and your heart."

Catie adored her brother-in-law. It had taken time and a few more knocks, but she'd taken his words to heart. As she had her mother's.

"Clive was a mistake," Jacqueline had said to her once, then, in a rare moment of softness, added, "The only good thing I ever got out of that relationship was you." A touch of Catie's hair. "But don't pin your hopes on him, Catie. He's just not built to treasure them." Sadness in her voice.

Catie had taken her mother's hand, and they'd stood there, staring out the plate glass window of Jacqueline's penthouse apartment in Auckland city, a rare moment of sympathy between mother and child.

But Danny wasn't like Gabriel and Sailor. He'd grown up with not only two loving parents but two amazing big brothers. She couldn't expect him to understand what it was to have a gambling addict for a father, an addict who'd nonetheless been there for her at the worst possible time in her life—he hadn't ducked out to gamble even once.

Nothing was uncomplicated when it came to her relationship with Clive.

"Catie," Danny began.

"I'm going to use the gym for a bit. Don't join me." She made the last an order before she headed to her room to change.

Danny was nowhere in sight when she reappeared, so she figured he'd headed into his bedroom, but the whole apartment smelled delicious. Whatever he still had in the oven was making her stomach rumble despite her cookie feast.

"Exercise first." It wasn't only about maintaining her athletic strength but about keeping a healthy body overall because it all fed into her speed and skill on the track. It also helped stave off injuries—though nothing was guaranteed.

She pushed thoughts of her mentor Posey's latest injury out of her mind and strode to the gym on her running blades. They weren't the ones she used on the track, rather a pair she'd had customized for gym or treadmill use—she always packed one set of blades no matter where she traveled or for how long.

Sometimes it felt like she was flying when she ran full-tilt on her blades. No limitations, no stopping her. She *was* the wind.

She kept that mantra uppermost in her mind as she walked into the spacious gym area and got to work. Just because she was a runner didn't mean she didn't also need upper-body strength—especially as a double lower-limb amputee. She did a lot of work with her upper body when she wasn't wearing prostheses. The latter was a rare occurrence these days, but Catie wasn't about to be caught flat-footed—no pun intended.

Her lips quirked at the unintended joke.

Her mood got better with each rep and each lift until she felt more even-keeled at last. Movement always did this for her. It had been her inability to move that had most badly impacted her after the accident. She'd talked a good game, but she'd been so scared she'd be stuck in a bed forever, her body mangled beyond repair.

She'd been so lucky that her therapist back then had figured out the truth and the hospital physiotherapist had managed to put together a program that she could do from her bed until she was in a position to progress out of it.

At first, given her injuries, it had been as basic as simply squeezing a soft foam ball with her left hand, then her right, for a specific number of reps. Sounded like nothing, but it had meant everything to Catie to reach those goals—then blow past them.

"Ahem." A knock on the side of the wide doorway that led into the gym area. "Is it safe, Small Dragon? Do I risk being crispy-fried?"

She would *not* laugh.

Stomach aching from the strength it took to hold in her mirth, she gave Danny a haughty look and saw that he was in workout gear too. "What do you want?"

"Figured I could warm up while you cool down." Scuffing at the floor with his sneakered foot, he lifted his shoulders in a shrug, his expression sheepish. "I usually work out with the team during the season or with one of my brothers during downtime."

"That's the difference between us, Daniel," she said. "You're a team player and I'm out for myself." But she moved so he had room to stretch on the mat next to her.

"BS, Caitlin." He did a few moves that looked more like yoga than anything else. "You're on the relay team. Or is that another Caitlin Moonbell River?"

She glared at him. "*M*," she gritted out. "We only ever say Caitlin *M*. River unless we wish to be decapitated." Jacqueline had still been in love with Clive when she gave birth to Catie, hence the fact Catie had the hippiest middle name to ever hippie its way into the world.

"Do we?" A wild grin before he dropped to the floor to do push-ups. He was wearing a sleeveless gray tee, but she could see the fluidity of the muscles moving in his back, the curves of power in his biceps, the way his thighs and calves were tightly, heavily muscled.

Jeez, Catie, snap out of it. This is DANNY.

Clenching her jaw, she continued with her cooldown but couldn't stop from asking, "Your tat finished?" All four brothers had tattoos that celebrated Samoan culture. Though Gabriel and Sailor hadn't been born into it, Joseph was the man they called Dad, and they wore their tattoos with pride. As the youngest, Danny had been the final one to start the ink, and last she knew, it was still in progress.

"Yeah, it's done. Wanna see?" Bouncing back to his feet with the ease of an athlete at the top of his game, he pulled up the edge of his workout shorts to reveal one superbly muscled thigh circled by an intricate tattoo that had been done piece by precise piece. Dots and angles and lines that formed a one-of-a-kind piece of art.

Catie found herself reaching out to touch, snatched back her hand before he could realize what she was doing. She'd never live down petting Danny's thigh. "Your uncle does amazing work."

"Right?" He beamed and dropped the edge of the shorts before she got her fill. "Worth every bit of pain. I've been talking to him and Dad about getting more ink down the road." He touched his upper chest. "Maybe on one of my pecs."

As he went back down to the floor to finish his

push-ups, Catie took a deep breath and told herself she was losing it. Because she'd been *checking Danny out*. Ugh, this whole abnormal situation was obviously getting to her. She'd have to keep on top of herself not to give in to the fake dating thing and start to think it was real.

It wasn't that she thought Danny was a bad guy. No, he was one of the good ones. But well, it was *Danny*. The bane of her existence. And a man who honestly deserved a lover far more emotionally balanced than Catie. He was so wholesome and *normal*, and she wasn't.

Forget her parents, losing her legs hadn't exactly helped with her sunny disposition either. She was moody and grumpy, and yeah, she'd scare Danny off in five minutes flat if they actually tried to get together for real.

Nope. Nope. Nope.

Even if they hadn't been so wrong for each other, she loved his family too much to mess things up by making it uncomfortable between them. That would be an absolute horror show. The two of them avoiding each other at barbeques and pretending everything was normal when it so obviously wasn't.

No, thank you.

"The call went better than I thought it would," Danny said, switching to do raised-knee crunches, his breathing even despite his pace. "I was worried Dad might not approve, but even he got in on the bets."

"You have a wonderful family, Danny," Catie found herself saying, her mind continuing along its earlier train. "Don't ever take them for granted."

A pause, Danny glancing up at her with a slight flush on his cheekbones before he looked away and continued on. "I know they're amazing," he said. "I lucked out." Sincerity in every word, and yet...

She frowned, sure she was missing something. That was when her phone, which she'd brought in so she could stream her music, pinged with an incoming text. Picking it up, she found a message from Laveni: *I'm sneaking a break while Suz covers for me. Only have five minutes. Call now or I shall fly over there with my thumbscrews. Are you two really a thing?*

Catie had no secrets from her best friend, so she stopped what she was doing to step out. "Going to talk to Veni."

"Tell her that ice water gave me a head cold. I hope she feels guilty."

Grinning, she wandered into the living room as she made the call.

"I knew it!" Veni crowed when Catie confessed that the hookup rumors weren't true. "So why did you sneak off with him?"

Catie found herself in a quandary. She and Veni told each other everything... but Danny had been so vulnerable last night and this morning, his hand tight on hers. She wanted—needed—to protect him. "I had a good reason, Veni, but I can't tell you what," she said, deciding on another kind of honesty.

"Hmm, I'd accuse you of shifting loyalties to a boy, but I know you better than that," Veni said. "And don't you think I didn't notice that that sexy hunk Viliame left with you two." She whistled and Catie could all but see her fanning her face. "I've never seen him up that close before, and oh my lady parts, that man is *fiiiiiine*. Almost as fine as my Ben, but not everyone can be a delicious scrumptious sex god."

Laughing, Catie leaned up against the counter. "Thanks for not getting mad that I can't tell you everything yet."

"I know you, Cates. You wouldn't do it if it wasn't necessary. So I'm all good to tell the others the media is blowing smoke up everyone's butts?"

Catie took a deep breath. "About that."

8

NOPE, NOPE, NOPETY NOPE (AND NOPE!)

Her ears were still ringing with the sound of Laveni's hysterical laughter when she walked back into the gym. "Veni gives us three dates before we blow our cover and start lobbing virtual pies at each other's faces." She scowled. "Charlie is now my favorite person."

"World ain't seen nothing yet," Danny said, still doing those crunches but with a little more heat to his face now, a touch of sweat on his brow. "If we can be that bad alone, imagine how much chaos we can create together."

"Hmm." Still, nudged on by her best friend's lack of faith in their acting skills, she snapped a pic of Danny as he sat up after completing the crunches. Hair a touch disheveled and gray tee contrasting against the brown of his skin, a little stubble on his jaw, he looked disgustingly good.

"You okay with me posting this?" There were rules in their ongoing war—that they didn't post private photos of each other was one of them.

She had a lot of images of him playing rugby with the family or just hanging out. Mostly because she'd been taking photos of everyone else and he'd been in them, but she'd never posted any of those images. Family was private, was to be held safe.

Danny gave it a glance. "Yeah, sure. What're you going to write?"

Catie got an evil look on her face as she tapped away without telling him. Knowing her all too well, he grabbed his own phone and wasn't the least surprised to find she'd written: *This rando followed me home last night. Should I throw him out into the snow? Vote yes for yes and no for yes.*

"Oh, like that, is it?" he muttered and typed up a comment even as the post began to rack up likes at the speed of light.

Caitlin, we talked about this. Be nice, or I won't give you what you most want in the whole wide world.

As he'd expected, his comment set the thread on fire. Everyone thought he was talking about sex. Flame emojis. Tongue emojis. Eggplants. And it degenerated from there.

"What?" he said innocently when she glared at him as her notifications went nuts. "I was talking about the cookies."

Still glaring, she stomped out—which was difficult to achieve since she was wearing those blades that made her move with a light bounce to her step. But her grace wasn't only because of the prostheses. It was her. He'd seen her in motion on the track, and holy hell, the woman was pure liquid lightning.

He was a runner too, burst into punches of motion on

the field, but he didn't move like Catie. She moved like she'd been born to run, where to him, running was just one part of his toolbox for the game. After a lifetime of training, her entire body was streamlined for her chosen sport. But as a sprinter, she had curves aplenty. Especially those glutes that were toned and round and—

Whoa.

Wait.

Where the fuck had that come from?

He did not think about Catie's butt!

Okay, fine, he'd admired it now and then—hell, it *was* fantastic. He'd have had to be blind not to notice. But he'd noticed in a way that wasn't this conscious. It had just been a passing thought. That hey, Catie was curvy there and it was hot, and then the thought had been gone because it was *Catie.*

Except now they were pretending to be in a relationship and he was going to be getting a lot closer to those tight, round curves.

His cock *reacted.*

Horrified, he glanced down with a stern "*No.*" He was permitted the odd admiring thought or two, but never would he actually act on them.

It would mess up their whole thing.

She was his nemesis, and that brought him an immense amount of joy. It'd be so incredibly awkward to turn that into a sexual thing that, given his track record, would no doubt crash and burn—and then they'd be familiar strangers. The thought made him want to shudder.

Nope, nope, nope.

His thoughts about Catie's curves—and the attendant

physical reaction—could go right back into the mental box in which they belonged. He repeated that admonishment more than once as he went through his workout.

What he could actually do with was a hard run. Since he couldn't go out on the streets, he powered up the treadmill, set it to his preferred speed and incline, and got on with it. After breaking once to check on the cheese-and-ham muffins he had in the oven, he picked up where he'd left off.

He'd used some frozen shredded zucchini he'd found in the freezer—because of course Jacqueline had something so random stocked—as a base for the muffins, so they were healthy in the overall scheme of things, but he was really there for the cheese. His mum had taught all her boys to cook, but it had taken Danny a while to get into it.

When he had finally hit his groove, he'd discovered that while he enjoyed cooking well enough, he absolutely *loved* to bake. His next challenge was pastry from scratch —that stuff was fricking hard, especially since he wanted to make these particular pastries that he'd eaten once in Paris.

Frowning, he kept himself occupied with thoughts of how to refine his recipe as he finished up his run, then decided to do a cooldown. Since, according to the weather report, he'd be stuck in this apartment for today and tomorrow at least, there was no need to push it all in during one workout. He could pepper things in through the day.

His phone rang just as he was finishing up.

Seeing his coach's name on the screen, he felt his gut twist.

. . .

CATIE CAME out of her bedroom, dressed in her beloved velour sweat suit; a designer item, it would've been ridiculously rich-girl OTT if she hadn't found it on special at an online retailer that was trying to get rid of excess stock. She tried not to spend her money frivolously—and she never touched Jacqueline's money for anything private beyond her prostheses.

The latter she could justify because what she saved on those, she could pass on to other amputees, *and* she was often a guinea pig for various new prosthetic developments and adjustments for which she had to give detailed feedback and go in for multiple fittings and tests. It felt like a fair exchange.

"You're just a money hoarder," her father had said more than once with a cheerful laugh. "Baby girl, your mother is filthy rich. Tap that well."

And *that* was the difference between her and Clive.

Sniffing the air, she headed unerringly to the delicious cheesy smell coming from the kitchen. A set of perfect golden muffins sat on a cooling rack that she hadn't even known was in the apartment. She reached to grab one, snatched back her hand. She did have *some* manners.

Since Danny's door was closed, he was likely in the shower after his own workout. She'd taken a bit longer because she'd wanted to wash her hair and shave her legs. You'd think the tasks would be quick enough, but with getting into different legs for the shower and all the rest, it was a bit of a mission.

Deciding she had the self-control to wait for Danny,

she set the table for lunch, then made a couple of smoothies. She knew the kind Danny drank while he was training, and it wasn't hard to put together with the ingredients on hand. She was just placing his green concoction by his plate when he stepped out of his room.

His hair was damp, his body clad only in a T-shirt and a pair of old shorts that barely covered half his tattoo. Jerking her misbehaving eyes up to his face, she smiled. "You look cheerful. Good news?"

"Yeah." Padding over to the kitchen area on bare feet, he grabbed the butter as well as a side dish of fresh salad he'd prepared at some point, added both to the table. "Talked to my Harriers coach, and he'd already talked to management beforehand. They made the call to touch base on this with the national team too."

Blowing out a breath between smiling lips, he said, "In summary, my medical records came through, the doctors and Vili backed me up, and apparently the fact I filed a police report was the icing on the cake. I'm good."

Joy sparked bright in her veins. Not thinking about it, she threw her arms around him. "That's great, Danny."

Wrapping his own arms around her, he lifted her off her feet in a huge bear hug. Catie normally hated being treated this way—but the men of the Bishop-Esera family were an exception. Maybe because when it came time to talk sport, they never talked down to her. They discussed her career with the same dead seriousness they discussed the rugby careers of Jake and Danny.

After Ísa hooked up with Sailor, Catie'd had a Bishop-Esera presence at every one of her meets. One time, when Ísa and Sailor couldn't come because Ísa was *wayyyyyy* pregnant with Emmaline and about to pop, it was Joseph and Danny who'd driven down to the meet, complete with a giant homemade fluoro-orange banner to cheer her on.

It had been horribly, wonderfully embarrassing. Her friends had teased her for days. And she'd loved every minute of it.

"Put me down, you animal," she said, but she was laughing.

Grinning, Danny put her on her feet with a care that was kind of annoying for reasons she couldn't quite put into words. "I have excellent balance," she muttered.

"I know," he said easily.

"Ugh." She pushed at his shoulders before she walked away.

He threw up his hands. "What did I do now?"

"Nothing." Except be annoyingly even-tempered. It was unnatural. Surely he should have some off days, some days where he was moody and temperamental? That was how people were—they weren't just cheerful all the time.

Or maybe golden boys were.

"Do we eat or what?"

Screwing up his nose at her, he brought over the muffins, served her one, then got one for himself.

She split hers open with her hands and breathed in the fragrant steam. Her mouth watered. "Okay, fine, you're a good cook."

"Gee thanks, princess." He buttered half his muffin, the heat melting the butter within seconds. Then he took a giant bite. "Mmm." The sound was low and deep and... interesting.

Again, that twitch low in her belly, a twitch that

threatened to spread to the space between her legs. What was *happening* to her? Dread dried up her mouth. It couldn't just be proximity. They'd been proximate plenty of times before at various family events.

Family events.

Key word being *family*.

Never alone.

Just the two of them.

Stuck in an apartment while the snow fell outside.

Shoving a buttered piece of muffin into her mouth in an effort to derail that dangerous line of thought, she found herself moaning in a way that would've been embarrassing if it hadn't brought a delighted light into Danny's eyes. "Ish good," she managed around her mouthful.

"Yeah?" He took another bite, chewed, seemed to think about it. "Yeah, I think I have the ratios just right."

He was so serious about it that she paused, gave him a searching look. "You decided to become a chef or something, Daniel?"

Color on his cheekbones, followed by an eyebrow-lowered look worthy of a mafia don. "Don't say a word to my family. Swear on that necklace you never take off."

The necklace in question—a fine gold chain with three small stars hanging off it—had been a gift from Clive a long time ago, back when she'd been a little girl and had still believed in him. Sad that she couldn't give it up, but hey, dreams were free and it was a good memory of a lovely day.

"Fine, I swear." She held up her necklace as she made the vow. "Though what's the big deal? All your family cooks."

That too was another thing that had surprised her when she'd met Alison and Joseph's clan. In her family, Ísa was the only one who cooked. The times Catie was with Clive, it was either Martha who prepared the food—or, if Martha was off—it was all prepackaged meals Catie put into the microwave. She'd been doing so since she was at elementary school. With Jacqueline, a chef did everything.

It had astonished her to see Sailor so at home in the kitchen. He'd made her and Ísa pancakes that first time, and while she'd tried not to show it, Catie had been goggle-eyed by the situation. Then she'd met Alison and Joseph and the others and learned that cooking together was a family thing. Which included Catie if she was in the vicinity.

She'd pretended to be aggravated by the tasks given her—like peeling potatoes or chopping carrots—but secretly she'd felt like she'd been dropped into the middle of one of those perfect sitcom families. She hadn't been able to believe her luck that she was being welcomed by them.

But she had—and she'd also learned to cook. A lot of dishes, she'd learned to cook with Danny. The two of them were so close in age that whoever was doing the teaching would often rope in both of them for the lesson.

"So you can feed yourselves as athletes without relying on anyone else," Joseph had once said.

Catie was grateful for the lessons, but where she was a functional cook, Danny was brilliant, had always been the better of the two of them. "Danny."

"You know what I studied at uni," he muttered, folding his arms across his chest—unknowingly drawing her eyes to the veins that ran over his forearms. "That's the field I'm meant to be going into after I retire from sport."

Which wouldn't be for a decade or more—he was in the prime of his life. As her body had begun to notice far too much for her peace of mind.

"BS." Wanting to shake herself for her reaction to him, she took a sip of her smoothie, then began to butter the second half of her muffin. "Nobody in the family cares what you do post-sport so long as you have some kind of plan for it."

That was a tenet with which they'd beaten Catie over the head too—figuratively speaking and with lots of love. Sport wasn't forever, not at their level. They'd both run and play until they dropped dead, but at some point it wouldn't be as highly paid professionals. The sponsorships would fall off as their influence waned.

If they were smart, if they saved and invested well, they'd be set up financially speaking—but they could also turn into emotional wrecks without direction if they didn't know what to do with the rest of their lives.

"Reality of professional sport," Gabriel had said to her once. "Don't let it kick you in the ass. Be ready so you can take the next stage of your life by the horns."

Which was why she didn't get Danny's reticence. "You want to open a restaurant or something?" she asked. "I mean, if Gabe's still investing for you, you'll have more than enough money." Gabriel Bishop was also investing half of Catie's retirement savings while Jacqueline was doing the other half.

The two had an unofficial contest going to see who could get the best returns, though they'd never admit it.

They just tried to sneak bits of info out of Catie by talking about her overall portfolio.

"It just feels..." Danny thrust his hands through his hair. "Catie, my big brother owns half the city, my other big brother started an empire in his early twenties, and my *third* big brother is the vice-captain of the national team—a team which he made while having a kid as a teenager and losing the love of his teenage life."

Breath harsh and the volume of his voice rising, he slapped both hands down on the table. "My dreaming of a future making pastries is not going to cut it!"

9

IN WHICH THERE ARE ABS OF STONE (AND "INTERESTING" TWINGES. UH-OH.)

Catie blinked, stared, took a sip of her smoothie. "Whoa." She'd never, not once, thought about what it might mean to be the fourth sibling in the Bishop-Esera family, but when Danny put it like that... "Big boots to fill."

"Tell me about it." Expression glum, he slumped back in his seat.

But Catie wasn't done. "Jake says all the time that he'd never have made the team without your support." Danny had actually been picked for the national squad first, though Jake was two years older.

"He always talks about the family support that got him through and how if other teen parents had that kind of support, they'd be able to achieve so much more." Jake was actually an ambassador these days for a youth program that supported teen parents. "He never ever tries to say he did it on his own."

"Sure," Danny agreed, having drunk half his smoothie in the interim. "But you know he just started a degree in automotive engineering *and* he's already getting broadcasting gigs? I wouldn't have believed it if you'd told me a year ago—Jake can be weirdly shy, but these days I turn on the screen, there's his face."

"Exaggeration much?" She raised an eyebrow. "Jake is doing a single paper this semester, and he has *one* show that he films around his rugby and other commitments."

"It's on prime time," Danny shot back. "Highest ratings of any new sports shows in the past ten years. And all I want to do is make pastries and cakes and muffins and not have a restaurant empire."

"You know your entire family would buy out your bakery and tell all their friends in support of your new career?"

"I know." If anything, he slumped farther down in his chair. "Your mum ever lean on you to follow in her footsteps?"

"Nope. Not since Harlow came through back when we were teenagers." Her stepbrother was Jacqueline's true son when it came to the business world.

Jacqueline respected Harlow even more because he'd left her company and worked internationally for several years, gaining valuable experience—and doing it all on his own. Catie was her brother's chief cheerleader and loved how he didn't flinch at butting heads with the Dragon.

Funnily enough, she thought Jacqueline might enjoy the verbal duels just as much.

"Mum's expecting me to go into the charity sector because of my camp," she added, "and yeah, I can see it."

Danny nodded. "It's amazing, what you do."

"You helped. Thanks." It wasn't so hard to choke that

out. "The kids get a kick out of having you come and spend time with them." With rugby a certified national craze, getting to interact with a player as admired as Danny was a major deal.

"It's fun, especially seeing their faces light up when you and the other instructors join me for a game of touch."

Their eyes met, a simple, powerful understanding passing between them in that moment. Then it shifted, just a fraction. A problematic fraction. The eye contact held a moment too long, the intensity of the connection a little too deep.

They both jerked their heads away, suddenly deeply focused on their meals.

Ignore, ignore, ignore.

Her phone buzzed. Buzzed again. And again. Thanking the heavens for the interruption, she grabbed it from her pocket. "My girlfriends," she said. "They must've just seen my post. They're going nuts in our group chat. Veni's playing along."

"Of course the rest of them are hyped up." Danny leaned back in his chair in that sprawled-out male way and held out his arms. The position emphasized the sleek musculature of his chest, showed off the line of his biceps, made the light shine on his far-too-sexy forearms. "Because I'm superhot."

"This is hell." Catie threw up her hands in lieu of strangling her fluttering stomach. "What did I do to deserve it, that's what I want to know."

"Oh, you doth protest too hard, Caitlin. I think the fans are right. You're madly in lust with me." He widened his eyes. "Should I lock my door tonight? Will you be able to resist the urge to break it down and attack my fine bod?"

Catie would not laugh. She. Would. *Not*. Laugh.

But a snort escaped her nose, and then it was all over. Only Danny could do this to her—make her laugh so hard that her stomach hurt. Especially when he joined in with that infectious, warm laugh of his.

Wiping away tears a long time later, she pulled up the chat. "A whole bunch of 'you're a sly one' followed by 'we're so happy for you!' and oh, they want to know if you're good in bed?"

She looked up just in time to catch dark red bloom across Danny's cheeks, his mouth falling open before he snapped it shut and pushed back his chair. "I'm going to clear the table."

Bemused at that reaction from Danny Esera, Sexiest Man in Sport, as voted by the masses, she didn't regale him with her friend group's other cheeky comments. She also didn't reply to the nosy parkers. Thirsting on an actor or sportsperson she'd never met was one thing, but she *knew* Danny. He wasn't just a picture on a wall she'd never meet.

He was all too real... all too sexy, all too funny, all too smart.

And she was going to be in serious trouble if she didn't find a way to squelch this soon.

"You cooked," she said and got up after setting her phone aside. "I should clear up."

Ignoring her, he kept on with it. Her lips pursed, her blood hot without warning. "I *said* I can do it." She hated it when people tried to "help" her, all the while disregarding her autonomy and abilities as a full-grown adult.

"Catie," Danny said, giving her a narrow-eyed glance that was pure steel. "Are you treating me like some ableist fuck? Because no, just no. That's not how we do things."

The blunt question and statement brought her up short. She'd reacted instinctively and, honestly, not that sensibly. This was the same man who played touch rugby with her like they were on a professional field and he needed to win the championship. Never in a way that would hurt her, but with *serious* intent. Not once in their relationship had he treated her as anything but his equal.

"Then why are you keeping on with the washing-up when I said I had it?" she argued back.

"Because my mother would whup my ass if I sat around while a woman cleaned and tidied around me." No give in his tone. "You know she would."

Okay, he had a point. No one sat on their butt in Alison's kitchen unless they'd done another chore. "You cooked," she pointed out again. "Your mum always says the cook is excused from the cleaning."

A scowl followed by an exhale. "Yeah, okay. I just didn't want to sit anymore. I feel—" Putting the dishes in the sink, he gripped the edge of the stainless steel and sharply square bowl. "A stranger put something in my drink and suddenly, I had no control. It's..." He swallowed hard.

Putting down the dishes she'd grabbed, Catie placed one hand on his muscular back. The heat of him burned through the fine cotton of his tee, his muscles all bunched up under her touch. "I know," she murmured. "Realizing that other people can change your life without any input on your part? It sucks."

Danny glanced at her, his eyes shiny before he looked

away and blinked. "I'm blowing this out of proportion, aren't I? I mean, compared to what happened to you—"

"That's not how it works, hotshot." She poked him in the side because the two of them, they messed with each other. It was their normal. "It's not a misery Olympics. Things can both suck in different ways."

He glared at her while rubbing his side. "What? You sharpen your claws now?"

She waggled her pretty polished nails at him. "What do you care? Your body's like stone." She'd meant that to be some kind of insult, but it didn't come out quite that way.

Thankfully, Danny was too distracted to cotton on to the fact she'd accidentally complimented him. "Where did you learn that? What you said? Therapy?"

"Nah, that was courtesy of another kid I met on the ward. Cillian, one of the counselors at my camp. You remember?"

"Yeah, sure. He gave that talk about how he lost three limbs because of a blood infection."

"That's him." She hitched herself up to sit on the counter. "Anyway, I met him during rehab, and I felt bad talking about my own stuff because at least I still had both arms. But Cill, he's a true farmer's son—or as he'd put it, blunt as a rusty axe.

"He basically said, 'You lost two legs, Catie, and you're a runner. That sucks. I'm a future farmer who lost two legs and an arm and that sucks too. And that other kid we met had cancer that might come back and it already took his left leg. That sucks too. It all sucks. It's not like a competition.'"

She smiled. "He's so wise I always tell him he

should've been a monk, meditating on the meaning of life. He points out that monks don't have sex and he likes to have lots of sex, thank you very much."

A flicker in Danny's eyes she couldn't quite read before he nodded. "He's right. It sucks. I just... I mean, a stranger almost took away everything I value on a whim. It unsettles me. Like nothing I do matters. I know that's BS thinking, but it keeps going around and around in my head."

"Trauma." Catie patted his shoulder. "Take my advice and attend that session with the headshrinker. It feels super awkward talking to a stranger about things at first, but if they're good, it starts to feel better after a while. And if they're bad, you find someone new. Because you gotta talk it out, Danny, or it will eat you up."

CATIE'S WORDS rang in Danny's head as he set himself up for the remote session late that afternoon. The two of them hadn't spoken much after lunch, both busy with their own things. But he knew she was right. Which was why he didn't try to bullshit the doctor. He cooperated fully, and it turned out the guy was good.

Younger than Danny had expected—young enough to understand Danny's world—but experienced enough to help Danny sort through the mess in his head.

Closing his laptop after it was done, he exhaled. He already felt a little lighter, not so many snarled threads in his brain. It was far from game over, but it had been the right call to do this while the wound was fresh; he could see the path ahead now. At least on this point.

As for his rugby career...

Jaw tight and a burn in his gut, he put aside the laptop and got up. He didn't want to think about the sword hanging over his head—it had been hanging there for the entire season, and he knew it was going to fall one of these days and cut out his fucking heart.

And the same media who'd hyped him up when he made the national squad at nineteen would exhibit glee at calling him a washout at twenty-five.

Unable to even think about it, he spent the time till dinner doing another bout of training, this time focusing on weights. He was just finishing up when he heard clattering in the kitchen.

Alarmed, he ran out to find Catie pulling out a pot; the remaining fresh vegetables from the fridge sat alongside a package of chicken breasts. "What horrible death are you planning for those innocent food items?" he asked, slinging his towel around his neck.

Catie gave his bare upper body a dismissive look, then went to wash her hands. "Shut up. I'm not that bad. I feed myself fresh, healthy stuff."

Danny forced himself to stay in place. Catie was a passable cook—if he gave passable a generous interpretation. "Have you learned how to use garlic and ginger and herbs yet?"

"I'm holding a knife, hotshot." She chopped down hard on the green beans she'd just washed, then made searing eye contact... and chopped again.

"Fine, fine." Holding up his hands, he backed away. "But I'm going to supervise."

"You're really making me feel stabby," she said in a calm tone. "And you don't need ginger for a stir-fry."

"Oh dear Lord in heaven, please save me." Leaving

her for a bare couple of minutes to throw on a tee—sexy half-naked cooking pics might be the thing in some circles, but he did not want hot oil splashed on his stomach—he returned to the kitchen.

"You want me to show you?" he asked, a bit wary because this *was* Catie after all. Annoy her too much and the woman might decide to dose his food with a cup of salt.

She smirked. "I should make you crazy by ordering you to sit and watch... but you did make the muffins and the cookies, so okay, fine."

"Hallelujah." Heading to the pantry, he hunted out the bottles of soy sauce and sesame oil he'd seen in there, then grabbed a couple of frozen chilies from the fridge as well as the jar of precrushed ginger. "Fresh is better," he said, holding it up. "But this will do in a pinch."

He then found the honey and even a small packet of sesame seeds. "Kudos to your mother's chef."

"What are you doing?"

"Watch and learn." He began to put together the ingredients for a spicy sauce with the barest hint of honey. "This'll give flavor to everything without the need to add extra salt. It's already in the soy sauce, and with the stir-fry loaded with veggies, it's healthy. Good way to pack in flavor without compromising on the health side of things."

Danny's body was the tool of his trade, and he took care of it. He also found food a pleasure, so he made an effort to balance necessity with delight. "You can also fiddle with it to highlight flavors you like. Me? I love ginger and chili." Dipping his little finger into the sauce, he held it out without thought. "Taste."

Catie's eyes caught his and the moment hung, the world falling silent around them.

Stomach clenching, he was about to pull back his hand when she reached up and swiped his finger with her own, then put that finger into her mouth to suck off the sauce. He was glad he was wearing his T-shirt, because his abdomen was now rock hard. And other things were starting to threaten hardness too.

Shit. Shit. Shit.

He wished he could blame the drugs, but his system felt good. Normal. This was just his body being a dick. That's what it was. Nothing to do with Catie's soft lips and heavy-lidded eyes as she savored the flavors he'd created.

"Mmm."

His dick twinged. Hard.

10

THE HALF-NAKED MAN WITH THE THIGH TATTOO

Mixing the sauce with a little too much enthusiasm, he tried to think of the non-sexiest things he could imagine, even bringing out the full-on horror of how, at age eleven, he'd once walked in on his mum and dad in the middle of "naked cuddling." He hadn't seen much, but oh hell had he been horrified.

His parents?

Had sex?

More than the twice it took to create him and Jake?

No. As far as he was concerned, they were celibates who happened to sleep in the same bed. Yes, he was quite content with that ludicrous fiction.

"That's so good, Danny." Catie's voice held real admiration. "And you did it with a few basic ingredients. Will you write it down for me? I'm pretty good at following recipes."

Chest expanding, a ridiculous warmth in his cheeks,

he smiled. "Yeah, sure. You can flex the recipe lots of ways. I like using balsamic vinegar sometimes too."

The smile Catie shot him before she got back to cutting up the vegetables, it held none of her usual snark or attitude. It was just Catie's smile. Sweet, open, kick-to-the-gut beautiful.

Mouth drying up, he replaced the saucepan with a wok he'd found in the cupboard and added a little garlic-infused olive oil. Of course Catie was pretty. He'd always known that. In the same way he knew his sisters-in-law were pretty. Just knowing without really *noticing*. But he was noticing now.

The way her roughly tied-back hair suited the delicate lines of her face, how her eyes sparkled with intelligence and humor, how her lips were naturally pink and probably soft as anything.

He brought his thoughts to a screeching halt when his mind wanted to keep on wandering down her body. He seriously needed to rein it in. A little cabin fever, that's all it was. "Is the snow meant to let up at all?"

"Tomorrow maybe," Catie said. "I had a look at the latest report just before. Apparently there's a front coming in that might mean sunshine."

"Great, then Leon's play should still be able to open." Having quickly chopped the chicken into strips while they'd been talking, he dropped it into the oil to fry, stirring all the while so nothing would burn and the chicken would cook quickly and evenly.

The rich scent of the garlic in the olive oil filled the air.

"You still okay to be my date?" he asked.

"Deal is a deal," she said, her eyes on the wok. "You're using a higher heat than I normally would."

And because cooking was safe, Danny went off on a mini essay about perfect chicken-searing temperature, et cetera, et cetera. That Catie actually seemed to be paying attention tangled him up inside, his pride a hot thing in his gut. Man, he was fucked. *This* was fucked.

He needed to talk to someone. Jake?

No, nope. He did not want anyone in the family getting wind of his sudden obsession with Catie. Or his friends. In fact, he didn't want to talk to anyone. He'd sleep on it and he'd wake up cured. The end.

"Chicken's done," he said, the words coming out a touch too fast. "We then put it aside while we stir-fry the veggies in the sauce. I like to drizzle a little of the sauce over the chicken while it sits. Helps it soak in a bit more."

Stop babbling, Danny!

Clenching his jaw tight, he kept his eyes on the food. It took a few short minutes to get the vegetables to the right level between raw and still crispy but seared. He then added the chicken back in, mixed, and they were done.

"Damn." He scowled. "We forgot to make rice or noodles."

"There are emergency microwavable packets in the pantry."

"Only because I'm starving. Next time we make it fresh." He didn't even realize what he'd said until the words were out.

Next time.

As if they'd be cooking together again soon.

Just as well Catie was busy getting the packaged rice and didn't seem to notice.

Releasing a tight breath, he set the table while she sorted the rice, then he carried the wok over to place it between them on the table.

Two minutes later, they both dug in.

"Yum." Catie finally spoke after eating half her meal. "I give you permission to say 'I told you so,' but the timer is on." She tapped at her wrist and her nonexistent watch. "Permission expires after thirty seconds."

He laughed, delighted and happy—and not about to miss this opportunity. Whipping out his phone, he recorded her as he said, "I told you so."

Catie made a face at the camera, but it was a cute face. Her entire face was just cute.

Maybe he'd taken a knock to the head while drugged. That had to be it. Or it was this whole situation where she'd basically rescued him. Didn't people imprint on their rescuers? He'd snap out of it.

"So," she said after swallowing another bite, "what's the dress code at this premiere? Is it super fancy or just nice?"

"Fancy," Danny said, glad to have a non-emotive topic on which to focus. "Leon figures a flash premiere might lead to more eyeballs on his work. He put together the play on a shoestring budget, but his dream is to stage a full-fledged historical. Costumes, huge sets, the whole shebang, and for that, he needs to make a splash, get the attention of the right people."

"He'll definitely get eyeballs on it if you're going," Catie said, but she didn't ask what many people would have—what he'd charged to attend. Because Catie knew that Danny valued his friends. If he could give them a leg up just by showing up, why the hell not?

Especially when it was the only help Leon would accept. Danny had offered to help finance the play, but Leon had turned him down flat. "You can come onboard when I'm sure I'm going to make a profit," he'd said. "Until then, it's a terrible investment risk for you—and I won't take from my friends to chase my dreams. I need to make it on my own first, need to own any future success."

Danny understood that need far better than Leon could ever comprehend. He knew his sporting prowess was due to his training and discipline—because even the most naturally talented player wouldn't make it if he sat around on his ass. But Danny also knew he'd been born into a place of privilege in terms of rugby.

Only this rugby prince's halo was starting to develop rust.

"With the two of us," he said, shoving aside the cold truth breathing down the back of his neck, "it might end up a circus."

Catie speared a snow pea pod. "You sure he wants that attention?"

"Oh yeah. Any mention of us will also mean a mention of his play." He suddenly thought of something. "I brought my tux down from Auckland. Left it with the hotel laundry to get pressed—it'll still be there."

He made a mental note to pick it up when the snow stopped. "Will you have to buy a fancy outfit?" She'd only come down for a short break with her girlfriends—one of whom happened to be dating a member of the Southern Blizzard. That was how they'd ended up at the same club.

Catie frowned. "These days I'm usually sponsored by

a label, but when I'm not, I try to give local designers the spotlight." She glanced at the clock on the kitchen wall. "It's last minute, but let me ring around and see if anyone can fit me into one of their samples. They usually have to do alterations—I've got too much muscle for most samples."

What she also had were very sexy curves. As a sprinter, her body was built differently to the ethereal slenderness of a long-distance runner's; she packed a ton of power into a taut, tight frame. And for all that was holy, Danny's brain needed to *shut the fuck up*!

Grabbing his glass of water, he gulped it down.

And proceeded to talk about car stuff—his brother Jake's passion—until Catie pretended to pass out from boredom. At least it got his mind back on the right track —which was not ogling Catie.

After dinner, Catie decided to call Ani to see if the publicist could hook her up with a local designer. "I know it's short notice," he heard her saying as she wandered into her bedroom, "but it's for an event with Danny. Yes, I know I didn't warn you about that photo post…"

Grabbing his own phone as her voice faded off, he called Viliame. "Hey man."

"Yo, Dan. How you doing?" Genuine concern in his friend's voice.

"Good. Back to normal." Except for his alien obsession with Catie. "Thanks for having my back."

"No thanks needed." Viliame continued on. "Did you see that international between Argentina and South Africa?"

"No, I haven't had a chance to catch up."

"Fucking brutal, man. But the South Africans have some interesting new moves. You should watch it."

When Danny checked the TV after he and Vili hung up, he found that Jacqueline had every channel known to man and then some. Easily locating the subscription service that held streaming rights for the rugby internationals, he settled in to watch the replay.

He was still good at this, at the technical analysis of a game.

Catie emerged from her room ten minutes into the game and came to sit on the other end of the couch. Ten minutes after that, she was yelling at the TV, he was up on his feet in outrage, and it was a good thing that this apartment had thick walls because otherwise they'd have been dealing with noise control.

CATIE WOKE AT SIX FORTY-FIVE, the world yet dark outside.

When she lazily picked up her phone to read the morning news, she saw that Ani had sent her a text at eleven the previous night, alerting her that a local designer was coming by at *seven* this morning to do a fitting.

Jerking into a sitting position, she rubbed her gritty eyes; she and Danny had stayed up late, arguing over the game—agreeing on some points, hotly contesting others.

While he was the rugby player, she'd grown up with the game thanks to his family, so she'd held her ground. And gone to bed so exhilarated and energized that it had taken her another hour to nod off. At which point she'd dreamed of a man with powerful thighs and wide shoulders who looked a little too familiar.

Shoving that glitch in her imagination to the back of beyond, she put on her legs with her eyes still half-closed. She could've left them off while she got herself sorted, but it was habit now. A habit she'd purposefully cultivated as an older teen after realizing how easy it would be to skip one day here and one day there until it just got too hard.

That kind of approach wouldn't work for her and what she wanted from her career. Catie saw every day as a chance to practice, become better—not in the sense of working herself to the bone but of putting herself in the right frame of mind; for her, that meant her prostheses were a seamless part of her life.

Which was why her eyes snapped wide open when she felt a touch of swelling on her left stump. Her heart skipped a beat, her cheeks burning, then going ice-cold. She checked with careful fingers all the way around, exhaled a shuddering breath.

Nothing major. Just a slight touch of irritation.

She had no trouble attaching the prosthesis.

Sitting back up, she took a moment to allow her heart rate to ease before she headed to the en suite shower. She'd just emerged from the steamy enclosure when there was a knock on her bedroom door.

"Catie, some dude just arrived—he insists he's here to dress you." Danny's voice was full-on suspicious.

Cracking the door open with the towel wrapped around her, she saw a seriously grumpy male face, Danny's hair all rumpled up and dark bristles shadowing his jaw and his chest on full display since he'd only pulled on a pair of black shorts. Shorts that revealed his thigh tattoo.

Her mouth watered.

Tightening her hand on the door handle, she said, "It's the designer." A cough to clear the rasp out of her voice. "Give him a cup of that delicious coffee I can smell and tell him I'll be out in ten."

"Just wear your underwear!" a stranger's voice called out. "I need your measurements!"

When Danny, his expression a thundercloud, put his hands on his hips and began to turn toward their guest, she poked him in the shoulder with one finger. "Shoo. And don't eat him."

Then she shut the door and pressed her back to it for several long seconds, telling her misbehaving hormones to get with the program. Danny was off-limits. Now and forever.

The end.

Her pussy clenched.

11

DANNY, DON'T EAT THE DESIGNER

Horrified, she looked down in the direction of that body part, desperately shook her head. And decided to bury her head in the sand for the time being because she had to get dressed. She wasn't sure how long the designer would be safe with Danny. The Bishop-Esera men could be overprotective.

Though, honestly, if she'd been in Danny's position and some man was demanding her friend come out half-naked, she'd have been suspicious too. As it was, she found a pair of bike shorts and a slimline sports bra to cover herself. Respectable enough while giving the designer what he needed.

Danny was still in glare mode when she entered the living room, but he'd made her a coffee exactly as she liked and now shoved it over. He was still shirtless, still ridiculously beautifully male.

"Thanks," she said and glanced around. "Where's the designer? I told you not to eat him."

"Outside." With that short reply, he took a seat on a

breakfast stool and turned his glower on the skinny and bespectacled Asian man of around forty who'd just wheeled in a whole rack of clothes.

"Oh my!" The man beamed, so dazzlingly awake that he clearly didn't need any caffeine. "You're even better in person than in the pictures. Those abs! And oh, you have cleavage! I have the perfect outfit!"

"You must be Jet," Catie managed to interject.

But he was already rustling through his rack to emerge with an "Aha!"

When he pulled the outfit free of the others, Catie raised both eyebrows. Nearly all designers put her in clothes that showed off her legs. That was fine with her. She often requested exactly that. She'd worked fucking hard to get to the point where she could wear prostheses full time, and she was also proud of her skins.

They not only protected the mechanical parts of her prostheses, they gave her legs shape when she wanted to wear jeans or other long pants. But they were also as cool as fuck—she'd designed her favorite set herself so they looked like bionic legs from the future.

Jet, however, was holding up what looked to be a pantsuit in a moody blue-green shade she'd never have chosen for herself. She really didn't think it'd suit her but set her coffee aside on the breakfast counter and did him the courtesy of trying it on. The pants fit well except for the waist.

"You have more muscle than my models," Jet muttered with unexpected excitement as he began to pin and mark before stepping back.

The pants were now jerry-rigged to hang on her hips

while she shrugged into the jacket. "What do I wear underneath this?"

"Nothing." Jet jumped forward and buttoned it up for her. "Oh my."

Danny whistled at the same moment.

Jerking her head up, she found him looking her up and down. "Gotta give it to the dude, princess, you look hot."

She frowned at him. "Be serious, Danny."

"Cross my heart. You have that whole— What's that actress's name? The one who wore that white suit you liked?"

"Zendaya?"

"Yeah, her. You're giving off that vibe."

Catie couldn't feel it, but when she walked into her bedroom to look in the full-length mirror, she sucked in a breath. She *did* look hot. And in control. The color did amazing things to her skin. And the way the jacket buttoned between her breasts but cut away over her abs to display her muscle tone...

Sexy and athletic at the same time. "I love it."

Jet, having come in behind her, began to fuss with the jacket. "It's not quite the right fit, but I can make it right by four today. Will that work?"

Sensing a prickle on the back of her neck, she glanced over to the doorway to see Danny leaning in it, his mug of coffee in hand.

"We have to do the entrance thing at seven," he told her.

"Then four will be fine," she told Jet.

"What will you do for shoes?" the designer asked her.

"I do have feet designed for heels, but I didn't bring them with me. I'll go with glittery sneakers."

"Perfect. Where are they? I need you in them to measure the pant legs."

It didn't take long to sort that out, and Jet was soon heading out the door with his rack of treasures.

"Jewels!" he called out from over his shoulder. "Definitely a pendant in your fabulous cleavage! Want me to call my contacts?"

"I'd appreciate that." She didn't have anything suitable on hand. "And thank you."

"No! Thank *you*, Catie. This will bring so many more eyes to my work!" He pulled the door shut behind himself.

Leaving her dressed in bike shorts and a sports bra while Danny stood next to her, his grump back on.

"Still not a morning person, huh?" she said to cover the flutters in her abdomen.

"Didn't sleep well," he grumbled before stalking off to the kitchen, where he pulled out a skillet, eggs, and a bunch of other things. "I have to eat, then go grab my tux. Snow stopped sometime last night and the street outside looks like it's been plowed, but if not, I can walk there and back in an hour. You want food?"

"Sure." Hormones out of whack or not, she wasn't about to turn down his cooking. "Let me get changed."

"Is that normal?" he said when she walked out in jeans and a simple black sweatshirt.

"What?"

"Designers just pawing at you?" He was chopping herbs as he spoke; that meant they'd officially cleared all fresh produce out of the fridge.

"Danny," Catie said with exaggerated patience, "your brother is an underwear model, and you front a campaign for athletic gear. You know exactly what designers are like."

"Yeah, but no one's talking about my boobs."

"I'd be worried if they were."

After shooting her a glare, he put the egg mixture into the pan and began to stir, and she realized they were having herb-scrambled eggs. Yum, she thought as she put in the toast. Which gave her the opportunity to *not* look at Danny's gorgeous body. It was just a body. One she'd seen plenty of times before.

Only today it was making things inside her go zing!

"Seriously though," she said, determined to keep things normal, "that really bothered you? To Jet, I'm nothing but a living hanger to showcase his work."

"I mean... maybe if he was a woman it wouldn't have, but that was a dude and he had his hands all over you."

Catie didn't quite know how to take that, and though she and Danny had never been less than blunt with each other, she was feeling off-balance enough as it was; she decided to sidestep it. "On another topic, have you seen the comments and likes on my post from last night? I think we broke the internet."

Instead of the scowl she was expecting, he shot her a wicked grin. "We're just getting started." He held out a fisted hand.

Laughing, she bumped it, and if she felt a flash of heat on her cheeks from the small contact, well, she could ignore it. Her relationship with the Esera family was too precious to her to risk screwing it up by actually acting on this unexpected physical spark.

It would pass the minute they were back in the normal world.

DANNY WAS SERIOUSLY glad to get out of the apartment after breakfast even if it was into a frozen white world with air crisp enough to burn. It was hell being around Catie when his body had decided to go off the rails where she was concerned. It had taken everything he had not to reach out and run his fingers over the sleek lines of her abs, the silk of her skin taut over muscle she'd worked hard to build.

Again, he thought about calling one of his brothers. Again, he put it off.

The front desk attendant at the hotel gave him his abandoned tux with a smile, too well trained to ask any questions. The same couldn't be said of the two teenage girls who were heading into the restaurant for breakfast with their family. They squealed when they saw him, then ran over to ask for a selfie.

Danny didn't usually mind this kind of thing—he knew it was because of his current age and place in the sporting world—but the girls were also gushing about him and Catie, and it was just not what he needed to hear right then. But he wasn't about to ruin their day because of his own issues; he posed for the selfie with a smile, then made his excuses and left.

The taxi he'd hired was still idling outside, and he got into its warm privacy with a sigh of thanks. That little interaction, he knew, was just the start. The New Zealand public and media weren't as voracious as in other parts of the world, so it was unlikely he and Catie would be jumped by a photographer hiding in the bushes, but the interview requests had already begun to hit.

And given both his and Catie's international profiles, some foreign press—or local photographers who sold to international press outlets—might decide it worth their while to stake them out in an attempt to get a lucrative shot. They'd be aiming for one that caught an intimate moment. Ugh. His sister-in-law, Charlotte, had a best friend who was married to a rock star. Some creepy fuck had actually put a camera in their hotel room, then sold the video!

He didn't have that high of a profile or that type of tabloid interest in his life, but it had definitely taught him to be wary. He'd have to be doubly so now that he was with Catie. If that took booking future hotel rooms under a pseudonym, so be it.

He'd rather be paranoid than risk people hurting Catie by taking away her choice in what she wanted to share and what she didn't. Like with her prostheses. She took them off at the children's camp all the time when she gave talks to the kids. Never once, however, had she posted social media shots of herself without her prostheses.

"Because soon as it goes online," she'd said to him once, "there's a high chance a creep will find it and add a fetishizing comment, and yeah, no thanks." She'd shaken her head. "I see it with Posey's profile—she doesn't care, but I get so angry for her. I'd probably go nuclear if anyone pulled the same shit with me."

"What does Posey say?"

"She sees it as being herself in all her glory and fuck the creeps, which I agree with—but she also accepts my viewpoint. We're different people with different thoughts on the whole thing. No one has a right to what we don't choose to reveal."

Danny would punch out a photographer himself before he let anyone steal that choice from her. "Thanks, man," he said to the cab driver when they pulled up to a stop outside the apartment building. "I know it's slow going on the roads today."

"No problem." The big Tongan man smiled, his teeth white against the black of the neat beard that framed his mouth. "You mind autographing this notepad? My boy plays rugby. He'll go nuts—and it's his birthday in a week, so I figure I can give it to him then."

"Sure, no problem." Danny paid the fare, took the notepad. "If you give me your address, I'll send you a bunch of team stuff for him too."

This time the driver's smile eclipsed the sunshine that lit up the snow.

Danny carried that blast of happiness with him as he walked into the building through a coded door for which Catie had given him the number. She'd also given him a keycard to get into the penthouse elevator *and* the access code for the apartment itself.

Jacqueline did not piss around when it came to security.

When he entered the apartment, it was to find Catie's bedroom door open, silence a lingering beat in the air. "Catie!"

Nothing.

Taking out his phone, he texted her: *Are you alive?*

Ha ha. I needed hair goop for tonight, and I ran out of mascara. What, you miss me?

Danny didn't like this apartment without Catie here. It was too sharp and modern and clinical. But he wasn't about to admit that to her. *Bring back some eggs. I want to make a cake.* He'd tried to bring up his interest in baking with a couple of dates over the past year, and they'd both taken it as a joke. Not that they'd been mean women—Danny didn't go for mean—but they just had this image of him in their mind, and the whole cooking and baking thing didn't fit.

He couldn't blame them. It wasn't like he put it out there. Then again, wasn't dating meant to be about getting to know people?

Oooh, can you do chocolate?

I'll see. He actually wanted to try an experimental recipe but wasn't sure if they had all the ingredients. After checking, he texted her back. *Don't worry about the eggs. I need to go out to grab a few other ingredients anyway.*

I'll meet you at the supermarket. You're going to the one around the corner from the apartment? I'm almost there.

Yeah.

He'd just grabbed a shopping cart outside the store when she wandered over from the parking lot. "Whose car is that?" he asked, having seen her drive into the spot on the other side of the cart bay.

"Jacqueline's."

Danny was aware they were attracting attention as they wandered the aisles, but he ignored it. It wasn't the people taking sneaky photos in a supermarket who were the problem. "Did you find your hair goop?"

"Yup." She put a huge bar of chocolate in the cart. "For the chocolate cake."

"Subtle, princess." But he didn't put it back. "Get me

118

that bar next to the one you grabbed." He pointed at the strawberry flavored chocolate.

"Ew." But she dropped it in the cart. "What are you going to do with that?"

"Something."

She poked him in the side, then pretended to have a broken finger. "Seriously, you're going overboard on the ab workouts."

Danny wanted to preen, fed his idiotic happiness into a joke. "What workouts? I'm a natural beauty."

As she laughed, he threw a packet of oats and one of mixed dried fruit into the cart. The secret ingredient when it came to making a healthy snack was to "trick" people into thinking it was bad for them—sometimes all that took was a hint of chocolate. Because Danny didn't just want to cook for sports people or others on nutrition-ist-informed diets. He wanted to cook for everyone.

"If I tell you something, will you keep it a secret?" he found himself saying.

12

TOP SECRET INFORMATION

Catie shot him a considering look. "Like a real secret?"

He nodded.

Her expression shifted, a solemn promise in her gaze. "Yes."

He believed her. He and Catie, they didn't backstab. That wasn't their kind of fighting. They got in each other's faces, and the best wins were always with humor. "Okay, but promise not to laugh too."

"Ha! Never going to happen."

"Evil wench," he muttered but took out his phone and opened up what he wanted her to see. "Here."

She leaned in close to him, her ponytailed hair brushing against his shoulder as she looked at the small screen. "Is this someone you follow?" she asked. "They take amazing pictures of their food. That fresh-fruit tart looks out of this world."

When Danny said nothing, she looked at him and her

eyes widened. "It's you?" she whispered. "Secret recipes page?"

He nodded. "Don't follow me." Her account was too big, and she had fans dedicated enough to stalk who she followed. "What do you think though?"

Having grabbed his phone, she began scrolling through his posts. There weren't that many as he'd only set up the account in the past six months, under the name of TheAnonymousWannabeChef. It was too long, but it seemed to have hit a chord with people and he'd somehow managed to collect a thousand followers.

That was peanuts in comparison to his main account, but these people liked his recipes, tried to make them, and reported back on their successes and failures. They weren't following him for his rugby skills or because they thought he looked hot in rugby shorts—hell, they'd never seen a single picture of him. They were there for his skills in the kitchen.

It felt good.

As did the admiration in Catie's eyes when she turned to him. "This is amazing, Danny. They're so dedicated to you."

Flushing, he said, "I get a real kick out of it when they post pics of things they've made using my recipes."

"I'd scream," Catie said with a grin. "What a rush!" After giving back his phone, she took out her own.

"Hey, I said don't—"

She waved away his interjection. "I have a supersecret account, duh. I use it to follow friends who prefer not to have the media hound them for quotes about me, and you know, fun stuff I enjoy but don't want the magazines writing articles about. Had it for years."

"I didn't know that." Oddly hurt by the fact she hadn't told him about the long-term private account, he glanced at the shelf of baking supplies to hide his reaction.

Then she said, "I don't post anything on it. It's only for follows—and I follow you out in the open where everyone can see me smoke you in our nemesis wars."

Right then, his account yet open on his phone, he saw that he'd just been followed by StringOfNumbersPlus-One. He snorted. "Seriously?"

"What? It's easy to remember."

They carried on with their shopping, though they didn't have to get that much. It was fun just browsing with Catie—she wasn't fussed if he spent time deciding between three different types of vanilla, and she happily hunted the shelves for his favorite ingredients. She did refuse to agree with his choice of "best baked beans," instead championing an utter abomination of a brand, but then, she *was* his number one nemesis.

"You said you're flying out tomorrow midafternoon, right?" he said after they'd paid and he was carrying the bags to the car.

"Yep. Which flight are you on?" When he told her, she shook her head. "I'm an hour later. I guess I'll see you back in Auckland."

An odd little skip in his heart. "Yeah."

THE APARTMENT WAS STILL REDOLENT with the smell of baking when Catie began to get ready for the night. She'd cursed Danny for making such delicious goodies when she was about to put on an outfit that was *not* designed for carrying a food baby.

"It's dessert for us, for after," he'd said with zero repentance on his far too handsome face. "We'll veg out in front of the TV and eat and discuss our nefarious fake-relationship plans."

That actually sounded amazing. *Too* amazing.

"Rein it in, Catie," she muttered to the mirror as she finished doing her eyeliner. "This is a result of the situation. Temporary blip."

Only, the thing was... it didn't look to be fading. Rather, it seemed to be careening fast in the opposite direction. For crying out loud, she'd had the best time just grocery shopping with him! Their ridiculous argument about baked beans had made her pulse race.

It freaked her out.

And it wasn't because she was afraid of parental disapproval. Alison and Joseph liked Catie. The same with Jacqueline when it came to Danny—the Dragon was not in any way a fan of sports, but she'd been known to give Danny a compliment or two.

"Determination and skill are determination and skill regardless of the field chosen," she'd said. "That young man has drive."

So yeah, approval wasn't the issue.

What worried Catie lay at the opposite end of the family spectrum: one hint of an actual relationship and everyone would start planning their wedding. The two of them could never have a casual fling—their lives and families were too entwined.

Sexy shenanigans meant serious complications.

Not that she was thinking about anything of the kind. God, it'd be embarrassing if Danny read her mind and caught her thoughts. He'd probably end up on the floor, laughing his head off at the idea of the two of them in a clinch.

The image should've made her angry, but it had her smiling instead. The idiot had a great laugh.

"Have you finished painting your face?" he yelled from the living room. "How much stuff do you need to put on there?"

"As much as I want!" Catie had, however, long gotten over her caked-on-is-the-best stage. The photos of her and Laveni's "glam" looks from their teenage years made her grin now.

Poor Veni, subjected to Catie's then-questionable skills.

As it was, Catie was also used to being photographed bare-faced—it wasn't like she wore makeup while running. Some sportspeople liked a bit when competing —Posey, for one, had been all about the mascara and the false eyelashes and she'd rocked it to the point that she was a spokeswoman for a makeup brand.

But Catie stuck with moisturizer that had good sun protection, her face otherwise naked and her hair pulled back in a ponytail. About as basic as it could get. But off the track? Oh, she loved makeup as much as she had as a teen.

"Is it safe to come in?" A masculine shout from outside her bedroom door.

"Yes!"

The next thing she heard was her bed giving a startled creak as a big male body flopped down on it. Shifting to glance over her shoulder, through the open door of the en suite bathroom, she found Danny lying shoeless and jacketless on the bed, his hands linked behind his head and his white dress shirt stretched over his chest.

Right on cue, that thing in her body that was acting up? It let out a "whoa" because Danny looked good in her bed. Damn good.

Forcing herself to turn back to the mirror, she put down her eyeliner brush. At least then she could ignore the fact her hand was trembling. She couldn't, however, ignore Danny—he was visible in the mirror.

"You're not even dressed," he said, squinting suspiciously at her fluffy white bathrobe.

"I don't want to get makeup on my outfit. It's not like it's a dress I have to get over my head."

Nothing for a while as she did a few touch-ups on the rest of her face.

"Huh, it's like surgery but with makeup." He sounded fascinated. "You did something with your cheekbones that made them all..." A frown she could all but hear. "Sharper, I guess? More like knives that will cut me if I look at you wrong."

Her shoulders shook, her grin creasing her cheeks. "Good. That was the look I was aiming for." She picked up the lipstick she'd chosen to pair with the pantsuit. A deep, blue-based berry red, it was the focal point of her whole look.

"How's this?" she said after putting it on, then turning around to show him.

"You look like a badass sorceress." Angling his head, he took a second look. "Yeah, you'd definitely cut a man who got out of line with you."

She knew, coming from him, that was a compliment. His mother might be a homemaker first and foremost, but Alison was one tough woman. Danny appreciated power in a woman. Which was why she didn't get one thing. "There's something I've always wanted to ask you."

"Yeah?"

"Why did you date that string of gigglers? You know, the ones who were all, 'oh Danny, you're so sweet, just the best,' giggle giggle."

Danny groaned, one hand over his eyes.

"Don't get me wrong," she added, "I have nothing against women being giggly bunnies." Catie's view was that the world should just let women do their thing whether that was slow or hard, giggly or staunch. "I just never saw you being inclined that way."

Dropping his hand, he grimaced. "It was a phase, okay? I wondered what I was missing when all my mates were heading in that direction—let's just say my FOMO did not end well and never again mention the subject." Before she could razz him about that, he pinned her with a sharp gaze. "What about you?"

"What about me?" She turned to the mirror to fine-tune her lipstick with a lipstick brush.

"That puffed-up bodybuilder you got with after dumping Ward the Dickwad," he said, purposefully drawing out the insult so it rhymed with Ward's name. "If he has two brain cells to rub together, I'm Albert Einstein."

Scowling, Catie resisted the temptation to shoot back a snarky response. Fair was fair. He'd been honest with her. "Brax is really nice. You'd like him."

When Danny made a choking noise, she hunched her shoulders up to her ears. "He's so nice I couldn't say no when he asked me out." Even though she'd known they wouldn't suit. Brax had agreed with every one of her opinions no matter if it was about food or politics or sports.

It. Had. Driven. Her. Bananas.

Catie felt like a troll for it. "He'll make some equally nice woman a lovely, lovely boyfriend."

"You? Feeling guilty crushing a poor helpless guy to mush? Hah."

Twisting around, she pointed the lipstick brush at him. "I can be super nice, thank you very much."

He rubbed his clean-shaven jaw. "One time you did give me half your chocolate bar," he said in a musing tone. "Then you shaved off half my hair while I was asleep!"

A laugh snorted out of her. "You deserved that, you ass. You made fun of my bikini." It had been the first time she'd worn one, and she'd been self-conscious about it. Danny hadn't been mean, hadn't commented on her body at all. All his digs had been about the color of the bikini—a perfectly innocent yellow—and about how she'd wasted good money buying it when he could've just cut up his old shirt for her.

Now he shrugged. "Yeah, I was a dickish teenage boy, but in my defense, I didn't know until then that you had boobs. It screwed with my mind to realize you were a *girl*."

"As opposed to?"

"Caitlin, the Nemesis." Like she was her own species.

That tickled her. "Fair enough. You're not like the rest of your family to me. You're Daniel, the Nemesis."

They grinned at each other before she turned her attention back to ensuring her makeup was as she wanted it. Then she picked up the hair goop and worked it into her hair. She was going for a slicked-down wet look. Simple but classy, and it would pull attention to her lips and clothes. Because she freaking loved the suit.

Daniel wolf-whistled when she exited the bathroom.

"Shut up, you idiot." But she was smiling as she went to grab the suit from the wardrobe. "Out," she said. "I need to put this on."

Rising in a fluid move, he sauntered out with that easy grace of his. She'd never tell him, but she loved watching him move on the rugby field. The media had called him a "young god" more than once and she had to agree. Yes, Jake was gorgeous too, and just as muscled, but in her secret heart, she thought Danny the better-looking and sexier of the two.

Not that she'd ever used that last word until now, not even in her own brain.

"Ignore, ignore, ignore," she muttered for the umpteenth time and shrugged off the robe to reveal panties of black lace and a bra she'd bought while out earlier. It was cut in a way that meant she could wear it under the jacket without it showing. Jet might want her naked under his stunning creation, but she liked the way the bra plumped up her boobs—which despite teenage Danny's shock—weren't exactly huge.

Cup size B was as good as it got for her, but they were nice and round, and she had no complaints. Bigger breasts would've made it difficult for her to run.

Pants on, she sat down to make sure her sparkly silver sneakers were solidly fitted to her prosthetic feet. She lock-tied the laces so they couldn't come loose. Because if they did, she might go ass over face. She also used the set of tools on her bedside table to double-check the connections between her rods and feet.

This was an experimental system that she'd been testing for a couple of months and so far she was loving its relatively lightweight design—especially given the extensive range of motion in the ankle and foot.

She dropped the most important tool in the little silver clutch she was taking tonight. That tool went everywhere with her. Then she got to her feet and pulled on the jacket, waiting until after she'd buttoned it up to look in the mirror. "Not bad, River," she said and turned to check the view from the back.

Happy, she slipped on the hypermodern diamond necklace Jet had sourced from a jeweler—on loan to Catie for the night. It dropped down against her cleavage in a slew of jagged icicles, lying against the vertical scar of a childhood heart operation. Postoperative complications meant the scar wasn't as faded as it otherwise would've been.

That line of rigid white against her skin didn't bother Catie, and she'd never bothered to try to hide it—it was the reason she'd survived as a baby, was a sign of life. She'd even done a photoshoot to help fundraise for the pediatric cardiac unit that had saved her life; the stylist had put her in a shirt of darkest autumnal brown, its open sides bracketing the scar.

After doing another twirl in front of the mirror, she said, "And I'm ready to rock." She checked she had her phone in her clutch along with a fifty-dollar bill and a credit card.

"Never leave home without enough cash to get back,"

Ísa had told her when she'd become old enough to go out on her own.

It was a tip Catie took seriously.

Walking out, she almost swallowed her tongue. Danny had pulled on and buttoned his tuxedo jacket and put on his shoes. Add in hair that was neatly combed, cuff links, and a perfectly knotted bow tie and he looked like a Samoan James Bond.

He glanced up from his phone. And did a double take.

A long pause fell between them as they stared at each other. Until the air thickened and Catie couldn't take it. "You clean up pretty good, Esera."

He coughed. "You too, River."

Walking across, she smoothed down the lapels of his jacket even though they bore not a single wrinkle. When he took out his phone and held out an arm, she tucked herself against him and smiled. He smelled so good that bubbles of champagne fizzed in her blood, the arm he'd slid around her back warm and muscled, his hand curving gently around her hip.

Click.

Lowering his arm, he showed her the photo, and her damn heart, it skipped. Because they looked happy, both of them smiling in a way that was so very *real*. "I like it." It came out softer than she'd intended.

"Me too." But rather than posting it, he slid away his phone.

She didn't poke at him about that. She didn't want that photo posted either. It showed a little too much, things she didn't want anyone else to see. Especially not their families. Because they'd *know*.

What exactly she was worried they'd know, Catie didn't want to face.

Danny's phone pinged.

Looking down, he said, "Limo's here" and squeezed her waist.

It was only then that she realized she'd stayed tucked up next to him. It had felt... natural.

Cheeks burning, she pulled away at last. He dropped his arm but then held it out, crooked at the elbow, his smile roguish. "My lady."

A smile cracked her lips as she accepted the offer. "I hope the theater is warm, otherwise I'm going to freeze." She'd decided not to take her coat since they were planning to go from the apartment to the car to the red carpet at the theater to inside, then back again the same way. If there was an after-party and they decided to attend, they didn't plan to walk.

"I shall be gallant and sacrifice my poor, shivering body and offer you my jacket," Danny said as they stepped out the door.

"Then I'll be wearing two jackets." She pulled the door shut behind them.

"Yeah, but mine would cover your stomach."

"Excellent point." She loved the way his jacket was cut, the fit flawless yet elegant—it gave her a glimpse into the future, of what Danny might look like with ten, twenty more years on him.

Good. He'd look good.

She pressed a hand against her stomach, certain the flutters were visible. "It's not looking poochy, right?"

Danny drew back, face stretched in a silent horror-movie scream. "Did you just ask me what I think you did?

Because there is no fucking right answer to that. Every man on the planet knows this."

His overacting was so bad that she started laughing and was still grinning when the elevator arrived. Stepping in, she said, "Sorry, had a bout of nerves. I know we're going to be the focus of a lot of cameras tonight."

He took her hand, squeezed. "You look awesome, Catie. Like your badass sprinter self."

That was the best compliment he could've given her. She almost leaned over and kissed his cheek, caught herself just in time. Jeez, Louise, she had to be careful or she'd give herself away, wreck everything.

On the other hand, she had to fake-like him for the duration of their agreement, so maybe she'd work through her unexpected fascination without anyone else being the wiser. "Let's go be fabulous and lie our faces off."

13

___

RED CARPET... KISS?

Leon was going to be ecstatic, Danny thought as their limo came to a stop at the end of the red carpet outside the stately old theater. His friend had gone all out, inviting everyone with even a smidgen of media clout—but, despite his track record working on major productions, he'd been ignored by the vast majority of his invitees. He'd told Danny that over their most recent video call, his face crestfallen.

Leon's theater buddies would've come en masse, of that Danny had zero doubt. They were as much a tight unit as any sports team—but most were currently appearing in shows in other parts of the world and could only offer their support long-distance.

Even the fact that Danny was a sure bet hadn't eased Leon's stress. Like Danny, he'd known that he'd need a few of the media darlings to turn up, the celebrities whose job it was to see and be seen and whose presence would ensure his play got mentioned online and in the papers.

Danny's sports clout didn't usually transfer over to this sphere.

Except tonight.

"Cameras out in full force," he told Catie after taking a look outside the window. "Not to sound big-headed, but I think it's for us."

Catie leaned over to take a look. "Day-um." She whistled as Danny pointed out the host of the biggest entertainment show in the country. "People are *that* invested in us being an *us*?"

"I guess so." It surprised him too—he'd expected a little interest, but this was next level. "Unless someone else super famous is coming and we don't know? Or it's a slow news day? Not that it matters. Still works for what we need."

But when Danny stepped out and turned to hold out his hand for Catie's, the camera flashes all but blinded him. Yep, the media had turned out for him and Catie. Which would have been kind of terrifying if Catie hadn't winked at him from inside the vehicle before she stepped out.

And suddenly he was grinning too. "Come on, princess," he said, the two of them far enough away from the cameras that no one was going to pick up his voice over the shouting of the photographers.

He made sure he had a firm grip on Catie as she stepped out. He didn't know how solidly Leon's crew had laid out the red carpet, and who knew if they'd cleared away any ice underneath.

Catie gave him a hard glance as she exited. "You trying to break my hand?"

"Nope. Just doing my best to keep us both from face-planting. Pretty sure this red carpet is from the dollar store." Leon had done his best with his meager budget, but the thing would only look like a plush carpet in pictures. In person, it was less carpet and more a curtain placed on the ground.

Catie glanced down for a second, and when she looked back up, the pinched look was gone from her eyes. "It's ripping at the corners." She pursed her lips after that whisper. "Your poor friend."

"At least people are too focused on us to notice." He angled his arm.

Tucking her hand into the crook, she said, "If we'd made a spectacle of ourselves before this, he could've probably gotten a sponsored freebie."

"Next time," he said, not thinking about it.

Before Catie could respond, the media's cries for them to turn around became an overwhelming chorus.

"Showtime," he muttered under his breath and slipped his arm around Catie's waist while she did the same to him.

Her sleek sprinter's curves fit perfectly against him, her skin warm gold under the bright lights and the glow from the standing heaters Leon had managed to finagle. Glancing at her as she laughed at something a reporter had said, he was struck by just how beautiful his child-hood nemesis had grown up to be, all sleek hair of dark auburn and sparkling bright eyes, her confidence stamped on her skin.

Leaving aside her uncharacteristic "poochy" comment earlier, which could be explained by the general craziness of the current situation, the only physical thing about which Catie was ever touchy were her legs.

Danny hadn't understood why when he was younger, but he'd grown up in the interim—and he'd seen how some people treated her. It infuriated him as much as it did her. She was so eminently capable that she could outdo most people any day of the week, and still there were idiots who tried to infantilize her.

He always had to fight his instincts to step in and put them straight. He knew better than that. Catie wouldn't thank him for playing knight in rugby armor. Instead, he'd learned to stand back and watch the show—as Catie took them down with acerbic wit and sharp commentary that drew blood.

She'd gotten very, very good at it over the years.

So yeah, he understood her touchiness on that point. He just wished that after so long, she'd figure out that he wasn't one of the idiots.

"What?" she said at that moment, having turned to look at him.

"Stop scowling," he said with a scowl. "How are we going to sell this if we're glaring at each other?"

She shrugged. "*Please*. No one will believe it if we're lovey-dovey." A sudden, dazzling grin, a wicked glint in her eye.

That same glint had led to sandburn on his butt back when they'd been teenagers. The family had gone camping near dunes that weren't a habitat for native birds or grasses and so were open for recreation. Catie had come up with the idea of sliding down the dunes on some cardboard boxes they'd salvaged, then flattened.

Since Jake had gone off on a beach walk with their dad, it had been just him and Catie.

The makeshift sand-sleds had worked fine the first five or so times.

That day had also been one of the only times Catie had ever accepted his help. It had been a bitch going back up the dune, and she'd finally decided that it would be no fun if she was still trying to trudge up after a single ride while he was sailing down again and again. So she'd allowed him to assist her back up—and even at fifteen, he'd known not to make a big deal of it.

And the thing was, it *hadn't* been a big deal. He'd have done the same for any mate who was having trouble getting up the slope. It was way more fun to slide down with Catie next to him, both of them whooping it up.

Then had come the sixth run.

When his box had come apart at the same time that his shorts got all but yanked off. He'd risen to his feet at the bottom, rubbing his sore butt—to see Catie on her back halfway down the dune, cackling with laughter. She'd laughed so hard that she'd "crashed" her own sled.

It was one of his favorite childhood memories.

"What are you up to?" he muttered now, well aware which of the two of them was the troublemaker—his mother might not believe it of "sweet Caitlin," but Catie was a demon child.

"Look happy," Catie said before sliding her hand behind his neck and yanking down his head.

He could've resisted, but with his skin going hot and his heart thumping, he didn't exactly want to. His breath kissed her lips, hers kissed his. Eyes of dark brown looked into his own, the specks of gold within as bright as her smile... and all at once, it wasn't a game and he didn't want to do this in front of an audience.

So he pressed his forehead to hers as if that had always been the plan. At the same time, she touched her fingers to his jaw, and her warmth burned right through skin and muscle to bone.

When they separated, it was with a shared awareness of a profound change between them.

Hoping his face didn't show the depth of his emotions, he smiled and waved at the cameras while Catie did the same. When she was asked to pose on her own, he happily stepped aside and just admired her, his chest all puffed up because this incredible woman was with him.

Fears for what this meant or not, he was already having the best night of his life by the time they sauntered on inside the old theater with its baroque touches, extravagant and flamboyant. Not a place you'd find in a city, but it had survived in this little town—thanks to the fact it pulled double duty as the town hall, a wedding chapel, the graduation hall, and the same for any other event that required the space for more than twenty or thirty people.

Leon, hovering just inside, out of sight of the cameras, all but pounced on Danny the instant they entered. His eyes, usually a calm hazel, were as bright as floodlights, the pale brown of his hair a messy tumble against freckled skin. "I love you, man!"

Staggering back from the force of his friend's hug, Danny said, "Whoa, dude!"

But Leon was too happy to care that he was strangling

Danny. Squeezing him tight, he smacked a kiss on Danny's cheek. "I love you. I love you."

The two of them had met playing school rugby. Leon looked every inch the big, beefy rugby-player stereotype and had the gruff mannerisms of a back-country farmer. He did not go around making declarations of love to anyone—Danny would be surprised if he'd so much as whispered the words to a girlfriend.

Finally releasing Danny, Leon turned to Catie, who was just slipping away her phone. He stuck out his hand. "Thank you."

Catie accepted his hand. "No, thank you for allowing in this gate-crasher. I'm so looking forward to the play—I read your post about *Chaos Bones* on your website, and it sounds amazing."

Danny's mouth all but dropped open. Because it sure as hell looked like Leon was blushing. *Blushing.* "Suck-up," he said to Catie.

Shooting him a smug grin, Catie tucked her arm into Leon's. "So, tell me more about how you put this production together."

When Leon sent Danny a worried look, Danny just rolled his eyes, then walked to fall into step to Catie's left. He knew what Leon didn't—that Catie was genuinely interested. It was one of the things he'd always liked about her. She was devoted to her dream, but she made time to listen to the dreams of others.

So he wasn't the least surprised when Leon ended up expounding exponentially on the project, a beaming human ball of joy.

"Danny."

Turning at that husky female voice, he said, "Hey, Mara."

She kind of arched toward him, but he stayed straight and glanced to the right as if distracted by something else. A sports reporter by trade, the curvy brunette was a beautiful woman. She'd also worked her way through most of the other single men in the squad. Danny had never been attracted to her, but having sown his own wild oats, he wasn't about to judge her for her exploits.

He *did* judge her for being a snake.

Because he was certain that Mara was here to stir the pot. He'd seen her work the same "oh, I just wanted to say hi" shtick on a happily married friend. The poor guy had ended up with a furious wife and no idea that Mara had been hitting on him. It was the latter that had saved him —he'd been so clueless that his wife had accepted he'd done nothing to attract the attention.

And while Danny and Catie might be faking their relationship—and shit, it was starting to hurt inside to think that—he wouldn't disrespect her by allowing Mara to play bitchy games. Especially since Mara probably had a plant in the crowd armed with a camera. Next thing he knew, she'd feed one of her entertainment friends an exclusive about how there was "trouble in paradise" or other similar stupidity.

An arm twining with his, a familiar body leaning into his, Catie's hand rising to pet his biceps.

"Mara," Catie said with a smile so genuine it could melt butter and give a church sermon.

Demon child.

"I didn't know you enjoyed avant-garde plays," Catie continued. "Aren't you so looking forward to seeing how

Leon explores the twin motifs of loss and belonging?" A glance up at a worshipful Leon.

Mara gave a thin-lipped smile. "I haven't had a chance to look at the media material," she answered. "Decided to accept the invitation at the last minute."

Like when she'd discovered that Danny was going to be in attendance, Catie thought with an inward bite of sarcasm. Worst of it was that Mara was an excellent sports reporter and Catie had been inclined to like her—until she'd seen the predator hidden behind the silky hair, spectacular boobs, and makeup so on point that it made Catie want to grit her teeth.

It should be a rule that shit-stirrers were bad at makeup.

Thank the universe that Danny seemed too smart to fall for her. From what Catie had heard in sporting circles, Mara was on the hunt for her final conquest.

"I'm getting on in age, darling," she'd said to a friend of hers while touching up her lipstick in the mirror of a hotel bathroom. One of Catie's running partners had been at the same event—and in a stall at the time—and had eavesdropped without shame.

According to her, Mara had added, "Time to put up the spurs and ride just one cowboy. Better make sure he's young and hung."

The woman was twenty-eight. She'd also never been near a ranch in her manicured and pampered life. Her father was a department store magnate who'd brought his "little girl" a Porsche for her sixteenth birthday.

Catie hated that she knew that, but a few years ago you couldn't turn around without running into Mara's face on a magazine billboard, seeing her on TV, or hearing her on the radio. Then she'd gone into journalism and Catie had figured the earlier attention-hound behavior for growing pains.

Nope. It was Mara's actual personality.

Today the brunette bared her bright white teeth. "I heard your friend Posey Greene is going through a tough time. Please pass on my commiserations."

Catie saw red. The only thing that stopped her from clawing off Mara's catty face was the squeeze Danny gave her hip and the way he dropped his head to murmur intimately against her ear. She didn't hear what he said—that wasn't the point. The point was to see Mara's eyes go as hard as stones.

"Oh, it looks like we're being ushered inside," Leon said with perfect timing, his glow undimmed.

Catie was glad he'd been oblivious to that byplay. This was his night and he should enjoy it. Channeling her inner Dragon and dismissing Mara without a glance, she turned with Danny and they headed toward the entrance to the seating area.

Danny kept his hand on her hip, and... it felt okay. Better than that. It felt nice. Big and warm and comforting.

Frowning, she went to pull away, but they were already in the stream of people moving inside and a sudden move would've sent her careening into a woman who was the epitome of the posh theater matron. Complete with a designer velvet shrug and actual opera glasses, her snowy hair perfectly coiffed in feathered spikes, and her lips a pop of pink.

She wore pink stiletto ankle boots.

"I want to be her when I grow up," Catie whispered to Danny after the woman had moved past.

"Wrong color lipstick for you," he said, deadpan.

Elbowing him, she found herself given another hip squeeze. This one made her face flush. Then they were inside the theater and the usher was showing them to the central block of seats that had been reserved for VIPs.

Where she would soon sit in the dark with this gorgeous man next to her.

14

DANCE WITH ME

Danny stood back and let her go first, which might've irritated her except she knew that was a Joseph Esera rule: the ladies go first. As a teen, she'd once tried arguing with Joseph about it, calling it an "antiquated leftover of the patriarchy."

He'd smiled at her in that gruff, fatherly way and said, "I'm so proud of you, Caitlin. Such a strong woman you're becoming."

She'd gotten it then. To a man like Joseph, these small acts of chivalry didn't mean he saw her as lesser or weaker. It was just part of his personal code. A code he'd passed on to all four of his sons.

She also had no reason to doubt Danny's opinion of her strength and independence. They'd raced more than once to get to something first, both of them fighting dirty. She'd pushed him into a slimy mud pool on one memorable occasion, while another time he'd gotten her into deliberate trouble with Alison just so he could win their secret race.

The memory of her silent rage and his glee made her smile as she took her seat. Shit, they'd been two hellion kids together. Kids who'd had an unspoken rule against adult intervention when it came to their bets and sneaky tricks in pursuit of glory. Jake alone had been privy to their exploits, and he'd refused to take sides, saying, "You're both equally nutso."

As Danny came down beside her, she turned to him, and he instinctively angled his head down to hear what she had to say. "Thank you," she murmured, breathing in the scent of his aftershave, his jaw close enough to kiss. "For keeping me from giving that witch Mara what she wanted."

"I doubt she wanted a broken nose and her eyeballs clawed out and crushed under your sneakers, but you're welcome." A nudge of her shoulder. "You know she was stirring to get media play."

"I know. I can deal when she's sharpening her knives on me, but she went for Posey."

Danny placed his hand over the one she had on the armrest, warm and a little rough and as familiar to her as her own skin... and yet it felt different tonight, in the whispering semidark of the theater. She wanted to slide her hand away but was all too aware of the eyes on them. It still took everything she had to keep it in place.

Then he was speaking, the deep timbre of his voice drawing her attention. "I get it," he murmured. He ran the pad of his thumb over her skin. "What I don't understand is why she got so catty with you. You're an athlete, and whatever else she is, she's a damn good sports journalist." The man looked genuinely mystified.

"Are you really that clueless, hotshot?"

When he raised an eyebrow, she said, "Ahem" and nodded to their clasped hands.

He stared as if he'd only just become aware of the fact he'd been stroking her... holding her. But he didn't break contact. "Oh right. She thinks we're..."

"Exactly. And you're on her hit list." She told him what her fellow runner had overheard. "Be careful not to be caught alone with her. Looks like she's out for a husband, but who knows? She might settle for a scandal and associated celebrity clout." Feeling oddly protective, she frowned and held his eyes. "Promise?"

Dark eyes looking into hers with a focus so absolute it stole her breath. "Cross my heart."

The lights went down.

Shuddering out a quiet breath, she faced forward... but she didn't slide her hand out from under Danny's. So if you wanted to get technical about it, they held hands throughout the play.

DANNY HAD TO BE HONEST. He didn't fully comprehend Leon's masterpiece. But that might've been because he'd been focused on Catie rather than the stage.

Leon had decided an intermission didn't suit the flow of this play, so Danny got to sit next to her all the way through, her presence a bright light: the light floral scent she liked that always took him by surprise, the slender bones of her hand, the softness of her skin—and especially how her face lit up when she turned to him as she laughed during a funny moment in the play.

Sharing the laughter with him.

Stealing another piece of his heart.

He was really in trouble, and he was beginning to think he didn't want to get out of it.

Fuck.

The single terrified word passed through his mind just as the curtain fell to rapturous applause. Danny rose to congratulate his friend, Catie beside him. He might not have caught all the nuances, but he could tell it was good. The kind of good that would get Leon the attention he needed to take his work to a bigger stage.

"That was brilliant," Catie said to him as she kept on clapping. "I could watch that again! We should go when he brings the show to Auckland!"

"Yeah," he managed to get out through his thickening throat.

The curtain went up again as the cast came to take their bows.

They returned twice more as the applause continued on—and they brought Leon out with them on the final round. He emerged with shining eyes, and tears were rolling down his face by the time he took his own bow as the cast stepped back as one to applaud him.

Danny put his fingers to his mouth and whistled.

It startled the more sober theatergoers around him, but Leon's local rugby mates as well as his extended family took up the whistle, adding loud yells of support, and they blew off the roof until even the "proper" theater people were laughing and clapping with their hands in the air.

Turning to Catie when the clapping finally died down and the cast and Leon had retreated backstage, Danny said, "I'm buzzed. You want to do something?" He didn't want the night to end, didn't want to stop being with Catie.

A nod, her eyes shining. "Leon said he's having an after-party at Vertigo." She named a fairly unknown club. "Mara butted in before he could tell you—anyway, he said he hired out a room, but he's not expecting many people aside from the crew."

"Oh, I think we can change that." He grinned at Catie, delighted at being able to do something to help his friend. "Can you rope in a few of the local glitterati?"

"Maybe." A dark scowl. "But don't call them glitterati." Sliding her hand down from her loose clasp at his elbow, she took his hand.

Danny closed his fingers around her palm, his heart pounding. "You okay to head home to change?" He tugged at his bowtie, suddenly too hot. "I want to get out of this thing."

"Let's do it."

It took them over fifteen minutes to get outside thanks to all the people mingling around, buzzing about the play, and the media who wanted to get their reactions. The two of them made sure to give the play a glowing review, and Danny heard others around them doing the same. Leon was going to blow up.

Danny couldn't be happier for his friend.

Once finally in the car and on their way home, they just collapsed and didn't say much. And it was fine. With Catie, silence was as comfortable as annoying each other for no particular reason.

"Thanks," he said to the driver when they came to a stop by the apartment. "We're actually going back out. Are you okay to extend your hours, or shall we call a new car?" He knew all commercial drivers had to follow strict safety regs.

"No, I'm good since I was on an official break while you were in the theater," the driver said with a grin. "I'll just give the boss a call and let him know you guys want me to hang around."

"We won't be long," Catie promised him. "Are you hungry? We can grab you food from the apartment."

"No, I had dinner while you were watching the play. Thanks though."

Leaving him to wait in his warm vehicle, they headed up to the apartment. Danny changed into clean blue jeans and a black tee, then pulled on the black jacket from the tux. "Does this look okay?" he asked, exiting his room. "I don't have another formal-type jacket on me."

She poked her head around the door of her bedroom. "Smoking," she declared.

Ducking his head, he was glad she'd pulled back and couldn't see his face. Because that face was hot. He raised his head back up just in time to see Catie step out. And almost swallowed his tongue. "Jesus, princess. You're going to give some poor guy a heart attack."

Laughing, she swiveled around to show him the back of her teeny tiny dress of glittering gold. It dipped sharply to the curve of her lower back, after which the designer had reluctantly permitted a measly few inches of glittery fabric that just covered her butt and hovered at the top edge of her thighs.

Thighs covered in creamy skin that made him want to loosen his nonexistent collar.

And the torture didn't end there. The dress spaghetti straps along with a slightly loose-on-purpose neckline that draped over the taut curves of her breasts. Which were braless. He knew that because his stupid brain insisted on putting two and two together and coming up with "holy hotness."

"You're wearing your favorite skins," he managed to get out, only then noticing the futuristic-looking prosthetic covers she must've been wearing under her pants tonight; he knew she used the skins under that kind of clothing to give her calves shape.

"I decided they went with this dress," Catie said with a grin. "Love my rods, but I wanted the gold."

Danny had to agree on both points—bare, her legs were incredible pieces of engineering that he'd been lucky enough to be allowed to examine close up. But these skins had a kind of bionic look to them, as if Catie were half machine—they were even specially painted to appear as if the lines of gold were alive. Electronic blood.

She'd also gotten rid of her glittery sneakers in favor of a pair of short black ankle boots without a heel. The makeup, however, was the same—which wasn't always a given with Catie.

"You got your wallet?" Catie said to him as she returned to her bedroom to grab her purse. "You had it in your pants pocket before."

"Right, thanks." He swung back into his room.

"Don't forget your coat," he said as they prepared to leave. "We'll probably have to walk a few minutes to the bar. I looked online, and there's no drop-off zone near there and the parking will be a circus this time of night."

"Yes, Dad," Catie said, the snark alive in her tone.

Danny narrowed his eyes. "What's with you? You just told me I was about to forget my wallet, and I thanked you like a normal human instead of going all Godzilla on your ass."

CATIE WENT to part her lips on a snapped response... and realized she was doing it again. Treating Danny like he was "other" instead of one of her own people. She didn't know why she reacted so defensively with him, especially when she knew that, to him, she'd always been just Catie. Not Catie the Poor Disabled Girl, or Catie the Inspiration, or even Catie the Paralympian.

To him she was Catie who liked makeup too much and always stole all the maple syrup on the table. "I did not go all Godzilla," she muttered instead of apologizing. Even accepting that she was being churlish, she couldn't make herself say the words.

"You still don't have a coat." Hands on his hips, he glared at her. "I'm not going to donate my jacket if you start to freeze off your bits."

Stomping into her bedroom because he was right, she grabbed her big pink coat with its splotches of golden glitter on the bottom half. You'd think it was designer, but she'd found the coat at a recycle boutique for twenty-five dollars, then splotched it herself. She loved it to pieces and it went with everything.

Danny opened the door for her, then pulled it shut behind them.

Catie fought with herself on the walk to the elevator, finally blurting out, "Sorry. Wasn't Godzilla, but might've been a smaller monster."

His lips kicked up, and boom, there went her heart all over again. "Let me guess—a mini dragon?"

"Ha ha." But she felt better now that she'd apologized. Ísa had brought her up better than to be an ass to someone who wasn't being an ass to her. Catie knew full well she had a chip on her shoulder due to many and myriad reasons, but that didn't mean she had to take the chip and beat defenseless people over the head with it.

The thing was, she almost never got snippy with even the most clueless people or those who misspoke. She didn't expect the world to understand her reality when she might be the first double amputee they'd ever met. Innocent cluelessness she could forgive, particularly if the person was open to being corrected if they'd made an error.

Generally, the only people at risk of coming face-to-face with her dark side were the assholes.

Tonight, however, she was going out with a certified non-asshole. And that, she admitted, was part of the reason she'd jumped down his throat. Because she was freaked out at how well they worked together, how easy it was to be his fake girlfriend.

"Ready to paint the town red?" Danny asked inside the elevator before drawing his eyebrows together in an ominous scowl. "The same red you painted my face while I was sleeping that time."

Shoulders shaking, she shoved the fear aside in favor of enjoying this night out of time. "City's going to be scarlet by the time we're done, hotshot."

As they walked through the street together after their driver dropped them off at the closest spot he could get into, she found that she was happy. She felt young and cheerful and content deep inside.

And if her hand kept wanting to reach out to take

Danny's, if her stomach kept wanting to flutter, if her mind kept circling back to that moment on the red carpet that had stolen the air right out of her lungs, well... it was only a temporary madness. This was all pretend, and it would be over before she knew it.

"There's the place." Danny pointed.

"Wow, look at that queue." She hadn't expected it of the hole-in-the-wall spot. "I only managed to round up a couple of folks who might get Leon some media attention. Jerri has a big local following—she said she'd give the party a shout-out." Catie and the model had connected online and had only met in person a couple of times, but it was a relationship Catie could see turning into a genuine friendship.

"Well, looks like she's made Vertigo *the* spot to be tonight," Danny said and reached out to take her hand. "I'll be the torpedo."

Since he was bigger and that queue of people had now spotted them, with a number having their phones out as they clicked and squealed, Catie decided to go with it. She had no wish to die an ignominious death in a stampede of women who wanted to aim themselves at Danny.

When his admirers kept their distance despite the fact they were all but bursting with excitement, she glanced at him to see that he had on what she'd always called his "serious shit" face. That face tended to come out on the rugby field when the chips were down and the team had to pull a win out of their butt. It also came out when there were important family things on the table.

Right now it told everyone to back the hell off.

For her.

Catie struggled with how she felt about his protective-ness. She was well used to defending and taking care of herself. Then again, she wasn't usually near a group just itching to stampede. So she held on tight to Danny and let him play protector. Just this one time.

The bouncer welcomed them through without a single question, his grin broad as he took in Danny and ignored Catie. Rugby fan.

"Wicked boots!" a female voice called out as Catie disappeared in the door.

Glancing over her shoulder, Catie saw genuine admi-ration on the face of a tall Indian woman with blunt-cut bangs. "They're not boots!" she yelled back, figuring it was the low light that had led to the mix-up. "Prosthetic legs!"

The woman's mouth fell open. "No shit! Oh, oh, you're the runner!" Up came her phone.

In a good mood, Catie tugged out a grumpy Danny and pasted herself against him for a shot before he grum-bled and tugged her back inside. "You're going to freeze. That coat barely covers more than your dress." He was rubbing the dip of her back.

Catie almost snapped back that most of her legs were metal, so cold wasn't an issue. But—and though it made her want to squirm—she realized that she liked the fact he was worried about her staying warm. Sailor was that way with Ísa, and her brother-in-law definitely didn't treat her sister as anything but a powerhouse.

She'd keep up her antennae of suspicion, but it was possible Danny could be trusted with the protective stuff without taking it too far. Then they were in the club, and it was jumping. The only reason they found the private room was that it literally had a neon sign that flashed the words VIP ROOM.

Inside, the party was raucous.

Jerri was holding court near the door and gave Catie a big hug and a kiss on the cheek. "Thanks for the invite, Cat. This party is *wild*!" All curly black hair and dark brown skin, she was a stunner—the modeling world called her plus-size, but to Catie, she was simply and unquestionably a bombshell.

"Thanks for the shout-out!" she managed before Jerri was asked to dance by an admirer.

Happy the other woman was enjoying herself, she looked around for Leon—and saw he was well on the way to getting drunk. He was a very happy drunk, and when he asked Catie for a dance, she agreed. Only to be bowed to before he took her hand and placed his arm around her as if for a formal waltz.

Of course, his balance was totally off, but it was adorable how he tried to act sober and as if he weren't stepping all over her feet.

Danny rescued her a few minutes later—after laughing his head off for the first half. Then she was in his arms and the music was booming and they danced.

15

COOKIES AND VENGEANCE

It had been the best night of his life.

After jumping quickly into the shower to wash off the sweat from dancing, Danny pulled on a pair of boxer shorts before he crashed into bed. He usually slept in his birthday suit but didn't want to be caught butt naked if Catie had to come into the room for some reason.

Images from the night played out against the wall of his mind. He'd danced with Catie most of the evening, and she hadn't seemed to mind. Hell, at one point, she'd been leaning hip to hip with him as they chatted to friends. It had—

Crash!

Snapping out of bed at the loud sound from the living area, he ran out the bedroom door. "Catie?"

A chill wind had him jerking his attention to the open balcony doors. And there she was, on the floor a foot inside the apartment, her legs splayed out just *wrong* and one hand pressed against the sideboard that had held a vase of smoky blue glass. That vase now lay shattered on the plush gray carpet.

The amount of noise it had made as it fell told him it must've hit either the wall or the sideboard on the way down—or maybe the noise had been caused by the sideboard itself slamming into the wall, but he didn't care about either of the stupid things. He cared about Catie.

Crossing the distance between them in a heartbeat, he went to kneel down, do what he could to help, but she snapped, "Don't! Go away!"

Frustration burned in his veins, but he didn't snap back. He'd caught the hint of wetness in her eyes, knew he had to deal with this right or it would hurt her. So he got up and, after closing the balcony doors, picked up one of the heavy dining table chairs and brought it over to set it on her other side. "Here, princess. I'll grab the dustpan to collect the big shards; then we can vacuum up the rest."

He deliberately kept his back to her as he walked to the kitchen. He'd spotted the dustpan under the kitchen sink earlier that weekend but spent at least a minute opening and closing cupboard doors as if searching for it. By the time he finally "found it," Catie was seated on the chair, one leg bent at the knee, the other stretched out in front of her, her party dress a golden shine.

"Fuck, fuck, fuck." Her voice wobbled.

"How bad is it?" he asked as he began to pick up the shards like he'd said he would. His muscles strained at his skin, his abdomen clenched against the urge to pick her up and hold her tight.

"I don't know!" It came out a yell. "Shit! I've walked in

and out those doors a thousand times. Why the fuck did I trip today?"

"Er, because you're human?" No matter the painful pounding of his heart, he knew better than to offer her sympathy. She'd murder him for that. "Did you damage the prosthesis?" Though she hadn't yet changed out of her dress, she had taken off her skins, and he couldn't see any obvious damage—to the rods or her body. But he knew she was in pain and it was taking everything he had not to react.

She didn't respond for so long that he thought she wasn't going to answer. Then she said, "It's my stump" in a voice so small and quiet that it hurt him. Catie was never small and quiet.

"You bruised it when you fell?" Putting aside the dustpan, he made himself go and get the vacuum. She'd stop talking to him if he made it a big deal.

"It's swelling," she said when he got back, then swallowed. "I can feel it."

He knew that meant she had to remove the prosthesis. "Can you walk on the leg?"

"I can walk on my stumps," she muttered.

"Sure, and get a shard in there." He raised both eyebrows. "You're just being dumb stubborn now."

Her lower lip quivered, shattering him. "I hate you sometimes."

"I know." He kept it together, kept things light, through sheer raw will. "But you also know I understand injuries, so let's get you to your room where you can sulk in luxury."

It took her three more minutes to say, "Fine."

Not saying anything in return, he just went to her

side, bent, and put his arm around her waist. She slid her own arm around his shoulders, then used him and her uninjured leg as braces to get herself up.

He caught the wave of relief on her face when her other leg held firm. But the spark of joy was fleeting, her expression settling back into grim lines as they walked toward her room. It didn't take them long to get there.

"Bed or chair?" he asked.

"Bed," she muttered through gritted teeth.

He left the moment she was down in a seated position on the edge of the bed. Catie would *not* want him nearby right now—that he knew without having to be told. But worry gnawed at him, and he couldn't keep still. The first thing he did was to track down both a heating pad and an ice pack. He'd known she'd have both; she was a runner.

Since he didn't know which one she'd need, he prepared the heating pad, then took both it and the cold pack to her door. Knocking, he wasn't surprised not to get a response. "Hey, I'm leaving a heat pad and an ice pack outside your door." Then he forced himself to get the hell away from her door and return to where the vase had shattered. He wanted to get that cleaned up so that Catie wasn't at risk of injuring herself on any stray shards.

He was all but done when he heard her door crack open, then close moments later.

He exhaled. At least she'd taken what he'd left.

But now that he was finished with cleanup, he found himself edgy and restless. So he did what he always did when he was stressed. He went into the kitchen and started hunting for ingredients. He didn't know what he was going to make until he found a half-eaten jar of morello cherry jam in the back of the fridge.

He already knew there was dark chocolate in the pantry along with all the other staple supplies. But when he found an unopened pack of pecans back there, he thanked Jacqueline's chef all over again. The man had great taste.

He got to adding together the ingredients, but halfway through, he went and knocked on Catie's door. "Are you alive?" It was the kind of question she might actually answer.

"I'm fine," came the curt response.

He caught the tone in her voice though. Shit. She was crying. He'd never actually seen Catie cry—she didn't do it in front of anyone. Or maybe she did it in front of Ísa, but she'd certainly never done it in front of him. He hated the idea of her crying alone in her room, but he also knew he wouldn't be welcome right now, so he forced himself to go back to his baking.

He still wasn't calm by the time he slid his first concoction into the oven, so he started on another mix. They already had leftovers from his previous efforts, but he'd go mad if he had to sit still. Most of it would freeze fine, he told himself, and Catie could thaw it out the next time she came down. They could also take a bunch of stuff back home to Auckland.

His phone, which he'd brought into the room with the idea of listening to one of his playlists and promptly forgotten about, began buzzing fifteen minutes into his second mix. Not in the mood to deal with even a text from a friend, he ignored it. But the messages kept coming.

Growling under his breath, he finished scooping out the last of the cupcake batter into one of the muffin pans he'd prepared, then went over and grabbed the phone. To find a long list of messages from Catie.

I can smell something.

What is it?

Don't you dare make cookies and not give me some.

HELLO!!

I'm wounded here and you're stuffing your face.

ANSWER YOUR DAMN MESSAGES, HOTSHOT.

That's it, I'm not forgetting this.

Revenge will be mine.

Grinning by the end of the string, Danny shot back: *Hold your horses. They're not done yet.*

Silence.

That was when he knew Catie wasn't back to her usual self or anything like it. Jaw tight, he took the cookies out of the oven, then slid the cupcakes in. The cookies needed a few more minutes to set. He spent that time warming up a tall glass of milk.

After which he plated four yet-warm cookies and walked over to knock on the door with his foot. "It's your food delivery."

He half expected her to tell him to leave it by the door, but she said, "Come in."

Face clear of makeup, her hair brushed out, she was in bed in her pj's. She'd pulled the duvet over her lower half and set her legs aside on the floor. Also beside the bed was a simple foldable wheelchair. He'd guessed she might have one here—he knew Ísa and Sailor had one in storage at their place in case Catie ever needed it during a visit. But he'd never actually seen her use one.

That she'd not only gotten it out but was allowing him to see it...

Fuck.

"Here, Your Highness," he managed to get out past the worry that was a heavy stone in his gut. After she took the plate, he put the glass of milk on her bedside table.

She was already taking a giant bite out of a cookie. Making a surprised sound when the chocolate melted all over her lip, she quickly licked it up and said, "Holy mackerel, hotshot. Where did you find cherries?"

"Jam," he told her. "Not perfect, but it'll do in a pinch."

Catie had stuffed the rest of the cookie in her mouth, had her fingers on another one. "Mmm."

Since she seemed to be feeling more herself, he dared go back out, get himself a drink and some cookies, and come back to join her. Putting his stuff on the other bedside table, he sat down on the bed with his back to the headboard and his body on top of the duvet.

"You lost your clothes?"

Only at her sharp question did he realize he was still only wearing boxer shorts. Dear Lord, he'd been so worried that he'd turned into a near-naked baker. At least he hadn't been at risk from oil splatters.

"You being lured by my luscious body?" he shot back in an effort to hide his cock's enthusiastic reaction to the fact Catie was looking at his all but naked self. He also drew up his leg to better hide the sudden interest in his boxers.

"You wish," she said and bit into a third cookie.

They ate in silence for a while until Danny said, "How bad is it?"

Catie loved cookies, but she was also an elite runner who usually only fueled her body with good, nutritious meals and snacks. One cookie binge over a weekend was a fun indulgence, but a second one? That was a sign something was very wrong.

"It's swollen," she said. "But I've had that kind of swelling before and it's gone down overnight, so it might be all right." A tightness to her voice.

"But?"

She put down her half-eaten cookie, reached to pick up the milk. After drinking a third of it, she put it back down. "You follow Posey online, right?"

"Sure. I met her that time she came to New Zealand, remember?" Catie had brought her friend along to a family dinner, and they'd all had a great time. "You're talking about the issues she's had this past year?"

Posey had been charting the issues with her residual limbs and how she could no longer wear prostheses as regularly as she'd previously done. She was in too much pain, her residual limbs prone to swelling.

Catie nodded. "She retired from professional sport on her own terms last year, so she's zen about it, just wants the doctors to get a handle on the pain. That's what bothers her most."

Danny had gotten that vibe from Posey's posts too. The former champion skier had a great off-field career as a writer and seemed to be at peace with having bowed out of her chosen sport at the top of her game. But she was also Catie's senior by a decade. "She's your mentor, right?"

Catie nodded. "She was a shining star when I met her as a kid. At that camp in the States—she came to give us a talk, tell us about her journey. I never expected her to reply to the letters I sent her afterward, but she did. I've always felt so lucky that I had someone like her to help guide me."

Setting aside the plate of cookies, she squeezed the duvet in her hands. "She was invincible, you know? All the things people said dual lower-limb amputees couldn't do? She did them, and then she did more."

Climbing mountains, diving out of planes, going scuba diving, Posey had grinned her way through each adventure while an excited young Catie followed along, hanging out for the next update.

I'm going to do that one day, she'd thought with each exploit. And she had. She'd also created her own adventures, conquered her own obstacles. But Posey... Posey had always been her benchmark. "Even now, she's being so amazing. Just going with the flow, this calm to her that's bone deep."

Danny didn't interrupt, instead just eating one of his heavenly cookies.

Which reminded her to take another bite of hers. After swallowing it down, she said, "But I'm also terrified." She hadn't admitted that to anyone, but it wasn't hard to tell Danny—he'd known her through some of the toughest years of her life, when growth spurts messed with the fit of her prostheses and left her struggling.

"What Posey's dealing with now? It could be my future too." That was what people didn't realize—being fitted with the perfect prosthesis and learning to use it wasn't the end of the story. "I've always known that complications could happen. My doctors prepared me. But I've become so used to living my life as I want. I hate the idea that it could be ripped out of my control all over again."

She stuffed the rest of the cookie into her mouth before she could start crying. She felt awful for her pity party when she'd suffered a minor injury in comparison to her friend and mentor's months-long ordeal to get back on her feet, but she couldn't stop the panic that fluttered inside her.

"I should probably say something uplifting about how I know you'll conquer all obstacles, blah blah," Danny said. "But we both know that would be soft-pedaling it. Injuries can end our careers. Lifetime of dreaming and working toward a single goal, and it's all over in a heartbeat."

Danny, she thought, had witnessed that firsthand.

It was as if he'd read her mind, because he said, "I mean, Gabe came out of his injury swinging, but it wasn't his choice to take another path. Not before the injury. We're at the mercy of our bodies, and it's fucking scary."

She glanced at him, picking up an edge in his voice. "Danny? Has something happened?" His form on the field had suffered a few glitches of late; he remained brilliant but wasn't the blazing star people expected.

Catie had thought nothing of it, figured he was just having a few off games. Happened to everyone. And Danny at his worst was better than most players at their best. The one thing she hadn't considered was that he might be struggling with an unseen physical issue. "Are you dealing with an injury?"

16

ONE NIGHT ONLY

anny shook his head. "A couple of the other guys just got benched for concussion-related problems and at least one might not be allowed back." He exhaled. "It's just... I feel like we only have a finite time to make our mark, and then it's all over."

He got it, at least when it came to the sporting side of things.

Catie's eyes went to the wheelchair she kept at this apartment. "I don't want to be in a chair," she said quietly. "Not every amputee can or even wants to use prostheses, and I'm all for having as many mobility options as possible." She never pushed prosthetic limbs on children or adults who didn't want them.

"All I want is for everyone to have a *choice*—and my choice was to become a full-time user of prosthetic legs and then a competitive runner." She squeezed her fingers into her palms, her shoulders tight and stomach churning. "I sweated blood to learn to walk again, run again, went through endless prosthetic fittings, put up with blisters, pressure wounds, and more to get to this point. The idea that I could lose it all... It makes me so angry."

It shoved her back into the hospital bed in which she'd woken disoriented and in pain at age eleven. She'd had moxie, that kid, had made up her mind to run again even if she didn't have legs. But she was no machine; there'd been dark times along the way, and in those dark times, she'd raged against the unfairness of it all.

A big warm hand closing over one of her tightly fisted ones. "It sucks," Danny said. "But—and don't punch me for what I'm about to say—it's not your reality right now. If you start panicking and let it take over, you'll have already lost everything."

She glared at him. "Did you get that off a fortune cookie?"

"No." He glared back. "Gabriel. He told me that when I had a panic attack soon after he got injured." A shake of his head. "My big brother was the one hurt, and I was the one panicking. I'm definitely the baby of the family."

Hearing what he didn't say, she flipped her hand to weave her fingers through his. "He was your hero, and you saw him fall." Just like she'd seen her own hero fall. "It's hard to handle."

"Yeah."

They sat, hand in hand, for a long time, just thinking. She knew he was right, and most of the time she managed to keep the fear at bay. "My aim is to be more like Posey, more zen about life in general."

"She's got a good, what, ten years on you? Maybe she was exactly like you at your age. You should ask her."

Perhaps she would, when her friend was feeling

better. Right now Posey needed all her energy for herself. "Want to watch some TV?" She needed to zone out, stop thinking about her leg and the damage she might've done to it.

"Sure." A dramatic sigh. "I'll even let you pick the show."

Catie had a TV across from her bed that she'd never before used, far preferring to sit in the living room. Watching TV in bed reminded her too much of being stuck in a hospital. But tonight, watching a science fiction space movie with Danny—and managing to fit in a warm cupcake, sans frosting, when those came out of the oven —ended up being fun.

They stayed up far too late, and she didn't know when they fell asleep.

She just knew that when she woke, it was with Danny's big body curled around her own. He was still on top of the duvet, she was still below it, but he had his arm flung around her and his face buried against her nape.

She'd never fallen asleep with a man in bed with her. Ever.

Not even with Ward.

She'd just never felt comfortable enough with anyone for that ultimate vulnerability. But today she didn't start. His scent was warm and familiar, his presence too entwined with her life for even her sleep-hazy brain not to recognize him. Instead, she yawned and snuggled back a little deeper into his chest.

He tightened his hold on her but kept on sleeping, his breathing deep and even.

Yup, not a morning person. Catie smiled. She knew he only got up for training because he had to—if Danny had his way, he'd stay up all hours and begin to develop vampire fangs. She, however, was now fully awake. As she lay there, she flexed her injured stump, testing its status. It moved well, felt good.

She'd gotten lucky.

Exhaling, she lay there and stared out at the balcony doors beyond which the city was waking up, one alarm clock and cup of coffee at a time. Soon, she and Danny would be heading to the airport, signaling the end of this strange interlude.

Her stomach clutched.

She'd miss him.

God, when had that happened? Her, missing Daniel Esera?

This time her stomach did a backflip. Because the ache inside her, that wasn't a random physical blip, a pulse of attraction toward a beautiful man. It held an emotional depth that was solemn, serious. As if they'd already been together for years, their connection a deep and important one long before she'd acknowledged it.

Terrifying. Yet she stayed tucked against the living burn of Danny's body, his breath hot against the skin of her neck.

When he stirred at last, she had to fight to keep from tensing. No way was she about to give away the confused longing inside her. That would screw up everything, wreck a critical foundation of both their lives. He loved and needed his family. So did she. Messing with that warmth and friendliness by dragging in a fleeting physical attraction? No, not worth it.

But when he stretched while rubbing his bristly morning face against her, she couldn't take how her stomach did another flip. "Hey, I'm not a scratching post."

Instead of backing off, he wrapped his arm back around her and rubbed harder while tickling her stomach.

"Daniel!" It came out a giggling screech—her stomach was the tickliest part of her body, which the demon very well knew. "I'm—going—to—kill—you!" she managed to gasp out between giggles.

Flipping to her back when he finally released her, she found an unrepentant Daniel Esera grinning at her. And boom, there went that fist of "like," right into her chest, clamping itself around her heart. "I'll get you for that," she threatened, hoping he'd put her husky voice down to having just woken.

"Promises, promises." Twisting, he bounded out of bed. "That was a good sleep." With that satisfied pronouncement, he spread out his arms in a full-body yawn, all rippling abs and brown skin that glowed with health. "Want an omelet for breakfast?"

"With cheese. And onions. *Lots* of onions."

"Weirdo. But okay." Then he was gone, flexing his arms back to stretch his shoulders as he padded out the door, his body on bold display. She'd seen that body countless times over the years, from back when it was skinny and lanky, then lightly muscled, then as it was now. It had never made an impact in a male-female sense.

This morning her cheeks burned, flutters erupting *everywhere.*

Exhaling loudly, she stared up at the ceiling. "I do not

need this complication," she muttered. "I have enough on my plate."

But her body wasn't in the mood to listen. Neither was her heart. Because it wasn't about Danny's admittedly spectacular body—it was about the fact he'd made her cookies he damn well knew she couldn't resist, how he'd come in here and sat with her, talked with her, watched TV with her, played silly guessing games with her where they tried to predict the plot.

Just because she'd needed it.

She had to admit it: Daniel Esera would make a wonderful boyfriend—for the right woman.

DANNY SLUNG the strap of his duffel over his shoulder, then grabbed Catie's small roll-on case with his other hand. When she didn't argue with him, just closed the door of their taxi and waited on the curb in front of the departure area of the airport, he knew her leg had to still be giving her trouble. Not enough for her to not wear the prosthesis on that leg, but enough for her gait to not be quite even, and for her to let him get away with playing knight in blue jeans and a gray sweatshirt.

She hadn't even bitched at him when he'd called the airline and had himself transferred to her flight. Once inside the departure area, she took over, checking them in on the machines and choosing seats side by side. Both their pieces of luggage were small enough to go in the overhead compartments, but since their frequent-flier status allowed one piece of checked luggage each, they sent them through.

The security queue was longer than Danny had

expected but moving along at a good clip when they joined it. Danny was aware of a few surreptitious glances, but no one approached them.

His muscles uncoiled.

He didn't know how long he could keep up this facade—he felt like such a fraud when people treated him like a rugby hero. He wasn't, and they'd all seen it from the stands or on the big screen over most of the past season.

"What's up with you?" Catie asked with a nudge of her elbow. "You're as jumpy as a cicada."

"That is the oddest comparison ever."

Catie frowned but left it for now. She'd dig out the problem later. At this instant, she was very conscious of all the ears around them. Most of these people probably didn't care one way or the other, but she couldn't take the risk that someone in the queue was a fan or just wanted a moment of social media fame.

A movement by her side.

Glancing down, she saw a boy of about seven staring at the prostheses exposed below her midthigh-length denim skirt. "Hey, little man."

He looked up, brown eyes huge. "Are you a robot?" he gasped out.

Catie winked at him. "Shh."

Face gleeful, he said, "Can I touch you?"

Having never had a problem with little kids and their curiosity, she said, "Sure, one time. My robot defenses might activate if you try it again."

He raised a super careful hand and gently brushed

his fingers against one rod of gleaming metal. "Cool." It was all air.

"Manaaki! Manaaki!"

His head jerked toward the back of the line at the sound of that feminine voice. "I gotta go."

"Bye," Catie said and waved him off.

That was the most exciting thing that happened in the queue as they inched their way forward. Especially since Danny had gone silent and seemed lost in his own thoughts. Something had been up with him since he'd received a text message just as they'd gotten into the taxi for the ride to the airport.

It couldn't be anything to do with his family because he'd have told her that straight off the bat. But it was clearly something important enough to weigh on him. It worried her. Danny was the most cheerful of all the adults in the family. And of the two of them, he was *definitely* the more even-tempered.

They reached the front of the security line right then, and as usual, Catie was waved onto the designated spot to undergo a manual check. That was why, no matter the weather, she wore either a skirt or shorts to the airport. It saved her the hassle of explaining that she was wearing prostheses, then pulling out her medical forms. She still had the forms in her purse, but having her prostheses out in full view tended to make those redundant.

The security officer she had today was a cheerful and petite blonde who was more interested in Catie's purse than her prostheses. "I've been trying to get something like that," she said after the purse had come through the detector and another officer had brought it over to where

Catie stood, waiting for her body scan. "Designer, I'm guessing?"

"Vintage find." Catie spread out her arms for the scan. "In an op shop," she said, referring to the thrift-style stores that existed throughout the country. Each one was unique; that was part of the fun. "Five dollars."

"*No.*"

"Steal, right?" Catie had actually felt so bad about the ridiculous pricing that she'd made a significant donation to the cause supported by the shop, but she still loved that she'd found the bag. It was like finding treasure. "I don't think anyone nowadays is making this style. I'd definitely haunt the op shops and garage sales."

"I would've never thought it, but yeah, I'm going to do that." The officer ran her wand over the back of Catie's sweater, checked her bra strap when the wand beeped, then said, "You're clear, hon. Have a good flight."

"Thanks. Have a nice day." She walked over to join Danny, who had his hands in his pockets. All he had on him was a wallet and his phone. Which of course meant he'd hit her up for tissues if he needed one, chewing gum from her stash, a pen if he decided to do the crossword in the complimentary airline magazine.

Men, she thought with a surge of affection.

She expected him to comment on her girly moment with the security officer, but he just said, "All good?"

"Yeah. Sweet." Waiting until they were in a quieter area, she poked him in the arm. "Seriously, hotshot, what's up?"

17

ADORABLE BABIES!

Danny's shoulders hunched in.

Catie blinked. Danny was about the most confident person she knew. This wasn't like him. Closing her hand gently around his upper left arm, she said, "What's wrong? I promise not to cackle like a hyena at your misfortune."

He didn't smile at her attempt at what would normally pass for a joke between them. Seriously worried now, she slipped her arm through his so they were even closer and fluttered her eyelashes at him. "Do I look suitably besotted?"

That got his attention. "You look demented." But a little of the tension drained from his face, and he thrust his free hand through his hair. "I have a meeting with my coach on Monday. The kind of meeting no player wants to have."

Catie thought of her earlier concerns about a secret injury. It was true Danny wasn't playing his best, but there was no question that he was still holding his own.

"It'll be fine. You're the best winger in the country, probably in the world." It was impossible to be around the Esera clan and not pick up on rugby news, so she knew that Danny had been on many lists of the "Best Wingers in the World."

"I was," Danny muttered as they headed for their gate. "I'm not anymore, and the team can't keep ignoring that. I'm screwing up over and over."

Catie frowned. "No team is going to cut a brilliant player over a few bad games."

Snorting, he said, "It's not just a few bad games. My entire season has been shit."

"But you guys are at the top of the league."

"No thanks to me. The fact the rest of the team is turning in stellar performances is hiding some of my sins, but not from the guys. They see it and they've been fucking legends covering for my errors." He pressed his lips together. "Dead certain I'm not going to be selected for the national squad."

She'd never, not once, heard Danny sound so defeated; playing for New Zealand's world-beating national team had been his dream since childhood—and that hadn't altered after he first made the squad at only nineteen. He treasured every single second he spent in the iconic black jersey.

"Have you spoken to Jake and the others?" His brothers and family were his staunchest supporters. "You know they'll help you figure it out."

"That's just it," he said quietly. "I keep on standing on their shoulders—and even with all the advantages that's given me, I'm still screwing up." His jaw worked. "My entire family set it up so my path was the easiest of them all.

"How many people have *the* fucking Bishop as their advisor on field strategy? How many people train on their off days with the vice-captain of the national team? How many people have a brilliant rugby mind as their father? I've got no fucking excuse."

Catie had no idea what had led Danny to this point, but his words made her think that the issue wasn't with his body or his reflexes. It was in his head. "Danny," she murmured as they reached their gate, "you might've been born into rugby royalty, but *you* put in the hard time doing the training, *you* played the games, *you* impressed the scouts. This isn't some royal lineage thing where you were anointed because of your family name. You won your place with sheer hard work."

Danny didn't answer, his jaw grim.

They boarded the plane soon after, and from that point on kept any conversation light and suitable for public consumption. Catie, however, was determined to continue their earlier discussion once they landed, get to the heart of the matter. But it wasn't to be, because when they walked out of the gate, it was to find Jake and Jules waiting for them with eight-year-old Esme and her toddler cousin, Joseph Connor, known to all as Connor.

Probably babysitting the little guy to help out Sailor and Ísa.

Esme screamed, "Uncle Danny!" and made a beeline for Danny while little Connor ran over to Catie. Guess everyone knew who each one's favorite was, Catie thought with a grin as she bent to cuddle her nephew's pudgy cheeks. Even so little, Connor had learned that he couldn't run straight at Catie's legs. Which was why Catie had zero patience for adults who didn't understand simple courtesy.

"Hey, my cutie, cutie pie," she said, her ovaries singing. She had no desire to have babies anytime in the near future, but gosh, Sailor and Ísa's baby boy was *adorable.* Happy and smiley and with those little round cheeks. Catie had no idea how her sister and brother-in-law got anything done around him.

Then again, they'd already survived Emmaline's cuteness—while Catie remained a total pushover for her niece. As she was for Connor. Prerogative of being a doting aunt.

After cuddling Connor, she rose with one of her hands holding his and leaned down so spunky and sweet-natured Esme could kiss her on the cheek. Esme had recently declared herself too big to be in anyone's arms. The sole exception was her Uncle Danny, but then only for a moment or two when she got excited.

"Catie, I like your eyes," Esme said with a sigh. "They sparkle like jewels."

"I'll show you how to achieve the effect," Catie said, having received permission from Jules and Jake to teach Esme a few makeup tips. Esme was only little, so for now it was like painting for her, a kind of art. She wasn't allowed to go out with makeup on and didn't yet have a palette of her own, but Catie knew exactly the products she'd get for her when it was time.

"Hey, you." Jules wrapped Catie up in her arms, her presence warm and strong; she was one of Catie's favorite people.

Jake, meanwhile, was hugging his younger brother and ruffling his hair.

"You guys on babysitting duty?" Catie asked after they drew apart.

"Was meant to be for a couple of hours, but we kidnapped the cutie for the airport run," Jules said with a smile, wrapping one arm gently around Esme's shoulders when Esme came to lean against the woman who was technically her stepmother but who'd embraced the role of mother wholeheartedly without ever trying to erase the young woman who'd been Jake's first love. "Your sister and Sailor went to the prizegiving ceremony at Emmaline's rugby club."

"Oh, of course." Catie's niece was a phenomenal player. "She told me about it when we spoke on the phone the other day."

Catie continued to hold on to Connor's soft little hand as they went to the luggage carousel to pick up their checked bags. Connor held his beloved "Gooey" with the other—a soft and squishy cloth doll in rugby uniform that Alison had made and that was Connor's constant companion and partner in crime.

Danny, of course, grabbed both their bags—while avoiding her gaze. She was sure Jake had figured out that something was up—why else would he have turned up to welcome them home when they could've easily caught a cab?

Oh, the Eseras were crafty when it came to looking after their own.

"I saw the social media posts from the play," Jules said.

"How did we come across?" Catie took her laser eyes off Danny; she'd get him to herself sooner or later.

"Brilliant." A sparkle in Jules's eyes. "As if you've been dating forever."

Catie's cheeks threatened to burn. "We should get the Oscars for best acting, right?"

"Um-hmm."

Catie wanted to squirm at Jules's noncommittal response. Thank goodness they were turning to head out. Esme and Connor went on ahead, Esme keeping a big-cousin's eye on little Connor. Catie recognized that protective look; she'd seen it often enough on Ísa's face.

"Mum and Dad invited us all to dinner," Jake said, coming up alongside his wife with Danny next to him and Catie on Jules's side. "But they said they understand if you two are tired after the weekend."

"It'd be great to see them," Catie said, cutting Danny off before he could squirrel out of it; whatever was going on, he needed to be around his family, not hiding off in a hole somewhere.

He shot her a pointed look but kept his mouth shut. She'd known he would. Danny wasn't the kind of person to make anyone around him feel bad. Even during their frenemy wars, he'd never once picked on anything that would make her feel *actually* bad. It was more about ramping up the annoyance and the aggravation.

Catie had responded in kind. Actually hurting Danny had never been the point. And now...

Things twisted inside her at the idea that he was in pain.

Well, she thought with stubborn determination, he'd get over his silence—or she'd *make* him. He'd lured her with cookies, hadn't he? She'd lure him out with bait just as good.

THE ELDER ESERAS had managed to gather the entire gang for this family dinner. Which meant Catie ended up being jumped on by her big sister and cuddled to within an inch of her life.

Grinning so hard that her face ached, Catie said, "It's only been a week since you last saw me, Issie," but she didn't mind the affection. At all. Her sister's arms were the most familiar anchor in her life.

After Ísa had satisfied herself that Catie was still in one piece, Catie found herself being wrapped up in Sailor's strong arms. Yeah, okay, she still had a little bit of a crush on her brother-in-law—in a strictly platonic way. He was the epitome of a protective big brother in how he treated her; Catie let him get away with it because he'd earned the right over years of love and care and steadfast support of her dreams.

Sailor had driven her to countless out-of-town meets over the years, been so openly proud of her at them that people who didn't know who he was had assumed he must be her brother rather than her brother-in-law.

It was some five minutes later, after more hugs from various members of the clan, that Catie was able to make her way to the corner armchair where Charlotte sat, nursing her newborn. Seraphina Pippa Bishop was her and Gabe's first child and the newest member of the clan.

"Catie." Charlotte's smile was as sweet as always as she reached up an arm to hug Catie even as she cradled

Seraphina with the other. When her spectacles slid down her nose, Catie nudged them back up with a finger.

"Look at her." Catie touched one plump baby cheek just as the baby unlatched and smiled a gummy smile at her. "Don't tell me that's gas. I want to pretend she's smiling at me."

Laughing, Charlotte burped the baby, then handed her over to Catie to cuddle. The first time one of the family had handed her a baby, Catie had been sure she was about to pass out from terror. They were so tiny and fragile, babies. But she was an old hand at it now, had even once babysat the whole brood in tandem with Danny.

They'd fed Emmaline, Esme, and Connor, plus two other small members of the wider clan, far too much sugar and takeout, watched cartoons on repeat, and had a grand old time. The kids begged to be babysat by them again, so Catie figured she was doing a good job on the auntie front.

"Where's Gabe?" Catie hadn't spotted the eldest Bishop brother.

"We somehow forgot Sephie's diaper bag—he's gone back to grab it." Charlotte laughed, her entire face aglow with love. "He's also planning on making a ten-step checklist for leaving the house with a baby."

"Ha! I can just see him doing that." Gabriel Bishop didn't own half the city by accident.

While Charlotte took the opportunity to pop off to the bathroom, Catie carried Seraphina over to Danny. "Look, she's smiling at me. I'm the favorite."

"You wish," he said and scooped the baby out of her arms without missing a beat. "Hey there, angel. I think you grew an inch while I was gone. You'll be a grown-up by the time of my birthday dinner next week."

As he smiled at the baby, Catie examined him. He looked better already, joy suffusing his face. *Good.* Being with his family was helping, but she knew that was only a temporary fix. She'd have to get him alone to get to the root of this.

The front door opened, Gabriel wandering in with the diaper bag in one hand just as Charlotte returned from the bathroom. Intercepting her, Gabriel kissed her until she blushed and told him to "Behave," though she had her hand pressed to his pectoral muscle and was kind of petting him.

Danny's eyes met Catie's at that moment, and things went topsy turvy in her stomach. She had never been more grateful for her sister than she was right then—because Ísa appeared and threaded her arm through Catie's.

"Come on," Ísa said, "you can help me keep an eye on the kids outside, make sure no one's bleeding."

"As if Emmaline would permit that," Catie said but allowed herself to be kidnapped.

Once out on the back porch, they confirmed that all three—Esme, Emmaline, and Connor—were present and unbloodied. Two dogs, one belonging to Esme, the other to Emmaline, went from child to child in happy excitement at having their number one people all in one place. Both dogs were very gentle with little Connor and had been known to lie unmoving the times Catie's nephew fell asleep on them.

Just then, Spot rewarded him for a pet with a lick that made him giggle.

Smiling at the scene, they sat down in the faithful old swing that had been on the porch as long as Catie could remember. Joseph or one of the boys sanded and painted it when it began to look rough, and Alison reupholstered the seat cushions every year. This time around, they were white with blue flowers.

As they swung lazily, Ísa's red hair glowing in the sunshine, Catie's sister said, "So, you and Danny."

"It's just a publicity thing, Issie." Catie rubbed her nails against the fabric of the cushion on which she sat, unable to meet her sister's eyes. "You know we get along as well as oil and water."

"Caitlin Moonbell River." Ísa's voice was pure big sister. "I've known you your entire life, so don't try to pull the wool over these eyes." She pointed two fingers at her gray-green irises. "I *know* and see all."

Dropping her head back on the seat, Catie groaned. "It's nothing, honest. Just proximity and his cookies."

"Danny does make great cookies," Ísa agreed before reaching out to stroke back Catie's hair. "There are worse things than falling for your best friend, you know?"

Catie's mouth fell open. Jerking up into a straight-backed position, she stared at her sister. "He is *not* my friend," she said, aghast. "He's my nemesis."

"Oh, my mistake." Ísa's lips curved in that annoying big-sister way that said she knew something Catie didn't. "Friend or nemesis, you two have been in each other's lives over a decade. Relationships are often born of such fertile soil."

"Not with us." Folding her arms, Catie looked determinedly ahead as Connor clambered his way up the toddler-friendly outdoor "gym" Joseph had set up for his grandson; it was the same one on which Esme and Emmaline had played at Connor's age. These days the girls preferred the trampoline or the climbing frame Sailor had recently built.

Connor got put on the trampoline now and then, though he spent most of the time on his butt. He loved being with his big sister and cousin, and they were careful when he was on there with them. Today all three were at different spots in the yard, doing their own thing while talking to each other and the pups as they played.

None of them paid any attention to Catie or Ísa.

"There's too much between us," Catie found herself saying when Ísa looked dubious. "Hypothetically speaking, even if I did feel a smidgen of a 'thing,' it's not worth the disruption to the family."

"Oh, sweetheart." Ísa pressed a kiss to her cheek. "No one is going to take sides if you two decide to date, even if it doesn't work out. We all love you both too much."

"I know. But it'd still be awkward." She pressed a finger over Ísa's lips when her sister parted them to speak. "And this is all hypothetical, remember? Please don't mention a word to anyone else. Danny would die laughing."

Ísa frowned, the cream of her skin gilded by sunshine. "Honey, are you sure? Danny's not that good an actor. And the way he was looking at you in those photos..."

Tightening her abs to contain the dratted butterflies, she focused her attention on the children. "The weekend wasn't real. It was all pretend."

A cocoon that was now broken.

18

BROTHERHOOD

Danny'd been surprised his brothers had left him alone at dinner the previous day. He should've known something was up. Because here they were, all three of them, at the door to his apartment at eight in the morning on a freaking Sunday. His building had a secure door, but he'd given his family their own entry code when he moved in a year earlier. They'd never before used it, always calling up to be buzzed in.

"This is an intervention," Jake said, poker-face in place.

Danny groaned. "I wanted to sleep in."

"Then why can I smell coffee?" Sailor pushed past him with a ruffle of his hair, an annoying big-brother thing that nonetheless made Danny feel like he was home. "Hope you didn't make it tar like you usually do."

Jake followed Sailor inside but didn't attempt the hair thing. The two of them were too close in age for Jake to get away with it. Instead, he just fake-punched Danny on the shoulder.

Then there was Gabriel.

The eldest of them all and the one to whom they all turned whenever life kicked them in the balls. As big and muscled now as he'd been during his playing days, Gabe was dressed in jeans and a faded gray sweatshirt from the local rugby club where he coached a young team. Power pulsed off him.

"Come here, little bro," he said and hauled Danny into a hug that felt as good now as it had when he'd been a scrawny kid in awe of his big brother. "You really want alone time?" he asked after releasing him from the hug. "If you do, say the word and I'll take us all home."

"No. It's good to see you." Even if being around them would make it very hard for him not to blurt out all the stuff inside his head. And that stuff had to *stay* inside his head. "Charlie and the baby?"

"They were cuddling when I left." He smiled the smile of a man deeply content with his life. "Also, Charlotte says I've been hovering. She all but pushed me out the door, said they needed some girl time."

Danny grinned, well aware of Gabriel's overprotective tendencies. "French toast?"

"Now you're talking."

As Danny got to cooking, his brothers shot the shit and laughed, and after a while, he found himself unwinding and laughing too. It struck him at one point that the only other person with whom he could be this way—totally comfortable, no walls—was Catie.

His mind filled with the image of her as he'd last seen her. She'd made "I'll call you" signs at him as she got into

Ísa and Sailor's SUV for the ride to her place. The signs had been more threat than promise.

Which was why he'd turned off his phone.

Yes, he was a chickenshit, but Catie could always wind him up... and she could make him talk.

"So." Gabriel leaned back in his chair around the breakfast table after they'd all started on the French toast. "You're having form issues on the field."

Trust his big brother to lance the boil. "I suck is what you mean."

Reaching over, Sailor squeezed the back of his neck. "Cut that out." A scowl in the vivid blue of his eyes. "You're one of the most brilliant players the country has ever seen, but you're not a machine. Blips are inevitable and expected."

Sailor was the only one of the four of them who'd never played—and didn't want to play—professional rugby. That didn't mean he didn't know the game inside out.

"I had a hell of a big blip during my season of injuries," Jake pointed out after swallowing a big bite of his toast.

"After which you came back hard—there's a reason you have the vice-captainship," Danny said and held up a hand for a high five. He was fucking proud of his brother; Jake was a brilliant leader on and off the field.

Jake met his high five, but he was shaking his head at the same time. "You've only had a few bad games, Da—"

"My entire season's sucked." Danny put down his fork and looked at Gabriel. "It has, hasn't it?"

Gabe took a drink of his coffee before replying, the steel of his gaze thoughtful. "It hasn't sucked," he said.

"Even at your worst, you can still outplay most others—what's missing this season is the brilliance that turns you into a lightning bolt on the field."

Danny swallowed. He'd known his big brother would give it to him straight, but it still hurt to hear his own fears put into words. "Yeah. I have a meeting with Coach Brook tomorrow," he said. "Think he'll cut me?"

Jake snorted. "As if. Like Gabe said, you're still magic on the field."

Where Gabe was the straight shooter when it came to his younger brothers, Jake had often been Danny's partner in crime and would always support him, even to the extent of not seeing his flaws. As for Sailor, he was the more analytical one when it came to the game. Which he proved now.

"I watched your last four games while you were away," he said. "What I'm seeing is that while you're making all the right moves in the technical sense, you're no longer pulling out those unexpected passes and runs that got you this far."

"Something's knocked your confidence," Gabe said, his tone quiet but his attention intense. "You gonna tell us what?"

Danny shrugged, his hands tight around his coffee mug. "I don't know. Honestly." No way was he going to spill out his confusion; not to these three men who had always, *always* been there for him. They didn't deserve to feel even a tiny bit of guilt for being who they were—which was simply awesome.

"Here's the good news," Sailor said, leaning forward. "If you're going to play technical rugby, we can come up with multiple moves you can add to your repertoire that will look like magic on the field. We keep doing that until we get to the bottom of this."

Danny rubbed his face. "I seriously don't know if I'll get a chance to play. Coach really hasn't been happy with me recently."

"Then we prep for the day when you do get called up." Gabe echoed Sailor's position. "And Dan, you know you can talk to any of us, right?"

"Yeah, of course."

But when his brothers left an hour later, having made plans to meet with him early that evening to go over a number of new plays that might bridge his rough patch, it was Catie he called.

"Oh hello, Mr. Chicken Poop," she said sweetly. "You turned off your phone."

"Maybe I had a hot date and didn't want to be interrupted."

Her snort made him grin. "We should probably go out and be seen," he said, his gut tense with how much he wanted that. "I dunno, post another photo or something."

"I was going for a run on the track. Need to stretch out for a bit. You wanna come with?"

The tension vanished like magic. "Yeah."

They'd decided to meet at the outdoor track, and Catie beat him there. She was warming up when he arrived, her blades sleek curves of silver. A lot of sprinters preferred black, but Catie was Catie. Her previous blades had been cheetah print. There was a reason she had all those endorsement deals. The best thing about it all was that Catie hadn't calculated that response—she'd just wanted cheetah blades, and now blades of lightning silver.

Other than that, she wore simple black running tights and a cropped athletic top in black with pink detailing along the bottom. He could see goose bumps on her shoulders and arms but knew they'd warm up soon enough.

"Don't leave me in your dust," he said as he limbered up.

She buffed her hot-pink nails on one breast. "I'll think about it."

Face flushing, he bent to check his perfectly laced-up shoes. He could not be thinking about Catie's breasts. Ever. Even if they were round and firm and made his mouth water.

Oh, fuck, fuck, Fuck.

"You ready?"

Coughing, he rose. "Yeah, let's do it."

They weren't the only ones on the track—the odd person shot a fascinated glance toward Catie's blades, but most of the regulars just grinned when they saw the two of them together.

One had the audacity to yell, "I fucking Knew it!"

When Danny gave him the finger, he just laughed and ran on.

As did Catie, with Danny at her side. He lagged deliberately behind now and then just so he could watch her move. She was pure grace on her blades, her body fluid with muscle designed for speed. When she challenged him to sprints with a glint in her eye, he groaned.

"I am not up for public humiliation. I'll time you if you want to do some speed tests."

She laughed and let him off the hook on the race, but took him up on the offer of timing her sprints. Though she'd kept to the rules of the track and chosen the otherwise empty outside lane for her sprint, *everyone* stopped to watch her run. He swore he felt the slap of a powerful wind when she snapped past him on the finish line.

"Holy hell, Catie!" he yelled. "You're hitting above your personal best! Faster than the time with which you won silver!"

That was insane when she wasn't currently on a full training schedule. As with most athletes, she took down time in order to allow her body to recover. Of course she was still running—she just wasn't doing it with the same focused concentration as when building up to a meet.

She jogged back to him, face beaming. "Seriously?"

He showed her the competition-grade stopwatch he'd borrowed from one of the other runners. The numbers were crystal clear.

"Paralympic gold," she huffed, hands on her thighs. "Here I come."

"I'm going to watch you win it." It was a vow.

She glanced up at that instant, a goddess in the sun, and he knew he'd blown it. He wasn't good at faking stuff, and right that instant, he was looking at her with all the admiration and need he felt inside.

Her pupils dilated. A glance down before she straightened to her full height.

Mouth dry, he was fighting to find the words to dig himself out of this uncomfortable hole when she said, "That's enough running for today. Let's cool down; then we're going to my apartment to talk."

Oh no, the dreaded TALK.

But since he'd been the one to screw things up, he didn't argue, and they got on with it. Though they also had to pause several times for Catie's admirers to come and gush over her. Grinning despite the fact his guts were in knots, Danny watched on.

A young Pasifika woman who was just barely showing her pregnancy, one hand absently stroking her bump, came to stand next to him while her husband went over to chat with Catie. "I follow her on her socials," she said to Danny, "but more for her work with children than the running."

"She's done amazing things in that area."

The woman nodded, the glossy black of her bobbed hair obsidian in the sunshine. "My brother lost an arm a couple of years ago, and you know, he's a teen. I don't know how he would've handled it if she hadn't been so visible at the time, being amazing with two artificial limbs." Sibling love was a song in her voice.

"Then Catie's foundation helped fund a bionic-looking skin for his prosthesis," the stranger added. "It's cosmetic, so it wouldn't have been funded otherwise. But it's *so* essential for a teenager. He felt a hundred times cooler, and these days if the kid's got a problem, it's that he's turning into a player."

Laughter in her eyes, she added, "It doesn't help that he joined the track team and immediately showed an aptitude for speed."

Danny's chest puffed out, but he kept the topic of discussion to the teenager. "Sounds like he's following her path in more than just confidence."

"He *idolizes* her." A beaming smile. "But I didn't come here to brag about Joey. I wanted to say that when I first saw pics of you two, I thought you were pranking everyone. But now that I've seen how you look at her..." Her gaze softened. "I'm so happy for her. Even though she doesn't know me, I feel like I know her. More than that, I respect and am deeply grateful to her—it gives me such joy to know that she's deeply loved."

Danny swallowed. Hard. The *L* word was even more terrifying than the idea of the upcoming TALK. Especially when he had no idea what was going on inside him when it came to Catie—much less how to label it. He blew out a quiet breath when the woman's husband jogged over at that moment, his face awash in smiles.

"She agreed," he said to his wife, who all but jumped up and down on the spot before breaking into excited chatter in a language Danny clocked as Niuean.

Leaving them to it, Danny and his freaked-out guts joined Catie, and the two of them headed over to the parking lot. "What did you agree to?"

"He invited me to his brother-in-law's eighteenth birthday party next month." She grinned. "It's going to be a family-and-friends thing out in Devonport. Wanna come?"

"Yeah, okay," Danny said even though they might not be on such good terms after the TALK.

Catie's smile faded as she looked at him, and he knew he'd revealed too much all over again. They didn't speak the rest of the way to their cars. Pulling out behind her, he felt his cheeks flush burning hot, then go ice-cold.

"Shit, Danny. You *idiot*." Slapping the steering wheel, he wished he was a mad scientist so he could build a time machine and take back that moment—but what was done was done. Chances were that Catie would tell him to pull his head in and stop acting strange, and they'd pretend it never happened.

Yeah, that would be good.

Except... his heart went all tight when he thought about ignoring what was happening and going back to how they'd always been with each other. Though... what the hell was he thinking? Him and Catie? It would never work.

Why not?

A question from the idiot in his brain who'd also taken over his body.

"We barely get along for one thing," he muttered to himself.

Lies. You two get along fine. You just get along in your own way.

Danny frowned but couldn't argue with that. He and Catie never actually fought. And when push came to shove, they were there for each other in a blink. They just also liked to rile each other up on a regular basis.

"Which is not the foundation for a relationship," he pointed out to himself. "And why the fuck am I even thinking that far ahead? Catie's going to ream me out for messing things up, our relationship will turn awkward for a bit, after which we'll be fine." Because the idea of a serious breach between them wasn't a fact he could comprehend.

He kept that thought at the forefront of his mind as he turned to park in a visitor spot in the underground garage of her apartment building. She'd pulled ahead of him during a traffic light change, so was waiting for him at the elevator by the time he got himself sorted.

Jogging over, he said, "Is it my imagination or did this place get a paint job?"

"The rest of the owners decided it needed a spruce-up. I think it's a garage and needs to look like a garage, but..." She gave a patently fake smile. "This is obviously why I pay mandatory property maintenance fees—to have a shiny garage."

He grinned. "Still not giving in to Jacqueline's offer for her to buy you a bigger place?" Catie had paid the deposit for this apartment with her own money, was keeping up with the mortgage the same way.

"Oh, I'm never budging on that, hotshot. I love my mother, but she likes control." Stepping into the elevator, she pressed the button for her floor. "Don't get me wrong. She wouldn't use a key and start coming over whenever she wanted—that's not Jacqueline's style. But just the awareness that she'd paid for the roof over my head, it would give her a subtle kind of power."

Danny found Ísa and Catie's family fascinating—in a vaguely terrifying way. Their relationships were so different from his with his parents and brothers. Since he'd been on a professional rugby contract from the time he was nineteen, the money question had never come up for him, but had it ever done so, he'd have been okay with his parents lending him the amount for a deposit or the like.

He'd have known he'd pay them back as soon as he could and that being able to help him would've made them happy. Same with his big brothers.

No worries about power and imbalance. Just family helping each other.

"What if it was Ísa?" he asked. "Giving you a loan or an outright gift?"

"That's different—a sister thing," Catie said as the elevator doors opened. "Issie wouldn't know how to hold something over another person's head if she tried—and she loves with all her heart."

An affectionate shake of her head. "You know she still buys me clothes even though I keep telling her I have enough? The worst thing is that she has perfect taste for me, so I can't even tell her I don't like the things she chooses!" Laughing, she fingered the loose knit sweater in a kind of champagne-type shade that she'd thrown over her workout clothes. "This is one of her picks, and it's my absolute fave for throwing on top of my athletic gear."

Sensing that they were making their way back to even ground, Danny felt some of the tension leave his body and he entered Catie's apartment in a far better mood than when he'd begun the drive.

He hadn't been here for a while—the last time had been when he'd helped Sailor carry up a small but heavy ornamental table Catie had inherited from a grand-aunt and couldn't bear to part with even though it didn't fit her usual rules for furniture. The chief rule being that she could move it around her apartment on her own.

The place was still as warm and as cozy as he remembered.

Catie had a thing for pillows and soft fabrics, so there were blankets thrown over sofa arms and cushions galore. Her sofa itself was a pale pink velvet with inset buttons covered in the fabric. While her four-person dining table was made of honey-toned wood, she'd upholstered the cozy seats of the chairs around it in the same shade of velvet. See-through curtains of gauzy white filtered the winter sunlight, helping to soften things even further.

The grand-aunt's ornately carved table—the top attached to a thick central leg that then flowed out into three curving supports—sat to one side of the doors that led out to Catie's postage stamp of a balcony; on the table was a lovingly tended potted plant with leaves of a striking lime green.

The walls were a warm cream, the pictures she'd hung up on them of family and friends. Even Danny made an appearance—in a group shot with his brothers, all four of them muddy from a rainy-day game of rugby in the local park.

But she'd given the most space over to the kids. Framed photos, paintings they'd done for her, even little baby footprints that Ísa had given her sister after the birth of Catie's niece and nephew.

The kitchen was in the far corner of the open-plan space. The simple but well-built cabinetry was painted a creamy white to echo the walls, the bench a gray granite with veins of gold. Color came from Catie's mismatched collection of antique dishes, which weren't just for display but for daily use.

"Hey," he said, "you still have that mug I found you." Delighted, he walked over to pick up the blue mug with its golden rim and—the pièce de résistance—filigreed handle. He'd spotted the unique and pretty thing in a tiny antique shop in a rural town, grabbed it without thought. Because Catie mattered to him.

Oh fuck, his brain was on the wrong track again. He

put down the mug in an effort to cut off that line of thought.

"It's my favorite for coffee in the morning."

Startled her voice had come from so close behind him, he turned... and she was right there. He'd have apologized for almost slamming into her, but he'd lost his ability to talk—because she was taking his face between two warm, slender-fingered hands and tugging him down toward lips pink and lush.

19

BOOM

The contact was an electric shock to his system, a bolt right down to his cock. Before he could get hung up on the fact he was thinking about his cock in relation to Catie, she licked her tongue over his lips and boom, his brain cells decided to stop functioning on any level but the most primal.

Grabbing her hips, he sank into the kiss, into the taste of her. She tasted as wild and as powerful as she was in every other aspect of life, a woman at home in her skin. Her hips were curved, the edges of her buttocks taut where his fingers brushed them, and when he hauled her even closer, his brain hazed at the round firmness of her breasts.

His own chest felt like granite against which his heart pounded hard as a drum. Wanting more, he opened his mouth over hers... and she opened hers in return before sliding her arms up his body to link her hands around his neck. Careful of her balance even in his addled state, he nudged her gently until her back hit the nearest wall.

Then he got down to the serious business of kissing his favorite nemesis.

CATIE COULD FEEL the hard ridge of Danny's erection against her, both of them still in workout gear that wasn't exactly armor. Even her sweater didn't blunt the rigid impact of him. And the man was rigid everywhere, from his wall of a chest to his biceps to his thighs. None of which was a surprise. She'd seen Danny play in his team uniform, and those rugby shorts and skintight playing tees did nothing to hide his stellar build.

But she'd known without *noticing*. It had just been Danny.

Today she was noticing. And *liking*. A lot. She loved how his body felt against her own, how his hand seemed to fit perfectly on the curve of her hip, how openly he enjoyed the feel of her. He squeezed and kneaded her hips before he lifted one arm to brace it over her head while slipping his other under her sweater to lie flush against the bare skin of her back.

She jumped, the sudden contact enough to shock her back to her senses. Breaking the kiss, she stared at him as both their chests heaved. "That's what I thought," she whispered, her voice coming out husky.

Pupils dilated and cheekbones flushed, Danny didn't pull away. "What? That we're both nuts?"

"Yes." Something inside her had snapped when she'd seen him looking at her *that* way at the track. Not just with heat in his eyes but open admiration and pride. "No point ignoring it."

Exhaling, he dropped his head so his forehead pressed against hers. "Catie, this is…"

She found herself stroking his hair. "It's okay, hotshot. This weirdness too shall pass."

He snorted out a laugh before finally pushing back.

She immediately missed the heat of his body. Catie frowned. She'd been taking care of herself a long time. Even with Ísa in her corner, given the custody arrangement, there'd inevitably been times when it had been just her and Clive. As a result, she'd long ago learned to handle the world on her own. So it was a shock to realize she'd liked the feeling of being protected by a big body.

Had to be her hormones acting up.

After all, she'd just kissed Daniel "Hotshot" Esera, Bane of her Existence and Nemesis Number One.

Shoving his hands through his hair, the action pulling up his tee a little, Danny said, "What are we going to do?"

She blew out a quiet breath. "Don't know about you, but ignoring it doesn't seem to be working for me." That part of her came from Jacqueline—calling a spade a spade, a problem a problem.

"Nope." Danny dropped his hands to his hips. "But it's not just about us."

"Exactly." On that, they were on the same page. She and Danny were connected by too many people who loved both of them; any screwups would have a far-reaching impact. "We could acknowledge it, then agree to blank it out forevermore."

Danny dropped his head a little, then looked back up, his hair falling over his forehead. "Nope. Not liking that option. I have you on the brain *and* the body, Catie."

She coughed, looked away, then sucked it up and told

the truth. "Yeah, same." It was hard for her, admitting vulnerability on any level, but fair was fair. "Then it has to be option two—we explore this until it burns out, without ever saying a word to anyone else."

A frown creasing his forehead, Danny stepped closer. "What if it doesn't burn out?" A soft question, his body a warm pulse against her.

Catie hadn't thought that far ahead, *couldn't* think that far ahead. Because if she did, what if she started to want things from him? A man like her sister's husband? Someone who loved without limits and put his mate and family first? They didn't grow on trees, and Danny was a young sports god who'd dated woman after woman with no sign that he wanted a full-on committed relationship.

He was like a honeybee, checking out all the different flowers.

Which was fine if that was his thing—but it wasn't hers. Catie had grown up with a man who couldn't commit to her. She was done with that. Finito. Over. The end. Friends with benefits was not a concept in her emotional vocabulary—there were too many fuzzy edges for her in such a relationship.

On the flip side, they had to face this and sort it.

"It'll burn out," she said firmly, to harden up those fuzzy edges. "It's like actors who fall in love on a set. They get influenced by acting at being in lust, and it spills over." That was far less terrifying an idea than that she might actually be falling for Danny. "Also, we might be terrible together physically, which will end things then and there."

Danny winced before rubbing a hand over his heart.

"Way to skewer a guy's ego, princess. Now I'm going to have to read the *Kama Sutra* to upgrade my skills."

Her lips twitched even as parts of her grew soft and wet at the thought of doing erotic things with Danny. "However long it takes to burn out, you agree we can't tell anyone?"

He nodded at once. "Can you imagine how awkward it'd be if our families knew we'd...?" He touched his lips, then pointed to hers. "As for the rest..."

"Yes." Everyone would assume it was serious, and she couldn't blame them—you didn't throw this type of grenade unless you meant it. And when they inevitably split up, it would break everyone's hearts. Not that the family would do anything but back their decision—but Catie and Danny would know the hurt was there.

Better to head it off before it began.

"So." He folded his arms, unfolded them, put them on his hips, then folded them again.

An unexpected tenderness bloomed inside her. Danny the Player was nervous. Cute. "This is already awkward," she said with a smile. "Maybe we've exorcised the lust just by talking about it."

Their eyes met right then, and whoosh, there went all the air out of her body. This time it was Danny who stepped forward, Danny who took her face in his warm, slightly rough-skinned hands, Danny who put his lips on hers.

Her eyes closed of their own accord, every ounce of her focused on the kiss. On the firm pressure of his lips, on the way he cradled her face, on the way his body pressed into her own as his breath became hers, his taste in her blood.

Shuddering, she wrapped her arms around him and kissed him back just as deep, no more thinking, no more analyzing. When he pulled off his tee to throw it to the floor, she stroked the toned muscles of his back, glorying in his strength as he returned to his adoration of her mouth.

Because that's exactly what it felt like: adoration.

Never had she been kissed with this much intent, this much concentration. As if every ounce of his being was focused on her lips. He didn't get handsy or start grinding his erection against her. It was as if the kiss was an appetizer he was bound and determined to enjoy to the nth degree.

As if he'd waited for this kiss and wasn't about to rush it.

She was the one with her hands all over him—and he didn't mind in the least from the way he stood so close and kept on with kissing her. Until she was breathless and her nipples plump and hard and it felt as if her breasts would burst out of her bra.

She got it now, why Danny always had a line of women out the door—and why none of those women ever had a bad word to say about him. Her childhood nemesis knew how to make a woman feel as if she was the most important person in his universe.

A pang hit her.

She pushed it aside, determined not to let foolishness spoil the pleasure between them. This was what it was; she couldn't change it—and she'd broken her own rules to indulge in it, so indulge she would. Until it came to an inevitable end. Some would call that nihilistic thinking, but Catie called it being pragmatic.

As her father was who he was, and Jacqueline was who she was, Danny was who he was. That happened to be a hot, young rugby star who wasn't against accepting the invitations handed to him on a silver platter.

Which brought up a point they *did* have to address.

Hands pressed flat on his chest, her own heaving, she pushed.

Breaking the kiss, he said, "Yeah?" and it sounded as breathless as she felt.

That did *things* to her. Serious, bone-melting things. But she had to be sensible about this. "Are you clean?"

"Why? Do I smell?" Lifting an arm, he sniffed at his armpit.

Shoulders shaking, she shook her head. "Not that kind of clean."

A blank look followed up by a blush so intense it glowed through the brown of his skin. "Jeez, Catie."

"What? I can't afford to catch cooties."

He shuddered. "I do not have any cooties, thank you very much. Verified by the last team medical—and I've been a monk since." A narrow-eyed look, hands on his hips. "What about you?"

Oh, she wasn't falling for that. "Clean, as per my last medical—and I've been a nun since. Want to see the certificate?" Fluttering her lashes at him, she gave him a beatific smile.

He made a sound deep in his chest, but then he was right there, kissing the life out of her, and oh boom. Nails digging into his hips, she held on for the delicious, sexy ride. When he finally put his hands on her, it was to push them under her sweater and start to peel it off.

Having made the decision to do this, Catie cooperated

and was soon clad only in her running tights and sports bra.

Danny stroked his hands down Catie's sides, ran his thumbs over the sleek architecture of her abdomen, her musculature a testament to her dedication to her sport. He fucking loved the feel of her, the strength of her. "You're so goddamn beautiful, Catie." He glared at her. "I can't believe you made that come out of my mouth."

She glared back at him. "Your abs are ridiculous." A poke at his gut. "An actual eight-pack? Seriously?"

Then they were both laughing because *they* were ridiculous, and a second later, he was all tangled up in her mouth again, and it was *so good*. Like ice cream and chocolate sundaes and fudge brownies and caramel cupcakes with pecan sugar frosting. Delicious and decadent and making him crave more and still more.

Groaning, he stroked his hands down her back, all the way to her very fine butt. When she didn't try to unman him for daring to touch her there, he squeezed and stroked and learned the shape of her.

Her hands, meanwhile, were all over him, and he loved it.

But when she slipped her fingertips underneath the waistband of his shorts to brush against his buttocks, he pulled back. "Can we do it here?" he asked, his breath so shallow he had trouble forming words. "I mean, against the wall?" Catie had a thing about being picked up and lifted without permission—he'd learned that years back.

She stared at him. "You want to?"

"Hell yeah. It'd be hot as hell to have you wrapped around me."

A pause before she said, "Yes, but I should get the protection now."

CATIE FELT OFF-CENTER, unbalanced, and it had nothing to do with her legs. While she hadn't run riot through the ranks like Danny, she'd had more than just Ward as a lover. All the men with whom she'd chosen to share her body, Ward included, had treated her well in bed, but none of them had ever been so hot for her that they'd suggested impulsive up-against-the-wall sex.

There'd always been a subtle element of "looking after" her that had frustrated her. Because she wasn't made of cold iron and baby Catie had liked those young men, she'd allowed that type of thing to pass at the start of her first physical relationships—back when she'd been nineteen, twenty. She'd figured they'd chill once they got used to her prostheses, realized she wasn't breakable.

It hadn't happened. So she'd walked away. Catie refused to be with anyone who saw her prostheses first and *her* second.

Ward had been her first and worst mistake as a full-fledged adult—because she hadn't been expecting his idiocy. He was an amputee himself, after all. He'd also been a flat-out charmer at first. She'd gone giggly with excitement, telling Veni that she might've finally hit the jackpot.

Ugh.

Hot hands on her hips, Danny kissing the back of her neck.

She shivered. "Hold on."

But of course he followed her all the way to the bathroom, where she'd stashed a box of condoms. Unopened, because training had taken the front seat for the past six months, and—after the disappointment of Ward—she hadn't run across anyone who made her want to shave her bikini line, much less get down and dirty.

Until Danny.

The man who'd seen her with stubble on her thighs, sand in her hair, and makeup smeared by sunscreen. And whose cock was stone hard for her.

One big arm came around her front, Danny tugging her back to him so he could attack the side of her neck with his sucking, kissing, nibbling mouth. Her eyes threatened to roll back in her head.

"Danny, damn it, let me open this!" Stupid plastic wrap.

He kissed her shoulder instead while stroking one hand down her side to her thigh. "Hurry up, princess. I might lose it in my pants and damn, that would be embarrassing."

Her hands trembled, her muscles quivering with want.

Sex had never been this way for her. Ever. "Are you always like this?" she asked as she tore open the box. Flat packets went flying everywhere. Two, however, fell on the counter in front of her, and she grabbed one. Right as Danny swiveled her around with a tug—so that she was the one who chose to do the swivel and could control her balance—and pushed up her sports bra.

"No, you just make me crazy."

20

NO HOLDS BARRED

Heart thudding, she lifted her arms and he pulled the tight fabric off over her head. Danny's groan made her thighs clench, her pussy flood. She wasn't ready for him to bend and put his mouth on her breast, sucking hard.

"*Danny.*" She clenched one hand in his hair, her other still clutching the unopened condom packet.

Her butt hit the counter.

Guess it wouldn't be the wall after all. That was fine. This was also something she'd never before done—gone nuts in a bathroom. Dropping the condom onto the counter, she put both hands in the rough black silk of his hair and let him devour her breasts. He used a hand to squeeze the taut mound of one breast while he kissed and sucked the other, then switched focus.

Unable to breathe, she pushed him off.

He looked at her, wild-eyed.

Feeling just as wild, she slid her hand into his shorts and palmed the rigid length of his erection. His skin was delicate and soft, his cock hard as rock. And bigger than she'd expected. By a good margin.

Jerking, he pressed his hands on the counter on either side of her. "Fuck, Catie." Teeth gritted, he pulled her hand away before wrenching off his shorts to kick them aside.

Before she could fully take him in, he had his hands on the sides of her running tights. And Catie's hot, sexy dream came to a screeching halt. "I'll need to get them over my prostheses." Designed to be aerodynamic, the tights might as well have been a second skin, they were so snug.

Hands on her hips, Danny lifted an eyebrow.

Cooperating with him even as disappointment chilled the heat in her skin, she allowed him to pick her up and put her on the counter. When he put his hands back on the waistband of her pants and said, "Lift," she got it at last.

It was her turn to blush, the heat returning full blast. If he peeled off the tights, he was going to be eye level with some *very* private parts. But the fact he hadn't balked or hesitated and that he was as painfully hard as he'd been...

Bracing her weight on her hands, she lifted her hips.

He got the tights over her butt quickly, then, as she watched, tugged them past her sockets... and while he was paying attention, he also kept being distracted by the fact she was all but naked.

Catie had never felt sexier in her life.

That ramped up even further when he finally got the tights off. Dropping them to the floor, he was on her like a hurricane. As if he couldn't keep his hands off her. She couldn't keep hers off him either. Grabbing the condom, she slapped it on his chest.

He took it, tore it open, had himself sheathed in three seconds flat.

He was hauling her forward a heartbeat later, her ass sliding on the counter and her hands on his shoulders. She looked down, was shocked by the carnal image of her spread thighs and his rampant cock. But it was the kind of shock that just made her hotter.

Sliding his hands under her thighs, he tugged her forward a bit more and she fell back to balance herself on her palms. Then, their eyes locked, he pushed into her in a slow, thick, rigid slide that had her making low sounds of pleasure that seemed to drive him even crazier.

Catie wasn't sure because she was losing her vision from the erotic heat of it all.

She used the leverage provided by her arms to push her body into his, and he thrust all the way home at the same time. After that, it was all over. They moved together like people possessed. At some point Danny lifted her up in his arms, she wrapped her thighs around him, and he swiveled to push her back against the wall.

Then he kissed her.

All the way through.

While she held him tight and kissed him back, no holds barred.

When she came, it was in a taut clenching of muscles that made her see stars. Danny was still moving, his back slick with sweat, but she heard his shout as he orgasmed, felt it in the powerful tension of his body.

Afterward, he slumped against her, his breath hot on her neck.

She found herself stroking his nape as she fought to catch her breath. When Danny staggered upright and made his way somewhat drunkenly to bed with her wrapped around him, she didn't ask to be put down. She'd been partnering with him for so long on the beach races that she knew he'd never drop her.

They fell into bed together, but Danny got up a moment later with a groan and went to take care of the protection. He returned in a short few seconds—to fall facedown on the bed next to her.

"Dead," he huffed out. "You killed me dead, River."

She patted his back lightly, the angle awkward since she was lying on her back. "Mutual." No point in attempting to hide it when her thighs were still quivering.

They lay there for several minutes, just trying to learn to breathe again.

When Danny finally pushed himself up onto his elbows, he shoved his hair out of his eyes and said, "I thought I knew sex, but I feel like a debauched virgin."

Catie scanned his expression to see if he was flexing a bit of the famous Daniel Esera charm. He never did with her—she knew him too well—but this was a strange situation. But no, he looked normal, not as he did when he was doing his smooth-operator thing. "Well," she admitted begrudgingly, "I can't say I was expecting that degree of fireworks."

"Fireworks, hell." He scowled. "That was nuclear." Leaning in, he pressed his nose to hers. "Admit it or I'll have to bring out the big guns."

"You dare tickle me, Danny, and I'll go into your place, mix all your sugar with salt and all your spices with each other."

"Way to hit below the belt," he said but flopped over onto his back. "So we're doing this again." Not a question, because of course it wasn't a question.

"Yep." She stared up at the ceiling. "How long do you think it'll take to burn out?"

DANNY SHRUGGED, though the word *NEVER* was starting to blare like a neon sign in his brain. He couldn't face it just now—thinking this unexpected thing between them might not burn out and *knowing* that were two different things, and the knowledge held the power to alter the axis of his universe. "I accidentally read a women's magazine in a doctor's office once—"

Catie fake-coughed. *"Accidentally."*

"Shut up." He turned to look at her, and his gaze threatened to get caught on the way one damp tendril of hair stuck to her cheek in a perfect curl. Why had he never noticed how pretty she was? He could just *look* at her like a goof.

"Anyway," he said after clearing his throat, "there was this advice-column thing, and a woman had written in to ask for advice because she was torn between two guys. One was a friend who made her feel good when she was with him, and they had heaps in common.

"The other was a new fling who made her 'orgasm like a fountain'—I remember those exact words, because da-yum—and they had the odd thing in common, but the main connection was the heat between them."

"Let me guess, the columnist told her to go for the friend."

"Nah, she did this whole pros and cons list, and one of

the cons was that the hotter a flame, the faster it burns out." Danny really didn't like the thought of that.

"Oh." Catie said nothing after that.

Neither did he.

When their bodies began to cool from the sweat, he reached down and pulled up the hand-knitted blanket at the foot of the bed. "Charlie make this?" His brother's wife had learned to knit from his mother.

"Yeah." Catie yawned. "Why are you doing that? It's lunchtime."

"I need a nap. You wrung me out."

Another yawn. "Okay, you win. I want to take off my legs first though."

"Hmm." His eyes were already closing.

But when he felt the bed depress on her side after she lay back down, he curled himself around her and nuzzled his face into her neck. Her hand came to lie over his forearm. They fell asleep that way while the sun poured in through the gauzy white curtains.

CATIE WOKE, feeling lazy-limbed and content—and warm. The sun was no longer on her, but there was a burning heater in the bed. She definitely wouldn't need her electric blanket when Danny was in bed with her.

Not going to last, she reminded herself as she looked toward the window. They were still spooning loosely, but he was now sleeping with this face buried in the curve of her upper spine. She didn't know why, but she found that cute.

Rolling her eyes at herself, she looked down at the arm around her waist and knew she'd wake him if she tried to move, so she stayed still. It struck her that at some point during her first time taking off or putting on her legs in the presence of a lover, she'd have felt a moment of awkwardness.

She wasn't awkward about it; it was her life and she was at home in it. But most guys were. Weirdly, even Ward had been that way even though he was also a user of prosthetics, having had his left leg amputated below the knee as a child. His discomfort should've been her first clue, but hey, her dickhead radar wasn't foolproof; at least she'd only made that particular mistake once in all her years on this planet.

What she'd learned today was that there would never be any awkwardness with Danny. No matter what. He'd been too long a part of her life, and she was too used to him—and he to her.

Shouldn't that have made them less likely to burn up the sheets? The whole familiarity-breeds-contempt thing? It certainly had been like that for a long time. Until they went from zero to nuclear.

...the hotter a flame, the faster it burns out.

Danny's words were still echoing in her head when she felt him wake behind her. A stirring of a bigger body, a yawn against her skin... and a cock that grew rapidly harder as it nestled against her buttocks.

When he kissed lazily at her neck, she sighed and let him do it. If they were going to implode fast and hard, she'd enjoy the ride to that inevitable final destination. Reaching back, she played with his hair as he kissed her while petting her breasts.

Then, feeling wild and carefree, she stroked one hand down her body to tuck it between her thighs, where she used a single finger to stroke the delicate folds of her pussy. Danny groaned and moved his hand over her arm until he was gently "pushing" his way between her thighs.

Of course, there was nothing of force about it. It was sensual play.

His voice was rough when he said, "Show me" and placed his fingers exactly over her own.

Mirroring her. Learning her.

Damn, it was hot.

Especially when he nudged her hand aside after several long, languid minutes and began to touch her exactly as she'd touched herself. She found herself twisting, writhing, and going tight as a vise around the finger he pushed into her.

His breath rough, harsh, he said, "Shit, all the condoms are in the bathroom."

She didn't like it when he withdrew from her and left to grab one. But he returned so quickly that he had to have run. Then he was back, the fingers of one hand playing with her engorged clit while he nudged into her from behind.

It felt different this way.

Not bad. Just different. And good. So, *so* good.

Arching back against him, she allowed him to set the pace while she stroked the thickly muscled ridge of his thigh and any other part of him she could reach. She should've hated being this out of control, but how could she when his breathing was rough and his rhythm lost?

Danny was in no more control than her—and it was *glorious*.

21

DANNY GOES TO THE DOGS (THE DOG THERAPISTS, THAT IS)

"Four times," Danny muttered to Spot and Domino the next afternoon as the dogs sniffed at the leaves around the path. "We did the horizontal tango four times between the time we got home and when I left at five in the afternoon. That's ridiculous. Even more ridiculous is that I was pumped for my evening training session with the bros—you'd think I'd be wiped, but no, I was buzzed."

Spot woofed, looked over to check on where Esme and Emmaline were playing on the swings, then went back to his sniffing. Domino just sighed. She was chocolate brown, Spot black and white, both rescues of indeterminate breed and both with affectionate natures when it came to their favorite small people.

Danny, who was walking the two dogs around the large park while keeping an eye on the girls as they used the playground equipment, said, "Some friends you are." And therein lay the problem.

Usually he could talk about woman stuff with Jake,

who was closest to him in age. He could talk with Sailor and Gabe too, but that tended to be about more serious things. Then there were his buds. Danny had never disrespected a woman by airing anything that went on in the bedroom, but he could usually talk in generalities if he wanted advice.

Neither was an option when it came to Catie.

Firstly, thanks to their social media posts, everyone would know he was talking about her. Secondly—and most importantly—Danny didn't want to share any of this with anyone. He felt protective of her. Strange, because of all the women he'd ever dated, Catie was probably the toughest and most independent.

He hated the idea of making her vulnerable in any way. No, what was going on between them was their business. As a result, Spot and Domino were going to be his only confidants. Just as well Esme and Emmaline didn't mind him stealing their dogs now and then while they were at school.

Today he'd been stressed about the meeting with his coach, but it had gone surprisingly well; they'd discussed Danny's form, talked about how he could improve, and made a plan of attack.

Afterward, feeling lighter, he'd volunteered to do the school pickup for both girls, made them some fruit-and-nut oat bars for after-school snacks, and stopped to get the dogs along the way. The pups had been hanging out at Danny's parents' place; Alison and Joseph loved them, and Spot and Domino loved staying over during the daytime when their families were at work or school.

Little Connor was with Sailor; he went to daycare part time for socialization with other kids his age, but after that, Sailor tended to take him to one of his plant nurseries. Connor had begun his visits as a baby strapped to his father's chest, but these days he had his own tiny gum boots and overalls, knew what plants he could and couldn't touch, and had Sailor's calm way about him.

The girls had spent plenty of time at the nurseries too, but it was Connor's number one *favorite* place away from home. Danny was fairly certain his nephew would be a horticultural genius by the time he began to talk in full sentences. As for the girls, Danny figured he might as well take advantage of the fact they were still young enough to consider chilling with him fun. A few more short years and they'd be teens with growing social lives.

He'd pushed them both on the swings for twenty minutes before taking time out with the dogs. "I mean," he said to his canine therapists, "four times that close together is a new thing for me, but I know four times isn't excessive for a guy my age." Especially after having heard some of the boasts from his mates.

Though he wouldn't be bragging about ten times in a night like one had done—because how long could each bout have lasted if it was all over within a few hours? "Quality trumps quantity," he told Spot, who decided now was the time to lift his leg.

Looking away to give him privacy, Danny spoke to an attentive Domino instead. "But now I've got quality *and* quantity."

It came out a touch smug, and he couldn't help himself. He *felt* smug. He knew he'd pleased Catie. She'd been soft and loose-limbed when he left, hadn't even snarked at him when he stole a kiss on the doorstep.

"The problem," he said as the three of them moved

on, "and I don't even know if it's a problem really, is that even after four times, I could go over again today and do it four more times with her."

Domino gave him a bemused look.

"Sex maniac, right?" Danny turned back toward the swings—most of the crowd today was mums with their kids, but he'd made sure to keep the girls in sight. They were his responsibility and he took that seriously. "But man, I want her."

His stomach flipped. Because the want wasn't only physical. He'd loved falling asleep with her, loved waking with her, loved making them both giant omelets during their recovery period. If he was honest, being with Catie just felt... good.

"It kinda sucks that it won't last," he said quietly. "I mean, I was just thinking—if we could make it work, it'd be the dream, right? We both do sports, our families are tight, and there'd never be any trust issues." Yes, he was still sore about that one date who'd tried to sell her story to the tabloids; she'd only failed because she'd had zero juicy material—they'd literally just met for a coffee in a busy Mount Eden café.

But a future with Catie was a pipe dream. The two of them were too combustible for it to last. They'd be back to their antagonistic relationship as soon as the lust went cold.

Spot leaned his body against Danny's, Domino echoing him on Danny's other side. Bending down, Danny patted one dog, then the other.

"Yeah, it sucks," he repeated, his chest tight and hurting. "But I guess that means I better enjoy it to the limit while it lasts."

. . .

HE GOT a chance to do exactly that two days later, when Catie texted him midmorning: *Going to see the new Star Gen movie with Veni and the gang. You want in?*

Yeah. He wasn't as big a fan of the franchise as Catie, but he'd seen all the movies. *When?*

Seven p.m. showing. Usual theater.

After confirming he'd meet her there, he blew out a breath. He knew a number of her friends—a result of the fact he'd known her so long—but they'd never had a mingled friend group. This was a serious departure from their norm.

He wondered if he should wear armor. He'd also forgotten to ask if he was going to be the only guy there, because that would be flat-out terrifying. The latter fear proved unfounded. Arriving at the theater, he found that two of her girlfriends had brought their guys. Ward was also present.

Danny barely stopped himself from curling his lip. What the hell was that loser doing here? Yeah, the dick was a top athlete, but he was also such a poser. The kind of person who was always "look at me."

Danny still didn't understand what Catie had seen in him.

But he kept a smile on his face as he was introduced around to the friends he hadn't previously met. He got narrow-eyed looks from the women, Veni included, that told him they were withholding judgment, and friendly hellos from the guys—all but Ward. Dude's smile was so fake-ass Danny didn't have high hopes for his rumored dreams of a Hollywood career.

"I got your ticket already," Catie said after he'd run the gauntlet and emerged mostly alive.

"Thanks. You want extra-buttery popcorn and a lemonade?"

"Yep."

Ward, the asshole, decided to join him at the concession stand. "You and Catie, huh?" More fake smiling, his mouth full of teeth and his hair a flawless golden blond. "Never saw that coming. She always used to say she didn't see the appeal."

Danny figured that "casual" comment was meant to hurt, but it didn't. Because before this, he hadn't seen Catie as a possible girlfriend either. She'd just been Catie, who annoyed him. "Guess she changed her mind."

Keeping it light in the interest of not ruining the night, he said, "How's it going with you? I saw you hooked up with that radio DJ." The relationship had been splashed all over the media—funny how Ward's private life always sprang a leak.

"Oh, that's over. I'm free and single again." A biting smile. "Catie's looking great."

"She sure is." And if this wet noodle of a man thought she'd be fooled by his manky ass a second time around, he had another think coming. Holding back the words because he wasn't about to give Ward the scene he wanted, Danny grabbed a giant tub of popcorn for him and Catie to fight over, two lemonades, then made his way back.

Catie was standing alone. "The others decided to go on up and grab our seats. You know the seat poachers like to try their luck." She took the tub of popcorn.

Danny decided fuck it with being mature. "Why is Dickwad here?"

She snorted at his alteration of Ward's name. "Apparently he's friends with Jen's new boyfriend." After a few kernels of popcorn, she said, "Here he comes."

Thankfully, their tickets put them at either end of the long row.

"I think he was hoping to hook up with you." Danny scowled.

"Man is dreaming." She shuddered. "I wouldn't touch him with a ten-foot barge pole."

Grinning, Danny slouched down in his seat. "So, *Star Gen* or *Glory Sky*?"

That argument, into which they dragged in both Veni and Jen, took them into the trailers, which they all shut up to watch, in agreement that trailers were to be savored. Ward the Dickwad, of course, was chatting away at the other end. Idiot.

But an idiot who'd lost Catie, leaving her free for Danny to claim.

His stomach did that flip thing again. *Claim* was a helluva strong word. Not a burn-up-in-a-hot-second kind of word. No, it was the kind of word that meant sticking and was related to other words like *forever* and *commitment*.

Exhaling quietly, he reached for the popcorn.

His hand bumped Catie's.

Instead of play-fighting with her, he picked up her hand and kissed the salty tips of her fingers. She stared at him, her eyes visible in the light from the screen. Had they been in the very back row, he'd have kissed her, but since they weren't, he smiled and leaned in to whisper, "Round five?"

He felt her jerk... before she whispered back, "Forty minutes to end of movie. Ten to shake everyone off. Twenty to make it to your place."

His cock pulsed.

Their plans, however, were thwarted by a sudden group enthusiasm for Chinese food after the movie. No way to cut and run without being rude as hell—and also scuppering his chances of winning over her girlfriends.

So it was that Danny had to eat Chinese food while his brain plied him with erotic internal movies of a naked Catie undulating underneath him—or on top of him. He wasn't fussy, liked her every which way.

But sexual frustration aside, he had a great time. Catie's friends were good people—hardly surprising, given who she was as a person. And they seemed to like him back, which made him relax in a way that was dangerous for all that it implied. If this was a fleeting thing, then it didn't matter if Catie's friends liked him.

It matters now.

After that firm admonition to the part of him that was beginning to panic at the idea of this ending as fast as it had begun, he dug into the food. Laveni, Catie's BFF since always, had made sure to be seated next to him at the round table, and she asked him several pointed questions under the cover of the conversation.

He managed to wriggle around most of them with responses that betrayed nothing private. But her last one made him realize the other woman had figured out the truth, knew that their relationship was nowhere close to fake.

He went motionless.

"You know she's wonderful, right?" Veni said, her eyes huge and dark brown in a gently rounded face under a mass of black curls and her skin the same shade as Danny's.

"Catie," Veni continued, "drove an hour and a half through heavy rain one night to pick me up after I finally left my abusive shit of a boyfriend and found myself out on the street with a backpack and no money."

Danny didn't offer sympathy because her tone said she didn't want it; she'd clearly moved on from that point in time, had only brought it up to make her point. "I know," he said, his eyes going to Catie. "She's fucking amazing, and I knew that even when I was an asshole kid."

That was why he'd always been able to mess with her —because he'd known she'd mess back with him as hard. His parents had raised him to protect those who were weaker than him, but he'd never—not once—seen Catie as that.

"I know I'm the lucky one here," he said, the truth spilling out of him in the busy chaos of the restaurant. "I'm never going to take it for granted."

Veni's expression thawed. "Hmm, I guess you might be acceptable."

Grinning even as his heart thundered at what he'd just admitted to himself, he said, "Pass the sweet-and-sour pork please."

Catie, who'd ended up seated across from him, raised an eyebrow when he next met her eyes. He winked to tell her all was well and that he hadn't broken under Veni's interrogation. The slightest shake of her head, a sparkle in her eye, and yeah, his heart really hadn't gotten the memo about this being a quick burn.

Rubbing the heel of his hand over the organ in the aftermath, he got up to visit the restroom. He was in the process of washing his hands when Ward entered the spacious area. Which was why Danny wasn't sure why the man had to come stand next to him at the sink.

"Is it serious, you and Catie?"

Danny was not up for a heart-to-heart with Catie's douche of an ex. "You're in front of the paper towels."

Stepping back, Ward watched him pull towels out of the dispenser. "You know you'll never understand her like I do." His eyes held a hard shine. "You have no idea what we go through."

Danny wanted to snort at the arrogance of the man saying "we." As if Ward was in the same league as Catie. But Danny had grown up in rugby—and sad to say, there were always a few assholes who thought that being physical off the field meant something. So he didn't snort.

Instead, he threw his used paper towels in the trash and put more space between them, then said, "Oh hey, I think someone's trying to get in the door behind you" and slipped out when Ward moved.

"No feeding the fuckwits," he muttered under his breath after he was out of earshot; his brothers had taught him long ago that while a burst of anger might feel good in the minute, it just led to a mess in the aftermath —and it gave the *instigator* control.

Yeah, no, Danny wasn't about to dance to Dickwad's tune.

Catie shot him a worried look when he slipped back into his seat, and he knew she'd clocked the fact that

Ward had gone into the restrooms after him. He waited to make sure no one else was looking, then crossed his eyes at her.

Her shoulders eased up, her lips struggling not to break out into a grin.

And he went back to his food.

"I've never seen you two together this long," Veni said from his elbow, dawning realization in her voice. "So I never understood how well you know each other."

His chopsticks loaded up with noodles, Danny frowned. "I'm sure I met you the year after I first met Catie—you and your dad drove Catie up to Auckland one time."

"I don't mean timewise." She waved a hand, her nails unpolished and clipped short due to her work as an ICU nurse. "It's *how* you know each other—you do that eye-talking thing all the time. It's fascinating to watch."

Not sure if he was embarrassed to have been caught at it or happy because she'd pointed out that he and Catie were intimate on more than just the level of the physical, Danny opted to shove the noodles into his mouth to give himself room to think.

It also gave him time to process the fact that Ward was walking back to the table with a noticeable limp—as if he'd injured the leg on which he wore a prosthesis. Forehead furrowing, he watched the other man slip into his seat beside Catie and lean his head toward her while shooting dagger looks at Danny.

Seriously? The dude was trying to set Danny up as a bully?

22

MEMO TO WARD: CATIE IS NOT HERE FOR YOUR BS

"Your new boyfriend thought it was funny to kick out my leg."

Catie almost stabbed her chopsticks into Ward's classically handsome face, which was all sharp lines and bright blue eyes. "Ward, you're just being an idiot now," she said calmly. "You're the one who cheated, remember? This dog in the manger stuff doesn't suit you."

Those pretty eyes glittered.

She wasn't afraid of violence. Ward was the kind of macho asshole who picked fights with men but didn't hit women. She'd never have gone out with him if she'd realized his fight-picking tendencies off the bat, but oh well, live and learn.

"Are you saying you don't believe me?" His voice rose.

She kept hers even and looked him full in the eyes. "That's exactly what I'm saying." A quiet statement punchy with withheld fury. "Now, unless you want me to call you a liar in front of everyone, you'll shut it with that fake story."

Ward stared at her, his mouth falling open. But he snapped it shut when she shot him another glare.

Danny was looking over with death in his eyes when she glanced his way. She shook her head slightly, her eyes communicating that she'd dealt with the situation. His own narrowed, but he settled back down.

Because Danny, unlike Ward, was the kind of macho idiot who knew Catie could deal with her own shit. Which made him not an idiot at all, she thought with a warm feeling in the pit of her stomach.

Laveni caught her gaze from across the table, her lush lips—painted a dark berry red today—pursed as she fought a laugh.

Catie realized she'd been busted mooning over Danny. *Mooning.* Ugh. It had to be the sex hormones. They'd been antagonists too long for them to become friends and lovers now.

Really though? It was the annoying part of her brain that liked to poke at her sensible thoughts. *He wasn't your antagonist when you two and Jake worked together to prank Sailor and Gabe.*

That had been back when she'd been sixteen, and she had to admit they'd worked well together. Yes, Jake had groaned at their constant snarking at each other, but—looking back—Catie could see that they'd only snarked because they'd found it funny to come up with ever more creative insults.

She and Danny had the same odd sense of humor.

What a strange thing to be hit by in the middle of a crowded Chinese restaurant with her sulking baby of an ex next to her and Danny deep in conversation with a smiling Veni. Ward had never once been the recipient of that huge, eye-crinkling smile. Neither had he ever managed to get Veni to dip her head toward him and share a grinning tidbit in the way of friends who got along.

Danny groaned right then, and a laughing Veni punched him in the upper arm.

Catie felt her own lips curve. Though she knew this was dangerous, she couldn't help but be happy that her bestie liked him and he liked her bestie. The same went for her other friends. So when no one was ready to call it a night after dinner and Danny seemed amenable, she didn't argue with the decision to pile into their cars for a quick trip to Tamaki Drive and a walk along the waterfront.

Danny slung his arm around her when they met up after parking their cars. "Yes, I'm deliberately doing this to annoy Ward."

"Some women would find that insulting," she said, slipping her own arm around his waist. "Good thing I'm not one of those women."

"Guess we're both shit-stirrers." He grinned.

She grinned back, and they walked on behind the others. Danny reminded her about his upcoming birthday dinner, she teased him by saying she'd gotten him socks, and he laughed, a beautiful man against the night.

When they reached the stretch of restaurants in Mission Bay, the area a buzz of pretty lights and conversation, Veni and a couple of others decided to get ice cream from the busy specialty shop on the corner, then they walked back. It was halfway during that walk that she figured out what Danny was doing.

His hand had slipped to her hip at some point, and every so often, it'd tighten a fraction, then release. She hadn't noticed earlier because it was so subtle, but now that she was paying attention, she realized he did it every time she hit an uneven patch of footpath.

Giving her a little extra stability.

Her hackles threatened to rise—until she snapped her gaze toward him after another such incident and found him looking out across the water, his attention on the glittering reflection of the city's skyline. "I always forget how good the CBD looks from here," he murmured. "Makes me consider moving out here, but then I remember the traffic and nope out."

"Yeah," she managed to get out past a rough throat.

He wasn't doing it on purpose, she realized, didn't even seem to know he *was* doing it. She didn't know how to feel about that. As she'd thought at the restaurant, Danny had full confidence in her strength. That thing he was doing, it was cutely protective in the way a good boyfriend might be about his girlfriend. Grabbing her hand if she stumbled or helping her scramble over rocks.

Catie was annoyed by any such thing... but now that she was past her knee-jerk response, she found she wasn't annoyed by Danny's unconscious gesture. She needed to think on that. Before she could, Danny stopped, turned to her... and kissed her.

Right there with the skyline of the city glittering across and to her left on the water and their friends wandering on ahead. He kissed her in the quiet space between cars on the road while the waves whispered below the seawall, one arm around her and the hand of his other gently cupping her cheek and jaw.

After it was over, they turned and walked on, and her heart... it developed another crack in its protective shield.

GIVEN the length of the outing, Catie wanted to go back to her own place, where she had everything she needed for her comfort. Danny seemed unbothered by her decision and cheerfully tailed her home.

Once inside, she yawned—to his vocal amusement. "Look at us! Such hot young things!"

Shoving at his shoulder as she started laughing too, she said, "Round five can wait till I've caught a bit of shuteye."

But then he tugged her close and kissed her all slow and with a smile yet on his lips and her body melted. She ended up naked in bed with him not long afterward. It was different this time around—softer, gentler, almost lazy as they lay facing each other and explored and touched and kissed.

She still had on her legs, hadn't really thought about it, but as he stroked his hands over her body, his skin slightly rough and all perfect, she found herself saying, "Do you ever think about the fact I have prosthetic legs when we do this?"

Had she planned to ask the question instead of it just coming out, she might've expected shock or perhaps anger. People didn't like being questioned—many took it as an insult when she was just curious.

Danny shrugged. "A couple of times at the start, when I worried I'd inadvertently hurt you in some position"—

he pressed a hand over her mouth when she scowled and parted her lips—"but then I realized d'oh, this is *Caitlin* I'm thinking about."

A wicked grin. "I know you'd tell me to get the hell off if I was hurting you or if I was causing your legs to twist or bend in an uncomfortable way. Just like you did when we were roughhousing as kids. So then I stopped worrying."

Had any other man said those words to her, she wouldn't have believed him. It was easy to say such things, harder to live them. But she could say with certainty that Danny never held back with her. The fact he'd had to come to terms with how to see her once they began having sex made sense too—she'd had to do the same after all.

"Harrumph," she said once he'd removed his hand. "I should've bitten you."

"Then you'd have to kiss it better." Grin more than wicked now, he nudged her onto her back so he could come over her.

She went, because she was feeling lazy and sexy and because he was gorgeous and funny and she... liked him. There. That hadn't been so hard to admit. She really liked Daniel Tana Esera.

Wrapping her arms around him, she sighed as he slid into her after grabbing the protection from the bedside table. They'd learned their lesson, kept it handy now. As they moved together with languorous ease, neither one of them in a rush, Danny nuzzled and kissed her throat while she kissed the muscled curve of his shoulder, and inside her, things grew warm and tight and it had nothing to do with orgasm.

Shoving aside the terrifying realization that wanted to bloom, she held on and focused only on the heavy warmth of his body, the way he moved in her, on her, how he touched her, how he felt under her own hands, and how at the end, they kissed with their eyes locked.

LAVENI PUSHED down her cat-eye sunglasses and looked at Catie over her latte, the drink delicately frothed and offered with a tiny cookie on the side. The two of them were sitting at an outdoor table at their favorite local café, the winter sunshine bright.

"You look like you got shagged," the other woman declared.

Catie almost snorted her cappuccino out her nose. After coughing and recovering, she pointed a finger at her best friend. "Says the woman with stubble burn on her cheeks."

Veni's hands flew up, the purple of her suede jacket a dazzling pop of color. "What? Where?"

Catie cackled.

"Ugh." Veni picked up her latte, took a sip of the foam, then licked off the traces on the dark plum curves of her lips. "So fine, we both got shagged. But I have a fiancé who *just* two hours ago returned from a long-haul trucking run."

"What are you even doing here, Veni?" Catie shrugged off the faded denim of her own jacket to reveal the rich cerise of her silky top with its V-neck, the long sleeves cuffed at the wrists; she'd taken care to match her lipstick to the top. Catie and her bestie liked dressing up for their girl dates.

"I expected you and Ben to be shacked up for the next forty-eight hours at least." Her friend worked twelve-hour shifts in the ICU, which meant that unless she decided to pick up overtime, she usually had multiple days off in a row.

Laveni waved a hand. "He's out like a light, my poor baby. Said hi by the way. I told him I'd pick him up his favorite goodies from the café and a fresh coffee so he can have a feast when he wakes."

She carried on. "So my love life already has a ring on it." She waggled her left hand to show off the elegant and understated ring she'd chosen after gorgeous, besotted Ben proposed over a candlelit dinner he'd made himself —with a little help from Catie. "I'm far more interested in talking about what you're doing with Danny."

"Why?" Catie asked, delighted that Veni had found such a wonderful, solid guy after the hellscape of her ex. "Does sex turn boring when you get engaged?"

"You can only hope for our level of erotic bliss."

"Erotic bliss?" Catie's shoulders shook.

Veni shrugged. "I call it like I see it, babe." Putting down her coffee, she leaned forward across the table. "Seriously though, Cat, you look good. Happy." Her smile turned soft. "The way Danny looks at you—has it always been that way?"

Catie squirmed, parting her lips to remind her friend that—the aforementioned shagging aside—it was all pretend. But she couldn't do it. Not after last night, when they'd slept cuddled up and he'd made her breakfast again and she'd wrapped her arms around him from behind and kissed his back on her way to make the coffee.

None of that had been pretend.

"We've annoyed each other the entire time since we met," she said at last. "This is... new." Her honest words opened the floodgates, and she blurted out the truth. "It's freaking me out."

"I get it. Big change in the relationship."

"It's not a relationship," Catie said automatically.

"Cat." Veni was the only person in Catie's life who could make that single-syllable nickname stretch out to three syllables. "You two have *always* had a relationship. It's just that before, it was a relationship of frenemies—"

"He was my nemesis, thank you very much."

"Whatever. You two were nemeses then." Veni took off her sunglasses just so she could roll her eyes at Catie. "Thing is, you guys have never actively *disliked* each other."

Catie parted her lips, shut them. Because Veni was right. She'd never not liked Danny. He'd just been the annoying teenage boy who irritated her but whom she'd cooperate with when it was to their advantage. "If we had actual potential," she said, her chest tight, "shouldn't we have come together earlier?"

"I dunno." Picking up her coffee, Veni leaned back in her chair. "Maybe he was an asshole until now and you were a diva."

"Danny was never an asshole," Catie blurted out.

Only to have her best friend grin at her. "You just defended your nemesis before yourself. You're in deep, girlfriend."

Making a face at her too perceptive friend, Catie leaned back in her own chair.

"Seriously though," Veni said. "Sometimes we meet

people at the wrong time in our lives. Like if I'd met Ben the week after I left the loser, I would've sneered inside and walked away—because on the surface, Ben is as blond and blue-eyed and arrogant as that asshole. I was too raw to see to the marshmallow heart beyond."

Catie chewed on that, had a glimmer of a thought too scary to share. Instead, she said, "Enough about my messed-up dating life. Tell me about you and Ben and the gathering of the parents."

It was exactly the right thing to say to derail Laveni's focus. So it was only after their breakfast, as Catie was walking back to her car, that she allowed that powerful, scary thought she'd stifled to bloom: What if the reason she'd never seen Danny as a potential lover was that she'd known it would never be just a flirtation between them? What if some part of her had known that it'd be deadly serious?

Catie hadn't been ready for serious for many, many years.

"It's too early to be thinking this way," she muttered to herself. "Even if he kisses you like a lover and not friends with benefits." Her stomach got fluttery at the memory of their kiss on Tamaki Drive, with the city glittering in the distance and Danny's hand warm and familiar on her back.

Something had changed that moment, but what it meant, she didn't know.

23

THE INFAMOUS WALL OF SHAME

S he turned up to Danny's birthday dinner the next day—Friday—with a box of macarons that were a favorite with the family. Alison and Joseph had thrown Danny a big party for his twenty-first, as they'd done for all their boys, but after that, he'd kept his celebrations low-key. Dinner with the family followed by drinks out with his friends.

Catie did it the same. Clive was sometimes around, sometimes not, and Jacqueline still had trouble putting family over business at times, but Harlow, Ísa, Sailor, and the kids never let her down—and since Catie always invited the Esera family, the guest list for her and Danny's dinners were remarkably similar.

The gatherings had always been a fun and laid-back affair, but—after her realization yesterday—she was feeling unsettled about facing Danny. Then she turned the corner into the living room, saw him laughing with Sailor.

And he said, "Hey, princess!" A glance at his watch. "What time do you call this?"

"Sorry, had an appointment to get my pet squirrel a haircut."

"You two," Alison said with a laugh and leaned in to kiss Catie on the cheek. "Oh, I think I spy a familiar pink box."

Catie passed over the macarons. "I got the jumbo size. Cleaned out the little bakery." That wasn't why she'd been late by fifteen minutes—she'd been stuck in traffic due to unexpected roadwork. "Sorry I'm late."

Alison patted her shoulder. "Don't mind Daniel. Jake and Jules and Esme aren't here yet—and Sailor and your sister only arrived a minute ago. Had to handle a toddler tantrum first."

"I can't imagine that cutie throwing a tantrum."

"Oh, Connor has his moments," Alison said with an affectionate smile. "But all in all, they're few and far between." She nodded over at Danny. "Connor reminds me of my Daniel. He hardly ever threw a tantrum, barely even made a fuss when he got hurt." Alison's gaze turned misty. "He's so easy, my boy, and I worry that we let him down."

Catie blinked. "Why?" Alison and Joseph were perfect as far as she was concerned.

But Joseph called through from the kitchen for Alison right then, and she headed away with a pat of Catie's shoulder. Frowning, Catie joined the others. At one point, she found herself looking at the photo wall that Alison had started when they first moved into this house.

It opened with a faded photograph of a young Joseph and Alison with two skinny boys. All wore paint-splattered clothing and held paintbrushes, their faces beaming. Catie smiled as she always did when she saw that first image of a family just begun. The resulting photos showed those boys growing taller and broader... and then there was one of Gabriel holding a tiny baby while the baby gripped Sailor's finger. The two bigger boys were grinning, the baby smiling.

More family portraits—of a family of five, then six.

This time, it was Sailor who held the baby in careful arms, while a toddler rode Gabriel's shoulders.

After that came the first photo of the four brothers all on their feet—though Danny was only upright because Sailor held one of his pudgy baby hands and Gabriel the other. Jake stood on Gabriel's other side, his hand tight in his big brother's.

It would've been expected for the older boys to fade away at some point as they began to live their adult lives, but they didn't. Even when she knew Gabriel and Sailor were of an age when they'd long moved out, they were in countless photos with their younger brothers.

One of her favorites was of Sailor holding a large surfboard on the beach while a much smaller Danny held a child-sized one. Both of them were in wetsuits with the tops peeled down, their hair slick and their faces awash in grins.

"He's a demon on the board." Sailor's voice as he came up beside her, putting one arm around her shoulders.

She leaned into him, more comfortable with him than she was with her own father. "I remember from when he aced those surfing competitions." Catie had been in the audience at his first competition, then again at his fourth and fifth; he'd placed better and better with each one. "Wasn't he weighing up which sport to go with for a while?"

"Nah." Sailor squeezed her shoulder. "It was always going to be rugby, but he liked the girl-pulling power of surfing—especially back when he was a skinny, scrappy rugby kid."

She laughed, well able to imagine Danny seeing surfing as a chick-magnet type of sport. "Did Harlow manage to get through to your place last night? He had the worst connection when he called me." Her brother was currently on a business trip to a remote part of India in order to meet a collective of crafts people.

He'd convinced Jacqueline that Crafty Corners needed to create a new arm where customers could purchase one-off pieces of craft from various regions of the world. The artist received the bulk of the profit while Crafty Corners received plaudits for good corporate citizenship. What only Catie and Ísa knew was that helping small artisans was Harlow's passion.

"Yes," Sailor said. "Emmaline is fascinated by the way he calls from all kinds of places. I've told Harlow to watch out or he'll open his suitcase one day to find she's stowed away in it."

"It's nice," she said, nodding at the wall. "Seeing how close you all grew up, how you and Gabe made time for Danny and Jake even after you were living away."

"Wouldn't change it for the world." Sailor pressed a kiss to the top of her hair with easy familiarity. "I want my kids to grow up the same with their cousins."

"I don't think you have to worry about that. The kids are like a tiny pack."

"One day, Brown Eyes," Sailor said, "your kids can join the pack." Another shoulder hug before he left to help with the barbeque.

Catie was still blinking over the idea of having kids when Jake, who'd just arrived, bumped into her. "Oops, sorry," he said with a grimace. "Shit, I think I managed to find the one piece of Lego on the floor."

Looking down, she saw him picking the offender off the bottom of his bare foot. "Ouch."

"Tell me about it." Wincing, he put the tiny colored brick safely on the mantel. "You checking out the Wall of Shame, huh?"

When Catie lifted an eyebrow, he began to point out images. "That's the one where two seconds after the photo was taken, I pushed Danny into a mud pit we'd created the day before. And that's where he put a rotten tomato on my chair—my shorts were gross while this photo was being taken."

Catie's shoulders shook. "Then why do the two of you have your arms around each other and are cackling like maniacs?"

"It was an excellent prank—I thought it was hilarious." Jake grinned, all dark eyes and dark hair that reminded her of Danny. "Oh, this is a good one. I wasn't born then, but apparently this is where Sailor decided to paint Gabe's hair while Gabe was sleeping."

Catie leaned in closer, finally saw the colors in Gabe's hair. "Hah. I never spotted that." The images had faded over the years—what hadn't were the scowls on both boys faces or their mulishly folded arms. "They're not happy."

"Sailor got grounded for the prank while Gabe got

grounded for retaliating by putting worms in Sailor's bed."

Catie lifted a hand to her mouth to stop her giggles. She'd never thought of the two older brothers as mischievous boys, was charmed by this glimpse into their history. "I think I need to hear more stories."

But Jake's gaze had softened, his eyes on a particular photo. Catie knew that one. It was from the day he'd been named acting captain and, for the first time, realized he was considered a leader by not just team management but by his fellow teammates. It showed Danny hugging him so hard that he'd lifted Jake off his feet, Danny's face aglow with joy.

"That was a good day," she murmured.

"Yeah." His voice was rough. "Every time I look at that photo, I feel so fucking lucky to have brothers who have my back. I might've played out my heart to earn the jersey, but I would've never even been on the field if they hadn't gone to bat for me when I couldn't do it for myself."

A sudden, sharp look aimed at Catie. "Danny, he's one of the best men I know."

Catie's skin burned, but she was saved from having to answer by the torpedo who was Connor. The toddler crashed into Jake's legs with a giggle and tugged him off to join a game. Catie, meanwhile, found herself looking at that image of open joy from one sibling to another. No jealousy. No spitefulness. Nothing held back.

She was still thinking about the sheer love in that photo half an hour later when everyone was outside, hanging out while the meat grilled. "That cake looks amazing," she said to Alison.

The older woman leaned into her. "Danny made it himself." She pressed a finger to her lips. "He honestly thinks I don't know, that I believe he just picked it up from the shop because it was exactly what he wanted for his birthday." She shook her head. "I'm his mother. I know everything."

Catie shifted on her feet, a fierce sense of protectiveness rising to the fore. "He's shy about his baking."

"I know." Alison's smile was pure maternal love. "I haven't mentioned it to anyone else, but I knew you must know. You two have always been as thick as thieves."

Alison spoke again before Catie could quiz her on that startling statement. "It gives me so much joy to see him so happy with this art—and it *is* art." She passed Catie a bunch of cutlery to set out on the outdoor table.

"He's one of the happiest people I know," Catie said, then decided to chance it. "Which is why I don't get why you're worried you let him down?"

Alison was quiet for a while before she said, "When Calypso died, we had a devastated Jake and a tiny baby Esme. Jake and Danny, they've always been tight. Friends as well as brothers, and Danny stepped up there—he was the driving force to get his brother playing again. Because he knew how important rugby was to Jake, and more than that, he was Jake's friend when Jake needed it most."

"I don't think he'd see that as any kind of sacrifice." Catie remained confused. "He knows his brothers have his back anytime. It's just how they are. Like me and Ísa." There wasn't a ledger.

"Oh, I know. And I'm so proud my boys have that." Alison rearranged a few of the salad bowls. "I just worry that because Danny's so even-tempered and easygoing, we forgot to watch out for him as much as we should have during those years."

"I don't think you have anything to worry about." Catie hugged Alison, the scent of her warm and familiar. "Seriously, I've never seen any sign that he feels ignored or sidelined."

Alison hugged her back. "Thank you, sweetheart. It does feel good to hear that... but there are things I wish I'd done differently regardless. I suppose parents always question themselves. One thing I do know about my boy —he never asks for anything, so I have to figure things out myself."

After Alison left to fuss with her secret salad dressing in the kitchen, Catie glanced over at Danny. Alison was right in one sense: Danny *was* the most easygoing of the four brothers. The kind of kid who was so chilled out that it'd be easy to forget he had needs too.

Not that she thought Alison or Joseph had done that.

Catie had been in the stands at Danny's first professional game—and so had they. Jake, too, had come, while Grandmother Esera babysat Esme for a couple of hours. No, she didn't think Alison had any reason for guilt. But that she did showcased the difference in who she was as a mother compared to Jacqueline.

Probably not fair to make that comparison, but Catie couldn't help it. The last time her mother had come to one of her childhood meets... was never. Not even when Catie had been up for a championship title.

So Catie was probably not the best person to understand Alison's worries.

A muscled arm around her shoulders that made her

stomach dip. "Why the frowny face?" Danny rubbed at the frown lines with one gentle finger. "You hangry?"

"If I am, you shouldn't be anywhere near me," she said, eyebrows lowered and teeth bared. "I can be dangerous when hangry."

"I can handle you, princess." A wall of heat next to her, he leaned over to grab a handful of potato chips out of a bowl without taking his arm from around her shoulders.

So she elbowed him.

"Ouch." He scowled at her. "What was that for?"

"Don't want the family to get suspicious of us being all cozy."

Removing his arm, he rubbed at his side even though all she'd given him was a nudge. "I think I have bruises."

She lifted her fingers to her shoulder. "Let me play my tiny violin for you."

"I'm serious, Caitlin. I think I need it kissed better."

Catching the glint in his eye, she felt her thighs tighten. "Behave," she muttered.

"Make me."

"Make you what?" Gabriel asked, having just walked over, a beer in one hand and Seraphina cradled in his other arm.

"She's not a rugby ball, bro," Danny said with a laugh. "Aren't you supposed to have her up against your shoulder or something?"

"She's fine. This is her favorite sleep spot." The baby snored in lovable puffs, happy and content to be tucked into the crook of her daddy's arm.

Leaning in, Catie touched her itty-bitty nose with a careful finger. "God, she is so tiny." It was impossible to believe that Gabriel had sired this creature. "Must be Charlie's genes."

"She has my eyes," Gabe said definitively. "Charlotte said so."

Charlotte was also madly in love with Gabriel. It was adorable. In fact, the entire Bishop-Esera family was adorable. No wonder Danny couldn't settle down—the couples in his family were a tough act to follow.

"Where is Charlie?" Catie asked. "I haven't said hi to her yet." In point of fact, she hadn't spotted her at all.

"Having a nap in the guest room." Gabriel's smile creased his cheeks. "Baby Bishop decided to keep us both up all night. I managed to grab a couple of hours this morning, so I'm a little more functional, but Charlotte's out like a light. I'll go wake her before the cake cutting."

Danny and Catie looked at each other.

Laughing at their shared dismay, Gabriel said, "Yeah, tiny humans are hard work, but damn, she's got my heart." Then big, strong, powerful Gabriel Bishop lifted his arm so he could bend down and kiss his daughter on the temple.

She smiled in her sleep, happy in the hold of a man who knew how to keep his promises.

Catie's heart ached.

24

DANNY POKES THE SMALL DRAGON
(OOOOH)

Danny walked up to the popular downtown bar an hour after things wrapped up at his parents, Catie at his side. Taking a deep breath, he told himself it would be fine. Catie had met his rugby mates plenty of times, but this would be her first time meeting his other close friends.

This was also the first and *only* time he'd be officially introducing a woman he was dating to them. It was different from running into a friend while out on a date. This was a *thing*. Especially since it was his birthday.

Then he walked into the bar and immediately forgot his nerves. "Leon, you asshole!" He hugged his friend. "What the fuck are you doing here? You have no money for a plane ticket!"

He could say that only because they'd all been tight since their school days—he'd have paid for Leon's ticket if he'd thought his friend would accept it, but where Leon had seen Danny's presence at the show as a mate helping him out, he'd never accept a financial assist.

Laughing, Leon slapped him on the back. "Jarod had air points and he twisted my arm."

Since Jarod—a slick and polished Samoan-born Kiwi who did play rugby but had never wanted to go professional—was an international sales rep who flew almost as often as most people drove, Danny could well believe that. And all of them shared perks from the job when they could, which was why Leon saw the air-points thing as okay.

Danny had scored the group free game tickets while Leon had gotten them into a backstage deal at his last big theater gig. Nirav, lanky and bespectacled with a small goatee, used to moan about not having anything to share in return, his job as a road engineer not one that threw up such opportunities.

None of them had cared, but Danny had been able to tell it bothered Nirav. Then Nirav had worked on a bridge in a remote part of the South Island, green bush and snow-capped mountains as far as the eye could see. He'd received permission from his bosses to take his friends across when it was finished but before any cars were permitted on it. The. Views. Had. Been. Insane.

"Hey, Catie." Leon hugged Catie after Danny released him.

Jarod and Nirav waggled their eyebrows from behind Leon, where Catie couldn't see them. Danny grinned, not giving a shit that they were going to rag him about this. He was proud to be with Catie. And yeah, that was getting into dangerous territory, but he couldn't keep from going there, couldn't keep from falling deeper.

Jarod's bubbly girlfriend, Noelle Lu, returned from the bathroom just as Danny was making the introductions. Formalities over, they got themselves drinks—then Nirav pulled out a gift-wrapped box about half the size of Danny's palm. "Happy birthday, man. This is from all of us."

Danny had already received a number of gifts from his family as well as from Catie. Some time back, after all of them began to earn a good income, they'd agreed to make the gifts personal and not necessarily bought new.

Tonight he'd received a hand-knitted beanie from his mum that he planned to wear on morning runs, a beautifully crafted picture frame from his dad, a plant that was perfect for his place from Ísa and Sailor, and a vintage bomber jacket from Jules and Jake. Jake had found it online, then Jules had embroidered the back with Danny's playing number.

Gabe and Charlie had given him a journal that Gabe had hand-bound, the art one he'd picked up due to Charlie's continued efforts to get him to relax. But prior to giving it to him, his big brother and sister-in-law'd had all the children in the family make their usual birthday drawings in the journal while the rest of his family—*and* his friends—had written messages inside.

Danny cherished every single gift.

Catie, of course, had stuck to their long tradition of pranking each other on their birthdays by getting him a bobblehead doll—of himself. That wasn't a sponsorship item, so she'd gone out and found a doll that she'd then customized so it looked like him... except that it wore a red bikini. He'd laughed so hard when he'd unwrapped it that he'd almost fallen off his chair.

Now he said thanks to the guys and Noelle and opened the box. Inside was a black enamel pin in the shape of a rugby ball engraved with his team number in the national squad and the number of times he'd been capped as part of that squad. It was thoughtful and beautiful and it punched the air out of his gut.

"Wow," he managed to get out. "This is amazing. Thank you."

Everyone smiled, but he could feel Catie's laser eyes on him. She knew him too well. She didn't say anything, however, as they made plans for the rest of the night. It ended up being a few drinks, dancing, then a late dessert stop at a downtown cookie bar. By then Noelle and Catie and Leon were best friends while Jarod and Nirav were giving him the thumbs-up every time he looked around.

"Thought you two were doing it for a laugh at first," Nirav said to him at the restaurant, after the women went off to the bathroom. "But she's really great. Why the fuck did you wait this long?"

Danny shrugged. "All good things take time," he intoned like some wise guru.

While his friends laughed, Danny battled a strange heaviness in his gut, formed by the knowledge that this wasn't forever. Not for Catie. She was sure they were going to crash and burn. He was beginning to think the opposite, but relationships weren't made by a party of one.

Husky laughter, Catie chatting with Noelle as they walked back to the table. Her face was alight with amusement, and the way people's eyes followed her... yes, his Catie was something special and always had been.

. . .

CATIE KNEW something was up with Danny, but she didn't mention it while they were with his friends. All of whom had turned out to be fun people with whom she enjoyed spending time. She and Noelle and Leon had hit it off particularly well, but she liked the others too. It'd be no hardship to have their friend groups merge during—

Her brain came to a screeching halt.

What she was doing? This—thinking about the future and about a relationship where they might hold events that brought their friends together—it was dangerous. Their current relationship wasn't about that. It was a thing far more fleeting. And she'd long ago learned to be fine with impermanence. The trick was to enjoy the moment and not make plans for the future.

Less chance of broken promises and hurt feelings, she thought, ignoring the twisting sensation in her chest at the thought of a future without Danny as hers. And regardless of anything else, she cared for him.

So, tucking her arm into his as they walked back to his car, which he'd parked in a multistory garage, she said, "Spill it, Esera. What's up?"

He stiffened. "I had a great time. Didn't you?"

"Yes. Your friends are nice people." And Catie wasn't about to be sidetracked. "I'm talking about the pin. It was a super thoughtful gift, but you were weird about it."

Groaning, he rubbed a hand over his hair. "Do you think anyone else noticed?"

"Nah. You covered it well. I've just seen your mug too many times to be fooled."

Brows lowering into a scowl, he looked away. But she knew the scowl was for show, Danny's worry having nothing to do with her. "Hey, you love the game." He'd asked for a cake in the shape of his playing number for his twenty-first, wore the national team's black jersey and his Harriers colors with open pride. "What's up?"

He exhaled, lifted his hand to his face, just held it there for a moment before dropping his hand. "You know how I had that chat with Coach about my form?"

"You said it went well."

"I thought it did, but he's called me in for a meeting with full team management this coming Monday. That's not good, Catie."

She didn't try to reassure him—he knew his sport far better than she did. "You're really worried they'll cut you from the squad?" Catie couldn't see that happening; Danny was a star player, and the team wasn't as strong as it was because it jettisoned members at the first hint of trouble.

Danny shrugged. "I have no idea, but I'm worried that the drugging thing might be part of it."

"Hell no." Catie jerked him to a halt. "They even try that, you shut it down. You did nothing wrong."

"I know. But coming on top of my bad form, I wouldn't blame them if they thought I was covering up a habit." He pressed his fingers to her lips. "It might have nothing to do with that. This is just me panicking."

Catie kissed the fingers he had against her lips.

Jerking, he looked at his fingertips, then smiled. "Cunning," he said but took her hand in his as they started walking again. "They haven't asked me to bring along a representative, so I keep telling myself it can't be that bad."

She squeezed his hand. "Okay, let's play the what's the worst thing that could happen game."

"Um, I get dropped from the Harriers, never claw my way back or make the national team again, and slink away with my career in shambles?"

"Could you still play rugby? If the Harriers dropped you, could you get another contract?"

Frowning, Danny took his time to answer. "Yeah," he said at last. "I'm a good enough player to make any number of teams. I'm just off my game—and you can't be off your game to play as part of one of the two top clubs in the country."

"But Danny, you'd still be able to *play*." Catie tried to put the value of that in her voice. "All you've ever wanted to do since you were a kid was to play rugby—and you'd still be able to do that."

Danny knew what she was trying to do, and it made his heart go all odd and achy. "There was a second part to that dream," he reminded her. "I wanted to play for my country." For the best team in the entire world. "I wanted to wear the black jersey. That hasn't changed, Catie."

"Yeah, but as long as you're playing, the dream's alive. I mean, look at Viliame."

Danny parted his lips, closed them. Because she was right. Vili had one of the most iconic comeback stories in the game. And he'd come back from *not* playing after a freak infection saw him in the intensive care unit, then in rehabilitation for months. Danny's friend had lost most of his body weight, so skinny and weak by the time he was taken off the machines that Danny had barely been able to breathe when he looked at him.

Not because of Viliame's appearance—but because of what it might augur. Danny had been sixteen when Jake's girlfriend—Esme's mother—died. He knew what could happen in hospitals, knew that sometimes, people didn't come out. And Calypso had been sick too. Meningitis. It had stolen her life before she'd ever had the chance to spread her wings.

So yeah, he'd been fucked up at seeing Viliame hooked up to all those machines. But he'd been there for his friend, as had Jake and the others on the team. They'd come and hung out with him at his rehab sessions, hyping him up each time he hit a goal. Then later, Viliame had always had a mate with whom he could train.

Four years on and he was an integral part of his club team *and* had made the national squad multiple times.

"I shouldn't moan, huh?" he said. "After Vili came back from that?"

"Ahem, not the misery Olympics, remember?"

He sucked in a breath. "Yeah, got it." Weaving his fingers through hers, he let everything move through his head.

Catie didn't interrupt, as if she could guess exactly what he was doing. She probably could. It should've been scary to be with someone who knew him that deep, but it wasn't. It was... peaceful. He didn't have to worry about any kind of shield or wall or image. He could be himself, flaws and scars and bad habits and all.

Catie gasped.

Following the trajectory of her shining eyes, he began to laugh, joy chasing out the remaining slivers of tension. "Come on. I'll buy you a bag."

One of Catie's long-term addictions was a particular franchise of roadside stands that sold freshly roasted nuts. Candied pecans with crunchy almond coating was her drug of choice.

"Why are they even open?" Catie said as they joined the queue of three. "It's after midnight."

The person in front of them turned around. "Concert," she said. "Stand hit the crowds going in and is probably waiting for them to exit for a second go-around."

"Good we got here before the masses," Danny said.

The other woman nodded, then headed up to place her order. Soon enough, it was their turn. After he'd paid and they were walking again, Catie happily munching on her snack while he took the odd one, he realized he was happier than he'd been for a long time.

Not that he'd been depressed or anything. He'd just felt... off. He still couldn't explain why. Or why that feeling had crept into his game. He just knew that things were different when he was with Catie.

Were better.

"Daniel Esera!" The high-pitched squeal had him wanting to hide behind Catie, but it was too late.

Two women in fluffy coats over party dresses tottered over on spiked heels. "I love you, Daniel!" one screamed. "Can we get a picture?" She thrust her phone at Catie.

Who looked annoyed because that meant an interruption of her pecan feast. But she grabbed the camera and hooked an eyebrow at Danny. He was in no mood for photos with strangers, but figuring it'd be faster to get this over with, he gave her a nod.

A few seconds later, with him making sure the tipsy women didn't get handsy, the photo was done. But then the squealer pulled aside her coat to bare rather impressive cleavage. "Will you sign me?" She somehow had a marker in her hand and was waving it in his face.

"Er," Danny began, taken aback.

"Against his contract," Catie said smoothly. "Could get him done for harassment." She sounded super sorry and serious.

The women's faces fell. "Oh no," the brunette one said. "What a bummer."

"You have the photo." Catie soothed them. "Oh hey, we better get going. Looks like the concert is letting out. We don't want to be stuck in the crowd." She was hauling Danny away before the women could argue.

He was supremely happy to be hauled.

"Is it because of stuff like that?" he asked after they were out of hearing range of the women.

Digging happily into her paper bag of pecans once again, Catie said, "What?"

And Danny detonated the grenade. "Why you don't think we could be real."

25

TOO REAL, TOO SCARY

atie stopped with a pecan halfway to her lips, stared at him. Tension simmered in the night air, taut threads he could almost see, almost touch. Then she grinned, put the nut in her mouth, and chewed. "We can't be real because of all the stuff we've already talked about," she said afterward. "The groupies are just the icing on the cake."

But Danny wasn't about to let it go at that. Not anymore. "I want solid and true and forever," he said, putting it all out there. "That's what I was raised with, and that's what I see with my brothers. I'm never going to be the guy who messes around on my girlfriend or wife no matter how many groupies throw themselves at me."

Catie shot him a look he couldn't decipher. "I'm not saying you would," she said at last. "But Danny, that's *after* you choose someone to be your forever. Till then, you're used to going from woman to woman, which is fine. No judgment. I'm just the latest flavor—and if we keep it uncomplicated, we can come out of it still friends, with no bruises."

Danny really *really* didn't like what she'd said. "You're not just the latest fucking flavor. Damn it, Catie. How could you even say that?"

She made a face. "Fine, fine, not the best choice of words, but you know what I mean. We're new, fresh, exciting. Let's not mess things up by talking about an actual future together until we get to the point where it's realistic."

Right then he knew without question that she never expected to have that conversation with him. He wanted to argue and point out that they were already having conversations he'd never had with any other woman.

But she was also right in one sense: the change in their relationship was bright and new and shiny.

His gut told him it didn't matter. One day or one lifetime, it would never be over with Catie. And—his heart kicked—that was fucking scary thinking, especially when she wasn't on board... But so what? She was still in this, and as long as she was still in this, he had a chance to convince her.

So when they finally got home, he kissed the life out of her.

Moaning deep in her throat, Catie pushed at his chest.

"What?" he grumbled, nuzzling at her throat.

"My nuts!" She shook the precious half bag she had left.

Chuckling, he grabbed the bag and put it on the nearest flat surface. Catie dropped her keys beside it.

He did a double take. "What is that weird-ass fluffy thing on your keys?"

"What? That's a raccoon. See his cute face?"

"It has crazy eyes—thing probably has rabies." Deciding the topic of her bizarre choice in key chains could wait, he got back to kissing Catie.

DANNY WAS hot and impatient and insistent, and it was frying Catie's circuits. Somehow shrugging off her coat, she went to tell him she couldn't just drop it to the floor— it'd be a trip hazard. But he was already grabbing it from her and throwing it behind him, where it wouldn't be a risk to her as they went stumbling toward...

She had no idea where they were stumbling, having lost all sense of direction under the dark heat wave that was Daniel Esera. Of course she knew he was sexy. She'd *had sex* with him, hadn't she? But there was an edge to him tonight, a smoldering intensity that had her nipping at his lips and shoving her hands under his tee when he threw off his own jacket.

Ping. Ping. Ping.

Danny had torn apart her fitted black shirt. She'd probably be mad about that later, but right now it revved her engine into overdrive. The fact he was so hot for her made her even hotter for him, the feedback loop a thing of violent pleasure.

His hand, big and warm on her stomach; his lips on her throat; his hair silky and thick under her fingers; his thigh pushing between hers as he nudged her up against the wall. She didn't argue or protest when he undid her black jeans and pushed them down. But unable to wait, she hauled him up for a kiss with her jeans and panties still only partially down her thighs.

"Fuck, oh fuck, Catie." His fingers brushed against her as he worked at his own jeans. The jut of his erection slapped against her belly, a raw erotic shock.

"I want you." Desperation in every inch of her, she suddenly realized they'd have to stop for protection.

"One second, baby." Danny reached into his jeans pocket to pull out his wallet. In which he had a condom.

A grin when she shuddered in relief. "I learn from my mistakes, princess." Then he was on her again, his tongue licking hers and his chest crushing her breasts.

She felt him even through her bra, her lower body pulsing against his.

"Shit, shit," he said and looked down to get the condom on right. That done, he put his hands on her hips and swiveled her so her hands landed on the wall.

Catie hesitated. She was strong, but him pushing into her from the back would almost definitely collapse her legs. "Danny."

"I know." He bent to press a kiss on her spine that went right through the fine fabric of her now-buttonless shirt. "Trust me."

Because this was Daniel Esera, her favorite nemesis, she let go. And he pushed into her in a slow and thick slide that exploded her brain. Barely any pressure on her legs, Danny using his big hands to grip her hips... and take most of the weight she'd otherwise have borne.

A second later and all she could focus on was how rigid and hot he felt inside her, sliding in and out. In. And out. In— "Oh God, Danny!" A short, sharp scream as her internal muscles clamped down on his cock.

Biting off a harsh word, he wrapped her up in his arms as he came in hard pulses inside her.

Her chest was still heaving, her brain not quite right, when he gasped out, "My legs are now noodles. Help."

She tried to laugh, didn't have the breath. "Shit."

They both somehow slid to the floor, controlling their descent by leaning on one another so they ended up uninjured and braced against the wall. It was only when Catie felt carpet on her butt that she realized her jeans and panties were still stuck halfway down her thighs. Danny had pulled up his clothing, but the zipper lay open, the line of hair leading into the waistband drawing her eyes to the part of his body that had just been inside hers.

Her face flushed.

She looked away even though it was stupid. They'd just had sex. But this, it was different. Somehow more intimate. When Danny put his arm around her and tugged her close, she resisted.

Then he said, "Come on, princess. I need a cuddle after sex," and jeez, how was she supposed to resist that?

Giving up the fight, she cuddled into the warmth of his body.

And had to poke him in the side a few minutes later when his breathing got a little too even. "No sleeping on the floor."

He moaned and complained, but the two of them got to the bedroom, stripped, cleaned up, and were in bed about to crash when Catie remembered something. "I got you a serious present too." She took it from the drawer of the bedside table.

Suddenly wide-awake, he sat up, the sheets crumpled at his waist. "Really?"

Feeling oddly shy, she pulled the sheet up over her naked breasts and passed him the box. "Yes. Since we're not being full-time assholes to each other now."

Grinning, he ripped at the paper like a little kid. She waited, hoping he'd like it and telling herself it didn't matter if he didn't. But it did matter. She'd made a special rush online order for him and paid for overnight shipping because she'd thought the gift would make him happy.

Paper confetti on the blanket, Danny stared at the box. "Wilton cookie cutters." An awed whisper. "So many shapes." He began to tear at the plastic that encased the cutters. "I think I can use these to make Linzer cookies."

"That's why I got this set. You said once that you didn't have the right cutters for Linzer cookies." He'd been muttering about having a special recipe for the beautiful cookies that had a cut out center most often filled with jam.

"Man, look at this!" He held up a cutter in the shape of a crescent moon, then another in the shape of a star. Delight suffused his features. "These are amazing, baby!" Leaning in, he kissed her cheek, then went back to looking through the cutters.

As openly happy as a child with a coveted toy.

It turned her heart to mush.

She loved seeing him so happy, loved knowing she'd put that joy on his face. It was a good feeling. And terrifying. So, so terrifying. Because she believed every word she'd said to Danny: he might have begun to think that they could be forever, but the two of them had barely begun to walk this path.

And Danny's track record with women was impossible to ignore. He'd soon get bored with her as a lover. It hurt her to think that, but it would be worse if she wasn't realistic, if she didn't prepare.

This way she'd be ready for the inevitable end—until then, she'd enjoy every last second. There'd be bruises, no doubt about it. She'd deal with them as she'd dealt with the other blows of life.

MONDAY CAME AROUND TOO SOON. Danny woke with his stomach in knots, the meeting with team management the first thing on his mind. He was jittery, jumpy as he put on a dark gray suit for the formal meeting. All his brothers had called to tell him he had this, but his skin still felt too tight over his body. Gabe, Sailor, Jake—each and every one had offered to drive him so he'd have support on the way to the meeting, could talk things out, but Danny had turned them down.

His brothers had conquered their battles, done the hard yards, with no one holding their hand. Being the youngest of their quartet didn't mean he could rely on them forever.

Right then, he swore he could feel Gabe's glare from across the city.

His big brother would burn him to ash with his eyes if he heard him thinking that way. Gabe was of the same mindset as their father: family was forever, and it was always there to back you up.

"No feuds in this family, no getting angry at each

other and not talking for days or weeks," Joseph had declared the first time Danny and Jake had a big child-hood blowup. "We're aiga, and you are uso, are brothers. And a brother will walk by your side all your life.

"You see how Gabriel and Sailor are there for each other and for you two? That's how it should be between uso. If you have a disagreement, you talk and you figure it out. This aiga *loves*, and it sticks together. There is nothing any of my four boys could do or say that'd make me reject you—and you don't get to do that to each other either."

Because Jake and Danny idolized their big brothers, they *had* figured it out. With maturity had come a deeper understanding of the value of their father's words. That didn't change the fact that Danny was the youngest of the group, the one who was following in the footsteps of giants.

Decorated captain of the national team turned cele-brated corporate rebuilder.

CEO of a garden business that was now the biggest in the country.

Current vice-captain of the national team—and a student in an automotive engineering program, one who was already working with high-performance-motor-vehicle companies.

No wonder Danny had a complex.

Yet he'd change nothing of his brothers' lives or achievements. He was so fucking proud of them. *He* was the problem. It'd be one thing if he wanted to go his own way, do something other than sport. But while Danny loved baking, that was for after rugby.

In this time and in this place, he wanted to play. More,

he wanted to leave a legacy on the field, to be remembered as his big brother was remembered. As a player who'd elevated the game and whose plays were still considered some of the best ever made.

His one goal.

And he was failing. Over and over again.

His stiff shoulders jolted at the sudden knocking on his door. Wouldn't be his family, and the residents of this building were all high profile enough that they were careful about not allowing strangers to slip in behind them.

Had to be a neighbor.

Welcoming the opportunity to distract himself, he went to the door and glanced absently at the image shown on his little security screen. What he saw had him wrenching open the door. Because he'd forgotten that he'd recently given an entry code to his building to one other person.

"Catie. What the hell are you doing here?" he said even as he fought the urge to haul her close to him—right where she should be. He'd hated sleeping alone last night but had decided it was the best option given the early meeting.

"Good morning to you too, hotshot." Dressed in jeans and a comfy sweatshirt in dark green, she walked inside.

He couldn't help but brush his hand over her abdomen as she moved past. "Not that I'm not happy to see you, but I have to leave soon."

"I know." Turning, she cupped his face in her hands and kissed him until he was hard and his heart thundered. "How's that for a distraction?"

He pressed his forehead to hers, let her stroke his nape. "Wish I could take you with me."

"I, unfortunately, will not fit in your pocket, but I got you something just as good." Reaching into her citrus-orange handbag, she pulled out a small green stone.

He stared at it for a while before starting to laugh. "No fucking way! You still have it!" Taking it from her, he stared at his handiwork. He'd been sixteen then, and for whatever reason, had decided to give Catie a pet rock. He'd painted it green, put googly eyes on it as well as a button nose of a tiny black pom-pom, then left it on her pillow when they went camping. "He still has his eyes!"

"Of course. I take care of my pets. His name's Rick the Rock." Her lips twitched. "You were a weird boy, Daniel."

"Yes, but you like me weird," he said, then—without thinking—leaned in to kiss her. It felt good, like life flowing into his body. "Thanks, princess." The latter came out soft, tender, and he wanted to blush, but she was looking at him with eyes that weren't hard or amused or scared off, so maybe it was all right.

"You're welcome, hotshot. Keep him with you—and each time you start to stress, remember that weird kid with his dreams." A hand pressed to his chest. "Your dreams have value. Don't ever forget that."

Closing his hand over hers, he swallowed, nodded. "Thanks." It came out rough.

"You're welcome. And Danny, don't forget what we talked about. You can always climb back to the top."

"I don't want to be relegated... But yeah, I can work my way back."

A ping on his phone.

"That's my alarm to make sure I'm heading out the door."

Nodding, Catie walked out with him after he grabbed his wallet and phone. When she slipped her hand into his, he closed his fingers around it and squeezed. She squeezed back, and it was good.

She came with him all the way to the underground carpark and his car. Where she kissed him one last time before stepping back.

"You've got this." Her voice was fierce, her confidence in him unyielding.

26

CHANGES

Danny held Catie's words close as he walked into the meeting room. It encouraged him to see the setup wasn't super official, was instead a round table on which sat a carafe of coffee, a large glass pitcher of freshly squeezed juice, and a jug of water. Condensation beaded along the outsides of both the latter.

"Look, Dan," his coach said after they'd all sat down, "I won't lie, we're worried about you."

"I know. My form's been shit." No point in sugar-coating it.

One of the others around the table snorted. "Dan, your shit playing is still better than ninety percent of the players in the world."

"That's not good enough. I want to be better than ninety-nine percent."

He got thoughtful looks and nods in return. Elite sport wasn't for the tenderhearted or those without drive.

It took grit and will and the ability to take tough criticism and use it to improve your game.

Sliding his hand into his pocket and closing it around the rock he'd given Catie, he looked toward his coach. "I've been working on the things we discussed to lower my error rate, and I've also been working through suggestions made by my brothers." He listed them.

"I'd say we were impressed," Coach Brook said, "but we are talking the Bishop-Esera crew." A fond smile. "Those are all brilliant ideas and mesh well with what we talked about."

Danny squeezed his fingers around Rick the Rock. "But?"

The people around the table looked at each other, and his chest clenched. Then he remembered what Catie had said: *What's the worst thing that could happen?*

Yeah, he could work his way back. He was more than good enough. He just needed to get his head in the right space.

What he didn't expect was for the team psychologist to take the lead in the conversation that came next.

He was still reeling over what the other man had to say when he walked out the door. The first thing he did was text his family: *Still in the squad.* He added a smiley face to make it seem everything was okay.

He knew they'd respond, but it'd be by text. They all knew to give a person space around something this big and stressful. As they knew that Danny would share everything when he was ready.

Right now, however, he found himself wanting to talk to only one person.

You free? he messaged.

Catie's response came quickly. *Of course I am. I was waiting to hear about your meeting.*

I'll come over.

Auckland traffic meant it took him around a half hour to make it to Catie's—and he still hadn't figured out how he felt about what had just taken place. When the elevator doors opened on Catie's floor, he looked up to find her standing in the doorway to her apartment, waiting for him.

He strode to her.

"Hey, hotshot," she said, slipping her arms around him and hugging him tight in that way of hers that was so warm and intense and wonderful.

Exhaling, he wrapped his own arms around her in turn, squeezed. The heat of her body, the scent of her, the feel of her, it felt right, so right.

"Come on," she murmured at last and stepped back. "Let's go inside."

He let her take his hand and tug him into the apartment, let her nudge him to the couch while she pushed the door shut. He took off his jacket and tie along the way, left them hooked on a stool at the breakfast bar. But he didn't truly relax until Catie came down on the sofa too.

She sat in her favorite spot—at the far end, with her legs stretched out. He shifted so that those legs were stretched out over him and he could stroke her thighs as he spoke. "Good news is that I'm still in the Harriers squad if I want to be."

Catie frowned. "If you want to be?"

Shoving a hand through his hair, he dropped his head back against the sofa. "Yeah." The fabric of her tights was soft under his palm, but he wished it was her skin. "Shrink says I need a break."

CATIE SHIFTED until she was almost in Danny's lap. One hand on the back of his neck, she massaged his tense tendons.

"They think it's stress related?" she asked, not quite able to compute that. Danny was the least stressed-out person she knew—he took the world in stride.

Rolling his lower lip inward, he bit down on it in thought before saying, "Not so much stress as... mental wear and tear, I guess." He angled his head so she could get at another spot. "They pointed out that of all the people in the squad, I made the team at the youngest age —*and* I've been selected nonstop since then."

Catie had never really thought about it in those terms, but the psychologist was right: Danny had been playing professional rugby since he was only nineteen. On the flip side... "High-performance sports is a young person's game." A simple fact of life. Catie would always run, but she knew that her body would—at some point— stop being able to keep up with younger athletes.

That was when she'd retire from competitive running and flow into the next stage of her life. A next stage that she had all planned out thanks to the Esera family's example and her own mother's type A genes, which Catie had inherited in a certain measure.

"That's what I said," Danny muttered, arms folded. "I told them there was no point in me taking a few months off. I'd just worry about losing conditioning, and *that* would stress me out."

Shifting her legs off him, she rearranged herself. "Put your head in my lap and I'll give you a proper scalp massage."

He didn't argue, just did as she'd ordered. Eyes closing, he let her play with his hair, massage his scalp, and she could see the lines fading from his face. "What did they say to that?"

Eyes still closed, he said, "See, that's the thing." Tiny frown lines that she rubbed away. "They have an idea that I'm actually considering."

"What? Are you into cliffhangers now?" Catie pretended to strangle him.

Laughing, he flicked his eyes open, the warm brown of them as familiar to her as her own eyes. "They pointed out that I've never done the usual young-Kiwi thing and gone off backpacking somewhere or found a job in a bar in another country while I see the world." He reached up to tug on a lock of her hair. "You did that."

"Kind of, sure." She'd trained in different parts of the world and had always tacked on at least a couple of weeks to explore.

While in high-altitude training in Kenya, she'd added an extra two *months*; Laveni had flown over to meet her, and the two of them had traveled through several countries on the continent in a battered old Jeep Cherokee that they'd bought off a departing backpacker for the grand total of five hundred dollars. The thing had been losing parts by the time they ended their trip, but they'd still been sorry to say goodbye to it.

"I remember seeing your posts when you were in Africa," Danny said, "and being kind of jealous but not really. Like I wanted to do that, but I wanted to play rugby more, if you get what I mean?"

She nodded. Because people didn't all have the same dreams. "Back when my friends were taking off to parts unknown, a lot of them didn't understand how I could stay put. But I always knew I was never going to take an entire year off to travel and explore. I can do that when I retire." Which, for an athlete, came at a far younger age than it did for people in most other professions.

"Yeah." Danny nudged at her hand with his head.

"Greedy," she said with a laugh but started the massage again. "So what's their idea?"

"That I go play a season somewhere else—maybe Japan or over in Europe." Danny's words were stones dropping into a still pond, the ripples immediate and cascading.

"Harriers talked to the national selectors too, worked it out so I'd remain in the running for national selection after that season. By joining an overseas club team, I could stay in form but still have time out, do a bit of travel in the region that I choose."

Two things happened simultaneously inside Catie.

Happiness for Danny. She could see exactly how this could be the best of both worlds for him.

And panic because this would speed up the inevitable end of their relationship.

Heart squeezing tight, she said, "I'd jump at the idea, Danny." It came out rough, but at least her voice didn't shake. "You know how tough they are about that kind of switch up." No major team liked to lose players—for management to *suggest* Danny play for a club team in another country was a big deal. It was also a sign of just how worried they were about their young star.

Danny looked up, held her gaze with the dark brown of his. "You think so?" All at once, it was no longer just a conversation between one former nemesis and another; it was deeper, more intense.

Swallowing, she nodded. "Yes. You need the time-out, and you'll love the experience—and the memories."

Danny reached up to touch her jaw. "If I go, do you think you'll have downtime where you can come join me? We could see a bit of Japan together. That's where I'm leaning toward."

Catie stared at him, the ground under her feet shaky and uncertain. "You don't want to use your downtime to get drunk in some disreputable bar in a back corner of Tokyo?"

"Not without you to rescue me," he quipped before his face turned solemn. "Maybe I'll make the odd stupid decision, but I'll miss my nemesis. Will you come?"

Catie knew she should say no, should cut things off clean and fast rather than letting it fade slowly and painfully as he moved into a whole new life... but she wasn't ready, couldn't let go. And shit, shit, shit, she was in so much trouble. She had to stop this before it went too far, before it broke them both.

"It's going to be strange being so far from home for an entire season," Danny mused, and she knew he'd made his decision. "Looking forward to your visit will keep me from losing it."

Her walls crumbled into rubble. Unspoken was that their relationship would progress in fits and starts, around her training and events and his commitments to his club team.

"You'll love it," she reiterated, trying not to imagine him having so much fun that he forgot her.

Danny blew out a breath. "Yeah, I think it's time the baby of the family grows up and figures things out without the rest of his family riding to the rescue."

Catie tugged gently at his hair. "Not everyone has that support structure."

"I know. And I will never, ever be sorry to have a family like I do. They're my fucking world."

God, the way Danny *loved*. So openly. So without boundaries.

"It's just that they tend to take care of me without realizing they're doing it."

Making herself think about it instead of just reacting, Catie nodded slowly. "They're always there, ready to step in with an assist."

"Exactly. I've never had to fall on my own and pick myself back up." He bent one leg at the knee. "Maybe that's what's been bugging me. The need to grow up in a way I can't here."

Catie thought suddenly of how she'd called the hospitals that one time. Danny's life, she realized, was the exact opposite of hers—and strange as it was to think, such a life, such a family, could have its downsides.

Especially in a small country where the Bishop-Esera clan had a huge profile. Danny *couldn't* fall, could never fail, without it becoming a major incident. He couldn't stretch his wings. He had to leave New Zealand for that.

And he was asking her to stay with him while he flew.

Catie knew he'd pull away as soon as he found his

feet, and oh, it would *hurt*. But so be it. Danny needed this, and she found she couldn't say no. Not to this man who never asked for anything.

"Family's going to figure it out," Danny murmured. "About us." A question in his eyes.

"I know." Leaning down, she pressed her lips to his, the promise within the touch a thing of dazzling hope that hid the panic in her heart.

27

GOODBYE, HOTSHOT

T hings seemed to move at the speed of light after that, though Catie knew that was in her head. It took time to set everything up, arrange what was effectively a limited-time transfer. But with Catie away at international meets during large segments of that period and Danny in training at other points, they didn't have much time together.

It felt as if the string that had begun to tie them together was fraying with every day that passed, until by the time she stood at the airport with his family, ready to wave him off for his flight to Japan, she thought it would snap with only a little more pressure.

Ísa slipped her arm through Catie's, squeezed. "Hey." Soft eyes. "The Bishop-Esera men? They hold on tight. And you're unforgettable. It'll be fine."

Catie wasn't even mad that her sister had figured out the truth. Leaning her body slightly into Ísa's, she said, "We're so new, Issie." It was a hard thing to admit even to herself just how much Danny meant to her. "And he's

279

getting to experience a part of life that he's never before done. I'm going to come a far distant second to all the new experiences he's about to have."

Issie gave her a searching look. "Oh, baby girl." Rising on tiptoe, she stroked back Catie's hair. "Danny's not the kind of man to forget or to make empty promises." In her eyes was the knowledge of another man, the one who'd made Catie so many promises—and broken all of them. "Trust him."

Catie swallowed. She didn't know if she had the ability to trust any man in so deep a way, and she knew full well that made her seriously screwed up. But when Danny turned to give her a shaky smile, she said to hell with it and went into his arms to squeeze him tight. "Fly safe," she whispered huskily against his ear.

"I'll message you when I land," he promised, holding on for a long, long breath, all warmth and a scent so familiar she ached at the thought of it fading from her apartment.

Then he was letting her go and turning to head toward the departure gate. He looked back right before he disappeared around the corner, his eyes meeting hers for a long second that felt like an unspoken promise... or maybe a request. To trust in him. To trust in *them*.

As her demons howled, Catie clung fiercely to the memories of the time they'd spent together since everything changed. The problem was, they'd changed so recently that the memories felt far too few... but what she did have were all the years and years of memories of her number one nemesis.

Perhaps it would be all right. Perhaps they'd make it.

But as she went through the rest of her day, doubt began to creep in like a tiny insect. Danny had always liked women, and women liked him right back. And now he'd be far from the girl who'd annoyed him for half his life and with none of the softness and urgency of the physical fire between them.

Long-distance relationships were tough to begin with, and she was trying to have one with a sexy young sports star who had a legion of admirers. Many of whom would be more than happy to jump in his bed.

"What's gotten into you today?" her coach asked when she jogged back after zipping past him a few seconds earlier. "You're putting in stellar times." He patted her on the shoulder, the two of them having been together so long that he was like an uncle to her—a stern and tough-talking uncle who never let her get away with any crap.

"Just in the zone," she said with a grin that hid the panic beneath.

The panic enraged her. She'd made it a point to *never* let any man get into her head. Never again would she allow someone else's thoughtlessness to destroy her days and her life. How dare Danny do this to her?

"Catie, you're sounding insane even to yourself," she muttered as she put in an hour on the weights that evening. She'd already done enough for the day, but she was antsy and this would take the edge off. "Danny's still in the air, and he's not responsible for your clingy dependence."

She closed her eyes even as she muttered those last words. She *knew* she wasn't clingy or dependent, could actually be independent to a stupid fault. But her father's throwaway words haunted her. Clive wasn't evil or abusive or mean. He was just... thoughtless.

All those times he'd said, "You'll be fine, doll. You don't need to be dependent on your dad." Or when he'd smiled and patted her on the cheek. "Men don't like women who cling, kiddo."

She hadn't even been a teenager at the time! And her crime had been wanting her dad to show up to one or two of her school athletics meets or even to a parent-teacher conference. She'd have taken anything. Of course it was Ísa who'd come. Always Ísa. Catie's one rock in life.

Having laid off the weights before she did herself an injury, she was in her pajamas when her doorbell rang at nine that night. The timing and the fact security had buzzed up the person meant it could only be a neighbor —or one of a very short list of people she'd cleared for automatic access.

And since she had no messages on her phone alerting her to a visit or asking for a place to crash, that narrowed things down even further. Ninety percent chance it was one specific visitor. It wasn't that her other friends or family didn't ever show up unannounced—but only one person in her life *always* turned up without warning and with no regard to the time.

"Hi, Dad," she said when she opened the door.

Clive River smiled that big and slightly goofy smile that went perfectly with his mop of silvery-blond hair and square-jawed face. His shirt was sage green, open slightly at the throat and tucked into faded blue jeans that hung on lean hips. He looked like an aging surfer dude—but one who'd aged *well*, complete with a flat belly, muscled arms, silver that glinted in his hair, and lines that flared out from around the edges of his eyes.

Not a man who'd fought the march of time—both because he didn't have to and because Clive wasn't vain. Strange how of all she knew of him, that had always surprised her the most. Or maybe it was no surprise— why be vain when you'd been genetically blessed?

One of her friends had recently called him a "silver fox," and while everyone else had laughed and told the friend to shut it before Catie threw up, all Catie had felt was a bone-deep sadness. Picking up younger women was just up Clive's alley—he'd see no problem with hooking up with a friend of Catie's should the opportunity come up.

"My Kit-Cat," he said and hauled her into a huge hug.

Her eyes prickled because at this moment, she could almost believe he was the father she'd always needed. A man with strong arms to hold her tight against the ravages of the world, protect her in his warmth.

She'd blinked back that emotion by the time they drew apart. That single second of weakness was all she ever allowed herself around Clive. She knew him too well to permit any other vulnerability.

"I didn't know you were in the city." Half the time, she didn't even know which country he was in.

"Yeah, Gloria and I are in town tonight. I thought I'd take my baby girl out for dinner." Another huge smile filled with Clive's brand of love. "What do you say, Kit-Cat? Date with your old dad?"

Danny's flight wouldn't land for an hour yet; after that, he'd have to go through customs and immigration. It might be two hours before he called her... if he remembered. She wouldn't blame him if he didn't; he'd traveled a lot, but this was different. It was the start of an adventure.

Her stomach all twisted up, she dug up a smile. "Sure, Dad. Just let me pull on some proper clothes. Where are we going?"

Clive wandered in after her. "That fancy restaurant at the top of the Sky Tower. Gloria was so excited about it she booked it in advance."

Catie didn't ask which one of them would be paying. If Clive was flush, he'd splash out. Otherwise Catie would pick up the check. She never expected him to pay—life was far less stressful that way.

"When did you and Gloria meet?" she asked from behind her bedroom door. It seemed to have escaped his notice that she had no idea who this woman was beyond being Clive's latest hookup.

"Oh, it's been two months," Clive called back. "She's the sweetest thing. You'll love her, Cat, you really will."

"I'm sure I will," Catie said, having every intention of being polite to the woman. Some of her father's lady friends were sadly *actually* in love with him and believed his protestations of love, while others were just out for a good time—same as Clive.

No matter the category into which Gloria fell, Catie wouldn't interfere. She'd learned her lesson a long time ago when she'd tried to warn one particularly lovelorn woman that her father was fickle and that she should be careful how much of herself she invested in him. The woman had immediately put Catie into the role of "evil future stepchild" and was horrid to her whenever Clive's back was turned.

Catie had borne it without complaint because she'd known the woman would soon be out. And she was— within the month, when Clive was "no longer feeling it."

"Don't ever hang on to a relationship when you're no longer feeling it, sugar girl," Clive had said with the air of a man giving sage advice. "Life's too short to waste on anything less than total and absolute passion."

As Catie considered what to wear, she decided she was in no mood to answer questions from a stranger who'd vanish as quickly as she'd appeared. With that in mind, she chose wide-legged black pants in a flowy material, pairing them with ankle boots and a slinky black top with long sleeves that held a fine silvery glitter. She threw on a necklace with a dangly charm on it that landed just below her breasts, brushed out her hair, flicked on a bit of mascara and lipstick, and was done.

Her father was looking at the photos Danny had printed out and left for her on the kitchen bench—a surprise she'd found when she returned home and one that had made the lump in her chest expand until it threatened to fill her. All the pics were either of the two of them... or just of her. Photos that made her look beautiful and strong and full of laughter.

Was that how Danny saw her?

"That's one of Ísa's brothers-in-law, right?" A sudden sharpness to Clive's eyes. "You two hooking up?"

Taking the photos from him, she put them aside. "Too late to play the concerned father now, Dad." She softened the rebuke with a kiss on his cheek. "Tell me more about Gloria. She sounds lovely."

Chuckling, Clive allowed her to distract him, and they went off to join his latest paramour. It turned out that he and Gloria were staying at the hotel directly across from the Sky Tower, so Gloria met them in the lobby of the iconic tower that speared into Auckland's night sky and was visible from all over the city.

"Oh, I'm so happy to meet Clive's baby girl at last!" Gloria beamed.

Tiny and dark-haired with bronzed skin and bright eyes, Gloria looked surprisingly close to Clive in age. Her hug was as warm as her smile. Catie swallowed a sigh. Oh dear, she was one of the nice ones, the ones who believed in Clive's spiel about finally finding "the one."

He meant it every time; that was the thing of it. He conned everyone—including himself. In fact, Gloria was so nice and sweet through the ride up to the restaurant that Catie was seriously tempted to break her "no inter-ference" rule when Clive left for the restroom after they'd been seated.

"You really love him," she ventured as they looked at their menus.

Gloria gave her a soft glance. "So much." A pause. "It's all right, sweetheart. I know who and what he is." Smile fading into a quiet sadness. "We used to date when we were younger. He broke my heart then too."

Catie blinked, put down her menu. *This* was the one type of conversation she'd never had with one of her father's girlfriends. "If you know, why would you subject yourself to this?"

A lopsided smile that put the sparkle back in Gloria's eyes. "Love makes us stupid," she said, then laughed. "I'm divorced now with two adult children. I got married to the son of a family friend at twenty-three, was a good, faithful, and loving wife—and my ex traded me in for a younger model who dresses him in purple shirts and tight jeans that make him look like an overstuffed eggplant."

Catie was glad she hadn't taken a sip of her water. She'd surely have snorted it all over the table. "That bad?"

"Oh honey, you have no idea." The way she waved a hand as if swatting a fly said she was long past the pain and could afford to be amused. "Now that I'm free, if I want to have a wild fling with a man who's all wrong? I figure I've earned it."

Catie had caught more than a hint of steel in Gloria. "I think my dad might have met his match."

Gloria lifted one delicate shoulder. "Whatever happens, your charmer of a father will never see me cry —don't you worry about that. If anything, I intend to leave him crying." A wink.

Catie shook her head in mingled amusement and admiration. This should be interesting. "You know he hasn't changed at all?"

"Sweetheart, we've been hitting casinos both in Australia and here. I know." Gloria took a sip of her wine. "But like I said, it's my time to be wild and make terrible mistakes."

Catie liked her. She had a "no fucks given" quality about her. It would all end in tears one way or the other, but she silently wished Gloria luck. At least she was going into the situation open-eyed.

As had Catie.

Into a love affair with a sports star who was the favorite of women around the world. If it were acceptable to throw underwear onto a rugby pitch, Danny's position on the field would be festooned with them.

Gloria shifted her hand as she put down the menu, and Catie couldn't help spotting the time on the woman's delicate gold wristwatch.

Danny's plane would've just landed.

Her phone, which she'd put into a slender clutch that she had on the table beside her, vibrated at that second. Her heart thudded even though she knew it was stupid. There was no way he'd be messaging her right now. He was probably still on the tarmac.

Clive returned to the table while she was still arguing with herself, and he and Gloria began to talk about the menu. Glad for the cover, Catie slipped out her phone, telling herself to expect a message from Jacqueline. The Dragon had a way of messaging at late hours.

Catie had a sneaking suspicion that Jacqueline had actually put Catie on her schedule so she didn't forget to stay in touch—but that didn't bother Catie. It wasn't the greatest that her mother needed to put her in her diary to remember her, but then again, Jacqueline only put important things on the schedule.

Taking a deep breath, she touched her screen to bring up the message. The message ID said: **Hotshot**

And her heart, it went boom.

28

THERE MIGHT BE A SEX SHOW

After quickly using her face to unlock the screen, Catie read what Danny had written: *Landed. Time zones aren't that far apart, but I still feel like a zombie after sitting that long.*

A zombie emoji that made her grin.

Sun hasn't set yet, but captain said it's cold out. Meant to be picked up by someone from the club, but if he's not there, I'm planning to book myself into a love hotel and play with all the erotic gadgets.

Catie stifled a giggle before quickly typing back a message: *I've always wanted to try a love hotel. I saw one online that has a slide down to the bed. I mean, I could do a lot for a man who took me to a hotel where you literally slide in to bed.*

Done, came the reply. *I am now on the hunt for the slide. Gotta go, princess. They're gonna let us off soon, so I better sort myself out. (They gave us free socks. I'm saving them for you to use to protect your stumps when you don't want to wear your legs—they're nowhere close to the proper type you usually order, but they're seamless and kinda soft and stretchy, so might be good for lounging around. I know, I know, big spender.) xx*

Catie rubbed a fisted hand over her heart and put down her phone. When she looked up, it was to see that Clive and Gloria hadn't noticed her lack of engagement. She was glad of it, quite sure her face was the epitome of goofy right then. For Danny to not only *remember* her but to make her a priority?

Yeah, it meant something.

THIS WASN'T Danny's first time in Japan, or even in Tokyo, but the city still hit like an adrenaline shot. All energy and huge skyscrapers and glimpses of ancient temples around unexpected corners.

The rep from the club, Takuro, was a junior medic attached to the team. His haircut was so edgy it was a razor blade, his handshake firm, and his grin wide.

The two of them hit it off straightaway.

Takuro pointed out various clubs and other hot spots as he drove them to Danny's accommodation. "You're not in the city," he said in his flawless American-accented English. "Too disruptive for players here. But it's less than thirty minutes on the express train, so you can visit anytime."

"That's fine." Danny took a long pull of the pink sports drink he'd grabbed at the airport; he couldn't figure out the flavor, but it was good. "I'm not planning on clubbing until my girlfriend gets here for a visit." Yes, he was going to call Catie his girlfriend, and she could take it up with him when she arrived. "I actually want to see a lot of the older stuff—the temples and castles."

Takuro shot him a startled look. "Really?"

"Yeah? Why?"

The other man shrugged. "Other guys your age who come to play, they want to go out and party. Tokyo has a big club scene."

"I want to check it out, but I'll have way more fun with her."

Takuro's glance was lingering this time, the vehicle having stopped at a red light. "You're serious about her."

"Yeah. Very."

"Well, good luck." A fatalistic look to him as he turned his attention back to the road. "I mean that. I've just seen it all before, you know? It's hard to keep love going so far apart."

Danny set his jaw. "This time it's going to work." Because if there was one thing his mother had always said about her boys, it was that they were all stubborn as boulders. They *would not move* when they didn't want to move.

And Danny sure as hell didn't want to move away from Catie.

He was wide-awake when they finally reached his accommodation. It proved to be a quarter of an old-fash-ioned-looking house—Takuro told him it was basically an apartment.

"You have your own suite, complete with a kitch-enette. But there's a bigger kitchen downstairs that every-one's welcome to use. Club pays for a cleaning service once a week, so no hassles there." Takuro put the vehicle in park. "Other residents are all part of the team too.

Club's found that players who come in from outside the city or outside the country do better if they have company. But if you really want your own place, it can be arranged."

"No, this'll work." Homesickness would bite sooner or later; at least this way, he wouldn't have to mope about alone. "Great house."

To his eyes, it looked intrinsically Japanese with its curved black roof and fine white-and-black paneling, all of it accented by a perfectly manicured garden complete with a tiny maple and other topiary plants.

Taking out his phone, he snapped a photo and sent it to Catie without thinking: *Home, sweet home.*

He didn't get a chance to look to see if she'd replied until he was in his apartment. That took about fifteen minutes since the other three residents all turned out to welcome him to the team and to the house. Two were Japanese—Daichi from the tropical south and Haru from the frozen north.

They tried out their rough English on him while he responded with his even rougher Japanese—he'd thrown himself into studying the language as soon as this trip was a go. Both grinned in a friendly way at his terrible pronunciation and ridiculous grammar while also giving him the thumbs-up for trying.

Then there was James, an Australian player against whom Danny had played more than once.

"I suppose we'd better bury the hatchet," Danny said with a grin as they shook hands.

James pretended to glare. "After I take you down once for that tackle in the game last year."

Takuro translated the rapid-fire exchange for Daichi

and Haru, everyone laughed, and it felt good. Comfortable.

But he was still glad to get up to his apartment. Tired or not, he wouldn't sleep now; he was too hyped. What he needed was a shower and to get into fresh clothes—and then to go for a run. He hated being confined in an airplane.

Takuro had made it a point to drive past the team's training field; it was close enough that Danny could run to it along the narrow streets in this part of the city. There weren't any major parks or other open areas nearby, so the best place for a run without obstacles was on the training field itself; Takuro had already given him his access pass so he could scan himself through the gates.

But Danny wanted to explore the streets, and this residential neighborhood was quiet enough for him to get away with it. He'd get a few looks, no doubt, but he'd wear one of the team jerseys that Takuro had told him he'd find in his closet, and that should do the trick of reassuring people as to why this unknown man was pounding the night-dark pavement.

The first thing he did when he got to his room, however, was check his phone. No return message from Catie, but she might already be in bed. He still couldn't help the little dip in his heart. There was one from his parents. He'd messaged them from the car and knew they'd pass on the word to his brothers that he'd arrived safely.

Leaving the phone on the small table beside the large and comfortable futon-style bed in his room, he wandered into the shower and got clean. He heard a message come in as he was drying off and quickly wrapped a towel around himself before he walked out to pick up his phone. His mood lifted.

Princess: *Is it nice inside?*

Instead of messaging back, he hit the button to make a face-to-face call.

She answered within seconds, the face that looked back at him familiar and pretty and oh, he was fucking homesick.

"You're all dressed up," he managed to get out.

"Just got home," she said. "Dad."

That was all the explanation he needed. "With a woman?"

"Always." Catie was having trouble keeping a silly, happy smile off her face. Danny looked so good with his wet hair and his bare chest and the way he was smiling at her. She wished she could reach through the screen and touch him, kiss him. "How's your apartment?"

"Here, I'll give you a tour. I haven't looked properly myself yet." Holding out his phone, he began to show her around the space, which was small by Kiwi standards but spacious by Tokyo ones.

"I have everything I need to live independently," he said, showing her the tiny kitchenette. "But there's a larger kitchen downstairs. I might take that over now and then if the other guys don't care."

"They will once they taste your cooking," she said, already missing the way he'd make her breakfast when he stayed over and how he'd lure her to talk with cookies. "They'll be pushing you in there at every opportunity."

His laugh came from off-camera, the phone still

pointed outward as he showed her the small balcony from which he could look down at the beautifully maintained garden. "Takuro said our landlord is the gardener. And also a huge rugby fan, so I'm sure I'll be meeting him soon." A yawn cracked his voice. "Shit. Must stay awake. Must stay awake."

Heading back into the room, his face back on camera, he sat down on something. "Your job is to keep me awake as I get dressed for my run."

"Oooh, do I get a sex show?"

"Perv." A wicked grin. "I don't give out on the first date."

Laughing, she chatted with him as he put down the phone and began to get changed.

"So," she said, "Dad won this hundred-thousand-dollar jackpot in Brisbane and he's currently king of the world. He bought me a diamond bracelet as a gift." She looked down at the sparkle and glitter of it. "I tried to tell him he should've saved the money, but I knew I was wasting my breath."

"Did his newest fling give you dagger eyes like the redhead that time?"

She gasped. "Oh man, I forgot about that!" Danny had been with her for some reason back when she'd been eighteen and packing to move into her first flat during her university days. "That's right! You were helping me move my stuff."

"I got voluntold to do it," Danny grumbled. "You've always been my mother's favorite."

Catie grinned at the mock complaint. "That redhead was something, wasn't she?" The woman had been a simperer when Clive was around and a total bitch when he wasn't. And she hadn't liked it at *all* when Catie's father slipped Catie a few hundred dollars to "help her out."

Catie had taken the money, knowing that sooner or later it'd be going back to Clive. Her father's flush days never lasted long. "Gloria's lovely," she said. "She thinks she knows what she's getting into, and maybe she does. I like her, but I've decided it's still none of my business."

"Probably a wise move. People get weird when they're into someone." A pause before he returned to face her. "Just so you know, I'm into you, Catie M. River."

Catie sucked in a breath, parted her lips, but the words wouldn't come. She knew this was Danny, the thorn in her side who'd turned out to have sticking power... but he'd just left her. Who knew how long he'd remember her? She couldn't put her heart out there for him to discard when someone better came along.

"You have excellent taste" was what she managed to get out.

Narrowed eyes followed by a sudden wicked grin. "I stole something of yours before I left. I'll give it back when you visit." He hung up without any other clues.

Of course, she then had to wander around the apartment, trying to figure out what the hell he'd taken. He was probably just messing with her, she thought as she finally gave up and went to take off her makeup.

After she'd cleaned up, she stared at the bare vulnerability of her face in the mirror. No masks, no shields. Just a woman with the most fragile hope in her eyes.

"What if he *can* stick?" she murmured to that scared young woman. "Do you have the courage to reciprocate?"

She'd witnessed love between a man and a woman up

close and personal with Ísa and Sailor. It was there in the smile they exchanged across a room and in how Sailor would kiss Ísa as he came in the door, the act seeming to be as necessary for him as breathing.

He'd spent hours and hours refurbishing an antique desk as a surprise for Ísa. When he saw that Ísa was itching to write, he'd grab the kids and take them off to the park or into the garden with him so she'd have an hour of quiet.

Catie had also seen Ísa pack Sailor a thoughtful lunch bag even though she was busy and Sailor was happy to throw things together for himself. And when Sailor had to go away for work, Ísa faithfully followed his instructions on how to water the myriad plants that turned their home into a small jungle.

Most of all, Ísa looked for him too when she walked in the door. She kissed him with just as much joy each time they came back together after being apart, whether for an hour or for a weekend.

Give and take, back and forth, generosity on both sides; that was how love thrived. Even the most bighearted person couldn't keep giving and giving and giving without ever getting anything back. It would eventually break them—and even when he'd been her nemesis, Catie had known that Danny had a big heart.

As a boy, he'd rescued fish stranded in rock pools and shared his favorite snacks with her and Jake. As an adult, he was never too busy to throw a ball around with neighborhood kids who came by Alison and Joseph's house when they saw Danny was visiting; he donated time to her foundation with such grace that the kids had begun to expect him to turn up at camp; and he was there for his family come rain or shine.

Danny deserved someone with a heart as generous.

Catie was terrified her own heart was too armored against pain and abandonment to ever be that open to anyone. Breathing harsh, broken, she gripped the edge of the sink, a roar of fear and need and hope in her ears.

29

DANNY, THE DASTARDLY KIDNAPPER

She was still feeling heavy when she picked up her car keys the next morning. It took her a second to see it: her demented raccoon dangle was missing. Her shoulders shook. "Idiot," she said, affection in every syllable.

Trust Danny to choose the strangest possible thing to steal.

She said as much to Ísa when she met her sister at the café where they were having a late breakfast together to celebrate the beginning of Ísa's sabbatical from her teaching position. "He knew I'd notice, but he also knew it'd take me a while. Smart aleck."

Ísa's gray-green eyes were soft with laughter. "I can't believe you still have that. It looks like it got chewed by a rat."

"I dunno. I guess I'm attached to it because..." Her smile faded. "Dad gave it to me after one of his trips." Then she said something she'd never said even to her sister. "I suppose it's a reminder of a time when he remembered I existed even when he was off gambling with his new woman."

Her sister didn't give her words of comfort. She knew Catie was long past that. She just reached out and squeezed Catie's hand, "Tell me what else Danny said."

Happy to talk on the subject, Catie told her about the apartment and the cute garden, then said, "How's the sabbatical going?"

"Well"—Ísa glanced at her watch—"I'm officially two hours into it and all I've written so far is a text to you to tell you I'd found us a table."

Catie laughed. "Oh, we had to kick it off in style." Ísa could've long ago given up her job as an English teacher. It didn't have anything to do with Sailor's successful business either. No, Ísa was a unicorn in the literary world—a poet who made a livable income from her work.

She thought Ísa was as surprised by that as anyone else. Ísa wrote poetry because it was part of her psyche and it gave her peace. That her words had resonated with hundreds, then thousands, then tens of thousands of people around the world was somewhat of a joyful shock.

But Ísa also loved to teach, and her students adored her. The sabbatical would, however, give her a solid block of time to work on a project she'd been playing with for a couple of years. "You still intend to focus on that long-format piece?"

Nodding, Ísa took a sip of her tea. "Sometimes I feel like that old joke about how do you eat an elephant?"

"One bite at a time."

"Yes. Except I'm trying to build my elephant." She put down her teacup. "It'll be good to dig into it though."

As they ate, they spoke more about Ísa's work and

about Catie's upcoming meets. But Ísa wasn't Catie's big sister for nothing. "What is it, Catiebug?" she asked gently after their plates were cleared away. "Something's gnawing at you, and it's stealing your sparkle."

Catie swallowed hard. "I don't want to dump on you."

"You know I'll just worry if you don't tell me." Ísa patted her cheek. "You're saving me from my own anxiety. I think of you like my own kid, you know."

"I know." And it was messed up that Ísa'd had to take on that role, but she had, and she'd made sure Catie always had a strong pillar on which to anchor herself. "I'm scared of messing things up with Danny."

Then she let it all out. Her fear about her own ability —or lack of it—to allow anyone in that deep, her worry that she was too scarred on the inside to be a good partner... and most of all, her fear that he'd forget her.

Ísa listened to it all, then touched Catie's hand again. "Oh, sweetheart. I wish Clive had been a better father, a better man."

"Yes, but he is who he is." She'd accepted that long ago and knew Ísa was one of the few people who truly got it—she'd had it even worse in many ways. It didn't matter that Ísa's father was a high-flying CEO. He still hadn't been present in his daughter's life. "I shouldn't complain. You didn't have anyone, and I always had you."

But Ísa shook her head. "No, Catiebug. Don't minimize your hurt that way. I might've had absent parents, but neither one is a roving gambler. I know how much Clive hurt you." Fierce love in her voice. "Have you spoken to Danny about this?"

She shrugged. "Not really, but he knows, you know?

301

He's been around me long enough to have figured Clive out."

"Yes, I suppose so." Ísa frowned. "Then have you ever told him how important it is to you that the people you love stay in touch with you?"

Catie colored. "I'm clingy, aren't I?"

"Catie, if you were any more independent, I'd put a tracker on you so I could find you when I need to." Ísa's tone was full-on teacher-stern. "Honey, that's Clive talking," she said with far more gentleness. "You never ask too much. You just ask for what any normal human being asks—that your loved ones don't leave you hanging, leave you worrying."

When Catie would've spoken, Ísa shook her head. "Are you obsessing over what Danny is doing right now? Did you not sleep all night obsessing over that?"

Catie frowned. "No." That would be ridiculous. "I mean, after I talked to him and knew he'd arrived safe and sound, I was fine."

Ísa raised an eyebrow. "How is that clingy? Hmm? He's far away from you, and you just needed to touch base to make sure he was okay."

Biting down on her lower lip, Catie said, "The thing is, Issie, I don't know what's normal." She flushed again. "I've never really wanted to be with someone this much before." It was a whispered confession. "I don't know if it's normal to message him now and then with random comments... and I want to."

"Sometimes I really want to strangle Clive," Ísa muttered darkly. "Catie, I messaged Sailor three times this morning after he left for the main greenhouse complex."

She held up three fingers. "Once to send him heart emojis because I adore him. Second was to remind him about a meeting that he'd noted down on the jotter next to our home phone and I knew he meant to add to his diary, and last but most importantly, I texted to tell him something hilarious that Emmaline said while I was dropping her off at school."

Catie was grinning. "Heart emojis?"

"I'm a poet. I'm emotional." Ísa grinned, unashamed. "He sent me a cactus emoji in reply."

Catie might've taken that for some kind of dig if she hadn't seen the collection of tiny cacti in hand painted pots that lived on the windowsill of Ísa's study at home. All of them gifted to her by her husband over the years. Catie didn't know the full story behind them, but she knew they meant something romantic—Ísa always got a silly smile on her face when she was checking on them.

"My point," Ísa said, "is that you don't need to worry about things like that with someone you love and who loves you. There's no account book, no keeping track. They might think you're a dork, but they'll love you for it."

"It's not... you know... love." She shifted awkwardly in her seat. "We're just getting to know each other as more than annoying teenagers."

"Then don't hide," Ísa whispered gently. "Be who you are—don't show him just the armored steel you show the world. Show him the sweet Catiebug who sits Emmaline and Esme for hours, playing dolls or robots, and who delights Connor by watching the same movie over and over with him.

"Show him the Catie who saved up her pocket

money to get my first published book bound in leather with my name embossed in gold." Ísa's eyes shimmered. "Show him the Catie who has a heart so soft that she donates ridiculous amounts of money to animal shelters."

"How do you even *know* that?" Catie squeaked.

"I know things," Ísa said, tapping at her temple. "Baby, you're a gorgeous, sweet, strong woman who *loves*. You're also the bravest person I know. Now you have to be braver than you've ever before been because this—what I see with you and Danny—I know you well enough to know you'll kick yourself forever if you don't try your hardest to see if you can make it work."

"What if it fails?" Catie whispered. "It would really, really hurt, Ísa." That was as far as she could go to admitting how much Danny already meant to her.

"I know." Ísa's voice was thick. "But regret hurts too. I can't make that choice for you, but I want you to know that you're stronger than you realize. We both have a bit of the Dragon in us after all."

Catie held her sister's words close to her heart as she went through the rest of her day. She knew she could be brave. She didn't have any doubts about that part of herself. She'd come through the fires as a child and it had forever altered her. But emotional bravery of this kind... it was hard.

Then she got a text from Danny. A raccoon emoji. That was it.

Snorting out a laugh, she responded with a picture she had on her phone of her missing dangle, typing the word: Stolen across it in red text.

Five minutes later, he sent back a photo of the dangle

with packing tape wrapped around it as if it were being held hostage.

Laughing, she felt her anxiety drop once more. He was thinking of her, and he obviously didn't mind this kind of contact. So maybe... maybe they could make it work.

THREE WEEKS later and Danny knew two things.

One: he was hopelessly head over heels for one Catie M. River.

Two: she didn't feel the same.

Oh yeah, that hurt, but he was no chicken. He was also used to fighting for what he wanted in life, and he wanted to call Catie his own. The only problem was that he couldn't figure out what he was doing wrong.

That thought was uppermost in his mind when Sailor, Ísa, and the kids gave him a video call. It was good to see their faces and hear the children's chatter. He ordered them not to forget their favorite uncle, listened to Connor's earnest toddler talk, and soaked in Emmaline's excitement over her team's recent win, then told them about Japan.

After the kids wandered off, Ísa patted Sailor on the shoulder. "You two have some brother-to-brother time. I want to make a new recipe for Sunday lunch with the family."

A deep pang in Danny's heart. Sunday potluck lunch at their parents' place wasn't compulsory—with such a big family, all with busy lives, including children who played weekend sports or did other extracurricular activities, and adults who were involved in various endeavors, it wasn't a given that everyone could make it. But *someone* always did.

One memorable weekend, Danny had walked in late to find the table occupied by Alison, Joseph, Jacqueline and her professor husband, Oliver, all of them a little tipsy from wine and laughing uproariously over something.

He'd quietly tiptoed back out.

"How are Mum and Dad?" he asked. "I chatted to them a week ago but haven't heard much since." His parents had tended to baby him even after he reached adulthood, until he'd gently reminded them he was a full-grown man; he knew it was still a struggle for them to rein in the protectiveness, so at times they went a bit over-board with giving him space.

"Ísa still finds it bizarre that Mum has become such good friends with Jacqueline, but that seems to be hold-ing." Sailor grinned. "They went out antiquing, and Jacqueline apparently pulled out her credit card to buy this ten-thousand-dollar armoire that Mum admired. Mum had to explain to her that admiring things that are ridiculously expensive is part of the fun. The joy is in finding affordable treasures."

"I can't quite see the Dragon grasping that." Catie's mother had a way of thinking money solved any problem.

Sailor lifted both hands, palms upturned. "Yet they get along. I don't get it either, but Mum is happy and so is Jacqueline."

"Is Dad still doing that extra coaching with the kindergarten team?"

"Yeah, and the kids are freaking great. One made a try

in the opposite direction the other week and all the players clapped and happy-danced." Sailor laughed, his cheeks creasing and the blue of his eyes bright. "Dad says they remind him that at the heart of it, sports should be about joy."

The words struck a chord with Danny. He was finding his joy again too, playing on a team that was competitive but that didn't have the expectations of an entire city or country on its shoulders. Baseball was the top sport here, rugby *far* down the popularity ladder.

"What about you?" Sailor took a sip of the lemonade at his elbow. "Settling in okay?"

Danny nodded and told him about the day trip he was planning on one of his upcoming days off. "I'm going to see a sumo match with my housemates." He grinned. "I can't fucking wait. Those wrestlers are pure power."

"I've watched a couple of matches on TV, but being there in person, that'll be something else," Sailor said and they chatted a bit more on the traditional sport before Danny gave in and said, "Have you seen Catie lately? How's she doing?"

Sailor raised an eyebrow. "Great," he said. "You know she put in a blistering time at the latest trials."

"She told me." He scuffed his foot on the floor, unable to explain why he felt as if he were fighting to hold on to air.

"Come on, baby bro, spit it out."

"Don't call me that," Danny muttered, but he wasn't truly angry. He knew his brothers would be calling him baby bro when he was seventy-five and heading into a retirement village.

"Dan, what's wrong?" Sailor frowned. "Hold on. I'm

going to close the door. Emmaline knows not to come in without knocking if the study door is closed."

He returned soon afterward while Danny was still struggling with what he wanted to say. He wasn't sure he wanted to say anything at all—because he and Catie, it was something important. Private.

"You and Catie having problems?" Sailor nudged, and when Danny scowled at him, his brother shook his head. "I have eyes in my head. I saw the way you looked at her at the airport, saw the way she hugged you. You two aren't pretending anymore."

Danny got all hot, his face burning. "Did Mum and Dad notice?"

"Probably, but you know them. They're not going to say anything until you do." Sailor leaned closer to the screen. "No pressure in either direction, Dan. We love you both too much."

Exhaling hard, Danny shoved a hand through his hair. "It's just hard to get a handle on things when I'm so far away."

"You two are talking though?"

"Yeah."

"Dan?"

"She always replies when I message. Always."

"Ah." Sailor leaned back. "But she never sends the first message, is that it?"

Danny stared at his brother. "How do you know that?" It was what had made him realize he didn't mean as much to Catie as she did to him.

"Because I know Catie." Sailor rubbed his jaw. "Look, I'm in a tough position. I feel protective of both of you, so I'm not going to talk about one to the other behind their back—but I will tell you to use your brain and not react emotionally. Think about why Catie is the way she is, and then think about what it says that she always replies to your messages."

Sailor pointed at Danny through the screen. "Use your smarts, baby brother. You *know* the answer."

30

DANNY GOES MIA

It took three days of sending Catie messages and getting funny replies that made him grin before Danny got one that shifted his brain cells into gear. He'd said: *Clive still in town after his second jackpot?*

Catie's reply was to the point: *I went to his hotel today to meet him for coffee. Checked out. Left me a note with the desk. He found a great deal on a flight to Perth, had to take it. At least Gloria's with him.*

Danny found himself staring at that message, getting angrier with each second that passed. He knew without asking that Catie wasn't angry—were she right in front of him, her voice would've been pragmatic, her tone without surprise. With Clive, the only certainty was a lack of certainty. A lack of care.

He missed a great coffee date, he wrote back instead of the expletives he wanted to pile on Clive's head.

Are you still going to Kyoto this weekend?

Yes. With Takuro and one of the other guys. I'll send you pics and we can go again when you visit.

I can't wait. I've always wanted to see Kinkaku-ji.

They stopped the text chain then because Danny was joining his housemates for a run and Catie was gearing up for the rest of her day, but Clive's thoughtlessness ate away at him. Catie might be blasé about it now, but what must it have been like to be a kid with a father who was so thoughtless and careless? The fact he'd had a kid had never stopped Clive from taking off for the next big score.

Yes, Catie had had Ísa, but Clive was her dad. Meant to be one of the strongest foundations of her life. Only he'd been nothing but a charming and feckless gambler who couldn't be relied on for anything. He'd stood up his own daughter. No wonder—

Oh.

Danny sat up in bed that night, finally understanding what his brother had been trying to make him see. Catie, strong and tough and otherwise courageous Catie, *couldn't* put herself out there. She'd done that too many times with Clive and been rejected or ignored or forgotten.

But she always replied to Danny's messages. *Always.* If he sent them after she'd gone to bed, she replied first thing in the morning. If she was training when he sent a message, she replied as soon as she picked up her phone. Not once had she made him wait longer than a few hours, and most of those times had been because of the time difference.

"Oh, princess," he murmured, his heart swamped by a crashing wave of tenderness. "I'll be first then. Forever, if that's what it takes for you to feel safe." Then he picked up his phone and sent her the emoji of a runner, adding a blast of wind behind her to indicate speed.

Just to let her know he was thinking of her.

It had been two months since Danny moved to Japan, and they'd talked every day since. Sometimes it was nothing more than a quick text, other times a longer conversation. Catie kept expecting him to get more sporadic in his communications or to leave her hanging in other ways, but he never had. Not once.

Until the day he did.

They'd made a time to meet up online and cook the same meal together—with Danny biting his tongue most of the time against her culinary crimes. Dorky, but it worked for them, was a way to stay connected that felt almost real.

Almost.

She missed touching him, missed having him around, missed his hugs most of all. But she could see how well he was doing in Japan, the stress melting off him.

Thanks to a little help from Laveni's tech genius of a brother, she'd managed to subscribe to an online sports channel from Japan just so she could watch his games, and his last couple of games? Sparks of magic on the field, Danny doing things with his feet and the ball that stunned the opposition and had the crowd chanting his name.

Daniel Esera was on his way back to top form.

And the two of them? They seemed to be making it.

Except now as she waited for a call that was well past late. Knowing the app they used could be glitchy, she made a direct call instead.

No answer.

Her stomach dropped. He'd never bailed on her, she told herself and tried again. No response. Staring at her phone, her face hot, she thought about just leaving it and going off to do her own thing. *No one* got to do this to her, got to treat her as disposable.

But all those times he'd messaged her, the silly emojis, the woo-hoos after she clocked great times... it all counted. So she swallowed hard and sent him a message: *Hey, hotshot, where are you?*

Nothing.

Panic burst to life in her gut, an ugly twisting thing that was all too familiar from the days when she'd tried to track down her father, terrified that he'd been in a crash or something else equally awful—only to discover that he'd fucked off to a casino or shacked up with a new ladylove.

Shoving away from the table, she strode out to her balcony and took deep gulps of the cold air. "Snap out of it," she told herself. "You knew this was coming."

Except she hadn't. Because it was Danny.

Danny, who'd carried her on his back for countless races and never dropped her even when that meant he went down face-first instead. Danny, who spoke to his nieces and nephew every weekend like clockwork. Danny, who'd messaged her first every single time since he'd been away.

She'd told herself to be better, to reach out first, but the fear was a choking hand around her throat.

Danny wasn't her father.

He was also a young and sexy male in a foreign country where he was considered a star. She knew it bothered him a little, that the spotlight had turned on him even so far from home. But over there, it seemed focused more on him as a man and less on his sporting prowess, which he was able to laugh off.

"I have a brother who is a damn underwear model," he'd said when she teased him about the adulation. "Trust me, I know I'm just flavor of the month."

He hadn't mentioned the attendant female attention, but Catie had a brain, could figure it out. Danny was hot, and New Zealand or Japan, women noticed that. It was late afternoon heading into early evening in his part of the world now, so he could've just forgotten their online date and gone out for dinner.

Striding back to grab her phone, she checked the screen. Nothing.

Stomach acid burning, she decided to leave it and work out. But all those things she'd just thought about Danny, they made her hesitate. So, though her cheeks burned, she went to the part of her phone where she'd stored the emergency contact information he'd sent her. His family all had the same information, and they'd surely have told her if anything had gone wrong...

She hesitated, not wanting to feel foolish and stupid and clingy.

Two months. No missed calls or ignored texts.

It still took everything she had to call the number for his friend Takuro. Better to start there than with the head of the club. The phone rang and rang, and she was just about to hang up when it was picked up.

"Hello, Catie," said a male voice from the other end, his accent indistinguishable from that of a New York native—it was where Takuro had apparently gone to university. None of which explained how he knew it was Catie on the line.

"Takuro?"

"Yes," he said. "I was about to call you."

Her heart thundered. "What's wrong? What's happened?"

"It's okay," he reassured her. "Danny is in the hospital—"

"What!" It came out a yell.

"But he is fine." Takuro rushed to reassure her. "He had bad pain in tooth damaged long time ago in game and went to dentist, and dentist sent him to hospital."

The fact that Takuro—whom Danny had told her was totally fluent in English—was dropping words and not using contractions just stressed her out even more. "Why?"

"Infection," Takuro said. "It goes from tooth to heart if doctors don't stop."

Trembling, Catie sat down on a breakfast stool. "Where is he now?"

"Sleeping," Takuro said. "Doctors give him medicine for infection but also to make him rest. He forgot his phone at home, asked me to call you—he *really* wanted me to call you."

Mouth dry and chest aching, Catie ran a trembling hand over her hair. "Have you told his parents yet?"

"No. Danny said call Catie first because Catie's waiting for my call."

"You have my number programmed into your phone."

"Yes, you and his family." Takuro sounded calmer now, his breathing even. "For emergencies."

Catie's nails dug into her palm. "I can talk to his parents. But first give me all the details."

Takuro went above and beyond, even going to a doctor and asking questions, the answers to which he then translated for Catie. The doctor reassured them that they'd caught the infection early and Danny would be out of the hospital within a day or two. Mostly they were just keeping him for observation—the sleeping meds were because he'd stayed up the previous night as a result of the toothache.

Once she had all the info and was calm enough that she wouldn't freak out his family, she hung up with Takuro and immediately called Alison.

The entire family knew within the hour. By then Takuro had been joined at the hospital by a couple of people from club management, and all three of them conferred with the doctor and were assured Danny would be fine. Catie still couldn't concentrate or sleep or do anything in the hours that followed.

So she was wide-awake when her phone lit up with a message at three o'clock in the morning.

A sloth emoji.

A laughing sob broke out of her. Fingers shaking, she found the tooth emoji and the sick smiley with a thermometer in its mouth, sent both back to him.

He sent back the cute smiley with the big, sad-looking eyes along with the words: *Pity party of one.*

"Idiot," she whispered, wanting desperately to talk to him. *Are you allowed calls?*

Her phone rang in her hand a moment later. "Why are you awake?" Danny whispered.

She took what felt like her first breath of air in months. "Why are you whispering?"

"Nurse was very strict, told me to rest. I fear her wrath."

Cheeks aching from her smile, she said, "You're feeling better."

"Yeah."

"Did they pull the tooth?"

"No, the old repair was good, just got cracked—maybe in a recent game. Docs say I can have it redone after they spring me. Area's still a little tender, but I've done worse with overenthusiastic brushing of my teeth."

He was downplaying things so she wouldn't worry. Pure Danny. "You have to message your parents and brothers. They're worried and probably not asleep either." Danny might be an adult, but he was also in the hospital in a country halfway around the world.

"I'll do it now," he said. "We can keep talking."

So they did, and toward the end, he said, "Sorry to stand you up, princess. We good?"

"Yes," she said but sat there staring at her phone long after he'd hung up.

Danny was literally *in the hospital*, and he was worried about her reaction to the fact he'd missed their call.

Her entire face went hot, then cold.

He shouldn't have to worry that she'd freak out because of an unavoidable emergency on his end. Yet he did... because Catie had done nothing in this relationship to make him think otherwise. She'd kept him at a distance, never quite committing.

I just worry that because Danny's so even-tempered and

easygoing, we forgot to watch out for him as much as we should have...

Alison's words from that barbeque what felt like a lifetime ago came back to haunt her. Danny, calm and laid-back and funny. Danny, who could be relied on by family and friends. Danny, who never demanded anything from the people he loved.

Catie understood Alison's worry at last.

It wasn't that Danny was consciously self-sacrificing or a pushover. That type of personality would've never meshed with Catie's. No, Danny had his dreams and he knew how to aim for them. He could be incredibly stubborn when he felt like it. But he was also generous by nature, generous enough to always be the one to reach out to Catie... because he knew she couldn't.

Swallowing the big lump in her throat, her back braced against the headboard of her bed, she clenched her hand around her phone. Was this the person she wanted to be? A woman who never committed, never allowed a man—never allowed *Danny*—to depend on her commitment? Didn't that make her just like Clive?

She spun away from the horrific thought, but minute after minute, hour after hour, it haunted her. Clive was terrible at commitment because he was constantly distracted by the new and shiny. Catie was nothing like that... but did the reason matter when it led to the same end result?

She felt sick to her stomach.

Yes, Danny was young and hot and currently far from her, but he was also a man who knew how to commit. To his family. To his sport. To his friendships. When Danny Esera said he was going to do something, he did it.

And still panic gnawed at her. Because if she put herself out there and he let her down, it would hurt a hell of a lot. Regardless of what she'd told herself, she'd fallen for him... fallen far harder than she'd ever intended.

Now she had to decide if she had the courage to open herself up... or if she should shut it all down before he could do the breaking up.

Because even the most generous heart couldn't give forever.

31

LOVE SOUP

Danny was just walking out of the hospital when he received an emoji text from Catie: an orange and a glass.

Orange juice for the invalid, he deciphered with a grin.

He sent back a nurse emoji. She sent the smiley rolling its eyes.

Grinning, he slid into the passenger seat of Takuro's car.

"You're in a good mood for a man who was just in the hospital," his friend said.

"Catie." Danny's grin deepened. "She sent me a funny message." Other people wouldn't get it, might even consider it a juvenile way to communicate, but it worked for the two of them. They got it, got each other.

"You know," Takuro said, "when you first came to Tokyo, I thought for sure you'd be single again in a month tops. I've seen it happen many times. But you two are the real deal." He shot Danny a quiet look when they stopped at the lights. "She was so worried about you."

"I'm madly in love with her." It was somehow easier to admit it to Takuro than to anyone else—maybe because the other man didn't know Catie or his family and had no stake in the game.

"Dude, I know." Takuro laughed. "I can always tell when you're reading a message from her. Your face lights up like the sun."

Breathing in the frenetic energy of Tokyo, Danny said, "She's a lightning bolt to my system. She'd love this city. All the energy it has—she'd fit right in."

"Is she going to visit you?"

"Yes," he said, but he wasn't as sure as he sounded. Catie remained skittish. It might take him far longer than a single rugby season to convince her that she could trust him to keep his word. But Danny hadn't gotten to where he was in life by giving up. He'd teach Catie to trust him, step by small step.

What if it doesn't work?

A whisper from the back of his brain where his fears liked to hide.

What if she never trusts you enough to commit?

Danny had been running from that thought since the day he realized they were more to each other than just friends, and he kept on running from it the rest of the day. It became far, far easier when one of his housemates came up with a delivery order that had just been left at their door.

"Chicken soup for you," Daichi said in Japanese. "Smells good."

"Thanks, Daichi," Danny said in the same language;

he was *far* from fluent, but he could understand most simple sentences now as long as he had the vocabulary—which he continued to add to, day by day.

"No problem." This time it was in English, Daichi as invested in improving his conversational English as Danny was in improving his Japanese. The two of them often spent an hour over a beer, each speaking the other's language.

When Danny checked the receipt after Daichi left, he found Catie's name on it. She'd ordered him food all the way from New Zealand. His heart went all soft, and he didn't care. They'd be fine, he told himself as he opened up the soup. No need to imagine problems that didn't exist.

But that night, as he lay down to sleep, he found himself wide-awake and staring at the ceiling, that scary "what if" question circling and circling in his mind. The chicken soup had been wonderful, but Catie *was* wonderful. Her willingness to look after her friends and family had never been the problem.

He fell into a fitful sleep hours later and had no answers by the time he woke... but he did have a message from Catie: *Brush your teeth, hotshot.* It was followed by the emoji of a tooth.

A snort burst out of him. Yeah, Catie got his weird sense of humor.

As for the what-ifs, they could wait. Because he was planning on fighting for Catie and fighting hard.

A MONTH after Danny's hospital stay, Catie saw that she had a three-week block of open time coming up. She'd still have to keep up her training, but she could do that anywhere as long as she set up a stable routine.

When she checked Danny's schedule using their shared online calendar, she saw that he had one game toward the start of that period, then a full week off. Only two days training the week following. Add in a buffer for travel and recovering from jet lag and they could have almost two whole weeks together.

Despite all her resolutions to be better than her fear, it still took incredible willpower on her part to send him a message with all the details of a possible trip. That was a cowardice too—writing rather than calling—but she could only go so far so quickly. Even just asking had made her break out in a cold sweat.

Asking for things meant people could turn you down, could reject you.

The only people from whom Catie ever asked anything without fear were Ísa, Sailor, and Laveni. Ísa because Ísa was her rock and the core of her family and the reason Catie was in any way a balanced adult. Sailor because he'd come into her life at a time when she'd still had a few threads of trust left in her—and he'd shown her that he'd never breach that trust.

And Laveni because her best friend had been with her since they were in kindergarten—they'd grown up together, each having the other's back. Of all her friends, Veni was also the only one who hadn't, in some way, treated Catie differently after her accident. She'd moaned about school during her hospital visits, grabbed notes for Catie so she wouldn't fall behind, smuggled in nail polish to do her nails, and otherwise been totally normal.

Catie trusted Harlow too, but their relationship was

different from the one they both had with Ísa. Because of his own upbringing and the involvement—or lack thereof—of his biological parents, Harlow had always been hungry for his stepmother Jacqueline's approval. That hadn't altered when she became his ex-stepmother.

Though younger than him, Catie'd still felt like she couldn't put her own problems on him when he had so many of his own. But if she called, she knew Harlow would respond at once. The same with Martha—the woman who'd watched over her as a child loved her to this day, as Catie did her. They still caught up regularly. Catie wasn't about to take advantage of Martha's generous heart, but she knew that Martha would never gainsay her if she asked for help.

And that was it, the whole sum of the people on whom she relied.

She loved her other friends, but *she* was the one they called in an emergency. Everyone other than Ísa, Sailor, and Veni just accepted that she'd look after herself. That's what she'd taught people to accept, what she wanted them to accept. Only... Danny had never quite done that, had he? He'd somehow found an impossible balance between treating her as a fully capable adult while being there for her at the same time.

He'd baked her cookies because she was sad and angry and scared.

He'd pinned her against the wall for the best sex ever.

He'd tickled her without mercy when they had a tickle fight.

He'd shaken his head and told her to get out of her prostheses one day when he could tell they were bothering her. "I promise I won't sell them on the black market, princess... though, come to think of it those are experimental, right? Maybe I'll take up industrial espionage after all"—he'd begun to twirl a nonexistent mustache—"set myself up for life."

She'd laughed despite herself.

So many moments, none of them in a stereotypical pattern.

Which was why she could message him, could suggest a visit.

He responded after his afternoon training session. *Hell YEAH! Let me run this by team management and see if they'll let me off on the training days too. Should be okay I think—we have that big gap because there's a traditional holiday that all the local players go home for and not everyone will be back for training that week anyway. Message you once I have some news.*

She smiled stupidly at her phone.

She was still smiling weeks later as she packed for the trip. She and Danny had decided to meet in Beijing as he wanted a bit more time to learn Japanese before he showed her around his adopted city.

"In Beijing, we'll be equally lost," he'd said with a laugh.

Odd that she, a woman who'd never liked being lost and who always wanted a roadmap, would be so compelled by the idea of being lost. But not just being lost. Being lost with Danny. This man who kept on upturning her world.

"He freaks me out," she finally admitted to Ísa.

Her sister was sitting on her bed, keeping her company and offering comments on her clothing options as Catie held up various pieces. She'd left the kids with

Sailor, who was apparently teaching them how to propa-
gate plants.

While Connor was the more horticulturally inclined
of the siblings, even mad-for-sports Emmaline enjoyed
the small growing experiments. She was planning to gift
her successful baby plants to friends.

"Danny?" Ísa smiled. "I figured. You're not acting like
my cool and controlled Catiebug. The last time you asked
me my opinions on your clothes, you were fourteen and
had a crush on that boy. What was his name?" She
clicked her fingers. "Tae Lim, that's it. You asked me to
write a love sonnet for him."

Catie groaned. "Do you have the memory of an
elephant?"

Smiling the smile of a big sister, Ísa said, "The people
who matter freak us out before we figure things out. It's a
law."

"I hate it," Catie muttered and threw a pretty top into
the bag. She didn't need to pack pretty tops. They were
going to be climbing a remote part of the Great Wall,
walking the streets of Old Beijing, and heading out to
explore more rural areas.

But she didn't take out the pretty top.

"I know." Ísa's voice was gentle. "Just remember that
Danny isn't Clive."

Freezing, Catie looked at her sister. "I know that. I
just…"

"Oh, baby girl." Ísa rose and took Catie into her arms.
"I could murder Clive for what he's done to you—and I
could murder Jacqueline for being party to it." Her hug
was warm and tight, the wild flame of her hair in Catie's
watery vision as she clung to the big sister who'd never

let her down. Not once.

"Commitment is scary." Ísa kissed her on the cheek. "Trusting someone is scary. Trusting someone who can hurt you? That's scary to the power of ten." A stroke of her hand over Catie's unbound hair. "But when that trust is reciprocated? When that commitment goes both ways? It's a wonder, Catiebug. A joy unlike any other."

She pressed a kiss to Catie's temple. "You've always been brave, little sister. Now you have to be even braver and risk not your body but your heart." Another squeeze. "Don't let your childhood shape your future. Don't let those scars control you."

Sniffing into her sister's neck, Catie told herself not to cry. "I love you, Issie," she managed to rasp out.

Ísa stroked her hair again, pressed another kiss to her temple. "Your love is a fierce, wonderful, precious thing. So is Danny's. He knows how to love. If he loves you, you'll never doubt it. That's how the Bishop-Esera men do things. Give him a chance to show you."

Ísa's words spun in Catie's head as she set foot outside her arrival gate at Beijing airport. Because there was Daniel Esera. With a giant heart balloon. Her flesh and blood heart went pop, and then she was moving as fast as she could to him.

He was faster, wrapped her up in his arms and lifted her off her feet. "I missed you, princess. I *missed* you." A kiss pressed to her mouth, another hug that filled her with warmth, more kisses on her cheek, the scent of him so familiar it made her soul ache.

She felt utterly adored and utterly safe.

"Come on," he said, taking her hand after tying the balloon to the pack he'd already grabbed off her. "I made friends with a taxi guy. He's waiting outside."

"How did you already make friends with anyone?" She laughed, giddy and young and happy. "You only got here two hours before me. And that balloon!"

"I bought it in Japan," he said. "Had plenty of time to blow it up while waiting for your flight to land."

Seeing a little girl's tiny hands fly to her mouth at the sight of the balloon, Catie undid it from the pack and gave it to her. "Here, sweetie."

Though she couldn't understand the child's language, her excitement was a blazing light in her eyes.

"Hey," Danny mock-complained afterward. "I spent good air on that balloon."

"I don't need the balloon, Danny. I have you."

His cheeks colored at her soft words, and he looked almost shy before his grin returned with megawatt force. "Let's go show this town what we're made of, princess."

In her case, that turned out to be jet lag. She crashed at eight that night, was out like a light for twelve hours straight. When she woke, it was in a sunny room with an empty space beside her on the bed. Slightly disoriented, she sat up, rubbed her eyes... and smelled coffee just as she heard masculine whistling.

Her lips curved, her stomach flipping. She was happy and it was terrifying, but she wasn't about to let her issues screw up her joy.

Shifting to the side of the bed where she'd left her legs, she stretched with a groan. *Mmm*, she felt so much better now that she'd had a good sleep. Her stomach, too, was well rested.

It grumbled.

A chuckle from the doorway. "Good morning, sleepy."

When she glanced over, it was to see Danny lounging against the doorjamb, dressed only in loose gray sweatpants.

Lord, he was beautiful.

Smile deepening as if he'd read her thoughts, he wandered across with a mug in hand. "An offering," he said, holding it out.

She took a long sniff of the rich aroma, shivered. "I want to swallow it in a single gulp, but my stomach is so empty. I think I better eat something first."

Setting the mug on the bedside table, Danny leaned down to kiss her first on one cheek, then the other. It was so soft and sweet and romantic that if she had toes, they'd have curled.

She put a hand on his bare chest, smiled. "What are you up to?"

"Trying to get lucky." The grin turned wicked, and oh, things in her just melted. "But I know the true way to said luck is through your stomach. Which is why I've been slaving in the kitchen since I woke up."

Instead of booking a hotel, the two of them had taken a chance and rented a small home on the outskirts of the city for the first week of their trip. They'd also picked up a few groceries from a local market.

Wanting to just nuzzle into him, she poked him in the stomach instead, her nerves getting the better of her. "Shoo. Off you go, back to the grindstone. I want my meal hot."

"Don't take too long." Then he picked up the coffee and was gone.

She waited until he was out of sight to slump back on the bed. She'd forgotten how lethal Danny was to her system. Especially half-naked and with that heartbreaker grin out in full force.

Her stomach grumbled again.

"Okay, okay." She got moving. The air was redolent with delicious smells by the time she made it to the kitchen after a lightning-fast shower. "You made pancakes?" Her stomach danced.

"Buckwheat," Danny told her from his position at the stove. He'd added a plain linen apron to his outfit.

It just upped his hotness factor by a zillion.

"Couldn't find maple syrup in the shop yesterday," he added as he returned the fry pan to the stove after flipping the pancakes onto a plate, "but I did snag fresh preserves and a bottle of cream. I've whipped it up, chopped up a bit of fruit to go with it, and ta-da." He came to the table with a pan on which sat caramelized bananas.

"You're gonna get *so* lucky," Catie said and grabbed a seat. "Lucky out the wazoo."

Laughing, Danny put down the bananas, then undid the apron while Catie began to dish up plates for both of them.

"Can you put a spoonful of sugar in my coffee?" she asked. "Don't tell my coach."

"It's our secret." Seated across from her, he doctored her coffee as she'd requested.

The small table was drenched in sunshine, and it struck her then how very good he looked in the sun. A young god in the prime of his life. And the emotion in his beautiful eyes when he glanced up and caught her staring...

Unable to breathe, she looked away, began to fuss with her pancakes. Then the beauty of what he'd created hit her, and she wasn't fussing anymore. She was biting off pieces and eating.

The sounds she made were more moans than words.

Danny's smile grew darker, more intense, but he didn't interrupt her food lovefest until after she was done.

"I can't believe you managed that with the few ingredients we picked up yesterday." She patted her stomach. "I'll have to watch the food belly when we live together."

She didn't even realize what she'd said until his eyes burned hot.

"Trust me, I'll make sure you exercise it off."

She might've panicked had he pushed at her inadvertent slip, but he let it go with that.

The idea of living with him lingered.

And Catie realized she wasn't against it.

She gulped. "More coffee."

"Yes, Your Highness," he said with a grin. "So what do you want to do today? I have our list of things we looked up and that electronic portfolio you made up."

Catie parted her lips, went to say they could go down the list. Then hesitated. Because this was Danny. Easy-going Danny who didn't often ask for anything. "How about you choose," she said. "Let's treat this as the start of your travel adventure."

"Yeah?" Danny's smile went lopsided. "In that case, we could just wander the streets of Old Beijing. I really like looking at the old buildings and checking out the little shops—we can explore until we get a little lost."

"You want to get lost on purpose?" Catie took a fortifying gulp of coffee. "Come on then, let us go horrify ourselves."

Laughing, Danny rose with her and wrapped her up in a hug, big and warm and of home. That's what Danny felt like, she realized with a lump in her throat. Home.

32

LOST IN BEIJING

Catie was ready to get off her prostheses by the time they wandered into a tiny little restaurant down what might've been a dark alleyway if everyone hadn't been awake and energetic and going about their business. Just a few minutes earlier, they'd walked past a small square where a group of elderly people had been flowing into the graceful forms of tai chi.

"I thought New York was the city that never slept," she said as a harried member of the waitstaff waved them to an open table in the narrow place filled with the smells of soy sauce, ginger, and things fresh and green.

"Yeah, looks like Beijing didn't get that memo," Danny said, stretching before he took a seat.

She saw three women at the table next to theirs give him surreptitious looks before whispering to each other with smiles on their faces. The kind of smiles that needed no translation: they said that dude was hot. A moment later, two of the women looked at Catie—who'd worn shorts today—then back at Danny, and put their heads together again.

"Why are you rolling your eyes?" an oblivious Danny said as he grabbed his seat.

"No reason." If there was one thing growing up an amputee had taught her, it was that shallow people were shallow. There was no great mystery. That's who they were and that's who they'd always be. She was never going to tie herself in knots because a few strangers had decided she wasn't up to Danny's level.

She'd never understood what that even meant. People were either into each other or they weren't. And Danny was into her. She knew that beyond any doubt—because he'd made sure she had no doubts.

"You're pretty amazing, you know that?" she said softly.

A sudden heat in his cheeks, but his grin widened. "Well, I try not to toot my own horn, but..." Brushing his nails against his T-shirt, he then lifted them to his mouth and blew them off.

Laughing because that hadn't been so hard, or so scary, she nodded at the menu. "You figure it out?"

"No freaking idea." He scowled at his phone. "I think I got scammed the $4.99 I paid for this translation app."

A server appeared at their side, reeling off something in Mandarin. Catie glanced at Danny. He looked at her. Then the two of them began pointing at things at random on the menu. They'd already figured out that the cost of eating out was incredibly cheap in comparison to home, so it wouldn't break the bank. And from the size of the dishes on the tables around them, they could expect small portion sizes.

They were right. And wrong.

Catie's eyes went huge as, a relatively short time later, the server rolled over a cart on which sat a huge bowl surrounded by lots of smaller bowls, all full of food, and started putting everything on the table one by one. She gave them a beaming smile afterward, said something else, then left.

Catie looked at Danny, raised an eyebrow. He shrugged.

And they dove in, trying one thing at a time and giving each other their opinions. Catie loved a red cabbage dish while Danny couldn't stand it. He, meanwhile, was intrigued by a dumpling so delicious he took another one apart in an attempt to divine its secrets.

The bowl in the center turned out to be soup, of which they both put away a big helping each.

As a result of their feast, they were stuffed by the time they left the restaurant. "How are your legs?" Danny asked, one arm around her shoulders.

"Good after that rest."

This far from the tourist areas, there were no hawkers, no trinket stalls, just people going about their day—or night. The tai chi group was gone, but in its place was a group learning to salsa.

"It's so alive." Not in the way of bright lights and neon. In the way of life being lived full throttle. And she thought: this is the life I want. Not this city or this place. But this sense of living life without the boundaries she put on things. The way she'd tried to put a boundary on her relationship with Danny.

Fake relationship.

Friends with benefits.

Long-distance lovers.

None of it fit anymore, had never really fit. And yet she still wanted to label it, to somehow contain it. Because open-ended things with people who held the power to hurt you were scary.

Turning, she pressed a kiss to his jaw. It was stubbled after the long day, and it felt intimate to touch him this way in the warm dark while dancers swayed and dipped nearby. "Let's go home, hotshot," she murmured. "I have to pay up for breakfast."

His eyes sparked fire, and suddenly he wasn't so into lazy walking. "Hurry up, princess!"

Laughing because he made her feel young and alive and wild, she held on to his hand as he led them back home, his sense of direction unerring. She never felt lost with Danny, whether they were exploring the back alleys of a strange city or sitting at home on the sofa. Or being pinned up against the closed door of the house that was to be their home for the time being.

She gasped at the heat of his kiss, her hands pressed to his chest. He was already pushing his own hand up under her top, the rough warmth of his skin a delicious shock to the system. Then he placed his hand on her breast and squeezed, and her thighs clenched on a gush of dampness.

Wrapping her arms around his powerful shoulders, she kissed him back with all the pent-up need inside her. They'd kissed and cuddled last night before she collapsed into her sleep coma, but she was starting to realize it would never be enough with Danny. She could kiss him forever.

Pulling at his T-shirt, she managed to get it off over

his head. Her own top ended up thrown over a piece of furniture not long afterward. The sight of his hand, big and strong against the pale pink lace of her bra, made her stomach clench, tiny lights exploding behind her eyes.

Breath coming hard and fast, she ran her hand over the ridges of his abdomen and lower to palm him through his jeans. He groaned, pushed into her with unhidden need, the ridge of his erection so taut that he felt enormous.

She stroked, squeezed.

"Fuck, Catie." A groan against her mouth, his hands slamming onto the door on either side of her head as she moved her fingers, undid the top button of his jeans, lowered the zipper... and slipped her hand inside his briefs to close her fingers over the warm steel of his cock.

He shuddered, dropping his head to kiss and suck at her throat as she stroked him exactly the way she knew he liked. It felt so good to touch him this way, to know she was giving him as much pleasure as he was giving her.

Pulling down the lace cup of her bra after pressing a tender kiss to her heart-surgery scar, he ran his thumb over her bare nipple. "I want to suck you everywhere, baby." His breathing was ragged. "Especially here." He dropped his hand to between her legs, pushed up with the heel of his hand.

Catie's nerves short-circuited. "I want you inside me."

"Oh fuck yes." Shifting back with alacrity, he kicked off his jeans and briefs while she somehow managed to undo her shorts and get them off.

Danny's hands on her hips, the slightest pressure. And she realized he wanted her to turn.

Damp heat between her legs, she did as he'd silently

requested and pressed her palms to the wall. He rolled her panties down her thighs, stroked his hand over one bare cheek.

"You are so goddamn beautiful." A rough whisper against her neck as he leaned in to press a kiss to her nape.

"Danny." She lifted a hand, moved it back to stroke his hair.

He nuzzled at her before pulling back, and she heard the familiar sound of a condom wrapper tearing. Then he was gripping her hips tight, the blunt head of his cock bumping against her in erotic pulses before he slid into her so slow and deep that she almost couldn't stand it.

Her body clenched around him, her hunger for him a raw need.

She'd thought she wanted fury, but she didn't urge him to go faster when he settled into a slow and intense rhythm that hit every sensitive spot inside her. All the while, he kept on saying the sweetest, hottest things to her until all her shields and walls lay in splinters at her feet, her heart in Daniel Esera's careful hands.

33

A BROKEN HEART

She didn't want to leave him. But here they stood at the departure gate as her flight began to board. They'd booked flights close in time so they could be in the departure area together, but hers was an hour ahead of his.

Throat thick, she threw her arms around him and hugged him tight. His own hug was as fierce. "Best holiday ever," he said, his voice rough.

She nodded, unable to speak. They were breaking apart all too soon and she turned to walk away. She couldn't draw this out. It was always better to cut things off hard and fast. It hurt less that way.

"Hey." Danny's voice stopped her.

She turned to see his eyes dark with emotion.

"Vietnam next?"

Her heart shuddered. Nodding, she managed to get out "Count on it." Then she was striding through the boarding gate.

But she turned at the last minute, looked back.

Danny was still there, watching after her. She carried that image with her as she walked onto the plane, found her seat. And, when the plane took to the sky, she imagined him watching her fly off.

"Vietnam," she murmured, and it was a promise to herself.

It, however, ended up a broken promise. Clive suffered a massive heart attack a week before she was meant to fly out to meet Danny. Dropping everything, she booked a flight to Sydney, Australia, where he was currently in the hospital, and took a taxi directly from the airport to the hospital.

A hollow-eyed Gloria sprang up from the waiting room chair where she'd been slumped. "Oh, Catie!" Tears waterfalled down her face as she threw her arms around Catie.

Panic was strangling hands at Catie's throat. "Is he okay?" If she was too late...

But the other woman nodded. "I'm just—" Gulping in air, she wiped her face. "I'm so sorry. That was terrible of me. But I've been alone all this time, and I—"

"Shh, it's okay." Catie hugged the distraught woman, well able to understand her fear and panic. As with Clive, Gloria had no family in Australia. She was only here because Clive was here, their relationship having lasted far longer than Catie thought even Gloria had expected.

Gloria squeezed her tight, then drew back. "Come on. I'll show you his room. I just came out here for a bit because the doctors were doing their checkup."

Her father's room proved empty of anyone but an unconscious Clive when they entered. He'd been put into a medicated sleep after his emergency surgery. Catie fought off her panic at all the wires coming out of his body, at all the machines to which he was attached.

Gloria touched her arm. "I think the doctor should still be here. I'll go find him so you can talk to him directly. I barely heard most of what he said." The kind woman then left Catie alone with her dad.

"Hey, Daddy," she said, her voice shaking as she bent to press her lips to his cheek. "Still sleeping in, I see."

Dropping her small daypack to the floor, she took a seat at his bedside. The daypack just held emergency supplies in case her luggage failed to arrive with her in Sydney. She'd prepared for a long stay and brought a full suitcase—it had landed safely and was now at the nurse's station not far from Clive's room. The nurses had been kind when she'd explained she'd come directly from the airport and had made room without hesitation.

As she took his hand, her heart got all tight and cold. Clive might be an unreliable firefly of a father, but he was still her father. She wasn't ready to lose him.

A rustle behind her, the curtains parting as the surgeon walked in.

Dr. Sung was a petite woman with sharp eyes and a firm manner. "The surgery went textbook well," she told Catie. "Your father is otherwise healthy and strong, which will help in his recovery."

"Will he have to worry about long-term effects?" Catie asked.

"No. He was lucky to be so close to the hospital when he suffered the adverse event. We had him in surgery within forty minutes. He's a lucky man."

"Always a gambler, eh, Dad," she said after Dr. Sung had left.

Gloria, having returned at the tail end of the doctor's visit, laughed a little wetly. "Isn't he just?" She brushed back Clive's hair.

"Why were you two so close to the hospital? Are you staying nearby?"

"No. I talked him into coming to the emergency room when he complained about feeling off," Gloria explained. "No pain, but he wasn't feeling like himself. Normally Clive would brush that off—you know your father.

"But he was sweaty and shaky and couldn't really argue with me when I bundled us into the taxi for the drive here. He had the heart attack as the taxi turned onto this street. Or maybe he was having it all morning. I don't know. The doctor will know. I just—"

"It's okay." Catie reached over to take Gloria's hand. Throat thick, she said, "You probably saved his life by bringing him here. Thank you."

Eyes swimming with tears, Gloria whispered, "I love him so much."

"Me too." She knew never to rely on him for anything, but she did love her father and always would.

When her phone buzzed in her pocket, she was glad of the distraction from the sight of Clive so quiet and still. Her father was never that way. Taking it out of her pocket, she saw a missed call from Ísa.

Her sister, of course, had sprung into action to help her. She would've flown over with Catie if little Connor wasn't sick with a bad stomach bug. Catie, herself, was worried about her nephew. She couldn't imagine the stress Ísa was under, seeing her baby in such distress.

"I'll just step out to call my sister," she said to Gloria.

Once in an open hallway far from any patient rooms, her back to a cold wall, she made the call.

Ísa said, "How's Clive?" as soon as she answered on the other end.

"He's okay. Not conscious yet, but the doctor says he should make a full recovery."

A jagged exhale. "Oh, thank God."

"Connor?" Catie asked, fingers clenching on the hard plastic of her phone case. "Is he any better?"

"Yes." Ísa's smile was in her tone. "Turned the corner a couple of hours ago. He's laughing with Sailor and Emmaline in the kitchen right now—be a few more days before he's back to his usual energetic self, but our poor little guy isn't throwing up anymore."

They spoke for a few more minutes before hanging up. After which, Catie found herself sliding down the wall to sit on the floor as tears threatened to overwhelm her. She swallowed them back over and over again. Then she called Danny. When his phone went automatically to voice mail, she left a message telling him that Clive was out of surgery and asking him to call her.

Because she needed him.

Needed his voice and his face and his warmth. Needed the way he could make any situation better.

But Danny didn't call. Not in the minutes that followed, or in the hours afterward when she took Gloria's advice and made herself go to Gloria and Clive's hotel room to shower and catch a few hours' sleep. Gloria would then do the same herself after Catie returned to sit with Clive. Neither one of them wanted him to wake up alone.

She woke to a silent phone.

Worry gnawed at her. Danny would never ignore her that way. She knew that beyond any shadow of a doubt. Remembering that time he'd ended up in the hospital, she tried to get ahold of him again, but it went directly to voice mail.

So she messaged Takuro: *Hey, Tak. I can't seem to get in touch with Danny. You know what's up?*

Takuro replied as she was heading down to the small café attached to the hotel to grab something quick for breakfast: *Hello, Catie! I'm visiting my village this week. Tea plantations everywhere! Want me to ask someone at the house to check on him?*

Catie chewed on her lip. She didn't want to intrude if Danny was just busy— No. She stopped that thought right in its tracks. That wasn't Danny. That had never been Danny. He never just blew her off. *Ever.*

Yes, she said to Takuro. *Just ask if they know where he's at, because his phone keeps going to voice mail.*

Okay, I'll ask. Not sure they'll reply quickly. It's a break weekend, so everyone's scattered.

Thanks, Tak. Message me when you know.

Though she picked up a muffin from the café, she couldn't make herself eat it. Instead, she drank an herbal tea, and on arriving at the hospital, offered Gloria the muffin. "I also got you a latte. I hope that's something you like?"

"Oh, you're a godsend." Rubbing at tired eyes, Gloria took the coffee but said she wasn't up to the muffin.

Catie put it on the bedside table. "How is he?" She placed a hand on Gloria's shoulder.

The other woman reached up to take it, her fingers

soft. "No real change. But the nurses say that's good. He just needs to rest for a while."

"And you? How are you doing?"

"Better now that you're in Sydney. I just felt so alone. So scared."

"I know." She hugged Gloria when the older woman stood, then nudged her out the door. "You need rest, like you told me to get. Even if it's only a few hours."

Exhausted, Gloria finally agreed and left. Taking a seat beside Clive's bed, Catie closed the fingers of one hand around her father's and glanced at her phone. No message from Takuro.

Her chest squeezed.

Just as her phone lit up with a most unexpected caller.

"Mum?"

"How is Clive?" Jacqueline asked in her direct, no-nonsense way.

After Catie gave her the breakdown, Jacqueline said, "He should have little to no medical costs given the coop-eration agreement with Australia, but if he has any bills that he can't cover, let me know and I'll handle it."

Catie swallowed hard. "Thanks, Mum." She knew Clive had done a number on Jacqueline, so this kindness was unexpected.

A sigh. "He was a terrible husband, but he gave me an amazing daughter." Then Jacqueline hung up.

Eyes burning, Catie gave a soft laugh and spoke to the air. "I love you too." That was the thing with the Dragon; she wasn't in any way maternal and had—frankly speaking—been emotionally neglectful, but Catie knew

345

without a doubt that Jacqueline would scorch the earth if anyone dared hurt her children.

"People are complicated, aren't they, Dad?" she said to the man who'd shaped so much of who she was simply by being himself. Unreliable, fickle, unable to hold on to money—and unwilling to shoulder responsibility. Yet he'd been an unswerving presence by her bedside after her accident.

He loved her.

He just didn't love her as she needed and deserved to be loved.

Throat tight, she rose to brush back his hair and press a kiss to his forehead. "I'm here, Dad," she murmured. "And I love you for who you are." She saw him and she knew what she could and couldn't expect from him, just as she knew the same about Jacqueline.

Rubbing her face after she sat back down, she picked up her phone. Nothing from Takuro and nothing from Danny. Worry crawled across her skin. This was so unlike him. But surely if anything had gone seriously wrong, his team would've contacted the Eseras? And Sailor and Ísa would've contacted her in turn.

Telling herself that Danny was fine—it was probably something simple like a flat phone battery that he hadn't noticed—she returned her attention to her father. And because she figured it couldn't hurt, she started telling him about her aim for gold at the next Paralympics. The specific training schedule she'd mapped out... and the ways she'd adapted it so she could see Danny. "Because he's important to me."

It came out solid, unshakable, that confession. "And I'm important to him." So strange to say that and to know it without question. "I can ask him anything and he'll give it to me."

That was when she got it.

Oh, of course he isn't answering his phone. He's on his way to me.

34

TRUST

It should've been a stupid fantasy thought that she dismissed out of hand. But it stuck. And kept on sticking in the minutes that followed. Until her stomach settled and she could actually eat the abandoned muffin.

A stir from the bed, her father's hand moving.

"Daddy?" She rose to see his eyes fluttering... and then they were open and looking into hers.

A moment of fuzziness before they lit up. "Sugar girl." His voice was a croak, his joy at seeing her open.

Swallowing back her tears, she leaned in to gently hug him before she pressed the call button.

After that, she had to back off to give the nurse and doctor room to evaluate him. Gloria, who couldn't have slept more than an hour, rushed in during the middle of all that and burst into smiling tears at seeing Clive awake.

Catie was surprised but happy to see the way Clive looked at Gloria, how he tried to joke with her to make her feel better. Maybe this might actually work. Perhaps her feckless father had finally found his match.

She murmured something along those lines to him when the medical staff cleared the room and Gloria excused herself to go to the bathroom. "Gloria's my favorite of all your girlfriends," she said. "Try not to get dumped, Dad." Clive was usually the leaver in a relationship, but she didn't think it would play out that way this time.

A shaky chuckle. "She'd kick my ass if I stepped out of line, wouldn't she?"

Catie laughed. "Yeah, I'd be careful there."

"I will, sugar girl." A patented Clive smile. "Your old man still has it, you know."

Happy and sad at the same time, she said, "I know."

Gloria bustled in right then. "Oh, look at you. So beautiful together. That same gorgeous smile." Taking out her phone, she snapped a pic. "I'll send it to you," she said to Catie.

"Thanks." Catie rose to her feet. "I'm going to give you two some time alone and go scout out coffee and snacks for me and Gloria."

"What about your old dad?" Clive grumbled.

"Sorry, Dad. You're on the hospital diet for now." As for any future prescribed diet, she'd leave that for Gloria to wrangle.

Catie had long ago given up the job of looking after Clive, but Gloria seemed to be okay with it. Each to their own, she supposed, and exited the room. She walked around a bit, found the cafeteria, grabbed the hot drinks as well as food for Gloria, then headed back up.

Clive and Gloria were making goo-goo eyes at each

other and whispering sweet nothings when she entered. They sprang guiltily apart, Gloria's cheeks a charming red.

Laughing, she left the food and waved off their offers for her to stay.

"But Gloria, you need more sleep," she pointed out. "How about you hang out with Dad for a bit more, then I'll keep him company while you go get that rest?"

Heavy-eyed, Gloria nodded. "Okay, yes, you're right. Now that I know my sweet man is okay, I'll be able to sleep."

Leaving the two for now, Catie took her own coffee out into the hallway and took a seat on one of the hard plastic chairs that seemed to come standard issue at hospitals. And when she looked up and saw a familiar man walking down the hall, a duffel bag in hand, she wasn't surprised in the least.

Abandoning her coffee on another chair, she got up and moved to him as fast as her regular prosthetic legs would allow.

Danny wrapped her up in his arms and lifted her off the ground... as she finally gave in to the fear-tears that had been trapped inside her since the moment she'd received the call. He just held her tight, kissing her hair and cheek and stroking her back until she could breathe again.

"He's all right," she managed to get out past the last of her sniffles. "I just—"

"Hey." He wiped away a tear. "I know you, remember? No explanations necessary."

Reaching up, she kissed him—then mock punched him in the chest. "Why didn't you message me that you were coming?"

He winced, rubbed his chest. "I didn't know if I'd get a flight—just turned up at the airport and hoped. Ran onto a plane right as they were literally shutting the boarding gate; then the flight attendant hurried me into a seat. By the time I got the seat belt fastened, she was back to tell me to turn off my phone."

Danny had thought about disobeying because he knew how much contact meant to Catie. But he hadn't wanted to risk being kicked off the flight. "I figured I'd message you using the onboard wi-fi, but turned out it was glitchy. I just couldn't connect. Sorry, princess. I know you must've worried."

"I thought something happened to you," she said with a scowl. But then her face softened, sunrise after a storm. "At least until I figured out you must be on your way to me."

Even as his heart cracked wide open, she pressed her hand to the side of his face. "If there's one thing I know, hotshot, it's that you'll always be there for me." No hesitation, no holding back. "I can trust you and I do. With all of me."

He staggered inwardly and, unable to speak, just held her until he could breathe again.

Afterward, she pressed a kiss to his jaw before pulling back. "Let me go wash my face; then we'll go see Clive."

He used those moments alone to get a handle on himself—except he couldn't. Catie hadn't been shocked or startled to see him. She'd *known*. Even though he hadn't been able to message her.

She'd known she mattered enough to him that he'd haul ass to be by her side. It wrecked him. That was as close to a declaration of love as he might ever get from her. Was he okay with that?

"Hell yes," he muttered to himself.

Because while the words mattered, what mattered more was feeling her absolute, unwavering trust in him. A man could live forever on that.

"Do I look like I was crying?" Fresh-faced and smiling, she stole his breath.

"Just pretend you were overcome with joy at seeing my beautiful mug," he said as he got to his feet.

"Hah," she said but then crooked a finger, and when he bent down, she kissed him soft and sweet. "I'm so happy you're here, Danny." A gentle touch to his jaw. "I was freaked out."

He ran his hand over her hair. This Catie, the one who trusted him and looked at him that way? Oh hell, he was never going to be able to say no to her. "I know," he said gently. "I'd be freaked too."

He'd known he had to get to her as soon as she'd told him what had happened. There were some things that were beyond logic and reason, things that required heart-driven actions. He was grateful his team had released him for the week, but he'd have broken his contract if necessary and taken the resulting financial punishment.

No way in hell could he have stayed in Japan while Catie dealt with this.

"Come on," she said, taking his hand. "Let's go see Clive."

Catie's father beamed at Danny when they walked in.

"Hello, boyo," he said, then seemed to notice their clasped hands. "Oh, like that, is it?"

Danny was all ready for the fatherly interrogation, but Clive clapped his hands and said, "Hell, yes! I'm going to call Jackie and tell her I told you so!"

Jackie?

Danny knew for damn sure no one dared call Jacqueline Rain that, but who else could Clive mean?

"Seriously, Dad?" Catie shook her head. "You're telling me you bet on us?"

"Yep." A smug grin from Clive. "Back at the party for your twenty-first. Jacqueline didn't see it, but I bet her fifty bucks that when I walked you down the aisle, it'd be to marry the Esera boy."

Danny suddenly loved Clive.

What he loved even more was that Catie didn't stiffen at the allusion to marriage. She just laughed and went to kiss her father's cheek. "Make sure Mum gives you interest on that fifty."

"Damn straight."

After being introduced to Gloria, Danny ducked out to borrow a chair from another patient so all three of them could sit together with Clive. "So," he said to Catie's father after he got back, "bit of an adventure, huh?"

With that, Clive was away, with Gloria filling in the bits where—according to Clive—"The lights in the noggin went out."

Catie perched on the side of her father's bed, and though she looked much better than when he'd arrived, he could see the worry that continued to gnaw at her. He could well understand why: Clive still looked small and sick and old. That, he hoped, would soon change. If he never saw Catie cry like that again, it'd be too soon.

Reaching out, he took her hand.

She smiled, wove her fingers through his. And kept them there when they took their leave after Gloria said she wanted to stay longer; Catie did make the older woman promise to nap in the family room if she needed it.

"And no excuses when I get back." Catie shook a finger, her tone stern. "You will be going back to the hotel to sleep."

Gloria laughed into Catie's hug. "Yes, I promise."

A pair of small kids were wrestling on the floor of the outer hallway when they walked out, their harassed parent talking to a doctor. The kids were attempting to maul each other but letting out small giggles now and then that said they weren't actually doing harm.

Danny grinned. "Given our genes, our kids will be energetic terrors, won't they?"

Looking over, Catie frowned. "I never really thought about having kids."

"Oh." Danny decided to just dive in. "Never thought about it as in you don't want any or just never thought about it?" He'd always wanted a big family, but he wanted Catie more.

"Just never thought about it." She twisted her mouth. "I guess part of me has always thought I'd be an awful parent after growing up with Jacqueline and Clive for role models."

"Your sister is a brilliant mum."

"Yes, but she was maternal to *me* back when she should've been a kid. I've never even had a pet." Biting down on her lower lip, she said, "You'd be a good dad though."

Lifting her hand to his mouth, he kissed her knuckles. "You'd be a great mum, Catie. I've seen how amazing you are with the camp kids—even the ones who are angry and throw tantrums and hate their life." No one was as patient or as understanding.

A startled look, a slow smile. "I've never thought about the camp that way." She swung their clasped hands. "Let me guess, you want a rugby team?"

"Half a team will be plenty." He grinned. "I mean, I gotta give my brothers some motivation to keep producing little mini-mes."

"It'll have to wait at least until after the Paralympics in three years' time."

"Done and done."

She narrowed her eyes. "How did you just talk me into having kids with you?"

"By being adorable and charming and so sexy I fry your brain cells?"

A slow, slow smile. "Yeah, maybe. But I think it's because you love me until I think I can do everything."

"I do, you know. Love you. To the stars and into outer space." No point in hiding his heart when she knew it was hers. "We just fit, princess."

"Yes, hotshot, we do." Then she tugged his head down and kissed him until his world spun. "I love you too. Right into outer space."

EPILOGUE
RUN, CATIE, RUN!

Three years later, Danny stood in the stands of the Paralympic Games, all ice-calm focus and love. "Go, go, princess," he whispered under his breath as the starter's gun went off.

There she went, a bullet out of the gate.

It had been a long, intense road to get to this point, her training schedule and his often colliding and with long periods where they'd been apart from each other. But they'd always found ways to come back together, found ways to drive each other crazy from continents away. And never, not once, had their bond threatened to break.

Takuro, who'd become one of his closest friends, called him the luckiest man alive. "She loves you like the sun," he'd said once in an awed whisper. "Such a love... It makes me believe in the stories of happy ever after."

If Catie loved him like he was her sunshine, he loved her as if she were his air. The two of them, they weren't into big public displays of affection or sappy social media posts—and had kept up their tradition of cheek and snark—but that they were a tight unit was simple, inalienable fact.

Whether he was playing for the Harriers or traveling as part of New Zealand's national team, her love was a constant glow that kept him company. He'd found his joy in the game again, but it hadn't just been the stint in Japan that had done it—it had been looking to Catie, and to Jake, and seeing that they both had passions outside of sport, something that gave their lives balance.

His decision to openly embrace his love of cooking had begun with a monthlong pastry course run by a local café, turned into him running a baking workshop at Catie's camp, and these days his teammates often chowed down on his experimental efforts.

The experience had also taught him the importance of living his truth. As part of that, and with Catie with him every step of the way, he'd penned an article for the largest sporting website in the country, describing his drug assault, his resulting feelings of helplessness and violation, and the importance of dealing with those emotions so they didn't become a shackle around his psyche.

In my case, he'd written, *the police managed to track down the perpetrator and bring them to justice. That's a fantastic outcome—but it took time. If I'd sat around stewing in my anger all that time, I wouldn't be the Danny Esera you know today; the anger would've burned away at me like acid, breaking me down until it consumed me.*

Finding a way—a healthy way—to handle things put me in the driver's seat. Me, not the a**hole who decided to dose *me. So yeah, I'm never going to apologize for talking it out with a therapist, and you shouldn't either.*

If anyone ever gives you grief about taking care of your mind and your heart, remind them there's a reason for the sports psychologists attached to major teams: the people behind the teams understand that a high-performing athlete is a whole—body and mind and heart in equal measure.

The response to the article had been a groundswell of support. But more importantly, it had opened the door for others—especially young people who looked up to him—to feel okay discussing their own similar experiences. If Daniel Esera, one of the Top 3 Rugby Wingers in the World *and* Sexiest Player of the Year, could do it, so could they.

Turned out Danny didn't mind his high public profile when it could do so much damn good. And from living his truth had come another passion—to work with youth sporting organizations throughout the country to put counseling services in place, or to upgrade and modernize those services to better suit the needs of the current generation.

As for Catie, her foundation continued to grow, and as well as her New Zealand camp, she now ran two camps in Australia and was in the process of setting up one in the islands. It would require more logistics since the future attendees were scattered across various Pacific Islands, but if anyone could do it, it was Catie. She'd also been talked into appearing on a local television game show thanks to the huge charity donation up for grabs, and though she hadn't won, her wry humor had made her a huge fan favorite.

Together, they'd been labeled the power couple of

New Zealand sport, and they leveraged that power to support both Catie's foundation and his work with the youth clubs.

Today, however, it wasn't about them or about him—it was about Catie and the sleek, muscular power of her as she raced down the track in the finals of the one-hundred-meter sprint.

"Go, baby, go!" Danny was up on his feet now, yelling his encouragement even though he knew she couldn't hear him down there.

Ísa and Sailor and their entire combined family—Jacqueline and Clive included—screamed beside him, as did the whole stand of Kiwi fans.

Catie was the wind, blowing past the finish line so fast that she was a blur on the big screen.

The entire stand erupted into wild chaos.

Danny's grin ate up his whole face. He hugged an ecstatic Clive, then turned back to roar his joy for Catie as she stood bent over, well past the end of the track—where she'd finally come to a stop. Her chest heaved when she straightened to her full height, the silver of her racing blades gleaming under the lights. Her grin was dazzling as she pinpointed him in the stands, exactly where he'd told her he'd be.

Grabbing the New Zealand flag he'd secreted away, he threw it to her.

She caught it with ease, draping it around her shoulders as she raised a hand to wave up at the fans who were screaming their joy. Danny's face ached, he was so damn happy for her.

When one of the camera crews went up to her, he looked at the big screen to make sure he could see and hear exactly what she was saying, not wanting to miss a moment.

"How does it feel to know that an entire country is celebrating with you?" the reporter asked. "You were the biggest trending topic in New Zealand after your spectacular time in the semifinals. Your win will have set the country alight."

"I feel like I'm full of fireworks." Catie grinned. "All those years of hard work, all the early-morning wake-ups and training sessions, it's all worth it to be here today."

"Now that you've achieved this dream, what's next for Catie River?"

"Oh, I've got a few more goals to hit—including in my other scheduled races," Catie said, her smile full of mischief. "But there's one specific dream that I'd like to set in motion today."

"Oh, what's that?" the reporter asked.

Catie shifted her gaze. "Hey, hotshot!" she said, meeting Danny's gaze. "How about it? You and me and a wedding?"

As the entire stadium erupted, Danny cupped his hands around his mouth to yell back, "YES, PRINCESS!" He thought of the ring burning a hole in his pocket and grinned even harder.

This was *her* moment, and he'd intended to wait until they were alone and in private so as to let her bask in the spotlight, but if Catie wanted to claim him in front of the world, he wasn't exactly going to argue. Especially not when he knew what a big deal it was for her to trust him enough to propose in front of millions of people.

It wasn't that his enthusiastic agreement had ever been in question—that they'd get hitched was a given between them, the proposal a formality. This, the way she'd done it? It was a joyous acknowledgment that she knew he'd *always* have her back, no matter what or when or where. Catie trusted him to be there for her, trusted him not to hurt her. Most of all, she trusted him to love her. Now and always.

Catie blew him a kiss, her own love ablaze for all the world to see.

∾

I HOPE *you loved Danny and Catie's story! If you haven't yet read Gabriel's, Sailor's, and Jake's stories, they are: ROCK HARD, CHERISH HARD, and LOVE HARD. All available at your favorite retailer.*

To stay up to date with my releases and get exclusive access to deleted scenes and free short stories, please join my newsletter at: www.nalinisingh.com. And if you feel like leaving a review, that would be awesome!

—xoxo Nalini

ABOUT THE AUTHOR

New York Times and *USA Today* bestselling author of the Psy-Changeling, Guild Hunter, and Rock Kiss series, Nalini Singh usually writes about hot shapeshifters, dangerous angels, and sexy rock stars. With the Hard Play series, she decided to write about a sinfully gorgeous set of brothers and their friends, all of whom will make your blood pump and your heart melt.

Nalini lives and works in beautiful New Zealand, and is passionate about writing. If you'd like to learn more about the Hard Play series or her other books, you can find excerpts, behind-the-scenes materials, and more information on her website: www.nalinisingh.com.

CPSIA information can be obtained
at www.ICGtesting.com
Printed in the USA
LVHW101141140822
725912LV00018B/234